T0166797

Pressure Chamber

Nir Hezroni

Translated by Steven Cohen

Legend Press Ltd, 51 Gower Street, London, WC1E 6HJ
info@legendpress.co.uk | www.legendpress.co.uk

Contents © Nir Hezroni 2021
The right of the above author to be identified as the author of this work has
been asserted in accordance with the Copyright, Designs and Patents Act
1988. British Library Cataloguing in Publication Data available.

First published in Hebrew by T'chelet Publishing in 2020.
English Translation by Steven Cohen.

Print ISBN 978-1-78955-9-033
Ebook ISBN 978-1-78955-9-040
Set in Times. Printing managed by Jellyfish Solutions Ltd
Cover design by Simon Levy | www.simonlevy.co.uk

Nir Hezroni was born in Jerusalem. His first two thrillers, were sold in two-book deals in six territories and have been optioned for film by Sony Pictures Television Inc. He now lives with his family near Tel-Aviv.

Follow Nir
@nirhezroni

Warning. Lucid dreaming, and how to induce lucid dreams, as described in the book, are very real. All people react to sleep paralysis differently, and some responses also have the potential to be problematic and could give rise to phenomena such as nightmares and psychological trauma. This book does not constitute a recommendation to experiment with lucid dreaming, does not purport to be a guide to lucid dreaming, and the author cannot be held responsible or accountable for any harm that may come, Heaven forbid, to any readers who decide to try out something from the book on themselves.

A second warning. The process of guiding someone into a trance that appears in Chapter 81 is real and shouldn't be tried without prior knowledge of hypnosis.

Sleep, little baby, sleep
Daddy has gone to the fields
Mommy has gone out to work
The demon with the hollow eyes
is waiting on your rooftop
Sleep peacefully, little baby
Sleep deep

1.

She used to run along the seashore when it rained. The sand would empty of people and she could run fast without having to weave around amblers or beachgoers sitting under umbrellas with children sowing minefields of colorful plastic toys in her path. In the winter, she runs along the waterline, her feet leaving quick-fire impressions in wet sand in the wake of the receding waves, like skin that tightens after someone holds your hand over the spout of a boiling kettle, like her father used to do to her when she was small.

Daphne!

It always happened if she misbehaved, and she always misbehaved, or most of the time at least, so he'd say. If she'd known how to behave, she would have, and then there'd have been fewer marks on her hands.

Daphne! Come here!

She tried, when she was very small, with all her might, but the slaps and fists never failed to materialize, and so she stopped trying, and waited for it to happen. Better to bring things to the boil quickly, to take the punishment and get it over with.

Heavy steps

Her bedroom door opens
A large hand grabs a small wrist and tugs

The waves rumble to her right, raindrops drum against the sand. Water, a chemical compound composed of hydrogen and oxygen atoms, boils at one hundred degrees and freezes at zero. A human body is usually at 38.6 when measured with a thermometer under the tongue. A third of the way between the blue pain of zero and the red of one hundred.

It's cold outside, but her body is warm, and she moves closer to the water's edge, running over the white foamy limits of the waves that lick the sand, paying no heed to the small rocks that stab her bare feet.

Everything's gray. Dulled. The pain, too.

PART 1

THE GUARDIAN

AUGUST 2016

2.

"Don't fight it."

He leans over her. A slender trail of blood trickles from her ear and drips onto the road, creating a bright red puddle on the black asphalt.

"Don't be afraid."

Her eyes open. She tries to say something, but her lips won't move.

"It'll be over soon."

Her right foot convulses in her white Nike running shoe and stills. He puts his ear to her mouth and feels no breath.

He slowly runs the tip of his finger from her hairline all along the bridge of her nose, her mouth slightly open, his finger skipping from the upper to the lower lip, chin, neck, chest, grazed stomach from the blow, with horizontal scratches in the region of her belly button, covered with small drops of blood. A piercing. Silver-plated clover leaf.

He touches the tip of her nose again.

"There we go, it's over. You see? It was quick."

That which dies, let it die; and that which is cut off, let it be cut off. Zechariah, Chapter 11, Verse 9. Nine Eleven.

He stands up straight and walks away. Slowly.

It'll take him years at this rate. He isn't putting enough into this cycle and needs to amend his priorities somewhat. So many things to do. Life is the sequence of actions you take in the limited period of time afforded to you. People can live their entire lives without doing anything meaningful. Without driving a spoke into the universe.

He inhales deeply, drawing in the scent of the flowers in the courtyards of the private homes along the winding street, the smell of perfume, the sweat and blood on the sweatpants of the girl lying on the road, the stench of the fur of the dog lazing in the yard of the nearest house. The humid summer air pulsates around him. The earth and the flora moves and breathes. People in small houses are fast asleep in their boxy middle-class existences.

He gets into the car, which awaits him open-doored, buckles up and drives off.

3.

Daphne is sleeping in nothing but a pair of panties. The three-room apartment she rents with Anna is equipped with an air conditioner in the living room only, and that died on them a few days ago. She tried calling the landlords, only to learn that they were in China, on an organized tour for senior citizens. "We'll take care of it the moment we return, in five weeks' time," they informed her before hanging up.

The fan she purchased does a good job of dispersing the humidity evenly throughout the room and cools her back somewhat by helping the sweat evaporate at a quicker rate. She of all people knows that the evaporation rate of a liquid depends on the type of liquid, its temperature, the surface area and the air flow above its surface. Under identical conditions, acetone will evaporate faster than benzene, which will evaporate faster than chloroform. She remembers the table of evaporation coefficients of liquids by heart.

The same nightmare keeps recurring. Her eyes move under her closed eyelids and the sweat on her back, comprised of water with the addition of sodium, calcium, magnesium and potassium, evaporates into the expanse of the room, mixing with the general humidity of the apartment and, through the open windows, the city of Tel Aviv as a whole. SCAMP. As a student of molecular biology, she used to come up with acronyms to remember the assortment of chemicals racing through the human body. Sweat is mostly SCAMP. Sodium. Calcium. Magnesium. Potassium.

She turns to the left in her sleep to lie on her side in the fetal position, exposing a sweat stain on the sheet. Sweat can be used sometimes for forensic identification purposes. Sweat can contain small traces of zinc, copper, iron, chromium, nickel and lead, and everyone has different amounts. Bodily fluids, skin cells, fingerprints, hairs – from the second we emerge from the body that has sheltered us, up to the moment we start to decompose and turn into other chemical compounds, after two and a half billion heartbeats, we're constantly scattering remnants of ourselves wherever we go. *The yellow brick road*, she calls it; though she doesn't feel like Dorothy – she feels closer to Elphaba, the Wicked Witch of the West.

She didn't set an alarm for this morning. She only got out of the lab yesterday at 11 p.m., and, arriving home at her dilapidated apartment on HaNevi'im Street after an hour-and-a-half drive from the National Israeli Police Headquarters, she immediately crashed into bed.

Her cell phone rings.

Still half asleep, and thinking it's the alarm she didn't set, she reaches out and silences the device. It rings again a few seconds later. She looks at the screen. The name of her team leader appears alongside the time: five-thirty.

"Nathan?"

"Daph, don't come into HQ this morning."

"You're an angel. I'm going back to sleep."

"No, what I mean is you need to get up now and get yourself to Kiryat Ono."

She looks at the half-closed shutter and the sun's rays penetrating it creating sunspots on the bed, then reads the time on her cell phone. "It's five-thirty in the morning."

"A hit-and-run, young girl dead at the scene."

"Shit." She rubs her eyes.

"Do you have the kit in the car?"

It takes her a few seconds to remember before responding. "Yes. What's the address?"

"It's 25 Trumpeldor Street. Kiryat Ono."

"I hope I make it there before they contaminate the entire scene. You on your way?"

"Yes, dressing and leaving Jerusalem in a few minutes. I'll be there in an hour or so, depending on traffic."

"See you there."

"Daphne."

"What?"

"Look with the eyes of a child. Ask yourself: What's different? What's happening on the street around the scene? What's there that appears…"

"…to be out of place. Doesn't belong there. On my way."

She sits up in bed and stretches through a yawn, then heads to the shower and stands under a stream of cold water. She needs to wake up. She has to be sharp. She can't afford to overlook a single detail.

Without Tel Aviv's as-far-as-the-eye-can-see traffic, which will kick in a little later in the morning, she's at the bottom of the hill, before Trumpeldor bends to the right, within fifteen minutes.

She parks behind a patrol car with flashing lights blocking the road, forming a barrier between the scene and the group of curious bystanders who have already emerged, coffees in hand, from the buildings on either side of the street. A second police car bars access at the other end. Between the two barriers stands a Magen David Adom ambulance. Two paramedics in white shirts with a red stripe at the end of their sleeves are busy packing up their resuscitation equipment and returning it to the vehicle.

Daphne gets out of her car, leaving the door open, and walks towards the scene.

"What's up?" A weary patrolman greets her with tired red eyes. "What unit?"

She plucks her police ID card from her purse and says, "Forensics. Who's been at the scene apart from you? Just the people I see here now? Any other cops who've left already? Another ambulance?"

He takes her ID card, briefly studies the photograph and then looks up at her. "No, just us," he says, and returns the card to her. "We arrived half an hour ago with the ambulance. When they saw there was nothing for them to do, we closed off the road."

"I'll get my gear from the car."

Without waiting for a reply, she turns around and goes back to her car, reaching into the trunk for the large metal suitcase, with its sticker reading *FORENSICS* in red letters on a white background that she received while on a crime scene investigators course. She opens the case, takes out a digital reflex camera and walks back over to the patrolman.

"Lift your leg."

The young policeman appears taken aback. "Aren't you going to the body?"

"It's not going anywhere. All of you, on the other hand, are wandering around it and leaving shoeprints."

He consents, and she photographs the soles of his shoes, then those of all the other people milling around the scene. The powerful flash of her camera casts an intense white light against the backdrop of the soft, orangey pink sunrise, emitting a faint beep as it recharges between shots. She also photographs the tires of the two police cars and the ambulance, their tread as well as the side of each tire that displays the details of the manufacturer and model number. When a driver brakes suddenly, it's easy to collect evidence from the road. The tires heat up when the brakes are applied, leaving skid marks, a black trail of burned rubber. But there was no sudden stop here. She has a good look around her. No signs of emergency braking. Nothing to suggest a sudden veering to one side, no foreign paint marks or signs of a collision on the vehicles parked on either side of the road. The driver of the car who killed the girl didn't see her at all. Drunk or under the influence of drugs perhaps. There are no glass fragments either, just a broken body lying on the road.

Daphne closes her eyes, inhales deeply, slowly releases the air from her lungs and then approaches the body: a young girl in a T-shirt and light blue sweatpants with black stripes running down the side. Her body is sprawled on the road, her head on the sidewalk. The fall must have culminated in a blow to the base of the skull against the curb. Bad luck – *flash* – her legs twisted in an unnatural position, exposed abdomen revealing scratches and grazes dotted with droplets of blood – *flash* – her head tilted back and a small pool of blood by its side, close to the curb – *flash*. Better that way. A sudden flash of pain and a quick death means a small pool of blood. The heart stops beating and doesn't pump blood out of the body through a ruptured vein or artery. Prolonged pain and a still-beating heart mean a large pool.

She looks about twenty. Younger even. A thin line of dark blood marks a trail from her ear down to her hair, some of which is soaked, and another thin trail of blood runs from the corner of her mouth across her cheek – *flash*.

Head facing the sky, black curls, open brown eyes, mouth slightly agape and half a shoeprint in the pool of blood alongside her. Whose? The soles of the shoes of the policemen and paramedics were free of blood – *flash-flash-flash*. Daphne retrieves a bottle of luminol from her case and sprays the reagent on the road and sidewalk around the body, before surveying the scene with a UV filter.

She follows a short series of glowing blue shoeprints from the body into the road. Four steps, that's all, that come to an end where the car had stood. He hit her, backed up, stopped, approached her to ascertain the extent of the damage, walked four steps back to his car and drove off. The blood marks left on the road by the tips of his shoes aren't smeared; he didn't run like someone who panicked and fled the scene. He stood over the body, surveyed it and drove away. She sprays more luminol but doesn't find additional traces of blood in the area.

"Piece of shit," she says to herself.

The policeman nearest to her looks up. "What was that?"

"Fucking piece of shit. He stood over her, watched her die, casually walked back to his car and drove off. In no apparent hurry."

"Maybe she?"

"What?" She turns to look at him, realizing she didn't bother to do so when she arrived at the scene.

"It could have been a woman driver."

"Not by the size of the shoeprint."

4.

She rests her camera on the hood of a parked car and lights a cigarette, noticing the glance from the policeman standing next to her.

"Want one?"

"Yes. Thanks."

She hands him the box. He helps himself to a cigarette and leans back against the car. Side by side, they smoke in silence. The orangey pink of the sunrise has been replaced by a bright blue sky and the number of curious onlookers beyond the police cars has increased.

"When you gonna clear that away?" asks one of the neighborhood residents from the doorway of the building in front of them, surveying the blocked road. "I need to get to work."

"*That*?" Daphne responds, standing up straight and taking a step towards him. "What's *that*? Are you talking about the dead girl lying there? Is she *that* to you? How would you like someone to say, 'Pick *that* up off the floor,' after a car's just flattened you on the street like a pancake? What the f—"

"Leave it," the policeman says, reaching out to place a hand on her shoulder. "Don't waste your energy."

She turns around, collects her camera and returns to the middle of the street, just as a siren sounds and an additional patrol car arrives on the scene. A young, bearded man with cropped black hair jumps out.

He flashes a badge to the patrolmen, ducks under the police tape and hurries over to her. "What can you tell me?"

"A hit-and-run. The victim's a young woman – nineteen going on twenty, I'm guessing. No ID on her person and her mobile's still working but locked with a password." She points to a transparent evidence bag containing white earphones and a white iPhone with a shattered screen. "It was thrown to the side from the force of the impact. I dusted it for prints in case someone touched it after she was run down. We're going to have to wait for someone to call her to know who she is."

"Anything else?"

"He didn't even try to stop before he hit her. It appears deliberate."

"How so? Maybe she jumped out between two parked cars and he didn't have time to brake? She was wearing earphones; perhaps she didn't hear him coming."

"In that case, I would have found signs of braking further along the road. The shock would have caused him to brake suddenly. He didn't. He continued driving, gradually slowed to a stop, backed up, got out, saw she was dead, walked back to his car and drove off."

"How do you know that?"

"He stepped in the blood," she responds, pointing at the shoeprint. "And there are another four distinct shoeprints here of someone walking away, then they disappear in the middle of the road. Look with the UV filter. That's where he lifted his foot, got back into his car and drove away. There aren't any others. They end too abruptly."

"Maybe he removed his shoes after a few steps, after noticing that he had stepped in the blood and was leaving tracks, and then walked the rest of the way to his car in his socks?"

"If he carried his shoes, we'd see a few drops on the way to his car. There's nothing here apart from the shoeprints. And why would he want to do that anyway?"

"Never rule out any possibility," Nathan says, kneeling over the dead girl to examine her up close. "He touched her. Look." He points to her exposed stomach and the belly button ring with its clover-leaf charm. "Her shirt was ripped open on contact with the road. The grazes and scratches are dotted with blood, but there's a small smear line running through them at a right angle, in the direction of her sweatpants. See? He ran his finger along here."

"Yes." She kneels down beside him and looks at the line of faint blood. She had missed that. "A necrophiliac perhaps? Maybe he did other things to her and then dressed her again."

"I don't think so. Not here in the middle of the street. He would have taken her to his place before getting rid of her, like in the case of that other guy. What was his name?"

"Yes, I remember reading about him during my studies." For the first time that morning, she feels nauseous, and she struggles to suppress the urge to throw up in front of her team leader, who's still examining the body. She tries to regain her focus and scans the lifeless girl once again. "There's something here on her nose. A small dab of blood. Can you see? It's not from the impact of the car. It looks like he also touched her nose with the same finger he ran across her stomach. Look."

"I think you're right. It's not enough for a print, but take one anyway. We may get a partial."

She gets up to retrieve the fingerprint kit from her case.

"Did you get pictures of her?"

"Yes."

"The surroundings? Her face? Position of the body? Personal items? Injuries? The plate numbers of all the vehicles in the vicinity?"

"Yes. Tires too, and everyone's shoes. I also collected biological samples."

"Biological findings from her proximity?"

"Only from her. I didn't see saliva or semen or blood anywhere else aside from what's here."

She tries to fight back her anger at herself for missing the finger trail. She should have spotted the small details on the body, just as she'd noticed the small details around her. Her subconscious caused her to be careless, to cut short her time examining the dead girl. She needs to make a note of that for next time. To be aware of it.

"What about them?" Nathan asks, gesturing in the direction of the paramedics who are still on the scene, waiting for instructions.

"They didn't mess with her much. They saw that her neck was broken and that there wasn't anything they could do. There was no attempt to resuscitate or hook her up to an IV line. They didn't move her. I took prints from them."

"Witnesses?"

"No. Just someone who was leaving for work and saw her lying here."

"So, we'd better find something. Let's scan everything again and then widen the circle."

5.

Oh my God, it's happening again.

I curl up under the comforter and the sense that something really bad is about to happen courses through me. It's like the walls of the room are closing in.

I peek out from under the comforter. I see the same old and secluded house. Wooden walls. A dark wood floor. Three windows. A shadow passes one window, flits by the second and stops at the third. It comes closer and suddenly a face appears, peering in, looking for me.

It's him again.

This is the only house for miles around, so even if I shout as loud as I can, no one will hear me. I tried it before and nothing happened. No one came to save me. The bed is in the center of a large living room. Not in the bedroom. The room is empty except for the bed and the small bedside table, with a white plate and two burning candles. The walls are bare. It's night now. There's no electricity in the house and the candles are the only source of light. The two small flames are dancing, and the shadow of the bed keeps time with them on the wall.

The face at the window disappears. I'm shaking under the comforter even though I'm not cold. I wait.

Then comes the loud banging on the door.

"Open up, I know you're in there!"

Maybe the door will bear up this time. I've been in this place so often. It always ends the same.

I jump out of bed and run to one of the windows. It's locked. I tug on the handle with all my might and a desperate scream escapes my lungs. I startle myself. I sound like a wounded animal. The window doesn't budge.

"Open the door right now!" The banging persists.

I run to the second window. Locked. To the third window. Locked.

Boom – Boom – Boom – Boom – "Open up nowwww!"

The door of the house won't hold up for long. The wood is starting to give in to a barrage of kicks. He has heavy shoes. Like the kind that lumberjacks wear. I run into the bedroom and look around. The room is empty. Windowless. It contains nothing but a large wooden closet – nothing I can use to defend myself.

I open the closet doors. Empty. Carved on the inside panel in large, jagged letters are the words: *He'll kill you. Get out of here fast.*

I return to the living room and see the wooden door of the house kicked in. He's standing in the doorway, panting. "You're done for."

In two quick strides he's on me and his fist slams against my jaw. I fall to the floor. On all fours, I stare at the floorboards swaying beneath me, dotted with drops of blood from my mouth. He slides his arm under my stomach and lifts me, throwing me onto the bed.

I land on my back on the comforter and he sits

on me. He smells musty, moldy. His giant hands are around my neck. I claw at them with my fingernails and try to scream, but no sound escapes my lips. He doesn't care. He smiles and tightens his grip. "Now I'm going to watch you die. Slowly."

And then I look to the right and see her lying next to me on the bed. Ripped light blue sweatpants with black stripes, a thin line of blood running from her mouth across her cheek, a clover-leaf belly button ring, a flat stomach with scratches dotted with blood. She looks at me and moves her lips, trying to say something, but I can't hear her.

I try to breathe – but can't. The room around me blurs, his fingers tighten around my throat, and I feel myself begin to lose consciousness.

Daphne bolts upright in bed, breathing heavily. The fan is humming beside her as usual and her heart's pounding. A figure appears in the doorway of the room.

Anna.

"Are you okay? You were screaming."

She steps into the room, her golden hair hanging loose over her shoulders. Even when Anna wakes up in the middle of the night and wanders around in her old pajamas and furry pink bunny slippers, she looks like a fairy to Daphne.

"Yeah. It's that nightmare again. The second time this week already."

"Poor thing. Can I get you some water?"

Daphne stretches her arms above her head and turns to get out of bed, placing her feet on the floor.

"No. I'll make us lemonade. I bought lemons yesterday and there's ice; I filled the trays. Want some too? Sorry I woke you. What's the time anyway?"

"A little after four."

"Fuck! I'm so thirsty." Daphne pushes herself up from the bed and heads into the kitchen. She turns on the light and squints against the sudden glare.

Anna follows her and leans on the doorframe, looking concerned. "Was it that same guy strangling you again?"

"Yes." Daphne goes over to the fridge. "But with a twist at the end this time: the girl from the hit-and-run in Kiryat Ono was lying next to me and trying to tell me something. I could tell it was something important, but I couldn't understand what she was saying. I could only see her lips moving."

"Your work is hardly conducive to a good and peaceful night's sleep."

"Hmm," Daphne says, focusing on slicing lemons.

"What's happening with that? Have you come up with anything? It's been two weeks already."

"Three." She adds sugar to the freshly squeezed juice and stirs vigorously. "No, nothing yet."

Anna gets the ice tray out of the freezer and empties cubes into two glasses. If she weren't on the police force too, in the Technology Control Center Unit, Daphne wouldn't be able to talk to her about it. In fact, Anna shouldn't be privy to details about an ongoing investigation. But Daphne trusts her not to say anything. In the same way Anna doesn't divulge the wage details of high-ranking officers she sees in the SAP system in her capacity as a human resources analyst. Daphne tried once to extract a few juicy details from her, only to be met with silence and an icy stare.

"They questioned all the neighbors. No one saw or heard anything. And we didn't find a thing. No DNA, no fibers, no fingerprints. Only a faint tire tread mark that we aren't sure about and a partial shoeprint. I told you about him stepping in her blood and—"

"And walking calmly to his car. Yes, you told me that about a hundred times."

"I can't shake that image from my head. Have you seen that pack of cigarettes I had here yesterday?"

"No."

Daphne rummages in a drawer under the kitchen countertop until she finds a pack, but it's empty, so she crushes it and throws it into the trash can under the sink.

They sit in the kitchen drinking lemonade to the sound of birds chirping outside.

"He simply killed a young girl and disappeared," Daphne says, staring out of the window at the new day dawning. "It's not just another regular accident. Nathan says he's never come across such strange behavior before. I have a really bad feeling about it. Even the biggest assholes in the world brake before fleeing in a panic. They scrape against other cars if they're drunk, they swerve off the road, they hit a tree. Something. Or they show up at the police station a few days later with a lawyer, when their conscience gets the better of them, or they realize they can't hide forever."

Anna rolls her eyes; Daphne knows she's heard all this before but she can't suppress the urge to talk about it. She reaches out across the kitchen table and picks up a ragged-looking paperback. "What's this book?"

"It's about lucid dreaming."

Anna reads out the title: "*Lucid Dreaming: The power of being aware and awake in your dreams.*"

"I took it out from the Mount Scopus library a few days ago after work."

"Stephen LaBerge?" Anna continues her investigation of the cover.

"He's a psychophysiologist – a pioneer of the practice of lucid dreaming."

Anna raises an eyebrow. "Just don't tell me you're joining a cult. It's not your style, Daph."

"Don't worry. Have you seen the movie *Inception*?"

"With DiCaprio? Of course."

"Well, this is the real thing. The movie's based on this book. It explains how to go into a dream while you're awake or how to wake up in a dream. I haven't read all of it yet. Maybe it'll help me to overcome my nightmare somehow; since conventional medicine has failed."

"Did you fire another psychologist?"

"Uh-huh." She nods. The last one wasn't very good, but at least he hadn't tried to fuck her like the one before, who must have had the couch in his office purely for that purpose. After explaining to her that intimacy would help move the therapy along and placing a hand on her breast, he got an elbow to the nose; and while he held a handful of tissues against his face to stem the bleeding, she invited him to file a complaint with the police. He didn't. She didn't either. She knew, just as he did, that it would only hurt her.

"It sounds like nonsense," Anna says.

"I don't think so. I did some online investigating in chat forums about nightmares, and I'm starting to think that lucid dreaming could be the solution. So I decided to learn about it and give it a try. That's who I am. An au-to-di-dact." She nods her head, spreading her arms out to the side in a regal gesture.

Anna laughs. "Take care not to screw up your head any more."

"If that's at all possible," Daphne responds, smiling and sipping her lemonade. Her thoughts return to the writing from the dream.

He'll kill you. Get out of here fast.

The red line of blood.
The open and unseeing eyes.
The partial shoeprint glowing blue.
Anna says something else, but she's no longer listening.

6.

He purposefully chooses a dark street. One with few streetlights and an incline so that the car can coast along in silence, in neutral, with its lights off. The sidewalk is strewn with uneven paving stones and trees in sunken flowerbeds, and she'll have to step off the curb and run on the road. He's familiar with her route. He's been following her for weeks. She's one of the options. He knows the days she goes out running, and at what time, and the route she selects on each occasion. The short route on Tuesday nights and the long route on Saturday mornings. Today's Tuesday. Day Three of Creation. Twice as good. At the end of each day of Creation, according to Chapter 1 of the Book of Genesis, *God saw that it was good*. But on Day Two, the work continued into Day Three, and *God saw that it was good* twice that day – once for the creation of Heaven and the Earth and then again for the creation of the plant world.

He needs to make sure that she doesn't die or end up in a coma. He mustn't hit her too hard like the previous one. Two months of surveillance work gone in an instant.

Slowly but surely. If he wants to do it right this time, he can't rush things. He needs her alive. He needs to inhale deeply, until his lungs are filled to capacity, and then to release the air slowly. To imagine that he's underwater. That if he doesn't count to one hundred before releasing the air, he'll drown and die. So easy to move from one state to another. Life. Death. It is all connected. The demise of one body is the beginning of another. Germs, bacteria, fungi, earthworms. He has to imagine that he's trapped in a dark and frozen lake that's covered with a layer of ice, and that he won't be able to make his escape before reaching the circular exit hole in the blue ice above his head.

The thought brings a slight smile to his face. When he watches movies, he always holds his breath with the hero who is diving underwater. Not as an act of solidarity but to check that the dumb director hasn't exaggerated a human being's ability to hold his or her breath voluntarily. Death by drowning is said to be worse than falling from a height. But why? Is the pain from hitting the ground somehow more bearable than inhaling water into one's lungs? Neither is particularly pleasant. If he's forced to end his life one day, it'll be a cold and calculated decision. He'll overdose on sleeping pills or fall asleep in his car after running a hose from the exhaust pipe into the interior of the vehicle. A peaceful and pleasant death.

He has time. Until the winter. What is destined to happen will happen then, and everything has to be ready and in place in time, otherwise it will need to be delayed another year. People stay indoors in the winter, taking cover from the rain as if they are made of sugar, hiding under umbrellas, unaware of what's going on around them. Not like him. He stands outside, allows his clothes to be soaked until the dampness and cold seeps into his bones, then raises his face to the sky and allows the rain to fall into his open eyes and mouth. Pure water. Clean.

He'll need a rainy day.

He knows she'll be turning onto the street soon, in red sneakers and red-and-blue sweats, her earphones in her ears, sounding a rhythmic beat to keep time with the pounding of her feet on the asphalt, where she'll be lying shortly after he hits her. Like the one before her. The one with the open lips, the clover leaf, the red dot on her nose.

The image of her body lying on the road appears in his mind's eye, and a wave of heat courses through him. Her last breath in his ear. The eyes of a doll. Unseeing.

He reminds himself again to be careful. Hit her hard enough to stun her but leave her in a state that will allow him to take her and use her. She's a vital part of the plan. There's no need to rush. If anyone comes down the street and sees, he'll pass it off as a regular accident. With tears in his eyes and in a broken voice, he'll say that the engine died on him all of a sudden, for no apparent reason, and then he'll flee the scene and dump the car.

She appears at the bend in the road and continues jogging down the incline. He waits a minute before releasing the handbrake, and the car begins coasting silently, picking up speed along the way.

7.

Lee is running to the sounds of Adele when a sudden blow to her left flings her to the ground. She doesn't hear the sound of the approaching vehicle because of her earphones, which confuses her; usually headlights serve as a forewarning. There were no lights this time.

She lies on the road, stunned by the blow and the sharp pain in her right forearm. She tries to clench the fingers of her right hand into a fist but she can't. The slightest movement sends waves of intense pain shooting up her arm and into her shoulder and head. It must be a fracture. Fuck. And in the very week, no less, in which she most needs her hands for school. She manages with a struggle to sit up, her injured arm folded across her stomach in the most painless position, her left hand pulling her earphones out before feeling for more damage because simply breathing hurts too. A cracked rib? Or two? Fuck. Fuck. Fuck.

Someone approaches and stands over her. She can tell he's studying her with interest. Maybe he's the one who hit her. Her breathing is shallow and rapid.

"Are you okay?"

"No, I'm not okay." She tries to get to her feet, but he places a hand on her injured shoulder and pushes her down onto the road again. He's wearing leather gloves, the kind that motorcyclists wear.

"What do you feel?"

"Leave me alone." His rude intervention, his unsolicited touch, the way he's looking at her frightens and angers her at once.

"Any internal injuries? Do you feel a burning sensation in your stomach or nausea or the need to urinate?" He remains standing over her as she tries to get up again. Only this time, he grabs her injured arm, and she cries out in pain.

"Your arm is broken."

"Leave me alone!"

"You need to come with me. I'll take you to the ER. I didn't see you. You stepped into the road without warning."

So, he is the guy who ran her down. It's evening now. He was driving without lights. Why was he driving without lights? Or maybe she just didn't notice. There's no way she's getting into the car with him, with this strange man. His calm manner of speech, the lack of emotion, sends a shiver of fear through her.

"Come. Get into the car."

"You can go. I don't need anything from you. I live nearby. I'll go home and my boyfriend will take me."

He knows she's lying and that she doesn't live nearby. He's very familiar with her route. Seven kilometers. He needs to act quickly before someone passes by and he has to take care of them too. The window of opportunity is closing.

His left hand, which is behind his back, rises above his head. She notices that he's holding something. His hand swings at her, and, before she has a chance to defend herself, a blunt instrument slams against the side of her head, sparking another wave of pain. A second blow lands. The world around her starts spinning, and she slumps to the ground, unconscious.

He places the iron pipe on the tarmac and looks around. The street is quiet and still. He picks her up and carries her towards the car. She's no more than fifty kilos and won't consume much food, he thinks. She'll serve her purpose well. She'll probably be excited to learn of the role she'll play in the creation of a new world.

The side of her head is bleeding a little, but her breath is steady. He lays her down on the backseat and looks at her. She'll end up thanking him later, but she's bound to put up a fight if she wakes during the drive. He ties her wrists with a thick black zip tie, then her ankles, before transferring her, cuffed and shackled, to the front passenger seat, which he reclines as far back as it will go. It'll be easier for him to keep her in check like that, in the event that she comes to before they reach the inner sanctuary. If he has to, he'll stun her with the pipe again.

Where's the pipe? He goes back and retrieves it from the road. A metal irrigation pipe, designed primarily to carry water. An IV line carries water and nutrients; the roots of a tree transfer minerals and provide sugar to the translucent web of fungi that links them to others. A forest is a living organism wholly connected within the depths of the earth. A single entity. Far from the eyes of those who tread on the earth, packing it tighter, is a parallel universe. Everything is interconnected. And some things are not always what they seem. Sometimes, what we can't see is the very essence of the thing. What we don't see and don't know will rise one day and bring about our demise.

Humanity is a huge collection of singular entities worshipping individualism and trying, contrary to all logic, to undo the connections, failing to grasp the immense value of the forest trees' connectedness to a single being. The power that comes from the unification of various life systems. It is something that people understood in the past. Everything appears in the ancient scriptures. The Father, the Son and the Holy Ghost; the Incas who sacrificed children to appease the gods; the Mayans who practiced bloodletting at every important event in the life of the royal family; the Aztecs who happily sacrificed themselves for the purpose of repaying the gods for the blood they shed when creating the world. The sacrificial offerings. The burnt offerings. The ram and the bull on the altar. *And the Cohen [the priest] shall take some of its blood with his finger, and place [it] on the horns of the altar [used] for burnt offerings. And then he shall pour all of its [remaining] blood at the base of the altar*. Blood for blood, blood to blood – everything's connected.

He'll make them all understand in the end.

He covers her with a thin black woolen blanket. Her head, concealed, is just a quick blow away if required.

He shifts the gear stick into drive and heads off.

8.

"If those tire marks really are his, they were left by Chinese-made Maxtreks, which you'll find on a third of the cars in the country. That doesn't get us anywhere."

Nathan is sitting on one of the chairs, leaning back and studying the photographs on the display board in the conference room. Some show tire marks on the road, and others are of partial shoeprints. *Anat Aharon* reads the caption above a headshot, a face with brown staring eyes framed by curls.

Daphne stands up, approaches the wall and looks at one of the photos, leaning closer until her nose almost touches the board. "And his shoes are Nike Dart 12s, also very popular."

"And he probably dumped them after getting home and noticing that he had stepped in the blood."

"If we find his car, her DNA could be on the floor mat on the driver's side." Daphne returns to the conference room table and sits on a chair next to Nathan.

"Yes," Nathan responds, his gaze still fixed on the photographs.

"When were you here till yesterday? Sorry for running out on you like that, but I was wiped," Daphne says.

"Around ten."

"I still feel bad about it."

"No worries." He turns his chair towards her. "I spoke to Eli from the Tel Aviv District Investigations Unit. They've interviewed all the neighbors, reviewed the footage from the security cameras of businesses along the nearby streets, and identified the owners of all the vehicles you photographed along the road where she was found. All but one of the cars belong to neighbors. The odd one out is owned by a woman who was a guest in one of the homes that night. They examined the car and found nothing on it."

"So that's it? They're putting the investigation on ice?"

"Maybe not."

"Why not?"

Nathan picks up a fresh photograph from the table and fixes it to the display board. "Lee Ben-Ami," he says.

"Who's she?" Daphne asks.

"Missing for two days. She went out for a run and didn't come home. They think the two could be connected."

"Why? How is she…" Daphne begins, before stopping to think. "Damn," she finally says, nodding her head. "They can be smart sometimes over there at Investigations."

"So you think there's a connection too?"

"That depends. Do they think Anat Aharon was an abduction attempt that went wrong and that he got it right this time? That the person who ran down Anat Aharon is now holding Lee Ben-Ami?"

"Is it unheard of for a young woman to simply run away from home?"

Yes, it happens; but the more she thinks about it, the more a possibility of a connection between the two incidents seems plausible. Both in the central region of the country. Less than a month apart. A similar victim profile – two young women who went out for a run and never came back. One dead. One disappeared.

"Did they find anything along Lee Ben-Ami's running route? An item of hers, blood stains?"

"They questioned her family and friends, as well as her live-in boyfriend. According to her boyfriend, she goes out running twice a week, for about an hour. But he has no clue where. When she failed to return, he drove around the neighborhood looking for her, then he called the hospitals. And then he contacted the police to report her missing."

"Lee Ben-Ami," Daphne says, getting to her feet to get a closer look at the photograph. Straight brown hair tied in a ponytail, smiling honey-colored eyes, freckles on her cheeks and nose. She studies the rest of the display board again too. "Let's go out for a smoke," she suggests, feeling a sudden need to get away from the images.

The Jerusalem air is already autumnal. They stand in the square under the arches on the ground floor, overlooking the large parking lot with the stone steps leading down to it. Nathan takes out his pack of Marlboros and removes two cigarettes. Daphne leans in towards the flame of his lighter. A female officer passes by in the parking lot and waves to Nathan, who responds in kind.

"She's still appearing in my dream. Anat Aharon."

"In that dream with the guy who strangles you?"

"Yep. And others."

Nathan drags deeply on his cigarette.

Daphne says, "Do you know that there's a technique that allows you to step into your own dreams? I've been reading about it."

He frowns at her. "What do you mean?"

"Have you ever been in the middle of a dream when suddenly you realize that you're dreaming in your dream and then you wake up?" She hoped she was explaining herself clearly.

"No," Nathan responds. "I hardly ever dream."

"Everyone dreams. A few times during the night. This book says that if you set an alarm for four and a half or six hours after you go to sleep, it'll wake you in the middle of a dream, and that if you keep a journal of your dreams, you'll develop a better recollection of them; not only that – if you conduct reality checks when you're awake, you'll eventually start doing so in your dreams too, and you'll realize that you're dreaming and be aware of it in the dream itself, then you'll also have the ability to call up a dream subject of your choice and to manipulate the environment of the dream while you're dreaming." She pauses. "Sorry. I'm babbling too much, this all sounds crazy but it makes sense when you read the book. Have you seen the movie *Inception*?"

"No. And I didn't understand a word of what you just said." He smiles at her, drops his cigarette butt to the ground and steps on it, then immediately lights another one. "The whole idea sounds strange but carry on."

"Well, I'm going to give it a try."

"Getting into your dreams?"

"Yes, to become aware that I'm dreaming; and then, if I can do so in the nightmare, I'll be able to change its outcome. To fight back. To resist. Stop being the victim."

> **Your mother's gone and she isn't coming back.**
>
> **Why?**
>
> **She said she doesn't love us anymore.**
>
> **That's not true!**
>
> **You're lying!**
>
> **Where is she?**
>
> **What have you done with her?**
>
> **What did you do to her?**
>
> *What did you do to her?*

"Daph?" The sharpness of Nathan's tone causes Daphne to look over at him; he's staring at her, concern in his eyes.

"What?"

"Are you okay? Did you hear what I said? You drifted off all of a sudden."

"Oh, it's nothing. I'm just tired, that's all. I haven't been getting enough sleep lately."

"So you're going to check if it works? Because let me know if it does. I'll book myself a dream with Scarlet and a hotel suite in Vegas. And she'll be wearing her outfit from *The Avengers*."

"No problem." Daphne smiles and stubs out her cigarette in the large flowerpot at the entrance to the building that had long since become a huge ashtray. "I'll set up a dream journal and start training myself to remember them. First, you have to write down: 'Tonight, I'll remember my dream', a few times before going to sleep. It says in the book that doing so creates expectations for your brain and then it starts to meet them. A self-fulfilling prophecy."

"Sounds a little simplistic to me," Nathan responds, still skeptical. "Don't get your hopes up."

"Okay. I'm going back to the lab. Are you coming later for lunch?"

Nathan looks at his watch, "No, there's an HQ briefing from twelve to two."

"Should I get you a sandwich?"

"No, thanks. I'll grab something from the cafeteria afterwards."

They stand quietly for a moment.

"She's probably hurt," Daphne says.

"Who?"

"Lee Ben-Ami. If he went with the same MO, he first ran her down to incapacitate her and then loaded her into his car." She speaks softly. He can hardly hear her voice.

"I don't envy her," he says. "This guy seems like a piece of work."

A shudder courses through Daphne.

"Me neither. Imagine you're hit by a car and, if you're lucky, you lose consciousness. And then you wake up in the company of a stranger in unfamiliar surroundings. Maybe you're tied to a wall or the floor. You're still hurt from the blow from the car. You know something bad is about to happen, it already has, and you have no idea how long it'll continue. Or where you are. Or if anyone will ever come to your rescue. And maybe you'll actually be dead in a few minutes. Or hours. Or months. You're helpless."

Nathan remains silent and simply stares at her intently.

"I'll find her even if I have to turn the entire world upside down," Daphne says, going towards the door and heading back into the building. Nathan follows in her wake.

9.

The Department of Obstetrics and Gynecology at Sheba Medical Center is part of a building that appears to have been assembled in a somewhat patchwork fashion. Whenever the hospital decided to expand, they simply added another wing, creating a mishmash of hallways and open spaces at varying heights linked to one another. He walks the length of a structure labeled *Obstetrics* in large gray letters, passing by a nurse in a black headscarf and a parking lot with a sign restricting access to authorized vehicles only. He then completes his tour of the circumference of the building, making a mental note of every detail of his surroundings, and returns to the main entrance to the wards. He doesn't go in.

Standing in the courtyard outside the entrance is a large ficus tree, its branches hanging over an unkempt patch of garden, a metal bench and a white trash can. He lifts the lid of the trash can and rummages inside, his torn sneakers and filthy sweatpants warding off any interest or concern from passersby. Many deliberately avert their gaze. A worn baseball cap keeps his face hidden.

As with any plan, patience is the key here too. Most keep it as a souvenir, but not everyone. One of the fathers will probably throw it away upon leaving the ward; and if not here, then perhaps in one of the trash cans in the surrounding parking lots. He'll have a good look there as well, until he finds one. Mothers would probably find a place for it in a pretty album together with the images from the first ultrasound scan. Nine months of assembling a human body from two cells, which transform into a skeleton, encasing internal organs, covered by muscles and topped with skin and a light covering of down. But one of the fathers is bound to dump it here. Patience is the key. Years of waiting and assembling are nearing their high point.

He removes a few empty drink bottles from the bin and places them in a trash bag that he's been carrying over his shoulder and is now lying open on the ground. If anyone wishes to come over and take a look, they are free to do so. Nothing to see here but empty bottles and cans. But no one shows any interest.

He catches sight of it at the bottom of the trash can. He wants to shout with joy. His plan is moving forward so well. He retrieves it and places it in the trash bag along with the bottles, before tying the end of the bag closed and starting to make his way towards the exit from the hospital grounds. He's come on foot; he doesn't want to run the risk of someone seeing him get into his car in the clothes that he's wearing. It will look odd, and could draw attention, and someone might remember him. He can't get sloppy now that he's so close. Now that he has a Guardian.

He planned his route ahead of time: He'll walk to a bus stop and take a bus to the fake house. To the stupid house with the stupid neighbors on Uziel Street in Ramat Gan, where he's been forced to sleep now and then so that they think he lives there. He'll get off the bus two stops before his destination, change his clothes in the backyard of an abandoned building that's undergoing renovations, clean his face with wet wipes, and show up ready to encounter the fools who live in that ant nest they call a residential apartment block. *Hello, Mrs. Maroz. How are you today? No, I wasn't the one who left a broken chair in the trash room. It's really not right for someone to do that. We need to convene a tenants' committee meeting. Yes. Absolutely. A committee meeting.*

One of these days, he's going to run into that busybody at the entrance to the trash room and hit her on the back of the neck. After making sure she's not breathing, he'll shove an apple into her mouth, like he's seen happen to a roasted pig in the movies, and he'll wrap up her ugly body in a sleeping bag and stuff it into the brown trash bin for organic waste. That's what she is. Organic waste. This entire street, this entire city, and the world as a whole are all organic waste. Viruses and bacteria that reside in hosts on two legs; the clothes that cover them serve as only a partial barrier between the filth and him.

He'll shower and change his clothes again at the apartment on Uziel Street and then he'll drive his car to the real house, where he's getting everything ready. To the white place. The clean place.

She's probably awake and waiting there for him by now. The Guardian.

He needs to be careful. To think about how he's going to approach things with her, about how much to reveal at each stage. To be vigilant. He needs to look after her. She may try to do something. Perhaps. In any event, he must make sure he doesn't kill her by mistake and then have to start all over again from the beginning.

He runs his tongue over his lips and remembers his dream from the night before. He was standing in the center of a dark concrete room, naked, basted in oil, with bubbles forming on the skin of his palms, like after a burn. And when the bubbles burst, they oozed bright red blood rather than clear liquid.

10.

She opens her eyes and can't see a thing. Total darkness. She doesn't know where she is, or what happened to her, and why her head and right hand hurt so much. A few seconds later, it all comes back to her at once. She was struck by a car. A man approached her. A blow to the head and then a blinding light and several dull sounds, and nothing after that.

Lee raises her hands up to her face but she can't see them. Could the blow to her head have blinded her?

"Is there anyone here?" she says out loud. She isn't expecting a response but wants to make sure she can hear. She can hear.

She feels around to get a sense of what she's lying on. A thin mattress, on top of a steel bed frame.

She sits up and places her feet on a smooth floor. She slept on a bed just like this in the army, during basic training, after which she completed a medic course and then served as an instructor. Basic training lasted just three weeks, but she remembers the structure of the bed well. A steel frame with springs stretched from top to bottom and side to side. She examines her aching right arm and feels that it's swollen. The sharp stabbing pains in her head are keeping time with the beating of her heart. She gently touches the epicenter of the pain in her head before holding her hand up to her face once again, trying to see if there is blood. But again, her eyes see nothing.

She stands up slowly and, despite the nausea and dizziness, takes a few steps. Her good arm stretches out in front of her, and her injured arm stays folded and pressed to her stomach.

The floor is cool. And she's barefoot. Where are her running shoes? And the clothes she's in – where did they come from? She isn't wearing the sweats she runs in but a pair of pajamas in a soft fabric, flannel probably. She stops to check – she still has her panties on.

She moves ahead cautiously, one step at a time, until her knee bumps into something. She lowers her outstretched arm until her hand touches a smooth surface at waist height. She taps on it and it gives off a metallic sound. She moves along the length of it, brushing her hand over the surface until it curves downwards into a bowl-like shape. She feels around it, realizing it's a sink.

She opens the tap and leans over and drinks from the stream of water. She's parched and the water is cold and thirst-quenching. Then she ducks her head under the stream, wetting her hair and detecting the sweet smell of blood as it rinses into the sink.

She straightens up carefully, the water from her hair dripping onto her shoulders, soaking into the flannel shirt. He must have undressed her and changed her clothes while she was unconscious. A shudder runs through her. Maybe her clothes are in the room somewhere? Her phone was in her running armband. If she finds it, she'll be able to turn on the flashlight and see where she is, and how to get out of here, and maybe make a call for help, if there's reception in this place.

She continues groping her way around the room, feeling wall-mounted kitchen cabinets above the sink, with unlocked doors and cylindrical tin cans inside them. A plastic curtain hanging on a metal rod, with a recess in the wall behind it – she moves her hand to one side until she feels a smooth surface. She runs her fingers along the lines of grout between the ceramic tiles. She reaches up and her hand runs into a showerhead. And next to it another one. And another one. And another one. A row of showers.

The tiles come to an end and she continues moving carefully along the wall until she encounters something new – a lintel, framing a door, with a handle. She presses down on it, but the door doesn't open. She locates a keyhole under the handle. The door's locked. If this is a door, then there must be a light switch nearby. She feels around the door until she finds a switch, then presses it.

A row of long fluorescent lights emit a series of clicks and her eyes are flooded at once with white light. She closes them tight. Now that they've gotten used to the total darkness, the sudden glare sparks an intense pain. But she's relieved to find she can see. He didn't blind her.

She slowly grows accustomed to the bright light. With her eyes shut to begin with, then shielding them with the palm of her hand, she opens them gradually until she can clearly see concrete walls, kitchen cabinets, a stainless-steel sink stained with the blood she washed from her hair, plastic curtains covering the row of showers. On one side of the room, across from the bed where she was just lying, stand four wooden cribs with mattresses.

On the wall opposite her, she notices another door. She walks over to it and presses down on the handle. The door opens to reveal a small cubicle, with nothing but a toilet inside.

Turning back towards the room, she sees that lying on the bed is a sheet of paper. When she moves closer, it's clear there's something written on it.

Welcome,
I'm pleased to have you here as my guest.
We'll meet soon, and after we talk, you'll have a good understanding of why you are here and the role you are to play.
Now, you're injured and confused.
I've gone out to run a few important errands.
Take care of yourself in the meantime.
The kitchen cabinet on the far right contains a first-aid kit with bandages, iodine, adhesive dressings and paracetamol. Take a tablet for the headache, rinse your head in the sink, apply iodine to your wounds and dress them.
The tap water is potable. Drink a little.

There's food in the cupboards. Eat a little. You suffered a blow, and if you eat a lot, your stomach will hurt. We want to make sure you don't have any internal injuries. I suggest two maple-flavored energy bars.

I'll take care of your arm when I get back.

Lee puts the sheet of paper back on the bed beside her. This is insane. This place, this letter, the weird creep who kidnapped her, it all feels like a bad dream. Why would anyone want to do this to her? To anybody? Is he going to rape her? Will he torture her? Lee notices her breath is quick and shallow. She takes a big breath and releases it slowly trying to calm herself down. She can't give in to panic. She has to think and act logically in order to get out of this place. She *will* get out of this place. She has to.

She finds the first-aid kit in the cupboard. The containers she'd felt in the dark were canned corn, beans and meatballs. In the drawer next to the sink are sealed packages of plastic forks and spoons. She opens another cabinet door – sheets, towels, sanitary pads, toothbrushes and tubes of toothpaste, soap, shampoo. Another door – detergents and trash bags.

He must have plans to keep her here for a long time. Maybe forever. She shudders at the thought.

She picks up a can of corn and gauges its weight in her hand. When he comes in, she can throw it at his face and flee. But she won't do that. Not before she figures out what this place is and whether he's armed. And not with a broken arm. She needs to regain her strength. She needs a plan. To be certain that her escape will not fail when she puts the plan into action.

She opens the cabinet door on the far left. It's filled with packages of baby food and baby bottles.

11.

Tonight, I'll remember my dream

Tonight, I'll remember my dream

Tonight, I'll remember my dream

05:05

We, the crew and I, are on a tour of the desert, and our hosts take us to a small village on the banks of a large reservoir. It's hot outside. The reservoir is very deep and we all dive into the water to get a closer look at the large groups of turtles living there. There are thousands of them, and we swim among them without any diving equipment.

I can breathe underwater and it seems perfectly natural to me. The turtles swim around us. Our presence doesn't bother them. A vehicle is parked under the water on the reservoir bed, with its lights on. It appears new, untouched by algae. Rays of sunshine illuminate the underwater landscape in wavy lines. Imprinted onto the white muddy reservoir bed behind the vehicle are two tire tracks. Maxtreks. Four luminous blue partial shoeprints.

We get out afterwards and dry ourselves off. "They purify the water." Our hostess, an elderly woman who runs the project, speaks Spanish and I understand her. "Before the reservoir was here, we used to drink from the river over there," she says, pointing in the direction of a river flowing on the other side of the village, "and many people would get sick back then. That was before we built the purification system with the turtles."

"Whose car is down there?" I ask, and she says, "It belongs to…"

I can't recall the name she mentions in my dream.

"He didn't manage to get out when they filled the reservoir with water, so the reservoir is named after him today."

Fuck. How could I forget the name she said in the dream? When I speak to her, she tilts her head slightly and smiles, as if to signal to me that she knows my Spanish isn't perfect but that she understands me anyway. I hope the reservoir is well protected and I offer my assistance. I tell her I work for the police. I try to remember the name of the man after whom they named the reservoir, but I can't.

It's hot outside. She takes us into her house on the edge of the reservoir and gives us cold water to drink from a thick glass jug. It's dark in the house. The water comes from the reservoir and tastes very good.

The woman leans over, her wrinkle-furrowed face close to mine. "Why did he run down the girls? What does he get out of it? Is he a serial killer? If he's a serial killer, then he'll continue. Do you realize that?"

"Yes. He'll continue."

"You need to talk to her."

48

"To Rotem?"

"Yes. You know she can help you, but you've put her aside. Try to think why."

"We haven't talked in a long time. I'm trying on my own first."

"She's the only one who can help you. Acknowledge it. The man you're after is smarter than you are. Smarter than everyone you know."

"But not Rotem," I tell the old woman.

"That's true." She smiles at me. "Not her."

She moves in even closer and whispers into my ear: "Even though it suits you to forget, you must try to remember. We're nothing more than our memories. What would happen if they were taken from us?"

I tell her that I don't know, and she walks away from me and goes to talk to someone else.

I hear a female voice say, "You get me."

I turn towards the speaker and recognize her. I've seen a picture of her.

"Lee?"

"Once, on a school field trip in the summer, we camped out for the night in a dry riverbed. Above us was a cliff, and some of the boys decided to climb to the top. One of them thought it would be funny to roll a rock off the cliff, and it landed between two sleeping bags – mine and my friend's. It was the closest I've ever come to dying. Apart from now. You know that. You know how it feels."

Daphne finishes reading the first dream she's recorded and places the notebook on the bed beside her. She jotted it down when she woke up, about an hour ago, and then went back to sleep.

She can hardly believe she wrote all of that.

She'd forgotten the dream completely, but it comes back to her as she reads, and that's good. The book says that first you need to

49

document your dreams. And then, when the brain realizes it's important, it'll start to get easier to remember them. That's the first step.

Anna's door is open. She's sleeping peacefully, curled up with her comforter in a fetal position, a thick book lying face-down on the bed beside her. Daphne enters the room quietly, barefoot, and leans over to read the name of the book. *Shantaram*. She stands still and listens enviously to the stress-free breathing of her roommate, who has no trouble at all when it comes to sleeping through the night. Anna goes to visit her parents in Holon every weekend, or they come to get her and they eat out at a restaurant. They invite Daphne to join them. Sometimes, she does.

She leaves the room and goes to the kitchen, breathing in the muggy Tel Aviv summer air. How can it still be so hot at six in the morning? She fills the kettle and, while waiting for the water to boil, lights a cigarette, standing at the open kitchen window and blowing out jets of white smoke. Two shot glasses are resting in the sink. She goes over and picks one up and smells it.

"Daphne!"

She runs to the living room in her cat-print pajamas.

He's sitting there with his friends.

They're very big. Big hands. Prickly cheeks. Nails with blackened tips.

There's a large clear-glass bottle on the square table in front of them. It's practically empty.

That familiar smell.

The smell that's usually there before something bad happens.

"Want to see something?" he laughs.

The back of her neck burns with a sharp pain and she jumps aside and catches sight of his hand stretched out behind her and orange sparks flying off the end of the cigarette with which he just burned her out of the blue.

"Like a grasshopper."

"Like a chicken."
They're laughing.
One of them has gold teeth.
She doesn't run back to her room.
It's forbidden.

The shot glass slips from her hand and breaks in the sink. The kettle switch jumps to the off position. The water is boiled. She stubs out her cigarette in the ashtray on the ledge outside the window, then picks up the pieces of broken glass with her bare hands and throws them in the trash. There are only two pieces. Small glasses don't shatter. She makes coffee and sits down with her mug at the kitchen table.

A cigarette butt can offer up numerous findings. DNA from saliva. A brand of lipstick or balm to treat dry lips, a bacterial culture. Every puff on a cigarette contains acrolein that binds with deoxyguanosine and creates DNA adducts, formaldehyde that rearranges and degrades chromosomes, isoprene that breaks DNA strands. She's aware of all of that, but even so she lights another cigarette in her car on the way to work. And then another one when Nathan tells her they have to go back to Tel Aviv.

"So why make me come to Jerusalem? Do you have any idea what the traffic is like out there today?"

"I received a call just now. Ten minutes ago. They found a Pandora bracelet in Givatayim. Lee Ben-Ami's."

"How do they know it's hers?"

"Three beads on the bracelet with her name. One with Lee, one with Ben, one with Ami. I've just spoken to her boyfriend and he confirmed it's hers."

She pictures the bracelet with the three beads. Good that she doesn't have a long surname. It would be tough to make a bead with the name Zilberberg.

"Who found it?"

"A woman spotted the bracelet on the road near the entrance to her building. When she saw the name engraved on it, she called the police."

"She probably put her paws all over it. We won't be able to lift any decent prints."

"Whoever snatched her wouldn't have touched the bracelet anyway. It must have fallen off her wrist as she was abducted. You coming? We'll pick up the bracelet from the Dan District HQ and take a drive to the location where it was found. Maybe we'll find something there."

They head out towards the parking lot in silence, then Daphne says, "I don't think he's going to stop. It's just a couple so far…"

Nathan stops walking and looks at her. "A couple?"

"If it's the work of a serial killer or serial abductor. If he killed Anat and abducted Lee, why would he stop there? He'll continue. He'll snatch others. He'll run others down."

"Not if we find him first."

They make their way from Jerusalem in separate cars so they can part ways at the end of the day. They tail one another through the heavy traffic all the way to the Dan District Police Headquarters at 122 Jabotinsky Street in Ramat Gan. There, they sign the appropriate paperwork and collect the bracelet in a closed ziplock bag. It was found by a sixty-year-old woman, who is standing outside the entrance to her apartment block and giving a statement to a Dan District detective when they get there. She points out the precise spot where she found the piece of jewelry.

Together, Daphne and Nathan examine the road and sidewalk, look for brake marks on the tarmac, then search through the yards of the adjacent buildings.

"There's blood here," Daphne calls out, pointing under a parked car.

Nathan comes over and lies down on the road beside her. She has a powerful flashlight in her hand and its beam is aimed at a purplish-brown blood stain.

"Close the road," Nathan instructs; and the two patrol officers who'd arrived on the scene along with the detective set up orange-and-white striped cones and no-entry signs to block any traffic.

"What would you use now?" Nathan asks Daphne.

"Luminol."

"Under the car?"

"Yes. Under the car with a UV light, and around it with a filter."

"Excellent. Go get it," he says.

She goes to her car, retrieves a spray bottle from the kit and sprays the stain. It's relatively dark under the car, and the stain glows under the beam of the UV light. They stand up and she sprays the asphalt around the car, and they use a UV filter board this time. A luminescent blue trail of small drops lead to the center of the road. They follow the trail of drops, spraying and exposing them until they come to an end.

The yellow brick road.

"This is where she was put in the car."

Nathan brushes off the road dust that stuck to his blue uniform, watching Daphne. "Daph?"

"What?"

"Did you do something to your hand?"

"No."

"So why are you playing with your fingers like that?"

"Ah, that. It's nothing."

"Come on now," Nathan persists.

"It's from the book about lucid dreaming," Daphne reluctantly explains. "It's called a reality check. You count your fingers, try to pull one and then read something, divert your gaze and then read it again."

"And what does that do?"

"If there are five fingers and they don't get longer when you pull on them, and if you read something and turn away and then look at it again and the text is the same, it's a sign that you're awake. If there's a different number of fingers or something strange happens to them, or if the text is different when you look at it again, then you're dreaming."

"A different text?"

"That's how it works. The brain's center of logic is inactive when you're dreaming, so you can't read like you do when you're awake. You can read, but the moment you divert your gaze, the text will be different when you look at it again. The book you're looking at, for example, will turn into an epitaph on a gravestone and then a billboard you saw once and then an airline ticket. All kinds of things like that."

"So why are you doing those checks now? You're awake, right?"

"That's the whole idea. You need to get used to doing them when you're awake and then it becomes a matter of routine, and your brain will do it in your dream at some point too. And once you start to do reality checks in your dream and realize that you're dreaming, that's when the lucid dreaming begins. It's the key to the door to that world. Pretty simple. You should try it."

"Have you managed to get into a dream yet?"

"Not yet," she says as she packs the samples they've collected in their appropriate places in her forensics kit. "I've only just started practicing, and the book says it takes a while before you get it right."

"Okay. Prove that it works and then maybe I'll try it."

From the corner of her eye she can see him staring at her as she sorts out the samples they collected. They've been working together for a year and a half now; she knows him well and knows he isn't the kind of person who thinks out loud. He goes quiet when he's thinking. He's giving her the same look she encountered during her first recruitment interview.

After finishing with all the standard technical questions about chemistry, he started on brain teasers.

"If one and a half chickens lay one and a half eggs in a day and a half, how many eggs will you get from a coop with thirty chickens during the month of August?"

She'd always loved brain teasers.

"Just a sec. Let me think."

It took her thirty seconds to come up with an answer.

"The classic answer would be six hundred and twenty, but I have some reservations. For example…"

"How did you get that number?"

"If one and a half chickens lay an egg and a half in a day and a half, then let's forget about the half chicken and say that one chicken will still lay one egg in a day and a half, which means two-thirds of an egg in one day. So two-thirds multiplied by thirty chickens multiplied by thirty-one days in August gives you six hundred and twenty eggs.

But there's no such thing as half a chicken or half an egg, and that makes the question a little problematic, and there's no data to indicate whether the number of eggs changes as a function of the months of the year. Let's say: Perhaps chickens lay more eggs during the heat of the summer? Increased metabolic rate? It sounds logical but needs to be checked. Who came up with it?"

She smiles to herself now, recalling how she'd tripped him up.
"What?"

"The brain teaser. One of yours?"

"No. From the Internet."

She'd taken a small notebook and pen from her purse.

"What are you writing?"

"A note to myself to find out who came up with it. He must have other interesting ones too."

He recruited her for his Forensics Unit team. She knew he'd had to fight on her behalf with the Human Resources Department, who didn't want someone with her background. A mother who disappeared when Daphne was nine years old. An alcoholic and abusive father who was a suspect in her mother's disappearance. A foster home from which she fled and to which she was taken back several times, until she was placed in a boarding school facility.

The police force didn't want her, but now she's a cop. The army didn't want to enlist her, but she insisted, and served as a combat fitness instructor at the Wingate Institute. To get into university, she first had to retake all her matriculation exams to improve her grades, and she funded her studies by working at the same time as a bartender at a pub in Jerusalem's Russian Compound.

"You're unstable. You're fucked up. You'll be out of here in a year." They went out of their way to shake her during the interview with HR. They presented her with a scanned copy of her personal file from the boarding school that included transcripts of conversations with her about all she had gone through with her father and with the foster family, things no young girl should ever have to endure. And she had sat in front of them, fists clenched, and explained that she was exactly the person they needed. A fighter. Determined. Uncompromising. Someone who will push on even when everyone tells her she doesn't stand a chance. All her life she'd been told she didn't stand a chance.

They work alongside one another, quietly documenting the scene, photographing every detail, collecting samples from the drops of coagulated blood. Daphne wonders if maybe they don't all belong to Lee Ben-Ami and they'll get the DNA of the person who abducted her. Perhaps she managed to put up a fight and something from him remained here at the scene.

The detective, who finishes questioning the finder of the bracelet, comes over to them.

"Find anything?"

"Yes. Based on the findings at the scene, we're dealing with a felonious assault and abduction."

12.

She opens the first-aid kit, empties its contents onto the bed and reaches for a triangular bandage, fashioning it into a sling for her arm so as to keep it bent without having to exert herself. She also looks for something she can fix to her arm with another bandage to form a splint of sorts to prevent the broken bone from moving, but she can't find anything suitable.

She gingerly examines her right forearm again. It isn't an open fracture. The ulna's whole and the radius is fractured. She can feel the point at which the bone is broken, and a cry of pain escapes her lips when she touches it.

What did he mean by: "I'll take care of your arm when I get back"? In their first year of medical school, Lee and her fellow students could recite the names of all the bones in the body and they practiced mending fractures on models. If the bones don't fuse properly, her arm's range of motion and symmetry will be compromised. And she'll require surgery to mend it – a surgeon will have to break the bone again so that it can re-fuse at the correct angle.

If she ever gets out of here.

She feels her head wound. It would have been better to stitch it, but it had already closed partially and was going to leave a crescent-shaped scar. She applies the iodine and fixes a gauze pad to the spot with two strips of adhesive tape in the shape of an X. She then removes her pajamas and examines her entire body. A few scratches and grazes. She cleans them with alcohol and applies iodine to them too, before carefully dressing again. No serious damage, she sums up, concluding her diagnosis; only a broken arm, a large blue contusion on her left thigh where she was hit by the car's bumper, and a head wound that's causing bouts of dizziness and nausea.

He's right – paracetamol would be a good idea; but she won't touch the medication.

She jumps as she hears a noise outside the door and then holds her breath and listens. Footsteps, and metallic clinking, like the sound of objects being scattered noisily on the floor. Tin cans perhaps.

"So where's it hiding?"

Someone is talking on the other side of the door. She recognizes the monotone, emotionless voice of the man who abducted her. She has no doubt it's him. But who's he talking to? Was she abducted by a group of people? Are there others involved too?

"Recycling is paramount. We have to save the planet. Water with chemicals in aluminum containers, filtered water in plastic packaging. Sewage flowing through concrete pipes en route to a purification facility. It hasn't gone anywhere. And even if it has, you can wander around there for hours and days without anyone noticing you. Like a ghost. Like an invisible onlooker. The herd won't spot the tiger until the tiger pounces."

What's he talking about? The cans roll and rattle across the floor. She hears the hum of a melody she doesn't recognize.

She goes over to the bed, places the first-aid kit in its box and returns it to the cupboard. She wipes down the sink with a small kitchen towel and lays it open on the counter, lightly stained with drops of her blood.

"Here it is. I knew it. It's here."

She sits on the bed and continues to listen.

13.

He finds the tag among the cans that are on the floor and places it on the desk. Then he gathers up the cans into a large trash bag and places it by the doorway to the first hallway, scanning the room to make sure he hasn't left a single can on the floor.

Order and cleanliness go hand in hand. Getting down to work is impossible if things aren't clean and tidy. You can't think. Everything has to be organized. Like an operating room before the patient is wheeled in. Like a dentist's clinic. Like the empty refrigerators at the morgue. Like the row of showers. Like the racks of protective gear. Like folders on your computer arranged according to subject.

He sits down and turns on the desk lamp and examines the tag from all sides. It was thrown into the trash by Doron Moskowitz. He's the father. The wristband grants access to a maternity ward.

It's made of light blue plastic and has a single-use closing mechanism that needs to be cut to be removed. A sticker with personal particulars. Name. Name of child. ID number. Ariel 16-point font. A severed edge. A date.

He opens a notebook and writes in it, reciting to himself in the process:

> *I adorned you with ornaments*
> *Put bracelets on your hands*
> *And a necklace around your neck*

He's going to need a small battery-powered printer to which he can send files from a mobile phone. He'll move to the computer room shortly to check where he can purchase such a device.

Using a hammer and a small steel nail, he fixes the light blue tag to the white concrete wall and then steps back to examine the wall with a sense of satisfaction.

Back to the desk.

He reaches for the raw materials and starts working. A flexible sheet of light blue plastic. A thin strip of transparent plastic. White paper. A lamination machine. A utility knife. Scissors. A perforator. White plastic snap fasteners.

After an hour of slow and precise work, he slips the finished product into a white envelope and places it on the table. He returns all the tools and accessories to their rightful places, and only then does he make for the door to her room. He's ready to deal with her now. Everything in its time.

With one hand on the handle and the other holding the key ready, he calls out, "I'm going to open your door now. Don't try anything foolish. You have no way of getting out of here without me."

14.

She's still sitting on the bed when she hears the key turn. Not the series of clicks you hear when a locked door is opened, but just a sharp and short one. The door opens and he enters.

After closing the door and slipping the key into his pocket, he stands in front of her. He's roughly her height, around forty, not too slim or muscular, wearing a black T-shirt and jeans. He is not intimidating, just an average-looking guy. A person she would not notice in a crowd. Lee holds her breath. How's she going to put up a fight? How's she going to push him off of her with a broken arm? What's he going to do to her? He comes over to the bed, sits down next to her and looks at her. The smell of iodine coming off her clothes mingles with the fragrance of his shampoo. She doesn't dare move and doesn't utter a sound.

He starts talking all of a sudden, in that same strange and hollow voice: "Since the beginning of time, there has been an element of purity in true suffering. Not the pain of a broken arm, not physical suffering. Mental anguish. For example, when someone's told he has Stage 3 pancreatic cancer and will live out the rest of his short life in agony. Or when someone is tormented all her life with the thought that she should have done something to save her twin sister a second before she ran into the road. Or when someone loses a child. That's the most severe torture. The loss of a child."

He closes his eyes and inhales slowly, filling his lungs. Lee watches him intently. Who is this man? He's a criminal; he abducted her; he's insane. But for some reason, she doesn't fear him. He hasn't undressed her with his eyes, and he's keeping his distance from her. She dares to hope that it isn't that kind of abduction, that he doesn't have plans to sexually abuse her. So what does he want from her? What's all this strange talk?

"That's why you're here."

"What?" is all she can say.

"There's a time for everything. I need you here now and won't need you afterwards. I'll release you at the end of the process. You'll be able to leave. I'm telling you this now so that you'll cooperate. You're here for a long time, but temporarily, for a finite period, at the end of which you'll be able to leave and return to your life. But before you can go, you'll have to work for me – attentively, with devotion and compassion."

"What process? What do you want from me?"

She's making an effort to remain calm. Not to yell. Not to annoy him. She's decided to cooperate with him, to go along with his madness; she thinks that perhaps she'll be able to figure out what's happening here that way.

"You'll find out soon enough," he responds dryly. "First, we're going to take care of your arm. I need both your arms in good working order." He rises from the bed. "Come with me. Don't try to escape. If you try to get away, I'll be forced to hurt you again, and I don't want to cause you any more harm." He sets out for the door. "Follow me," he says again, seeing her hesitate. "We'll take care of your arm."

He uses the key and leaves the room, and she follows him into the adjacent one. It's smaller and entirely different. She's standing next to a wall that's covered in a collage of pictures, and she studies them closely. They all depict something sick, distorted – a photograph she recalls from the newspaper of an Indian baby who was born with a second head growing out of his stomach; a black-and-white image of two men with narrow faces and straight hair who share one body, two arms and two legs; a picture of twins lying on a long bed, joined at the head with one long body; a photograph of a dehydrated fetus with two heads. More and more pictures, some old and in black-and-white, printed on photo paper or cut from newspapers; and some contemporary and sharp, in color and high resolution, with captions as if they've come from hospitals. What is the purpose of this place? Where is she?

She turns her attention to the opposite wall, which is covered by row upon row of large X-ray images mounted on white Plexiglas boxes and backlit by florescent bulbs.

The room gives her the creeps. She can't allow herself to believe anything he says. She has to try to remember everything. The smallest of details could be her way out of this horrible place. She scans the room, trying to take in as much as she can. A wall of photographs, a wall of X-ray images, a desk, a white envelope, a toolbox resting on a concrete floor, a large trash bag alongside another door, which he is opening with a key. He beckons her towards him and Lee follows him through the door. It slams shut behind them and locks automatically.

This room is very big, a hall of sorts, and is filled with medical equipment. In the center of the room is a horizontal surface, like a high bed, and above it the adjustable arm of an X-ray machine, another X-ray machine for chest-imaging in front of a wall-mounted panel, a mobile operating table, the kind of basin she's familiar with from hospitals, a trash can with a foot pedal mechanism to open it, a metal chair, closed steel cupboards like lockers. Large medical posters hanging on the walls – a muscle chart, a skeletal chart, a vascular system chart, an enlarged diagram of a heart, lungs, a digestive system. There is even an internal control room with clear windows – for the operator of the X-ray equipment, just like in a hospital.

She tries to etch everything into her memory, without missing a single detail. Maybe that's why he chose her of all people? Because she's a medical student? Will she have to operate these machines herself? The medical equipment is shiny and looks brand new. How did he get his hands on all of this? Who has this kind of access to professional X-ray equipment, let alone the money to purchase it?

He goes over to the only chair in the room and moves it closer to the X-ray machine. "Sit here and place your arm on the surface, and we'll take an X-ray."

She does as he says. He goes into the control room and observes her through the large clear window. "Don't move," he says; and seconds later, the machine emits its familiar humming sound. "Turn your arm to the side." Another hum. "Other side." Another X-ray. "Can you make a fist?"

She curls her fingers as much as she can, until the pain reaches her threshold of tolerance. Another hum. He studies the computer screen in front of him. "It's a simple transverse fracture. Your radius is broken. We'll have to straighten it before we set it externally. There's a deviation of three millimeters."

He knows the terms. Maybe he's a doctor. She isn't sure if she should tell him she's a medical student. But something tells her not to say anything yet.

"May I see?" she asks, turning to look at him in the control room while remaining seated with her arm resting on the metallic surface of the X-ray machine.

"Yes."

She stands up and goes to the control room. It's a clean break, and he's right – the two sides of the fracture are slightly out of line with one another.

"Come back to the chair and put your arm on the surface again." As she lowers herself into the chair again, he goes over to one of the cupboards and takes out a package of gauze pads. "Here, bite down on this while I straighten the bone. It's going to hurt." His voice is neither reassuring nor threatening. Simply devoid of emotion. And she has no other choice. Being at the mercy of this weirdo makes her want to scream. But she follows his instructions. She has to.

She bites down on the gauze pads as hard as she can the moment he takes hold of her arm. He pulls the two pieces of bone further apart and presses them together again. He does so skillfully and quickly, but the pain is intense, and she screams inside her muffled mouth, her entire body breaking into a sweat and her eyes filling with tears.

As he lets go of her arm she removes the package of gauze pads from between her teeth. She must find a way to escape. If she had something with which to stun him, she could reach into his pocket for the key. Not now, almost breathless with pain, but when her arm heals and she's fit again, he'll get a can or two to the head and then she'll make a run for it. Tears of rage mix with tears of pain as she promises herself she'll make him pay for what he's done to her.

He shows no interest in her pain and merely says: "Leave your hand in that position," before returning to the control room. Another X-ray, and another look at the screen.

"Very good."

She wipes her face with her flannel sleeve. "May I see?"

"Not now. Don't move your arm; I need to immobilize it first." He goes back to the cupboard to retrieve the materials he needs to make the cast – a thin layer of inner lining, and strips of plaster that he soaks in water and then winds around her forearm. He works in silence, efficiently and precisely, until her arm is covered from her elbow and down past her wrist, leaving the thumb and four fingers free. She can feel the plaster warming slightly on her arm.

"Let it dry for a few minutes." He stands up and washes his hands in the basin, before clearing away the remains of the materials he used and throwing them into the trash. Using a disinfecting wipe, he also cleans the surface of the X-ray machine and then throws away the dirty cloth. After washing his hands again, he returns to her to check on the plaster cast, which is hard now.

"Come."

She stands up and follows him to the control room. On display on the screen is an X-ray image of her arm. The broken bone is perfectly aligned.

"You have a pen and pencil in your room. You can draw on the cast whenever you feel like it."

15.

It's happening again.

I'm under the comforter, but something feels different. This isn't my room.

No. Not again.

Not that again.

Please, not that.

I try with all my might to fight the desire to peek out from under the comforter. If I stay out of sight, maybe it won't happen. But I can't help myself. An urge too powerful to suppress forces me to glance out at the three windows. They are shrouded this time in a thick fog through which I can't see anything at all.

And then his face appears at the middle window, between the palms of his hands that he plants forcefully against the glass. A cold shudder runs down the back of my neck.

He moves away from the window; I can hear him outside, screaming and cursing, and the powerful kicks against the front door begin. I decide that I'm not going to allow him in this time. I jump out of the bed and push it as hard as I can towards the door to barricade myself in. The bed is heavy, but I manage to move it little by little until the legs at the front get stuck against one of the floorboards.

I run around to the other side of the bed and try to lift it over the obstacle, but I can't. I try with all my strength but to no avail. I look down at my wrists to see strained tendons, and my Pandora bracelet, and its beads engraved with the name *Daphne Dagan* in curly letters glowing like drops under a blue light. The bracelet reminds me of something but I can't remember what.

I'm sweating. I give up on the bed and run to the other room to see if I can find something in the closet with which to stop him. I hear the door of the house give in to his kicking and a cry of: "You're done for!"

I open the door of the closet. It's empty and scribbled on the wooden side panel on the inside are the words *You're probably going to die tonight* in dried brownish blood. I turn around and he's standing in front of me, breathing heavily.

"So you're trying to block the door?" He looks back through the doorway at the bed. "Do you think that'll do you any good?" He lets out a hollow laugh, exposing his yellow teeth. "Let's play a little." He kicks me in the stomach with his heavy shoe and I double up on the floor. He lifts me up like a rag doll, walks into the other room and throws me onto the bed.

"You'll never get rid of me. You're my favorite toy." He's on top of me again. His breath reeks of decay. He's choking me.

The house around me spins as the oxygen in my lungs runs out.

She wakes up from the dream, heart pounding, soaked in sweat. She looks around, taking in her surroundings; the book she'd been reading is lying on the floor next to the bed, her sheets are crumpled.

The apartment's quiet; soft streaks of sunlight stream in through partially open shutters.

She touches the screen of her phone to see the time – 05:29. She gets out of bed, goes to the kitchen and fills the kettle. Her breathing is less rapid. She returns to her room, taking care not to make any noise and wake Anna, and picks the book up off the floor. She needs to remember to renew the loan from the Mount Scopus library.

She makes herself a cup of coffee and sits down at the kitchen table. She doesn't feel like going back to her room, which always feels like an intimidating place in the wake of a nightmare, as if the bed and walls and ceiling are somehow responsible for her dreams.

She lights a cigarette, opens the book and leafs through until she finds the page she was on when she fell asleep. If she wants to dream about something specific, she needs to add it to the sentences she writes in her dream journal before going to bed and play with the idea in her head. *Tonight, I'm going to dream that I'm flying*, for example. And to repeat it and memorize it and cram it into her head in the minutes before falling asleep, and her brain will do the rest. It doesn't happen right away. She understands she'll need to train herself. In the world of dreams, everything works slowly.

And there's also the matter of sleep paralysis. She needs to be wary of that.

On the kitchen table next to her book is the police notice she showed Anna the night before.

Dan District Police
Case No.: 447369 / 3822

משטרת ישראל

MISSING

The Israel Police is asking for the public's assistance in its search for Lee Ben-Ami, 23, from Givatayim, who was last seen at her residence – 16 HaLilach Street, Apt. 5 – on Sunday, August 16, 2016, before disappearing without a trace.

Description

Build: Slender

Hair: Light brown, short and straight

Eyes: Honey brown

Height: 5'6"

Clothing: Blue-and-red sweatsuit, red running shoes

Distinguishing Features: None

Anyone with information that could be of assistance in locating her is kindly requested to call the Dan District Police Headquarters at 03-6104444, or the Israel Police 100 hotline.

16.

She's more comfortable sleeping on her left side. The arm with the cast doesn't bother her as much that way during the night. And as for the pencil he left in her room, she uses that for writing in a spiral notebook she found in one of the cupboards, but mostly for scratching under the cast, which has started to irritate her skin.

It's been a week since she woke up here. And after setting her arm and returning her to the room in which she was imprisoned, he's disappeared. He left and hasn't returned. She has already managed to map and record the contents of all the cupboards in the notebook. The food will last her about a month; and as long as there is water flowing from the tap, she can drink. She washes the empty cans of food and fills them with water, which she changes every day, so that she'll have something to drink if the water supply is cut off.

She tries to listen for sounds of activity outside the room, but she can't hear a thing. The only noises are hers, the hum of the fluorescent lights on the ceiling, or the rush of the water she flushes down the toilet.

She has no way of knowing where she is. If she's ten miles from the location where he snatched her, or two hundred. Maybe she's in a building in the Negev somewhere, or a basement on the Golan Heights. She's tried digging into one of the walls with the sharp edge of the folded lid of one of the cans of food but only managed to scratch away a thin layer of plaster before running into impenetrable concrete.

She knows there are at least three rooms in the structure. The room in which she's being held, the adjacent room with the strange photographs, and the large room with the medical equipment. The air-conditioning system remains on all the time but makes no sound, and she can see the air vents in the ceiling.

The boredom is a killer. She's used to being on the go around the clock: going to school and her job at the hospital, seeing friends, nights out when she doesn't have a shift to work, Shai. What's he doing? He must have spoken to the police by now. He must be looking for her. Her mom and dad must be going crazy. Her friends too. She misses them all so much. The pain is real and persistent like a hole drilled through her heart. She recalls news stories about young women or girls abducted and then rescued after years of imprisonment. She won't be one of them. No. No way. Either she'll end up dead, or her abductor will be killed during her escape attempt – and that's not far off. She's not living for years on end in a closed room. Not her.

But she needs to bide her time. To recover. The cast will come off in a month's time. She'll keep a lid on her at all times – the metal lid she removed from a can and folded. She sharpened it on the concrete wall inside the kitchen cupboard under the sink so that he wouldn't see the marks. The lid has turned into a small knife. She'll wait for her opportunity. She won't miss.

She begins exercising. One set of stomach crunches. Back to her feet. A set of squats. Jumping on the spot. And then all over again. And once more. And again. Anything that doesn't require the use of both arms. Morning and evening. She perseveres, sweating, straining, feeling all of her muscles at work. She starts to feel better.

There's no way she's staying here.

After exercising, she wraps a trash bag around the cast and showers under a stream of cold water in one of the cubicles. The clothes she removes go into a large drawer labeled *Laundry* in red letters. And from the closet she retrieves a fresh set of neatly packed clothing, more and more of the same items – thin white sweatpants, a short-sleeved white shirt that's a little big for her, underwear, socks. All white.

She suddenly hears a door open and close in the adjacent room, followed by footsteps. She slides the improvised knife into the back of her sweatpants, the elastic waistband holding the weapon in place. In keeping with her practice runs, it's the best place for it – hidden and readily accessible.

She hears the key slip into the lock on the other side of the door and turn, releasing the pin tumbler mechanism with a click, and the door swings open to reveal him standing in front of a stainless-steel trolley, the kind you'd find in a hospital. She's pushed one around among patients at Ichilov Hospital countless times – the "Silver Platter" as they jokingly dubbed it. But his trolley isn't laden with medical equipment or medication, but tools, cardboard boxes and a set of steel handcuffs.

"Shackle your wrist to the frame of the bed."

He throws the handcuffs onto the bed. Lee doesn't budge.

"Shackle your wrist to the frame of the bed."

"Why?"

"I'm going to be working here in the room and will have to turn my back on you for part of the time. If you decide it would be a good opportunity to smash me on the head with something and flee, the handcuffs will prevent you from doing so."

He goes quiet and looks at her, scratching his chin.

"Actually, even if you were able to stun me and try to escape, you wouldn't make it out of here on your own. There are several rooms beyond this one and they're all locked. But let's leave things on the safe side."

She sits down and cuffs the wrist of her good arm to the frame of the bed, holding back tears of frustration, keeping an eye on him as he begins drilling into one of the walls. To the black metal fixture that he attaches to the wall, he mounts a television screen, which he then hooks up to an electronic device. Leading out from the device is a cable that's connected to the end of a second one, in a wall outlet. He works silently and efficiently.

He stands in front of her when it's done. "It's important for you to maintain your mental fortitude. I've set up a television feed for you. Not exactly cable or satellite TV, I can't risk you making contact with the outside world. This one facilitates reception only. You have access to programs from the two public channels and the music channel, and you can also get the Russian-language channel. I suggest you use the time to learn a new language. It could offer a challenge."

A challenge. Plunging the knife into his aorta would be a far more exciting challenge, she thinks. She'll get to do it at some point.

"Thanks," she responds, forcing herself to express appreciation to him. It's imperative he believes she isn't dangerous.

He rolls up the drill cable and returns the tools to the stainless-steel trolley, arranging them neatly again, and then he takes out a small hand-held vacuum cleaner to clear away the dust particles that fell to the floor as he drilled.

"How long do you plan to hold me here?"

"Until you've completed your task. Your mission."

"And what is my mission?"

"I'll brief you soon."

He produces a large black garbage bag and fills it with the laundry from the drawer. After placing it on the trolley, he leans over Lee. She draws back, as far as the handcuffs allow. He straightens up and shows her the key in his hand then leans over again and releases her.

He returns the handcuffs to the trolley and the key to his pocket and heads for the door, turning to her before he leaves the room.

"You may hear some drilling and renovation noises soon. My apologies in advance. You won't be bored for much longer. After we take off the cast and your arm recovers its strength, I'll arrange some friends for you."

He wheels the trolley out and the door closes behind him with a metallic click.

PART 2

THE FOUR

NOVEMBER 2016

17.

One hand gripping the steering wheel, he presses hard against his temples with the fingers of the other until the level of pain evens out. Great. He has the strength to get it done. The strength to take action. To take care of every tiny detail. To get in and to get out. To refrain from mistakes. He's played it over in his mind at least a hundred times already. He knows the place inside out.

Six-thirty in the morning. He's making his way along Route 4 towards Beilinson Hospital in a white Hyundai Tucson with tinted windows. He'd done a thorough check of the model, the keys and the type of alarm that had to be neutralized before deliberately choosing one owned by a family that lived in an area of private homes relatively far apart from one another. He then waited for them to go on holiday so as to avoid a stolen-car report. By the time they return, the car will be back in its rightful place.

But not in the same condition and with a slightly different smell.

Two hours, no more – that's how long he has to complete everything before they realize what's happened. Lying on the front passenger seat are two bags with everything he needs. A large bag and a small bag. Among various other items, the large one contains four sets of license plates – the one he's just removed from the Hyundai and replaced with another set, and three more sets to use later.

He turns on the radio and tunes in to the news, then opens Waze on his phone. Although he's practiced the trip countless times, he doesn't want to leave anything to chance; and if, God forbid, he's going to run into traffic or a blocked road along the way, he needs to know. Every now and then, the police radio scanner he purchased on eBay and placed on the dashboard emits a laconic report about an accident on one road or another. No irregular incidents to speak of. And it's raining. He raises his eyes and gazes at the heavy gray clouds above. Excellent. An ideal day. He won't deviate from his plan in the slightest and won't have to improvise. Unlike the bunch of clowns who work with him, who do everything in a half-assed way, without seeing things through to the end. He'll exploit their weaknesses.

Everything's in place. He's been preparing for this day for years, and they haven't. He has just the one attempt. After he does what he's about to do today, the procedures will be tightened. He knows that. If they had even an iota of intelligence in their empty heads, he wouldn't be able to implement his plan. But they don't have the ability to think one step ahead, a collection of fools who grasp something only after it's happened. He'll give them something to grasp. Soon. He smiles as he pictures everyone's reactions. The shock.

He drives into the hospital's outdoor parking lot and leaves the car, taking the small bag only. Dressed in a thick coat and carrying an open black umbrella, he makes his way towards the external entrance to the Maternity Ward, stopping at the door to shake the rain off the umbrella and close it before going inside. He then walks down the hallway straight to the men's bathroom, where he enters the largest stall, designed for the handicapped, and locks the door behind him.

He lowers the lid of the toilet, lays down the wet coat, folded, the umbrella and the bag, from which he retrieves a cordless power screwdriver, screws and a latch, and exits the stall. He's alone, and he quickly fixes the latch to the door of the stall with a few screws, checks that it closes properly and returns the screwdriver to the bag.

He gets back into the stall, stands in front of the mirror and rubs his eyes until they're bloodshot. He scratches the fake beard glued to his face. Irritating but bearable. Then he examines his eyebrows.

He applied gel to them that morning to ensure that not a single hair would fall out, and he shaved the rest of his body hair the night before from head to toe, but he had to leave the eyebrows so as not to appear odd. He needs to look tired but not strange. Chemotherapy patients lose their eyebrows and eyelashes too. But this is a different ward. Here, he needs to show lack of sleep. Every little detail counts.

He exits the stall again, leaving his equipment behind, and secures the latch with a small padlock. After pasting a sign on the door that reads: *Out of order. Undergoing repairs – sorry for the inconvenience*, he steps out into the hallway. He's familiar with every nook and cranny of the ward. He's done a walk-through on several occasions over the past year.

He goes over to the coffee machine and then walks around the ward with a cup of coffee in his hand, nodding hello to flustered nurses and exhausted new fathers. He walks past the wall with the large display window through which you can see the clear plastic cribs with their sheets of paper that note the particulars of the parents and the weight and gender of the babies. A blue one for boys. A pink one for girls. He smiles and gazes at the cribs and waves a greeting to a nurse who passes by.

A few minutes later, he returns to the bathroom, opens the stall and locks it from the inside. He takes out a light blue wristband with a name tag and a small portable printer. On the tag, he prints the name of one of the fathers from the blue sheets of paper he'd seen. An ID number. In the exact same font. A perfect replica. With the appropriate particulars. He secures the band around his left wrist and cuts off the superfluous strip of plastic. Before closing the bag, he checks to make sure that nothing has fallen to the floor. Everything's fine. He moves on.

He leaves the stall and locks it behind him again, then makes his way to the nursery window. He flashes the wristband to the nurse who's sitting inside and points to one of the cribs, the one that matches the name on the tag. The nurse opens the door and lets him in.

"Hi. Ruthie was thinking of trying to breastfeed before going to sleep for a while. Would it be okay now?"

"No problem."

He goes over to the clear plastic crib and the nurse checks again to make sure that the name tag on his wrist matches the particulars on the sheet of paper.

"He can stay with you in the ward for as long as you like."

"About half an hour. Ruthie's tired and I have to go to her parents to pick up all the equipment we've bought for the baby's room at home. She refused to allow them to deliver it to our place before the birth. Some sort of superstition."

"Yes, I'm familiar with that." The nurse smiles at him and he wheels out the crib containing the sleeping baby boy, wrapped in a fleece blanket. She closes the door behind him and he walks slowly down the hallway, engrossed in an imaginary call with his mobile phone pressed to his ear. When the hallway empties, he quickly makes his way back to his toilet stall with the crib, locking it from the inside again.

Reaching into the bag, he retrieves a baby carrier made of cloth and wraps it around himself. Taking great care, he then lifts the sleeping infant out of the crib and slips him into the carrier, still wrapped in the hospital blanket. He closes the bag and puts on the heavy coat. As he buttons the coat, the infant moves slightly and lets out a sleepy whimper, but his body heat and the darkness placate him. He doesn't wake up.

He picks up the bag and umbrella, locks the toilet stall behind him and leaves the building.

Back in the parking lot again, he opens the trunk to reveal four padded cardboard boxes. He places the sleeping baby into one of them, covers him with a blanket, closes the trunk, gets into the car and glances at his phone. Sixteen minutes have passed since he left the car. Less than the twenty minutes he allotted. Excellent. He'll have time to feed the baby the milk with the sleeping pill before he starts to wail in the car and attract attention. There's no need to hurry. The milk in the flask that's connected to the car's cigarette lighter socket has been warmed to precisely 98.6 degrees Fahrenheit. He'll empty the flask into a bottle. Soon. At the next stop.

Everything in keeping with the plan.

He starts up the Hyundai and drives off. The two bags are on the seat next to him. The baby is in the trunk. The radio is tuned to the news station and the volume of the police radio scanner is turned down low so as not to wake the infant. The heater in the car is set to exactly seventy-nine degrees.

18.

Ruthie Heller wakes up with a strange sense that something is terribly wrong. It's out of character for an optimist like her, but the feeling is very powerful. Something bad has happened. Something very bad.

The room in which she's lying isn't hers. After a quick glance at the armchair next to the bed, the bouquets of flowers, the chocolates, and the row of electricity and oxygen sockets on the wall, she remembers she's in the postnatal ward at Beilinson Hospital.

Perhaps the feeling has been brought on by all the anesthetics they pumped into her system. First, the epidural, then, when things didn't go as smoothly as expected, the anesthetist and two other grave-faced doctors rushed into the room explaining that a C-section was necessary, and something was added to the IV line that was already attached to her arm. She woke up only after everything was over and her baby was wrapped up and beautiful and perfect, and as he opened his eyes to gaze at her, she realized she loved him more than anything else in the world and cried with relief and joy.

That was last night. But today, something is wrong.

She sits up abruptly, ignoring the pain from the C-section, and gets out of bed. Her dizziness abates a few seconds later, and she shuffles as fast as the pain will allow her to the nursery.

It's just your mind playing tricks on you. It's probably only natural with a first child. The apprehension. Everything will be okay

when I see him again. I'll press my nose to his tiny body and smell
him again and calm down.

She shows the nurse her wristband and the nurse turns her head to glance at the row of clear plastic cribs. Her baby's crib is missing.

"Hi, honey. What are you doing up and about? You need to rest up in bed and be off your feet as much as possible." The nurse looks at the clock on the wall of the room. "Your husband took him about half an hour ago. Isn't he with you?"

The bad feeling turns into a shudder that runs through her entire body, freezing her blood. If Yonatan took the crib, then where is he? Why didn't he wake her? Maybe he wanted to let her sleep? She thanks the nurse and makes her way along the hallway of the ward. But she doesn't see them, her husband and her son.

Something's wrong.

Something's wrong.

She starts going through the rooms on the ward, opening door after door and peering inside. Yonatan isn't in any of them. After checking half the ward, she remembers her phone. Idiot. Why hasn't she called him? Her brain isn't functioning.

She returns to her room, disconnects the cell phone from the charger and calls her husband.

He answers almost immediately. "Hi, sweetheart. What's up?"

"Where are you?"

"In the car, on my way to you."

"What? Have you lost your mind? Have you taken him out for a drive?"

"What are you talking about? I'm on my way from home. I stopped at Jacob's to get you a proper croissant, not like the ones they sell at the hospital cafeteria."

"Is the baby not with you?"

"Don't be crazy. Do you think I'd take him out to do some shopping when he's just a day old? What's going on? Did you have a bad dream?"

She doesn't respond. The phone slips from her hand and drops onto the bed, and she stumbles towards the nursery, oblivious to her pain and exhaustion.

"He wasn't here!" she shouts at the nurse. "My husband wasn't here half an hour ago. He was home. He's on his way here now. Someone else took my child!"

The nurse looks confused. She couldn't have given one of the fathers the wrong crib. Simply no way. She always double checks the names to make sure, and she's never made a mistake.

"Take a seat here. I'm going to check right now. Maybe there's been a mix-up. I'll sort it out right away. Everything's okay."

But Ruthie knows that everything is not okay. Terror grows inside her stomach like a ball, rising to her throat. She can hardly breathe. She collapses to the floor, her back sliding down the wall. "Call the doctor; she's losing blood!" she hears someone call out in the distance, through a cloud of fog. It's a bad dream. It must all be a bad dream.

19.

Tonight, I'll remember my dream

Tonight, I'll dream about a pleasant hike outdoors

Tonight, I'll remember my dream

Tonight, I'll dream about a pleasant hike outdoors

Tonight, I'll remember my dream

Tonight, I'll dream about a pleasant hike outdoors

04:33

I'm a bomb technician in the Engineering Corps. The commander summons me to his office and closes the door behind him. He sits down in his chair and I take a seat across from him. He tells me that I have to go on a special mission, to work on the landmines of some general in the El Salvador army. I don't understand what this has to do with me, but he says: "You're the only one who can take care of it."

He hands me an airline ticket.

I'm in my room, packing a military kitbag. Some

of the things I put into the bag are really strange, but I don't remember what they were.

I land, and a group of soldiers in an army jeep are there to collect me, and we drive to the field. On the way, I see a tree with thick branches and no leaves. Lying on one of the branches is a naked body. It's smeared with mud in various shades, yellow-brown-red-black, and the arms are dangling on either side of the branch. I think initially that the body is part of the tree itself, until I realize it isn't.

The body on the tree looks a lot like Nathan. It may even be Nathan.

I have no sense of who killed him and why they left him there without any clothes on, smeared in mud, blending in with the tree. Black crows are perched on the branch next to him. I have an urge to call him to make sure he's not lying there. I'll soon see if he answers his phone or if the ringtone comes from the tree. Maybe they left his clothes next to the trunk. No. They must have taken them somewhere else. I have to photograph it. I try to remember where my cell phone is. Maybe I left it on the floor by the bed when I went to sleep.

I point at the tree and ask the soldiers to identify the man, and they tell me that he's their former bomb technician, that the explosive device he prepared for the use of the general didn't detonate.

"Maybe you'll get it right," one of them says with a smile. He's missing several teeth.

I'm not concerned. I quickly go over to deal with their landmine. I connect wires and tighten screws. I know it has nothing to do with landmines or bombs, but it seems like the right thing to do.

I work diligently, and the crew looks on, admiring my skill. We're all waiting for the general, who shows up, takes the mine and drops it from a helicopter.

The mine explodes; the quality of the blast is excellent and the general is satisfied. "Let's keep her here with us, she's better than Carlos," the general says to the soldiers standing next to me, and he points to Nathan's naked body among the branches of the big tree.

I look at the tire marks left behind by the jeep. They remind me of something and I can't figure out what. I tell the general that I have to go back because of an ongoing police investigation.

"I have to find this young woman – Lee Ben-Ami," I explain to them. "Someone abducted her and I'm going to put together an explosive device that will blow him to pieces. It happened three months ago, and no one has heard from her since. She's disappeared. I can't understand why everyone has been so quick to give up looking for her. I'm convinced someone is holding her against her will, that she's a prisoner. Alone. Frightened. The case must remain open because there'll be more like her if we don't stop the person responsible. If I don't look for her, she'll be forgotten. Her picture is no longer hanging in the squad room and the tack that was holding it to the drywall has left a small hole. I run my finger over it sometimes when I'm alone in the room. It will be filled in, smoothed over. But her family and friends can't fix the gaping hole that has opened in their hearts. They can't, and nor can those who loved Anat Aharon; and now they no longer have her to hug or see her smiling or singing or laughing or talking to them."

I approach the general and look into his eyes. "Do you understand?"

The general looks at me and then nods and says:

"Okay, you can go, but we'll call for you again in the event of additional mishaps."

"No problem," I respond.

"We have someone here whose body has been implanted with a database constructed from copper molecules," the general continues. "It contains all the particulars of the citizens of the country. It needs to be surgically removed. It hasn't been installed well; it takes up half of his stomach and is wrapped around his bones from the inside. It could cause an infection. We'll show you the next time you come here. You'll perform the surgery. See you at the hospital."

"Which hospital?"

"You'll see."

The jeep drops me off at the airport. My kitbag is thrown to the ground at my feet and the jeep disappears. I sling the kitbag over my shoulder and walk inside. On my way to the check-in, I walk down a long hallway with white doors. My foot bumps into something and I stumble and break my fall to the floor with my hands. I lift my head and look at the door in front of me. On it is a white plastic sign with an inscription in red: *Department of Upholding Oaths.*

Daphne records the dream in her journal and goes to the bathroom, then to the kitchen, where she pours herself a glass of cold water from the glass bottle in the fridge. After months of practice, it's become easier and easier to remember her dreams. The technique in the book really works, although it wasn't exactly the kind of outdoor hike she'd imagined before going to sleep. She tries to figure out why she's dreamt that particular scenario, in that specific location, and why the situation in the dream, which was frightening, hadn't scared her. She remembers having no fear at all. Not at the sight of the body of Nathan-Carlos in the tree, and not of the general or the soldiers who'd watched her with hungry eyes. She had known she

87

would do a good job and please him because she was a first-class engineering technician.

Everything seemed perfectly natural to her in the dream. Nathan-Carlos hadn't done a good job, so clearly he had to pay the price. Maybe she's on the right track to getting rid of her nightmares. She'll keep on practicing until she gets it right.

She finishes the water and goes back to bed, but she can't sleep. So she reads through her dream journal, the pages of which are filling up rapidly. Since starting to document them, the dreams are occupying more space in her mind, in her daily life. She thinks about them constantly, trying to figure out what they mean. Parts of them are obvious. Others remained closed, enigmatic. The two women are a regular feature. In her waking hours she can't shake the image of the dead body of Anat Aharon from her head. The person who killed her without flinching and then drove away could definitely be the same person who is now holding Lee Ben-Ami.

Maybe he abused her and murdered her and dumped her body somewhere, under a mound of dirt in the Jerusalem Forest, or the Modi'in Forest, or buried in the private yard of some house? What's better? To remain imprisoned for years or to die? Over the past few days, she's read online about several cases of lengthy abductions. Fusako Sano. Ten years old. Nine years in captivity after being abducted during a baseball game. Jaycee Lee Dugard. Eleven years old. Eighteen years in captivity after being abducted from a bus stop. Jessyca Mullenberg. Sabine Dardenne. Natasha. Andrea. Pamela. Sarah. Ingrid. Erica. An endless list of girls. Most were murdered. Some escaped. Others disappeared without trace and were never found. What's happening now to Lee Ben-Ami? Where is she? Who's holding her? What is he doing to her?

When she got to the case of Elisabeth Fritzl, she stopped and ended her research.

Daphne was so lucky to have escaped in time. It could have been her. It could have happened to her too. It was so close. So close. She has to find her. Has to find Lee.

She wakes to noises coming from the kitchen. Light is streaming through the window and she feels snug under the comforter. She pokes her nose out for a moment but then has a change of heart. It's so cold outside. But there's the smell of toast.

"Are you making breakfast?" she calls out from under the comforter.

"Yes, Your Majesty. Would you like it on a tray in bed?"

"Yes."

"That's not going to happen. Come on, up you get, it's ten already. I'm bored here on my own."

"It's a Saturday."

"Come on, Daph. Get up already!"

She grumbles to herself a little longer but finally peels back the comforter and makes her way to the kitchen, after pulling on gray fleece sweats and thick black woolen socks embroidered with a pattern of red-and-green bottles of Tabasco sauce. "You won't believe the strange dream I had."

"Haven't you had enough?"

"No, I'm fully into it now. I've already filled almost an entire notebook." She ignores the hint that perhaps Anna has had enough and tells her in great detail about her nighttime mission on behalf of the Department of Upholding Oaths.

"Have you managed to be awake in a dream yet? What's it called again?"

"Lucid dreaming. Not yet." Daphne fills the kettle with water and turns it on, while Anna, who's finished preparing a salad, washes the cutting board and places it on the countertop to dry.

"I'm surprised they haven't called you into work yet."

"Hmm?"

"Someone's snatched a baby from Beilinson."

Daphne freezes, holding the two coffee mugs she took out of the cupboard and staring at Anna. "What?!"

"Someone posed as a father and smuggled a baby out. I read about it earlier on Ynet. It's strange that they haven't called you. Maybe Nathan's no longer in love with you." Anna ducks just in time, and the kitchen towel that Daphne throws at her misses her head.

"I'll check my mobile. It may be on silent."

She goes back to her room and checks her phone. It's dead.

She'd connected it to the charger before she went to sleep, but the charger wasn't plugged in. "Fuck!"

She returns to the kitchen and connects the charger with the phone to the socket above the marble countertop, and as she waits for it to come back to life they both sit down to a breakfast that includes a finely chopped salad, toast that Anna had made from slices of challah, cheese and coffee. She loves Saturday mornings like this, before Anna goes to visit her parents in Holon in the afternoon and they can hang out together in the apartment. It gives her a sense of family. It's one thing to be alone, and another thing entirely to be alone on the weekend. She doesn't have many friends, and she's not the kind of person who finds it easy to make small talk and get close to new people. Anna's the same. They've been sharing an apartment for almost two years now.

Her phone starts emitting a series of alerts. Text message pings, WhatsApp notifications, unanswered calls, the beep of a voicemail message. She gets up from the kitchen table and checks: All the messages are from Nathan.

Call urgently

Where have you disappeared to?

Answer your phone, Daph

Call!

"Holy crap! He'll have my head on a platter." Daphne forms an imaginary gun with her fingers and aims it at her temple, and Anna simply smiles in sympathy. She calls, and Nathan answers on the first ring.

"Where have you been? Everyone here is on the go and you're nowhere to be found?!"

"My phone died. I only noticed now. What's happened? Are you talking about the baby who was snatched? Is there someone at the scene already? Do you want me to get there?"

"Scenes."

"What do you mean?"

"Four babies have disappeared."

"What?"

"Four."

"From Beilinson?"

"No. From four different hospitals. Beilinson, Ichilov, Mayanei Hayeshua and Tel HaShomer."

"Where's Mayanei Hayeshua?"

"Bnei Brak."

"So all in a radius of a few kilometers."

"And carried out over a period of less than two hours. One baby from each hospital. He simply walked in, left with a baby and disappeared."

"How could that have happened?"

"That's what we're looking into now. They've set up a joint squad of investigators from the Dan and Yarkon Districts, and forensics teams from National Headquarters are examining the scenes. We got Beilinson. I'm here already. Get yourself over here. I'm in the Maternity Ward."

He hangs up and she remains motionless, staring at the steam rising from her coffee cup, her phone still pressed to her ear.

"Mayanei Hayeshua? Ynet says Beilinson," Anna says with a mouth full of salad.

"Both. Four babies have been snatched." She's trying to digest the horrible news.

"What?"

"From four hospitals. Four different scenes in all." She pulls herself together and dashes to her room.

"Wow," Anna calls from the kitchen. "Do you realize how crazy things are about to get?"

"I don't even want to think about it," Daphne yells in response.

She dresses as fast as she can, grabbing her uniform from the chair next to her bed. Anna comes and stands in the doorway to her room.

"It's worse than any terror attack. Nothing's more sensitive than this. Newborn babies. The media is going to have a field day and drive the public and the police insane. I can already see interviews with weeping mothers, and the police commissioner's going to order a round-the-clock investigation. Should I lease your room to someone else in the meantime? Are you taking a sleeping bag?"

"Thanks for the encouragement," Daphne responds, jamming her feet into her shoes.

"Could it be an act of terror?"

"I don't think so. Too sophisticated. Well planned. Clean. Or so it seems from what I've been told; but I'll find out when I get to the scene."

"Good luck."

"Thanks. I need it," Daphne says, fixing her hair without using a mirror.

Anna turns around and is about to go back to her breakfast when her phone rings too.

"Hello."

"What?"

"Now?"

"To the Tel Aviv District?"

"At noon?"

"Okay. I'll be there."

She hangs up and takes one last sip of coffee. "Everyone's being brought in. The IT Unit too. There's a briefing with the commander in an hour."

Daphne replies with a wide smile, "Are you taking a sleeping bag? Should I distribute your food in the fridge to the homeless? It would be a shame to let it rot."

Anna sticks out her tongue and goes to her room to get dressed. Daphne leaves the apartment. She gets into her car and glances at the road and sidewalk in the rearview mirror. For the first time in months, she doesn't see Anat Aharon lying on the road.

20.

One hour and forty-seven minutes.

That's how much time he needed to take all four.

The procedure was replicated perfectly on each occasion. The locked toilet, the wristband, the coat. Nothing went wrong. Everything was executed exactly as planned. It was almost too easy to be true. He pinches the inside of his thigh the way she used to do when he was a small child. Out of love. That's what she'd say. With the color of the bruise and length of time before it faded as testimony to the intensity of that love. When they were small, they both used to vie for her attention; and even after the bruises had become nothing more than a memory, he still missed that pain, which overshadowed all the rest. And he knows that an individual well-accustomed to receiving pain or love is also well-accustomed to dishing it out. The divide between the two is extremely thin. Sometimes, they're one and the same.

He drives back to the address from which he'd borrowed the Hyundai early that morning.

The police scanner, this time, isn't quiet at all. It booms and thunders, spitting out messages at a dizzying pace and creating the impression that the police force has emerged from its Saturday morning coma to become instantaneously hyperactive. Notifications about checkpoints along the roads leading away from the center of the country; a closure imposed on the West Bank and Gaza; reports about upcoming briefings; the apprehension of suspects at all four hospitals.

His Waze app notifies him of the build-up of traffic congestion at various points – as a result, he assumes, of police roadblocks; he chooses alternate routes.

The Four are sleeping soundly in the trunk of the car in their cardboard boxes. He made sure to feed them all with milk laced with a sleep aid that would knock them out but wouldn't kill them. He can't run the risk of having the sound of a crying baby coming from the trunk.

The street is quiet, with no one out and about on a rainy Saturday, and he parks the vehicle in the precise spot from where he'd taken it. He starts up his silver Suzuki, which is waiting for him nearby, and turns the heat up to seventy-nine degrees. He then removes ten large containers of bleach from the trunk and replaces them with the boxes containing the babies. The bags go onto the front passenger seat, and he connects the police radio scanner, which continues to rattle on at a furious rate:

"Attention! Attention, everyone! The perpetrator or perpetrators are driving white Hyundai Tucsons, license plate numbers 29-521-68 or 61-864-49 or 51-574-93 or 31-308-41. They're all stolen plates. We may be dealing with one vehicle that's had its plates replaced four times, or four vehicles with stolen plates. This is for all cars and all checkpoints: Stop every white Tucson you see and turn it inside out. The plate numbers are being sent to your terminals right now."

So they've reviewed the footage from the hospitals' security cameras. Wakey-wakey, Israel Police. He empties the bleach containers into the Hyundai. Gallons of chlorine on the seats, the windows, the dashboard, the floor and the trunk. Into the Tucson's air vents too. He checks again to make sure he hasn't left anything in the vehicle and then starts it up, cranking up the heat to the maximum and closing the doors. The contents of the last container of bleach goes over the car from the outside – the roof, hood, doors and handles.

He leaves the key in the running vehicle and locks it with the remote control. The engine should tick for about seventy hours before the fuel runs out. A quarter of a gallon per hour in neutral. The bleach steam bath will erase all traces of biological material.

He lingers for a moment longer alongside the running vehicle and looks up at the gray clouds. The rain is coming down again, wetting his face. The low sound of thunder rumbles in the distance.

He crushes the empty bleach containers, stuffs them into the trash bag and places the bag on the back seat of the Suzuki, then checks on the four infants sleeping in the cardboard boxes. The boxes are padded with sections of a comforter that he cut into four pieces. Had he purchased four baby blankets at once, from the same store, someone would have remembered it, and the police must already be questioning the managers of baby stores. In addition to the sections of the comforter, each infant is wrapped in its hospital blanket. They won't find anything.

He checks: All the babies are breathing. They'll wake up in an hour or two. He needs to get going. He covers the boxes with a thin sheet, gets into the car and drives off. On his way to the white place, the clean and tidy place, he passes through two police checkpoints, waving and smiling at the officers on the lookout for a white Hyundai Tucson.

He'll add their pictures to the photo room. The four of them. He'll hang them on the wall along with all the others. Transparent plastic sheets in black and white. Pictures from before the change. Before the connection. To serve as mementos. When Hiroshima and Nagasaki were bombed, people standing close to the epicenter cast shadows onto the nearby buildings before they were vaporized, leaving white impressions of their souls on the burnt walls. It was a much slower process in Pompeii. There, they were buried under the ash of the volcano and decomposed over the years, leaving hollows in the hardened fallout. When wet plaster was cast into those spaces, the figures were reborn. Families curled up together on the floor. A man resting on his elbows. A sleeping baby.

Wet plaster that's cast into a space will assume its perfect and smooth form once it has set. After removing the plaster cast from the arm of the Guardian, he didn't throw it away. He kept it with the rest of the mementos. From time to time, he removes it from its vacuum-sealed packaging and breathes in the scent of her arm on the cast's cotton lining. Dead skin cells. Dried sweat, fine and delicate strands of hair, almost transparent, pencil eraser debris.

21.

Lee is busy doing push-ups when the door opens with a click. Her arm has healed completely, and since he removed the cast with the help of sheet metal scissors, she has got into the strict habit of exercising at least two hours a day in the flannel pants and shirt, which she's turned into a tank top by ripping off its sleeves. When the time to act was right, she'd be in good shape. She was using weights she'd fashioned out of various canned foods tied together with medical tape to work her arms, and lengthy and repeated sets of squats and step-ups onto the bed to strengthen her legs. She was familiar by now with every inch of her prison cell and had learned to make the best out of everything on hand.

She knows nothing about the conditions outside, since the room is always the same cool temperature maintained by the quiet central air-conditioning system. But the training warms her up, and the physical activity eases her mind and gives her hope.

He is standing in the doorway looking at her.

"The usual drill."

He tosses the handcuffs to her and she shackles herself to the bed.

"Show me."

She tugs her hand back to prove that the handcuffs are indeed secure.

He leaves the room and returns with the stainless-steel trolley bearing bundles wrapped in blankets. Lee watches him in silence as he places them one by one in four cribs. He does everything slowly, carefully, with reverence, his movements appearing almost ceremonial, like the careful action of a priest swinging a censer. She watches him in disbelief. She doesn't believe it's possible – that he's placing real babies in the cribs. Maybe it's some kind of a joke? Could they be dolls? Does he think she's going to play with dolls? He's out of his fucking mind. She has to get out of here. She remembers the cupboards with the bottles and baby food, and a wave of shock goes through her.

"What's going on?"

"I'd like to congratulate you. From this moment on, your true destiny is about to begin. From today, you'll be known as the Guardian."

She stares at him dumbfounded, then forces herself to speak. "Are those real babies?!"

"Yes. And you're going to look after them."

She stares at him, squinting her eyes. Don't lose your cool, be persuasive, she reminds herself. "I'm not the right person for this. I never had a baby. They would be better off with someone else taking care of them. You can still blindfold me and take me back. I have no idea where I am. Where I've been. I promise not to come looking for you afterwards."

"Don't insult my intelligence."

He goes over to examine the contents of the cupboards and empties the laundry drawer. "I'm not afraid of anyone. You're here on a full-time basis. You're young and strong. You have a background in medicine. You'll be able to take care of them even if they get sick, though the chances of that are slim. You've been here now for three months and can't be carrying too many germs. And I shower and disinfect myself before coming in. The air in here is well filtered. The temperature is constant. Tomorrow, I'm going to install a light that simulates sunlight. Make sure you turn it on for thirty minutes a day while they're in nothing but their diapers, to avoid Vitamin D deficiency."

Any doubt she may have been harboring disappears instantly.

He didn't run her down simply because she was there at the time. He chose her. Followed her.

"And what if I'm not cut out for this? I hate babies."

He loads the laundry bag onto the stainless-steel trolley and transfers clean clothes to the closet. "I've been nice to you and have taken good care of you until now. You don't want for anything in terms of nutrition, medical care and hygiene. I replenish your food supply and make sure you have clothes to wear and fresh and conditioned air to breathe. There's water in the showers and lighting in your room. All of that will change drastically if you fail to look after them. Your life and welfare depend on the life and welfare of the Four."

He tosses the handcuff key to her and she frees herself, throwing the items back at him one after the other.

He turns towards her before leaving the room. "You can't hate babies," he says. "It's not part of your genetic wiring. And stop ruining the clothes I give you. I'll get you some exercise clothes."

22.

Parked at the entrance to Beilinson Hospital are two patrol cars; more as a show of presence, to ward off curious onlookers and convey a sense of security, than an operational necessity. The crime has already been committed. The damage has been done. The gates to the hospital are closed, with only patients and their escorts allowed in following a stringent security check. It's a cold, gloomy, rainy Saturday.

The security guard says, "Where to, please?"

"The Maternity Ward."

"Sorry, no visitors allowed."

Daphne flashes her police ID. "Forensics."

He studies the ID and looks at her again. "I didn't notice the uniform. Come in, please. And good luck. Hope you catch the piece of shit who's done this."

"We'll most certainly try."

The guard raises the barrier and she drives to the entrance to the Maternity Ward, where she parks and then places a sign on the dashboard under the front windshield: *Police vehicle on duty*. As she goes around to the back of her car to retrieve her kit from the trunk, she's spotted by a group of news reporters who are waiting outside the door to the building, frustrated by the cold rain and the fact that they aren't being allowed inside. They're quick to pounce on her with their microphones and cameras.

"Any leads to speak of?"

"What about the rumor that it's terror-related?"

"What can you tell us about…"

She ignores the microphones thrust in her face and walks purposefully towards the police officer stationed at the entrance, who promptly opens the door for her.

In the ward itself, things are relatively quiet. The nursery is empty now. All the cribs have been transferred to the rooms and pressed tight against the respective mothers' beds. Despite the police presence, she can discern a distinct loss in all sense of security. Nurses are making their way through the rooms to make sure everything is in order or to take a baby to a check-up, in the company of both of its parents of course. No more leaving babies unattended. Not from today.

She continues on towards the nurses' station, where Nathan, a member of the hospital's security personnel and another police officer are sitting in front of a computer monitor. He sees her approach and motions her over.

The screen they're looking at is split into an array of square frames. "This is the video footage from all the security cameras inside the building," Nathan explains. "We've run it back to the point at which he enters the building. Here, look." The police officer next to him vacates his seat for her. "Here you see him walking in. Pay close attention and tell me what's out of line. What's off-color. What doesn't add up."

"The bearded guy with the black coat and umbrella?" She points at the blurry image on the screen. The kidnapper is of average height and build, his face can't be clearly seen. It seems he knows where the camera is and turns his head the other way.

"Yes."

Nine squares, each displaying a different camera angle, and various other people in black-and-white. She sits down in front of the computer and studies the images up close.

"He disappears here from the camera's field of vision. What's there?"

"Bathrooms."

"Okay. We'll check them. He may have left some DNA behind."

Nathan nods. The video footage from the security cameras continues running.

"There, that's him coming out, minus the coat and umbrella. Rewind a moment, to the point at which he enters the building."

The hospital's security officer responds immediately and the video jumps back.

"Look, he had a bag over his shoulder when he came in, and it isn't there when he emerges from the bathrooms. He leaves the coat, the umbrella and the bag in the bathroom and wanders around the ward without them. We need to check for fibers on the coat hooks in case he hung up his coat in one of the stalls."

"Good. What else?"

The video continues to run. She observes him walking around the ward. A knit cap on his head. Jeans, sneakers. Going over to the coffee machine, looking through the large nursery window, returning to the bathroom. Emerging from the bathroom.

"Pause a moment."

The video freezes.

"What's that on his arm?"

The security officer increases the size of one of the squares until it fills the entire screen. "It's a wristband."

"An ID bracelet of sorts?"

"Yes. You can't get into the nursery or take one of the babies out without one."

"Go back a little to the point at which he goes into the toilets."

The images run in reverse again. "That's it. Stop," Daphne requests. "See what I'm talking about? He wasn't wearing a wristband when he went into the bathroom. He put it on inside."

She continues to stare intently at the screen. He walks into the nursery. Talks to the nurse. Leaves the room with a baby.

"Has she been interviewed?"

"Yes," Nathan confirms. "He told the nurse he was taking the baby to his mother for feeding. She checked his wristband and the details matched. You can see her checking the wristband in the video footage."

"Are you telling me he stole the father's wristband?"

"No, we've spoken to the father. He's still in possession of his wristband," the police officer standing next to her says.

"So where did he find…" She pauses, but just for a moment. "Could he have made a wristband for himself in the bathroom? That would explain his first walk past the nursery – to find the details and then make an identical bracelet."

"Good. What else?"

"He's familiar with the ward. He knows where he's going. He doesn't appear to be looking for anything."

"True."

"So I'd like to see earlier footage. He must have visited here before in preparation. How far back does your footage go?"

"Three months."

"The detectives have already requisitioned the material," Nathan stops her. "Let's focus on the areas we'll have to work on, in keeping with the places where we see him wandering around."

The video continues. He walks down the hallway, talking on the phone. When no one's around, he returns to the bathroom with the crib.

"Are there cameras in the bathrooms?"

"No. It's not permitted."

He emerges from the bathroom with the black coat, the umbrella and the bag. No crib, no baby.

"Did he leave the baby in the bathroom?" she asks, not even daring to think of anything else he may have done to it.

"No. Take a good look at him."

The security officer enlarges the square displaying the footage from the camera at the entrance to the building.

"Got it. He's put on a little weight. The baby's under his coat. Is that it? No footage from outside?"

"The footage from outside shows him getting into a white Tucson and driving away. The plate numbers are visible."

Nathan leans back in his chair. "What would you examine now?"

"First, the crib he touched, and the bathrooms as a whole, where he spent most of his time – faucets, coat hooks, everything. And afterwards, door handles for fingerprints, the path he followed for shoeprints. You've sealed off the bathrooms, right?"

"Yes. Go on."

"The coffee machine for prints, possible tire prints from where the car was parked even though it's raining and I doubt we'll get anything from there, the coffee cups in the trash can. He drank from one of them, so we should get prints and DNA."

"He took it with him. He was carrying it when he went into the bathroom but emerged without it."

"Maybe he threw it into the trash can there?"

"Good. We'll check that too."

"So, we're going to start with the bathrooms?"

They walk the empty hallways towards the men's bathrooms. The place looks deserted. The corridors are empty and the parents are in the ward rooms with their babies.

"How's it going with the dreams?" Nathan asks.

At once, the image pops into her head. A naked body in a tree, smeared in colorful mud. Eyes open.

"Great," she responds.

"Have you managed to shake off the nightmare?"

"No. But I can remember my dreams really well now, and sort of aim to dream of something particular at night, in a general sense. I've yet to experience lucid dreaming, but I'm getting there. Little by little." She isn't going to tell him that he appeared in one of her dreams, not to mention the manner of his appearance. Never.

"I saw."

"What?" she asks.

"I saw you counting your fingers while we were analyzing the video footage."

"I wanted to make sure I wasn't dreaming. This all feels like a bad dream."

As they walk she shifts her gaze from Nathan to her fingers, resisting the urge to conduct a reality check in his presence.

"Are you listening?"

"Yeah, sure."

"Be careful with those games you're playing. It sounds like something that could screw up your head." More than a warning, his tone expresses concern.

"It really does sound a little weird to someone who hasn't read up about it and isn't familiar with it. But it's okay. I haven't lost it. I'm still sane."

"Okay then, you can sit me down to an orderly lecture after we catch the scumbag who's snatched the babies."

They stop at the bathroom door.

"Where should we start?" he asks as they go inside.

"Fingerprints from the faucet handles, the door handles, the coat hooks. Hair samples. An examination of the toilet bowls to see if he tried to get rid of something perhaps."

"There's something else that needs to be done first. What aren't we seeing?"

"Latent shoeprints on the floor. Electrostatic prints. Before we walk all over it. I'll get the kit. We can try that first. And then check with powder. The tiles are white. Black powder?"

"Yes. And use the blower for dispersal. We'll move on when we're done with that."

They lift and photograph shoeprints from the bathroom floor and progress gradually until the entire surface has been dusted. Nathan takes pity on her and shoulders the task of retrieving samples from the toilet with a handful of test tubes, and she goes over to the first sink to examine the faucet. She raises her head and looks in the mirror.

> **She returns home from the street.**
>
> **It's dark already and her friends are going back to their homes too.**
>
> **Lights are on in the windows of all the houses.**
> **Hers is always dark.**
>
> **She goes into the bathroom.**
>
> **Too bad she didn't pee outside in the bushes.**
>
> **The toilet is filthy and she flushes the water down first and then stands over the bowl so as not to touch it.**
>
> **There's no toilet paper and she pulls up her panties without wiping herself.**

He's sitting on the sofa in the living room in front of an empty glass bottle with a picture of two green stags with antlers.

His head's between his hands.

He lifts his head and looks at her when she walks in.

His eyes are red.

There's a full ashtray on the table.

The house smells of smoke.

Of alcohol.

She's twelve years old.

She remembers the moment like it's been etched behind her eyes.

"You had a little sister once," he says.

"We sold her.

For twenty thousand dollars.

She was two and a half years old.

She had black hair.

Slanted eyes.

I'm going to sell you one day too, but for less.

You're too old already.

No one will want you."

His head wobbles.

A memory of hands touching hands appears on the edge of her consciousness.

Two small black ponytails.

Mia.

Her name is Mia.

A voice calls out, "Wait for me, Daph," and then it all explodes.

Something inside her snaps like a rubber band that's stretched too thin and then tears apart with the sound of a whip shot.

She picks up the empty bottle with both hands, takes a swing and smashes it into his face.

She remembers his look.

The blood.
Her legs carry her far away. She never returns.

She grips the sides of the sink tightly until her knuckles turn white. Like all her flashbacks, this one came out of nowhere, and was so vivid. She takes a deep breath, releases her grip on the sink and looks anxiously behind her. Nathan is in one of the toilet stalls collecting samples. Thank God he didn't see anything.

She concentrates on examining the faucet. No fingerprints. She opens it and washes her face, then stands up straight to cast her eyes over the bathroom again.

What's different? What's out of place?

She looks at the door of the disabled toilet, then says to Nathan, "Take a look at this for a moment. Why is the toilet locked like this?"

She points to the lock on the outside of the stall and the sign that reads: *Out of order. Undergoing repairs – sorry for the inconvenience.*

"What's suspicious about that?"

"If a toilet at a boarding school or in the army was out of order, no one would bother to fix a latch to the door on the outside and lock it. It doesn't make sense. There'd be a sign at most."

"True."

Until then, they'd ignored that particular stall only because it was locked. Daphne goes over and dusts for prints on the lock and door before they remove the latch with the help of a screwdriver and hammer.

Inside the stall, next to the toilet bowl, is an empty crib.

She photographs and collects findings from the crib, the floor of the stall, the walls and the toilet bowl, while Nathan calls the command room.

One after the other, all the forensics teams from the remaining three crime scenes send in confirmation: each of them also found an empty crib inside the toilet stall for the disabled at their respective locations, all of them fitted with a latch and locked from the outside. They also found the same sign on the door. Clean of fingerprints.

23.

"Another day in paradise," Lee says out aloud while she goes over to the four cribs and peers into the first one, staring at the newborn baby lying there, wrapped up in a hospital blanket and fast asleep. She leans over, still refusing to believe her eyes; but yes, it's a baby – pink and breathing and warm and very real.

That's what she's here for. That's why he abducted and imprisoned her.

"Where did you get four babies from? You fucking lunatic. What did you do with their mothers? Do you have them locked up here too?" She talks to herself, as she's grown accustomed to doing to alleviate the silence, as she checks the other cribs, unable to believe this is happening. All four cribs contain infants sleeping soundly and peacefully. And they are all wrapped in hospital blankets. She notices that each blanket bears the logo of a different hospital. Four babies from four maternity wards. She remembers the terrible wall of photographs she saw. The babies here aren't quadruplets or sets of twins either.

She goes over to the cupboards and lays out bottles, a bottle heater, a container of Similac baby formula, a large bottle of mineral water, wet wipes and a package of Huggies Newborn diapers on the stainless-steel surface next to the sink. He didn't have to threaten her to force her to take care of them. Who can see a baby without wanting to take care of it?

She reads the instructions on the Similac container and prepares a bottle.

"It would have been nice of you to include in the instructions not only how many measuring spoons of powder to put in the water, but also how much a newborn baby should drink," she remarks, chastising the bottle as she places it in the heating device.

Bottle prepared, she sits down to wait for the babies to wake. A few minutes later, she hears the sound of crying. She lifts the baby out of the crib and sits down with him on the bed. She tries to feed it, but it can't suckle, and the crying turns into heart-wrenching screams. She quickly replaces the nipple with a different one, softer and more transparent, and the baby then manages to latch onto the bottle and feed. As it does so, the remaining infants wake up too, and she's surrounded by a chorus of wailing.

"It would help if you were to abduct someone else to give me a hand." She looks at the baby suckling on the bottle in her arms. Her tone is complaining but she smiles at the baby. After the silence of the past months, the noise is a blessing. They're crying the demanding cries of the helpless, but they're here. She's not alone.

"I'll get to all of you soon. Don't worry."

He chose her. He chose someone who's studying medicine. Who works in a hospital. Who looks after people. He wanted someone who could handle it. She's going to be here with them for a long time. She looks at the babies and knows deep down what's in store.

"*Не волнуйся, мои дети. Все будет отлично.*"

She speaks to them, practicing the flawed Russian she's picked up from the Russian-language television channel.

24.

When he leaves the Guardian's room with the laundry cart he passes through the image gallery room and into the X-ray Room, stopping alongside the X-ray machine and below its metal plate to retrieve a key he's fixed to its underside. From there, he pushes the trolley to the opposite wall and opens a heavy iron door. Stretched out behind the door is a long passageway with signposted doors on either side. And behind the one marked *Laundry Room* stands an industrial-sized washing machine and a large dryer. He empties the laundry bag into the machine, singing to himself as he does so:

> *From a chicken's dreg*
> *To a monkey's leg*
> *Whatever he's got*
> *He'll devour the lot*

"Another day in paradise." The Guardian's voice echoes in the Laundry Room. The hidden microphone he installed in the ceiling of her room is connected to the loudspeaker system and he can hear everything she says, no matter where he is. He stops singing, raises his head and listens.

"Where did you get four babies from? You fucking lunatic. What did you do with their mothers? Do you have them locked up here too?" Hmmm. What did you do with their mothers? Nothing. Could he have abducted four pregnant women and imprisoned them here? Or four non-pregnant women who he could have impregnated somehow? He had thought about doing so early on. When he first began investigating. Too complicated. Too long a process. Too risky. And no matter how well he planned it, he wouldn't have been able to ensure that they were exactly the same age. And he wouldn't have achieved that element of intense emotional agony that needs to be a part of the process. He waits, his eyes fixed on the speaker in the ceiling of the Laundry Room. When the silence lingers, he looks down and returns to his verse.

> *He'll ingest it all*
> *And grow strong and tall*
> *Lying in the street*
> *A carcass to eat*

After pouring in a generous measure of detergent and softener, he turns on the washing machine, and its large drum starts to revolve with a mechanical hum. He then returns to the hallway, which is cast in a yellowish hue from the old incandescent light bulbs fitted along its entire length. He makes his way to the last bulb, retrieves a key from behind it, opens the door at the end of the hallway and steps into the stairwell. He descends one floor, into a second hallway, and opens the first door on his right.

He goes over to the large generator situated in the room. He checks the oil, individually checks each of the batteries to which it's connected and which serve to start it up, greases several moving parts and cleans away a thin layer of dust that has accumulated. He then measures the amount of diesel in the tank at the other end of the room and dusts that too.

From there, he makes his way through the other rooms leading off the hallway, dealing with the equipment in each of them. When he's done, he climbs the stairs again, locks the door and puts the key back in its place. He then walks to the Admin Room opposite the Laundry Room. He retrieves a binder from one of the filing cabinets, pulls out a page with a table and begins filling in the fields. Date, Generator Checks, UPS Checks, Water Pumps, Chemical Filters,

Control Room, Electricity Boards, A/C System, Sprinkler System, Medical Equipment Rooms. He ticks all the boxes pertaining to checks that went well, and marks two of the fields with an X and adds comments.

X   Water filter needs replacing – Expired

X   FM-200 tank for Electricity Room needs replacing – Insufficient pressure

He'll fill out the required forms tomorrow and submit an acquisition request to replace both items.

Call and order chocolate, he jots down on a yellow notepad resting on the desk, adding a tick mark beside the text.

25.

"Daph!"

The cheerful voice at her back startles her and she almost spills her cappuccino. She gets to her feet to greet Rotem, who wraps her up in a long embrace.

"Wow, it's been so long."

"It's so good to see you again."

They're at the Ramat Hasharon branch of Aroma. Rotem orders an iced coffee, "...but from freshly ground beans, not from that machine of yours that's been churning there for the past six months. And with a double shot of coffee, and no sugar, and a drop of maple syrup and a green straw, not a black one." Daphne smiles to herself.

They met in the army, when Daphne was serving at the Wingate Institute and Rotem showed up as part of a group there for a month-long bonding seminar. Men and women, all post-military service. They did some physical training, some combat fitness, some Krav Maga, but spent most of the time shut up in the structure assigned to them, and all that Daphne's team was permitted to know about them was that they were from "the Organization".

Daphne put them through combat training drills, noticing Rotem during the course of one of them, intrigued by the tattoo just visible under the edge of her tank top. That evening, in the dining hall, Daphne asked her about it and discovered that it was a huge piece, a fairy, and that Rotem was someone she could talk to. Really talk to.

After dinner, they went down to the beach and sat on the sand and talked long into the night. Rotem was just a few years older than her, but she was the smartest person Daphne had ever met. She felt like Rotem was reading her. Rotem didn't tell her exactly what she did but explained that she managed a division that dealt in psychology. And she convinced Daphne that she should go to university and shouldn't be afraid because "there's nothing you can't accomplish if you're determined and strong. You can do anything if you release the pain that's pushing you down. It's not your fault. You're not to blame for anything that has happened to you. I'm telling you and you can trust me on this. I analyze people for a living. You're unique and special." She never forgot that. And when the seminar ended and the group from "the Organization" left, she stayed in touch with Rotem, and she was always there for her when she needed her.

And now was one of those moments.

"So what's going on with you, Daph? Anything exciting?"

"Nothing special."

"I actually thought there was. You were very mysterious when you called. You had me thinking you wanted to tell me about some new romance. Something juicy with lots of details." Rotem blinks her eyes dreamily, and Daphne laughs.

"I wish. Right now, I seem to attract only assholes and psychopaths. Both in life and at work."

Rotem sighs. "Tell me about it. I'm in the middle of writing a research paper about a lunatic we pursued through four continents and preparing material for two new courses at the same time, as well as reconstructing various tests and recruitment processes and—"

"And you love it."

"True." The waitress arrives to place a large glass of iced coffee with a green straw on the table in front of Rotem, who sips noisily from her drink. "Well then, talk to me."

Daphne gets straight to the point. "Look, what I need is to pick your brain about a case the police are working on. Just a few minutes. To see if it sparks anything in that head of yours."

"The kidnapping of the babies?" Rotem leans back, crossing her hands behind her head, examining Daphne.

"Yes."

"I'm assuming you've got every detective with an IQ above 60 working on the case."

"That's the problem. There aren't that many of those. And almost all are men." Daphne takes a sip of cappuccino.

Rotem chuckles. "Has he made contact?"

"Not yet."

Rotem leans forward, her face almost touching Daphne's, and talks in a quiet voice, "I don't have a problem helping you, but don't tell anyone. The last thing I need is for my bosses to get a roasting from the Prime Minister's Office about us poking our noses into police business. You know that our eyes are focused on the world outside and not on domestic issues."

"Not a single word," Daphne promises. "I'm in the same boat. Nathan will freak out if he hears I've discussed the case with anyone."

"Makes sense." Rotem pauses for a minute. "What do you have to go on?"

"Car tire prints, DNA, and fingerprints that are probably his but don't exist in any database. Neither ours nor Interpol's."

Rotem slurps through her straw again. "We need to figure out why he's doing what he's doing. Sex and money, combined with alcohol or drugs as a catalyst, are the two most common motives for serious crimes that aren't committed on the basis of religion or nationality. You're dealing here with something else entirely."

"That's why I reached out to you."

"He's not going to kill them. He didn't kidnap four babies just to murder them. It's not terror-related. He needs them for something. You've had another abduction incident recently, right?"

"Yes. Anat Aharon, a hit-and-run. And shortly thereafter, a second young woman, Lee Ben-Ami, who also went out for a run and didn't come back. Based on the findings at the scene, she was run down by a vehicle. We don't have anything to link those two cases with the case involving the babies, but—"

"Anat Aharon disappeared and then so did Lee Ben-Ami?"

"No, no, Anat was killed in the first hit-and-run, and Lee disappeared from the scene of the second one."

"It's him." Rotem is emphatic. "The same person who kidnapped the babies. He killed the first one unintentionally. He was more careful with the second one. He snatched her so that she can mind the babies for him while he does whatever he's doing."

"What? More kidnappings?"

"I don't know, but we'll find out soon enough."

Rotem falls silent. Daphne too. She sips her coffee and wishes she could smoke. A cigarette would go down really well right now. Rotem is staring at her intently. "It's Lee," she eventually says.

"What?"

She leans forward and clasps Daphne's hands in hers. "It's not just the babies. You called me because of Lee. She's the reason why the case is so important to you. To be imprisoned in a foreign location against your will, abused perhaps. It takes you back."

Daphne lowers her gaze. And at once, her throat chokes up and her eyes fill with tears.

"It's important for you to find her," Rotem continues. "You're projecting similar circumstances from your past onto the situation. The longer you remain involved in this investigation the more intense those projections will become. Keep reminding yourself that you're not Lee Ben-Ami. Don't allow things to get mixed up."

"She's appearing in my dreams." Daphne wipes her eyes and closely examines her cappuccino.

"Lucid dreaming will only heighten your emotions. Be careful."

"How do you know that I'm...?"

"You've already done two reality checks since the beginning of our conversation. You're awake, by the way."

"I know."

"Do another one."

One – two – three – four – five. A tug. Eyes on the menu, to the side, back to the menu. She's awake.

"Good. Don't ever believe someone who tells you that you're awake. The moment that happens, do a reality check right away to make sure: fingers, how you got here, whatever you need. Every character you ask in your dream will tell you that you're awake. Always."

Daphne isn't surprised to learn that Rotem is familiar with the subject, but she asks anyway: "How do you…"

Rotem responds without hesitation: "I use it sometimes to solve problems that my awake mind isn't able to process. But I try not to do it too often. I used to use it more."

"How I got here?"

"It's another kind of reality check. You ask yourself how you ended up in your current situation. If you know how, you're usually awake. If you don't, you're usually in the midst of a dream."

"What made you stop doing it too often?"

"Is there a character who guides you into the dream and accompanies you at the beginning?"

"No."

"Then we'll talk about it further down the line."

Daphne would like to talk about it more. Finally, someone who knows and understands what it's all about and isn't disparaging, doesn't make fun of it. But Rotem has other concerns. "Why are you delving into it?" she probes. "There are risks involved. Lucid dreaming opens doors that are closed for a reason. Even those that should remain closed forever. Maybe give it a try once the investigation is over? After we've caught him?"

Their table is positioned next to the café's large window. Daphne turns her head to look at the flowerpots outside and pauses to feel the warmth of the sun on her face.

"I've been using lucid dreaming for the purpose of getting into a nightmare and changing how it ends. They say that if you manage to remain lucid in your nightmare, you can deal with it. Do you know about…?"

"The same nightmare you used to have in the army?"

"Yes." Daphne looks back at Rotem.

"Why didn't you say so? I can help you with it. When you manage to experience lucid dreaming, let me know, and I'll take you to our Alpha room. It's too soon now."

"Alpha room?"

Rotem doesn't respond. Instead, she closes her eyes for a few seconds before opening them again. "He isn't raping her," she says.

"And he's not a pedophile either. Pedophiles usually abduct kids between the ages of nine and thirteen. He's a white male, between the ages of thirty and fifty. Intelligent. Pragmatic. Adept at planning and carrying things through. An analytical mind and access to a location where he won't be disturbed. A private house out of town, a secluded area. No one has reported seeing him show up with four babies and an unconscious young woman. Have you drawn up a profile on her?"

"On Lee Ben-Ami?"

"Yes."

"I haven't seen one, but I guess there must be one. I'll try to get my hands on it. I know that she's studying medicine and works part-time at a hospital to fund her studies and get some hands-on experience."

"And the one before her? Anat? Was she also studying medicine?"

"Yes."

"That's not good."

"Why?"

"What does he need a doctor for? What does he have in mind for the babies that would require a doctor?"

"I hadn't thought about it along those lines. I was thinking he wanted someone with the desire and ability to take care of others. Someone born to do so. Someone who's going to look after the babies without hurting them and without causing him problems because he could threaten to harm them."

"He could just as well have abducted a kindergarten teacher for that." Rotem beckons the waitress and orders cheesecake for the two of them.

"Pass on all you have about the abductee. Has he made any contact with the families?"

"No."

Rotem slurps up the rest of her ice coffee with a loud noise, attracting glares from the patrons at the tables around them. "Then we'll have to wait for him. The ball's in his court. And you're sneaky."

"Who? Me?" Daphne widens her eyes.

"Look how you've sucked me into this now." She shakes her head. "You knew I wouldn't be able to resist."

Daphne doesn't respond. She feels fortunate to have Rotem by her side.

Rotem leans back in her chair and closes her eyes again. "Whatever he's planning, we have to get to him before he manages to go through with it. And right now, there's nothing we can do but wait for him to make his next move. Call me when he does."

26.

I'm in bed in the house deep in the forest again.
Three windows. Darkness. Peeking out from under
the comforter. Everything's real. Everything exists.
Everything's here and now. The smell of the wooden
beams. The feeling of the comforter against my legs.
The mist outside. The thunder of heavy footsteps.
The paralyzing fear. The shudder down my spine.
His face appearing at the window. The banging on
the door. How am I going to escape now? It never
works. I wait for the shouting outside the door to start
and run to the empty closet in the other room. I open
its doors. Written in charcoal on the back panel are
the words: *You'll never make it*. I detach the closet
rod and hurry back into the other room. I slam the
rod as hard as I can against the middle window
and it shatters into small pieces. I move towards it.
The shards of glass on the floor slice up my bare
feet. I climb through the window to the outside,
and my hands and thighs and shoulders are cut by
the remaining glass in the window frame. I land on
muddy black earth and start to run away from the
house. I run along a narrow path among dark trees,
leaving behind a trail of blood. The mist is thick and
I can't see more than a yard or two in front of me,

and I'm scratched by branches that stick out along the path. I run fast, and I'm panting.

I need air.

I need air.

I need air.

I can't breathe.

I don't look back. He must be running after me. I continue running and his face suddenly appears in front of me. He's standing on the path, blocking my way, waiting for me. I can't stop. I run into him. There's white clay of sorts in his hair. White streaks smeared over the transparent layer of ice covering and distorting his face. His clothes are dirty and his heavy shoes are covered with mud too. His fist slams into my stomach and I fall to the ground, doubled up in pain. He picks me up and loads me onto his shoulder. I punch his back and scratch at him with all my might, but he doesn't react, just walks slowly back to the house. Inside, he throws me onto the bed like always, and sits on me. "It's a good night to die," he says and begins to strangle me.

No.

No.

Everything around me disappears.

She wakes up screaming and sits up abruptly in bed, breathing heavily. Her lucid dreaming exercises have upped the intensity of all her dreams, her nightmare included. The smells, the feelings, the terror. If she doesn't get the hang of lucid dreaming soon, perhaps it's better to stop. It's only getting worse.

She gets up to go to the bathroom, washes her face and goes to the kitchen, peeking into Anna's dark room on the way. Empty. The clock on the kitchen wall reads one-thirty. She's probably out having a good time somewhere.

After spending her entire Saturday collecting findings at Beilinson and then meeting with Rotem, Daphne returned home, took a shower and crashed into bed at eleven, sleeping deeply until the nightmare woke her up. She records it in her notebook, drinks a glass of cold water, and goes back to bed. She falls asleep again almost at once.

The alarm on her phone wakes her at six-thirty, and she joins Anna, who is already sitting in the kitchen in front of a cup of coffee.

"What time did you get back last night? I didn't hear you come in."

"At around three."

Daphne goes over to make coffee for herself too; the water in the kettle is still hot.

"Where were you?"

"At the department until twelve almost, then we went out to clear our heads a little."

"What were you so busy with until so late?"

"They've suspended all our routine work and have set up a number of teams to work on the Babysitter."

"Is that what you guys are calling him?"

"That's what everyone's calling him," Anna informs her. "We were working with teams from Google and Facebook, running algorithms searching for people who've shown an interest in things like pacifiers and diapers but aren't married or in a relationship. A bunch of cross-referencing with online purchases of large quantities of baby formula, searches for the names of the four hospitals, things like that."

"And did you find anything?"

"No. I mean, the Internet is always good for strange things, but we didn't find anything that could be a serious lead. If he bought baby products, he must have done so from various stores and paid in cash. What about you?"

"Fingerprints that don't appear in any database, shoeprints that don't appear in any database, DNA that doesn't appear in any database, tire prints that don't appear in any database," Daphne rattles off the list in frustration. "And I spent half a day in the bathroom. I showered for an hour and still have the smell of toilets in my nose."

Anna laughs. "Will you also be at today's briefing at eight?"

"Yes."

"Lunch together?"

"Sure."

Anna goes to take a shower and Daphne stays in the kitchen with her coffee and does a reality check. She's awake. She needs to make a list of dream signs and read it every night before going to sleep. Things that appear frequently in dreams. Things that require performing a reality check after encountering them.

She showers, dresses quickly in her blue uniform and heads to work.

After fighting the regular endless morning traffic jams, she parks in the Tel Aviv District Headquarters' parking lot and walks into the auditorium some fifteen minutes late. The briefing is already in progress, and a detective she doesn't recognize is busy with a review of everything known to the police so far.

"...and does the exact same thing four times. At each of the hospitals, he locks the bathroom stall for the disabled and hangs an out-of-order sign on the door. An empty crib was found in all four of the stalls..."

Nathan stares daggers at her and she shrugs her shoulders apologetically and settles into the chair he'd saved for her next to him, feeling bad she kept him waiting.

"...In all likelihood, we aren't dealing with a group but the work of just one individual. The same figure appears in the footage from all the security cameras. He was wearing a knit cap and avoided looking directly at the security cameras, so we don't have a definite profile for him. He may have an accomplice or accomplices who handled the logistics while he..."

"Sorry," she whispers to Nathan. "I was stuck in traffic for an hour."

"...we're working on the assumption that he used the same vehicle for all four of the abductions but with different plates each time. We've located the owners of the vehicles from which the plates were stolen the night before the abductions but didn't get anything from the scenes themselves. We're assuming he parked far away enough from all of them and walked to the vehicles wearing overshoes because we didn't…"

"That's no excuse," Nathan whispers harshly. "There's always traffic. Get out of bed earlier. I shouldn't have to be your alarm clock."

"…with the baby under his coat each time. We believe he changed vehicles or parked in the garage of a private home where the vehicle is out of sight. Following inquiries conducted by the teams at all four of the maternity wards, and together with the footage we have from the security cameras, we've put together a detailed facial composite of the suspect, but he may have since shaved off his beard and no longer…"

"Do we have anything left to do at the scenes?" she inquires in a whisper.

"No. The departments have been assigned to regular duties again."

"…we'll maintain a presence at the maternity wards until they implement new procedures to safeguard the identity of the mothers and fathers, since the existing system has proved ineffective. We're also concerned about copycats, criminal elements or terror groups, who may try to do the exact same thing…"

"So we're off to Jerusalem to go through all the findings once more?"

"Yes. We'll try to get some more insights from them."

"Perhaps we should—"

A policewoman sitting behind them places her hand on Daphne's shoulder, to the accompaniment of a "Shhhh!" and Daphne falls silent, turning her attention to the briefing. No one has a clue about the man's whereabouts. And they're not going to find him until he makes a mistake or chooses to surface again.

When the briefing ends, Nathan joins her and Anna and they get a quick lunch together at Dr. Shakshuka next to the Tel Aviv District Headquarters. The Babysitter dominates their conversation. Daphne spots Nathan stealing looks at Anna when he thinks she doesn't notice and she can't decide what she thinks about it.

After saying their goodbyes to Anna, who returns to the police station on Salameh Street, they head for Jerusalem to continue digging through the evidence they'd gathered under their microscopes. They have his fingerprints, there's DNA, there's a modus operandi; but they simply don't have a clue who he is.

At the end of the day, Nathan returns to his home in Jerusalem's French Hill neighborhood, a ten-minute drive from National Headquarters, and she begins her battle through the congestion on the way out of the city, then on the road down to Tel Aviv. She doesn't mind making the trip on a daily basis, so long as she doesn't have to live in or around Jerusalem. The city weighs heavy on her. Too much oppressiveness, too much obscurity, too many stones, too much religion, and too many people.

She walks into her rented apartment an hour and a half later. Coming from Anna's room are the sounds of rhythmic music and the faint smell of marijuana. Daphne changes out of her uniform and into her exercise wear and drives to the beachfront, leaving her car at the Gordon Street parking lot and crossing over to the promenade, before walking down to the beach. She takes off her shoes and socks, places them in a carrier bag, which then goes into her backpack, and begins running across the sand.

It's cold, and it starts to drizzle. The bathing season is still far off, and the waterline is littered with jellyfish that have washed ashore. Milky white, translucent bowls, upside down on the sand, glowing in the moonlight. She skips over the ones on her path. It's not supposed to be like this. One – two – three – four – five fingers. A glance in the direction of the Renaissance Hotel sign, a glance aside, a glance back at the sign. The text hasn't changed. She's awake. A few minutes into her run, she notices someone running behind her. When she slows down to let him pass, he slows down too; and when she picks up her pace to put some distance between them, he accelerates too.

She stops and turns towards him, standing firm, her toes kneading the sand. The man stops in front of her. He's wearing a T-shirt and workout shorts, and his panting face displays a distinct look of surprise. Perhaps he isn't used to meeting a woman who doesn't flee from him.

"Keep running," Daphne says.

He smiles, before dropping his shorts and moving towards her. Fucking pervert.

"I'm police."

His smile widens. "And I'm a firefighter," he says, reaching for her.

He's her height. And close enough to lay his hand on her, to touch her.

You'll see
  You'll be happy here with us
  You'll get everything you need right here
  But if you don't do what you're told, we're
dumping you
  You're going back to your father
  And he'll know how to deal with you just fine
  After what you did to him
  He remembers you every day when he looks
in the mirror
  Thinks about you all the time
  Hasn't stopped searching
  Just one phone call and he'll know where
you are
  So you're just going to do as you're told
  Everything you're told
  And then we'll keep you here with us
  You'll be happy here
  If you make us happy too
  Come here
  Come closer

Her hand reaches for his head and her fingers slide over his scalp, then twist into a fist that locks onto his hair. She tugs down on his head as hard as she can, bringing her knee up to his face at the same time.

"What's with you all? Why is every asshole in the world after me? Leave me the fuck alone already!"

He falls to the sand. His hand goes to his face and blood trickles between his fingers.

She stands over him, her eyes on fire but her voice steady and menacing: "Come near me again, and that will be the last thing you ever do."

She breaks into a run and heads away from him. As she runs she does another reality check. Awake.

Voices from the pubs along the beach carry all the way down to her on the shoreline. Tel Avivians without a care in the world raising toasts, the sound of clinking glasses mixing with music and laughter, the waves washing dead jellyfish ashore. The adrenalin coursing through her turns into speed that turns into sweat, which is soaked up by her tank top.

27.

"Police hotline. What's your emergency?"

"Hello. I'd like to report a car with its engine running but no one inside."

"Who is this?"

"Raviv. I'm a delivery driver for Zer4u, the flower and gifts shop."

"Raviv who?"

"Raviv Shavit. A delivery driver for Zer4u. I'm in Rishpon with a delivery for the Dotan family and they aren't home, but their car is parked here outside and the engine's running."

"Can you see anyone in the car? A child? A baby?"

"No. It's smoky or steamy inside, but I looked and I think it's empty."

"Did you check to see if anyone's home?"

"Yes. I rang the bell and I also tried calling the number I have, and I can hear the phone ringing inside, but no one answers, and I don't have a mobile number for them, just their landline."

"Have you seen anything that appears criminal in nature?"

"What?"

"Does something look wrong? Is the car damaged in any way? Is the alarm ringing in the house? Any signs of forced entry on the door?"

"No. Only the car with its engine running and the windows steamed up. And the fact that getting called out for a seven-in-the-morning delivery to a family who aren't home is pretty strange. Not our usual working hours."

"They may have left the car running by mistake and gone out in a different vehicle. Thanks for calling it in. I'll make a note of it and we'll contact them tomorrow to make sure they made it home. The Dotan family in Rishpon, right?"

"Yes. It's just that it looks strange to me. Sorry for troubling you; you must be up to your necks with the whole baby abduction thing that's all over the news."

"No problem."

"Thanks. Too bad about the Tucson though. I hope the engine doesn't burn out or something."

There's silence on the line for a brief moment, before the previously calm tone of the operator turns urgent and assertive.

"A Hyundai Tucson, you said?"

"Yes."

"What color?"

"White."

"Give me the exact address."

"It's 8 HaAlon Street. Rishpon."

"Stay where you are and wait for the patrol car to get there."

"Do you want me to open the envelope and read out what it says on the card attached to the box of chocolates?"

"No. Place everything on the floor and don't touch anything again."

28.

A feeble whimper transforms into a loud wail, then a second one begins, then another and another, the babies waking each other in turn to join the howling chorus.

Lee opens her eyes and gazes at the TV, which is tuned in to Channel 11, with the volume on mute. A clock appears in the bottom left-hand corner of the screen. Four-twenty in the morning.

"You've got to be fucking kidding me."

It's her second night with the four newborns, who she thinks must be two days old, three at most, based on the state of their umbilical cord stumps. Food. Diaper change. Food. Diaper change. Food. Diaper change. And no sleep. Each has its own internal clock, out of sync with one another, and certainly out of sync with hers, meaning she's gotten maybe a little more than thirty minutes of sleep in total throughout the night. Or that's how it feels at least. It's worse than a nightshift at the hospital. More exhausting than a night of guard duty during basic training. She completes a round of diapers and food, successfully soothes the babies and places them back in their cribs, then crashes into bed again. Her eyes have almost closed when a caption appears across the bottom of the television screen:

Up next: An exclusive interview with the interior minister, Gideon Hertzman, whose grandson is among the kidnapped babies

Lee reaches for the remote and turns up the volume.

"...exclusively here on the seven o'clock news. We can tell you now, following the lifting of a gag order, that one of the newborn babies abducted yesterday morning from the maternity wards at Ichilov, Beilinson, Mayanei Hayeshua and Tel HaShomer hospitals is the grandson of the interior minister, Gideon Hertzman. A spokesperson for the Israel Police has informed our crime correspondent, Adi Lifshitz, that the police and security forces are making every effort to locate the perpetrators, and that they've yet to find any evidence to indicate that the incident is terror-related. The Israel Police and its commissioner are coming under intense fire and have been strongly urged to declare—"

She mutes the TV again. That's all they've been talking about since yesterday, the kidnapping of the babies, and she's tired of listening to analyses and conjecture regarding their predicament, when in fact she's the only one who truly knows what's going on with them. She and the man who snatched her, and who hasn't returned since bringing them here.

But one of them is the interior minister's grandson. She gets up and looks at the sleeping babies, as if she'd be able to tell which one resembles the minister. It's good news at least. The police are going to come under enormous pressure; they have to find them. Meanwhile, she'll take care of them and make sure that the psychopath who abducted them, and her, doesn't try to harm them. Even though they aren't letting her sleep, they're tiny and fragile and haven't done a thing wrong.

She opens the cupboard and fills a bowl with Nestlé Crunch. It would be great to have milk to add to the cereal, but there isn't any. Yesterday, in a moment of curiosity, she tasted the baby formula. Disgusting.

And coffee. If only she had an electric kettle. She could have a cup of hot coffee in the morning. And wait for him behind the door with a kettle full of boiling water, aimed at his head.

29.

Tonight, I'll remember my dream

Tonight, I'll be in control of my dream

I'm strong and can face up to any character who seeks to harm me in my dream

Tonight, I'll remember my dream

Tonight, I'll be in control of my dream

I'm strong and can face up to any character who seeks to harm me in my dream

Tonight, I'll remember my dream

Tonight, I'll be in control of my dream

I'm strong and can face up to any character who seeks to harm me in my dream

07:20

I'm sitting on the edge of a pool and dangling my feet in the water. I look at my swimsuit and realize that I'm a child. A girl with almond eyes who I do not recognize is sitting next to me. I know she is my friend.

"Want to go on a journey?" she asks.

I look at her. Her black hair is wet and drops of water are falling onto her back and shoulders. My hair is wet too. We must have just gotten out of the water, but I can't remember anything that has happened until now. We're the only ones here. There aren't any people in the pool, and the surrounding green lawns and chairs under the red-and-white sunshades are empty. There's no one here but us. A gray bird lands next to us and taps lightly on the ground with its feather tail.

"Yes, I do," I say.

"It's a wagtail," she says. "Coming?"

"Yes, I'm coming."

We stand up and begin walking.

An orange desert. Sun. Lifeless heat everywhere. Oppressive. Heavy. Dust. A whisper. Silence.

The girl is gone.

Next I find myself with Rotem as a child and we are engrossed in a game of mud-ball, our feet kicking up clouds of orange dust as we run barefoot back and forth in the arid backyard. Rotem stops for a moment under the kitchen window and puts her finger to her lips. Mom is calling the rainmaker.

We crouch under the window, hiding in the vegetable patch. It hasn't rained in ages, and the bell peppers and tomatoes have started to shrivel on their stems and branches of plants are drying under the hot sun. The last time it was this hot, Mia was still with us. It was before the accident.

"So you'll be here at five-forty?" Mom schedules a visit from the rainmaker, and she closes the window above our heads. Before she closes it, I hear her mutter something about this insufferable dust and all the produce that'll end up in the trash if the rainmaker doesn't get here on time. Rotem says that Mom's upset because the orange dust reminds her of Mia and the accident and everything that happened, and that's why she's called for the rainmaker – because the peppers can easily survive a few more days without water. It's Mom who can't.

"How did she die?" I ask Rotem, and she gives me a look reserved for no one but an older sister.

"We don't talk about it," she says. "Let's go open the gate for the rainmaker."

"Is it true that the ship she was on disappeared?"

"We don't talk about it." Rotem kicks a large mound of earth, sending another orange dust cloud in the direction of the peppers on the vines. Her voice is strange, like she's choking. I think it's because of all the dust.

We open the gate, sit on the wooden fence and eat small red tomatoes and little heart-shaped pieces of dark chocolate that Rotem produces from a small box, without saying a word. The wind, hot and dry, blows my hair out of place. The world around us is both familiar and foreign. The sky boasts two suns. One big and orange, and one small and white. We each cast two shadows. One shadow for each sun.

The rainmaker arrives at precisely five-forty. "Hi, girls," he says, and we wave to him as he heads inside to talk to Mom. He then comes out to the yard and arranges his jars on the ground to form a hexagon. Around them, he scatters seashells and small white bones, and bundles of black feathers tied together with red thread, and tiny piles of white sand that you can hardly see from the fence we're sitting on. He spreads his arms to the side and calls for the rain to come.

I want to say to Rotem perhaps we can ask the

rainmaker to bring Mia back to us instead of the rain, and that it would be so wonderful if that were to happen because we'd be able to see Mom smile again, and maybe even laugh. But Rotem seems to read my mind and gives me the sternest big-sister look she can muster, and I remain silent.

Rain starts to fall.

"Let's go inside." I offer my hand to my sister and notice that one of my fingers is oddly slanted to the left. One, two, three, odd finger, five. What's happening here? I'm dreaming. I'm in a dream. That's impossible. It was reality just a second ago. Incredible. Wait, don't wake up. Don't…

Daphne wakes up. The dream was so beautiful and sad, and so vivid, and she remembers every detail.

She immediately opens her dream journal and records it, tears blurring her vision. Why did her first lucid dream have to be so painful? What's the dream supposed to symbolize? She feels a powerful, urgent need to understand what it means. Who was the girl in the swimsuit who was with her at the beginning? She didn't recognize her but knew in the dream that she was a very close friend. She looked a little Japanese. Slanted eyes and glistening, straight black hair.

She finishes writing and gets up to go to the kitchen, wiping her face on the way. She doesn't want a cigarette. She has a craving for ice cream, to drown her sorrow. She and Anna bought some really good gourmet ice cream the day before, and she's more than happy for it to be the first thing she puts into her mouth in the morning. She's eating straight from the container with a teaspoon when her phone rings. Nathan.

"Head straight to the scene in Rishpon without passing through Jerusalem."

She returns the ice cream to the freezer, throws the teaspoon into the sink and rushes back to her room.

* * *

"Did you catch the news on the way?"

They're standing at the bottom of the driveway of the home in Rishpon in their blue police windbreakers, smoking.

"Yes. The interior minister. What a mess."

"Was there no security detail assigned to his daughter?"

"No, she doesn't fit the profile. Only the prime minister's kids get a security detail. And bodyguards are reserved for the minister alone, not even his wife, and certainly not his children and grandchildren."

"That's all we need – more pressure," Daphne concludes.

A patrol car with two investigators inside is blocking the access road to the house. They ask Nathan if they can help in any way, but he declines, telling them he'd rather they remain where they are to avoid leaving additional shoeprints at the scene. His response pleases them. The cold wind and rain aren't particularly inviting, and they're taking a statement from the delivery driver in the comfort of a heated car.

Parked outside the entrance to the home, some twenty yards from them, is a white Hyundai Tucson with its engine running.

Daphne looks at the car. "If this is the vehicle, it's probably been here since the morning of the abductions two days ago. How come it hasn't run out of gas?"

"A car parked in neutral with its engine running consumes very little fuel. About a quarter of a gallon every hour. This car must have a tank with a capacity of at least twelve to fifteen gallons, so it can remain stationary with its engine running for two, three days no problem. What are we going to check for first?"

"Shoe and tire prints," Daphne responds quickly. "With all this mud here, we'll get some good impressions. I'll take prints from the investigators and delivery driver too."

They work methodically – taking photographs, pouring polymers into tire and shoe prints they find in the unpaved area in front of the house, collecting the impressions, and lifting fingerprints from the gift package the delivery driver left outside the front door. The package then goes into a large evidence bag, which they seal. And only once they've completed their examination of the area around it do they turn their attention to the vehicle itself.

"Can you smell that?" she asks.

"Bleach."

She peers inside. The windows are steamed up. Droplets of water running down the inside of the windows have cleared trails on the glass, and through them they can see that the vehicle is empty, nothing on the seats. Daphne lifts prints from the driver's side and Nathan from the other. Windows, handles, doors.

Nathan checks the doors. They're all locked.

"Should we break a window to get in?"

"Are you testing me?" Daphne smiles.

"You tell me."

"No. There could be prints on the inside of the window; besides, the fragments of glass will get in our way once we're in. Better to bring in a lock expert."

They radio for a police lock expert and go back to the patrol car in the meantime for an update from the two investigators. According to the storeowner the investigators spoke to, someone walked into the Herzliya branch of Zer4u yesterday evening, selected a box of Max Brenner espresso-flavored chocolates, handed them an envelope to attach to the gift, paid in cash and left. He had a beard and was wearing a black knit cap. The delivery driver hadn't seen him.

"Aren't you going to open it?" one of the investigators asks Daphne.

"Later. Back at the Forensics lab."

"Keeping the chocolate to yourselves, I see."

She stares at him blankly and doesn't respond.

When the lock expert arrives, they instruct him not to break anything or contaminate the scene. He sighs to himself, and, using a thin length of metal that he inserts through the rubber sealing around the window frame, it takes him just seconds to release the door's locking mechanism. "At your service," he says, gesturing chivalrously towards the vehicle.

Daphne opens the driver's side door, managing to peer inside briefly before stumbling backwards to the ground, coughing in a concentrated cloud of warm bleach vapor.

> **Don't waste the entire bottle**
> **It's expensive stuff**
> **Pour one cap onto the scouring pad**
> **And scrub the toilet bowls from the outside first**
> **And then from the inside**
> **Until all the stains are gone**
> **And then flush the water**
> **Don't you dare be lazy**
> **I'll be coming to check that everything is sparkling when you're done**

Nathan hurries towards her and drags her back, away from the door. Holding his breath, he then leans into the vehicle and turns the key. The engine dies, and apart from Daphne's coughing, everything goes quiet. She's still on the ground, trying to catch her breath.

"You okay?" Nathan asks.

One of the investigators comes over to them, then runs back to the patrol car, returning with a bottle of water. Daphne sips from it slowly, the cold water soothing the burning in her throat. Her eyes are watering and sore, and she sits on the wet road, trying to pull herself together. She's worried that her throat is scalded, that she won't be able to speak, but she gives the anxious Nathan a thumbs-up to say, "Everything's okay."

Nathan returns to the car and opens all the doors and the trunk. The vehicle is completely empty and functioning like a bleach steam bath. Fingerprints or traces of DNA could never have survived two days of that.

"There's nothing more for us to do here," he informs the investigators. "We'll go back to the Forensics Unit to process all the findings. Can you call in a tow truck to take the vehicle to National Headquarters? Let it air out in the meantime; and when they take it, make sure they work with gloves and keep their hands off it as much as possible. And send someone to Zer4u in Herzliya to collect a full set of prints from everyone so we can rule out the employees there. Get them to do it right away, on a computerized M-1003 form, so we can access the data immediately from the AFIS[1]."

Daphne can feel her voice starting to come back as she listens to Nathan. "Have you done a check on the residents?" she asks hoarsely, still from her position on the ground.

"Abroad. And the plates on the vehicle are the real plates. Registered to them."

"The screws look freshly worn," Nathan adds. "Someone loosened and tightened them several times recently. There's a good chance that this is the vehicle that was used for the abductions."

He reaches out to her, and although she can stand up on her own, she allows him to help her to her feet. His hand is warm.

"Feeling better?"

He's still holding on to her hand.

"Yes. Caught me by surprise that's all. I'm fine. Don't worry."

On the way to her car, she does a reality check; and on the way to Jerusalem she tries to call Rotem, but she doesn't answer. She'll try to get hold of her later.

---

1. Automated Fingerprint Identification System

30.

The Forensics Laboratory at National Police Headquarters in Jerusalem isn't very different from the labs of drug companies or hospitals. A light shade of linoleum flooring, white tables with attached cabinets, each displaying an array of microscopes, computer monitors, measuring devices, test-tube racks and containers of liquids. The only section that looks different is the area containing photography tables with powerful lighting from above and a wall of shelves of box files and sealed bags marked *Forensic Evidence*.

Nathan and Daphne, their hands clad in gloves, are standing at one of the photography tables. Nathan opens the evidence bag and removes the Zer4u gift package. It's smeared with the black powder they'd used at the scene to expose and photograph the fingerprints. Nathan gently starts to remove the wrapping paper.

"May I?" Daphne asks.

"Yes," he says, stepping aside. "Slowly. We're in no hurry."

She slowly removes the wrapping paper. Inside is a sealed cardboard box with illustrations of chocolates, along with a white envelope with the printed words: *We're just getting started.*

She opens the envelope and pulls out a white sheet of paper, a letter, also printed, and she reads it out loud:

Great upheavals in history don't occur slowly. They occur during the lifetime of a single individual over a period of a few years or several decades. A single individual strong enough to change the course of history – of a state, of an entire continent. Of the entire world. Take Theodor Herzl, for example, who sparked a series of events that led to the establishment of the State of Israel and a succession of upheavals in the Middle East; George Washington, who united a continent into a superpower; Genghis Khan, who ruled over half the world and whose direct descendants still make up one-tenth of the population of Asia and one in every two hundred people on the planet as a whole; Hitler, whose empire would still exist today had he not made mistakes and acted in haste. In recent decades, the world has lacked such an individual. Someone with the power to change history. The combination of Donald Trump and Kim Jong-un might spark a nuclear war, but it would do nothing at all to change the course of history. It would only lead to North Korea's temporary destruction and subsequent flourishing.

Growth and expansion come from pain. Take the birth of a baby, for example. A butterfly struggling to release itself from its cocoon. A chick from its egg. The greater the pain – either physical or mental – the greater the intensity of the change.

I am going to spark the next historical upheaval that will reverberate for generations to come. I'm not in a hurry. I will create the required pain and intellect slowly and cautiously.

Don't bother looking for me or the Four.

See you in a year's time.

"That's it?" Nathan asks, frowning.

"Yes. We're dealing here with a genuine lunatic. The kind you see in the movies, not in real life." She photographs the envelope and the letter, and while Nathan dusts them for fingerprints, she does a quick reality check. Five fingers. The text on the page hasn't changed. She's awake. He doesn't find a single print.

Nathan goes over to one of the computer stations and downloads the images from the Rishpon scene. He then uploads the fingerprints to the AFIS, which soon come back with matches. The Zer4u delivery driver. The employee who wrapped the gift. That's all. There are no other prints.

"They didn't waste time for once," he remarks to himself.

"Who?"

"The investigators who went to Zer4u."

Daphne nods. All the prints are indeed in the system already. And all of them had been identified. They were still none the wiser.

The prints from the car were of no help either. Nathan numbers them on the screen, in keeping with the order in which they were lifted. When he's done, he opens an enlarged image of the letter on the screen and runs a piece of software to scan it.

"Printed on an HP LaserJet Pro."

"Doesn't help us much."

"It's an office printer. Not something one buys for the home usually."

"But there are lots of them out there."

"True."

"Any sign of steganography?"

Nathan enlarges the image even more. The letters on the screen become huge, as he looks for the miniature yellow dots that note the printer's serial number and the date and time of printing.

"No. It's probably an old model, or he may have disabled the mechanism."

"Would you like an espresso chocolate? He didn't touch the chocolates."

"Are you crazy?"

"I'm joking. Don't get your panties in a twist," she responds, smiling at his frowning face and placing the box with its dark chocolate hearts back in the evidence bag.

Evening falls, and they're still in the lab, with sandwiches from the cafeteria and extra-strong coffee. They go through all the material that's been collected and feed everything into the police computer system.

"What do you think he means by this letter?" she asks.

"No idea. We know he's planning something for a year from now. To abduct more babies? He's stirred up a great deal of noise with these abductions, but they aren't going to change the course of world history. I honestly don't have a clue. How's anyone supposed to figure out a madman?" Nathan sends an email with the scanned letter to the Command Center that's coordinating police activities on the Babysitter case.

"How's your throat? Better?" he asks.

"A little sore, but okay. I should have been more careful. Next time I'll think twice before sticking my head into a car like that. We could smell the bleach from the outside too. I was careless." She swallows and feels the burning sensation again.

He pauses and looks at her. "We need to inform the Command Center."

"About what?"

"The bleach. There was enough there for a chemical attack. I can't believe I didn't think of it before. They need to question everyone who sells bleach in the central region of the country and check if anyone came in to buy a large quantity recently. We're talking about a huge number of places, but perhaps he made a mistake and bought the lot all at once from the same location. And maybe he even paid with a credit card."

"I doubt it. He's too meticulous for that. Just look at how he organized the four abductions. He wouldn't have slipped up with something so trivial."

The computer pings, and Daphne turns to look at the screen. It shows a green stripe with two images underneath it. Tire impressions, side by side, marked with a number of corresponding ellipses.

"I don't believe it!" she exclaims. "Take a look at this."

31.

Everything is perfect. The Four are in his possession. The Guardian is doing her job well, the abductions are dominating the news, the law enforcement authorities have no idea where he is. And everything is going smoothly at his place of work too, at his mundane, boring, dreary, stupid job, the kind fit for an ant in a colony.

The police must have read his letter and choked on the chocolates by now.

Run along little chicks
Peck here
Peck there
Maybe you'll find a seed
Perhaps a pit
From an avocado
Careful
Don't choke on it

He walks down the hallway carrying the toolbox and stops outside an unmarked door. Yesterday, he received and signed for all the deliveries outside, brought the cargo in and took it down in the freight elevator, and moved everything on wheel pallets into the room.

He unlocks the door, steps inside and goes over to the large wooden crate in the center of the room. He disassembles the walls of the crate and puts them aside, leaning them up against the wall in an orderly fashion, before removing the plastic sheeting and bubble wrap and then stepping back to assess his new acquisition in its entirety. A hot tub. Excellent. Exactly the right size. Spending hours online finding this particular model was worth the effort.

He works on installing the hot tub. When he's done, he cleans it with a pile of wet wipes. He surveys it once more, satisfied. And then he opens the air valves and water faucet, and the hot tub begins to fill up slowly. He flips the switch on the wall and sets the thermostat to ninety-six degrees. The model he purchased is expensive and sophisticated and allows for a precise temperature setting.

While the hot tub fills, he adds a mixture of chlorine to the water and checks the motor by turning on the range of bubble jets and whirlpool functions. When the tub is full, he uses a thermometer to check that the water has indeed reached a temperature of precisely ninety-six degrees and leaves only the water circulation function running.

The remaining cartons wait for him in the corner of the room, and he goes through them, opening and removing their contents. Four infant car seats, steel rods, IV needles, tubes and feeding bags, floats, and sheets of rubber.

He folds and sets aside the cartons, arranges the items and deals with each one in turn, checking the temperature of the water in the hot tub every ten minutes. All is in order. Half an hour later, he turns it off, drains the water and dries the surface with a towel.

With his focus entirely on the drilling, welding and installing of all the required components in and around the hot tub, the hours fly by. When he's done, he fills the hot tub again, makes sure there are no leaks from its bottom surface and then drains and dries it again.

He undresses and gets into the dry hot tub. He lies down, closes his eyes and soon falls asleep. An hour later, he wakes up and looks at the concrete ceiling with its row of fluorescent lights. No.

Such plain lighting is inappropriate for the most important place of all. It calls for orange-red lighting, low, and on the walls only. The ceiling should be bare. He decides to paint the entire room a dark red-brown-orange shade. Like the inside of a womb.

He stands up, raises his head and sniffs the air. Chlorine, wet

145

wipes, new black plastic, welding fumes, heat, drill dust, sweat. He needs to clean the room thoroughly and add a pleasant odor to the air. Nothing too strong.

He won't be cleaning and tidying for others this time. This time, it's for him. And when it's all over, he won't have to clean up after anyone ever again. They'll clean up after him. They'll bow to him. They'll worship him. Let them carry on thinking for now that he is serving them. He's a king dressed in the clothes of a simple peasant. A king who is building his castle right now. A king everyone will kneel to one day when he stands before them anointed with oil.

And standing behind Him at His feet, weeping, she began to wet His feet with her tears, and kept wiping them with the hair of her head, and kissing His feet and anointing them with the perfume.

He gets dressed and leaves the room. After locking up, he fixes a sign on the door with a single word printed in large black letters: *Temple.*

He returns the toolbox to one of the rooms and walks along the hallway and through the X-ray Room, making sure to lock each door and put the keys back in their place. The stainless-steel trolley is waiting for him in the room with the photographs, and he wheels it into the room with another sign – in large black letters – fixed to the door: *Guardian.*

32.

Nathan gets up and hurries over to Daphne's computer station.

"You've got a match?"

"Yes," she replies, pointing at the screen. Two identical tire prints.

Just as Rotem said. Now they had visual confirmation.

"Dan District Case 447369/3615. Anat Aharon. I remember that case number by heart. Look, the exact same defects. It's the same tire."

"The girl from the hit-and-run in Kiryat Ono?"

"Yes."

"And that's the Tucson's tire?"

"No. I lifted all the tire prints outside the house in Rishpon. This is a print from a car that was parked nearby. A Maxtrek. The same vehicle that killed Anat Aharon – the same person perhaps that abducted Lee Ben-Ami and is holding her somewhere."

"Or has buried her somewhere," Nathan says.

Daphne doesn't respond. He may be right. Anything's possible.

"No," she says, pulling herself together. "These three cases are connected. Anat Aharon, Lee Ben-Ami, and the four babies. Lee's alive and he's holding her and the babies somewhere. Don't you see? That's why he snatched her."

"To take care of the babies for him? Sounds a little out there," Nathan replies.

"This entire series of events is a little out there. I think he's holding them somewhere really remote, and he needs her to look after the babies while he moves ahead with his plans. He says in his letter that he'll be back in a year's time."

"Do you think he's going to demand a ransom?"

"I don't think he's concerned with the families at all. He's messing with us. He sent the chocolates so that we'd find the car," Daphne says.

Nathan nods. They both know the chocolates and the letter were intended for the police. "So you don't think his plan was to kidnap the interior minister's grandson?"

"I have no idea."

"In any event, I don't see the interior minister or his family bowing to terror."

"That's what everyone's going to see and hear on their TVs: fiery speeches from politicians. But behind the scenes, they'll pay whatever he wants to get their babies back."

"I think you watch too much TV. Coming for a cigarette?"

They go out into the Jerusalem cold and stand at the entrance to the building.

"I don't have time."

"For what?"

"Watching TV." She lights a cigarette and exhales the smoke while continuing to talk. "I'm either asleep and dreaming, or I'm at work. I don't really have a life."

Nathan lights a cigarette for himself.

"It took a while for Anat and Lee to stop appearing in my dreams, and now they're going to come back. It's all connected. All these incidents are part of one story."

Nathan's phone rings. "Yes, it's the same one that was suspected of being involved in the abduction in Givatayim. No, there weren't any tire marks there. These are only from the scenes in Rishpon and Kiryat Ono. Perfect, we'll fill you in if we come up with anything else. Sure. Thanks." He hangs up.

"Coming in?" he asks. "I'm freezing to death out here."

"Go ahead. I'll be there soon. I need some air."

She takes out her cell phone and calls Rotem.

Her friend answers. "You've caught me on my way to the gym. Anything new?"

"It's exactly as you thought. The same guy who killed Anat must have abducted Lee too. The tire prints match. And he left a letter."

"Where did he leave the letter?"

"He sent it to the owner of the vehicle he stole."

"Are they connected in any way?"

"No, no, they're abroad. He stole their car and then returned it to its parking place, with a ton of bleach inside and the engine running. Almost killed me."

"So how did you find the letter?"

"It was delivered with a box of chocolates, and the delivery driver called the police. He's playing with us big time." Daphne retrieves a folded piece of paper from her pocket. "I'll read it to you."

"Just a sec. Do you have anything else new on him, apart from the tire match?"

"No," Daphne says while pacing next to the building entrance to warm herself.

"Okay."

Daphne reads the letter; when she's done, she hears nothing but silence on the other end of the line. She waits several long seconds before Rotem speaks again.

"That's a first."

"A first what?" Daphne folds the piece of paper so she can put her free hand in her pocket to warm up.

"He's Israel's first psycho. He's going to make headlines all around the world. Like Charles Manson."

"So you guys are going to get involved?" Daphne pauses her pacing, hoping for some good news.

"No, it's a first, but it isn't ours. There was talk of him here today, and everyone agreed that we're not dealing with an act of terror, neither internal nor external, and that the police need to handle it. Barring explicit instructions, we're staying out of it for now."

Daphne goes quiet, hiding her disappointment.

"I don't think we'll be hearing from him again in the coming year," Rotem continues, "and it'll be very difficult to locate him if he chooses not to initiate contact again. He has good phonology. Too bad it isn't handwritten. Send me a picture on WhatsApp."

"Can't he be lured out of hiding?"

"What do you have in mind?"

"Let's say they were to air a report on TV in which he's ridiculed or said to be a pedophile? Or that he's a psychopath who must have been raped as a child and has never come to terms with it and feels good only around babies? Something that's going to piss him off and force him into a response? Or at least cause him to make a mistake?"

"Won't work. He'll catch on in no time, remain in hiding and take his anger out on his captive and maybe the babies too. That kind of thing may work in the movies but not in real life. And he's right, by the way."

"About what?"

"In terms of his analysis of major changes in history. It's true. The history of mankind is a sequence of interactions between individuals, and those who manage to attain positions of power and have sufficient charisma and megalomania to attract the following of entire nations are the ones who create the stone in the pond effect. The ripples from the stone they throw into the pond of history remain in motion long after their lives come to an end. I wonder what he meant by 'pain and intellect'."

"You've lost me."

"He writes about physical and mental anguish. About creating the required pain and intellect. He uses the word 'required'. Required for what?"

"How am I supposed to know? It's absolute lunacy."

"Or not. According to his logic at least. Fucking asshole. Take your eyes off your phone! I swear, Daph, everyone in the country drives around with their eyes on their phones. Someone almost ran down a kid on a crosswalk. The Four."

"What?" Daphne was struggling to follow.

"His letter talks of 'the Four'. That's interesting. Think about it. What word would you have used for them?"

"Babies."

"He doesn't see them as babies but as something else. Objects, entities, things. The letter needs more work."

"So what do you think we need to do?"

"Wait for him to make contact. Meanwhile, send me everything you have and Lee Ben-Ami's case file most importantly. The fate of the babies is in her hands now. Apart from his, of course. In what order were they snatched?"

"Beilinson, Ichilov, Mayanei Hayeshua and Tel HaShomer."

"And the times of the abductions?"

"About half an hour apart. The first occurred shortly before seven in the morning, and all four were taken within less than two hours. By the time they realized they were dealing with a series of abductions and sent out word to all the maternity wards around the country, he was long gone."

"He's someone who doesn't leave things to chance. He figured out traffic congestion patterns and arranged the sequence of abductions accordingly even though it was carried out on a Saturday." The line goes quiet again for a moment. "Mental pain," Rotem continues, although Daphne isn't sure if she's talking to herself or not. "What's that all about?"

The wind picks up and a shiver courses through Daphne's body. Droplets of rain begin dotting her jacket.

"Pain and intellect. The pain is mental, the anguish of the families who'll have to wait a year to get a sign of life from their children. Note, they're all boys. That's no coincidence. A year of mental anguish and then he'll move on to physical pain. Lee's physical pain perhaps. The babies' perhaps. Maybe he's going to sacrifice all of them as part of some ritual and broadcast it on YouTube."

"You really think he might do something like that? Kill them all?" Daphne was genuinely worried.

"Not really. He's planning something else that I don't have enough data to process. If you're in the left lane, why the hell are you crawling? Holy shit! I wonder why he sent the chocolate. Was there anything special about the chocolate?"

"No."

"Did you test for toxins and the like?"

"Nathan's doing all the tests now."

"Let me know if you come up with anything else."

"Great. I will. Thanks, Rotem."

She's about to hang up when Rotem asks: "What's happening with the dreams?"

"They're becoming increasingly palpable. Sometimes, when I'm awake, I have to check that I'm not dreaming, and sometimes I'm dreaming and have to check that I'm not awake. Last night I managed to lucid dream."

"You're progressing fast."

"But the nightmare hasn't disappeared."

"Wait, that'll come too. Meanwhile, make a list of your dream signs; and when you encounter them, do a reality check right away."

"I've done that already."

"What are your signs?"

"Sometimes, I feel like I'm missing something but I don't know what, sometimes I'm back in the army as some kind of an engineering technician, sometimes I'm naked or see naked people. It's embarrassing. I don't always document the embarrassing things in my dream journal. I don't want anyone reading some things if they ever find it."

Rotem chuckles.

"And sometimes there's also a small gray bird but less frequently. Is that normal or is it just me?"

"Not unusual. A third or half of lucid dreams are those kinds of dreams. And I don't mean the military engineering technician ones. That seems to be a personal thing of yours."

"Have you ever experienced sleep paralysis?"

"Yes. Hasn't everyone?"

"I read online that it could lead to a heart attack." Daphne sounds worried.

"When you dream, your muscles don't move; only your involuntary systems remain active."

"Yes, I know."

"So essentially, when you dream, you're paralyzed. It's no big deal. It occurs naturally a number of times during the night, to prevent you from running into a wall or falling off a balcony when fleeing a monster. When you dream, the only things that move voluntarily are your eyes, which race back and forth under your closed eyelids."

"Yes. REM."

"So when you start playing around with your sleep, you dream of waking up in your room. You're convinced you've woken up; but wait a moment and do a reality check. If it turns out that you're still dreaming, that's fine, keep dreaming. If you've woken up – cool, you're awake. If you can't bring yourself to carry out a reality check at all, you're in a state of sleep paralysis."

"So I'm awake, lying in bed like a mummy and unable to move?"

"Exactly. Being like that, waking from REM with your body still in a state of sleep paralysis, isn't very nice. It can be very stressful the first few times it happens. You're awake but can't move a muscle, you can't even open your eyes. And your brain will start playing tricks on you. You'll feel a heavy weight pressing down on your chest that seems to inhibit your breathing. Your heart rate will increase. You'll hear whispers, a voice calling your name. And even though your eyelids are closed, you'll see an indistinct shadow or shadows moving in your room. The first time it happens, you'll think you've lost your mind and pray to never dream again. It's terrifying at first, but eventually you get used to it and it's not so bad."

"Thanks a lot for the words of encouragement." Daphne laughs and shivers again. She looks up. Gray clouds fill the sky, and the rain is coming down harder. A gloomy day. A gloomy week. A shitty winter.

"So what do I do when it happens?"

"You mustn't try to flee in panic or get up because it won't do you any good; you can't move when you're in that state. You need to remain calm and view the situation like a scientist studying something and just keep experiencing the paralysis in a relaxed manner even though your heart is pounding like a jackhammer. The shadows around you and the whispers are your mind pranking you. There's a trick that sometimes helps you shake off the sleep

153

paralysis faster, and that's to keep trying to move your toes. It's never worked for me."

Daphne sighs. "That's all I need now, on top of the nightmare."

"I told you to be careful."

"Yes, you did."

Rotem doesn't respond.

"Rotem?"

"Huh?"

"You are the only person who really knows me."

"Don't go all mushy on me."

"I mean it. You're the best. Thanks for everything you're doing for me. Really."

"No worries, kiddo, go back to the lab before you freeze to death. I can hear your teeth chattering all the way to Ramat HaSharon. Keep me posted if you find something new."

PART 3

THE SWITCH

MARCH 2017

33.

Tonight, I'll remember my dream

Tonight, I'll lucid dream

I'm strong and can face up to any character who seeks to harm me in my dream

Tonight, I'll remember my dream

Tonight, I'll lucid dream

I'm strong and can face up to any character who seeks to harm me in my dream

Tonight, I'll remember my dream

Tonight, I'll lucid dream

I'm strong and can face up to any character who seeks to harm me in my dream

06:08

I'm lying in my sleeping bag in a tent, warm and cozy. It's dark outside and I can hear the chirping of insects.

"Are you awake?"

I turn to my right and see her, lying beside me in a blue sleeping bag, holding a small flashlight and aiming the beam at the tent flap, which is closed tight with a long zipper.

"Yes."

"It's frightening outside," she says. "There may be wolves."

I try to listen for howling but can only hear the chirping.

"I don't think so."

She squirms out of her sleeping bag barefoot, wearing long pajamas, and continues to aim her flashlight at the green nylon walls of the tent.

"Want to go on a journey?"

"Yes," I say and then everything changes.

The same whisper plays over and over again in my head.

Where do I start?

Where do I start?

Evening.

Reality check. I'm in. Conscious of my dream.

The sun's about to go down. The forest is huge, its treetops illuminated by sunset. Barefoot, I walk slowly along a narrow path between the trees, the ends of the branches scratching my naked body. The silence is absolute. No chirping of birds or light gusts of wind. Everything's completely still. The trees. The earth. The air. There's no one here but me.

Where do I start?

Something's following me. I can't see or hear it, but I sense it inside. I don't pick up my pace.

I'm hungry.

The treetops close the forest in from above. It's dark and humid here. Warm drops of water fall from the branches of the tall trees and trickle down my skin. I come to a circular clearing in the forest, the branches of the trees around it forming a huge dome-like structure, like a church, overhead. Standing around the edges of the clearing are stone statues facing the center of the circle. They're covered in moss, their facial features indistinct. Protruding from the earth in the middle of the circle is a slab of dark, smooth rock. I walk over to it and kneel down to read the inscription. I brush away the moss and read:

> *Rejection*
> *Abandonment*
> *Betrayal*
> *Humiliation*

Where do I start?

The dead, naked figure of Anat Aharon flits through the trees like a ghost. Her movement is barely visible, but it shifts branches and leaves. There is a sparkle of light from the metallic clover leaf on her stomach and a thin stream of blood trickling down her cheek from the corner of her mouth. Lee Ben-Ami is running after her, honey brown eyes, five foot six, blond-brown hair – straight and short – red running shoes and a blue-and-red tracksuit. She stops, turns around and looks at me, beckoning me closer. "Come here. Come here. Come here," she says slowly, without making a sound. She mouths the words in an exaggerated fashion, as if I'm deaf and she wants me to understand her.

I want to approach her but sense something breathing behind me. Hot air against my back. I'm not afraid. I turn slowly and see a large black she-wolf. We look each other in the eyes, yellow eyes into green ones. "Define a stopping point for yourself," she says to me. "A level below which there will be no more recursion. Otherwise, you will go on forever. You won't be able to stop. Every image will contain another image. It will occur and replicate itself within you again and again. Don't freeze time."

Where do I start?
Where do I start?
I tell her I don't understand.

"You have a lot in common – you and him," she says. "Neither of you has a defined stopping point. You were cast from the same mold. A forged sword. You could have been twins. A girl and a boy. To get to him, think about what you would do and how you would do it.

"There's the thrill of the chase, but it's no match for the thrill of the kill," she continues and then goes quiet. She sniffs the air of the forest. Steam is rising from the damp ground. I hear the calls of crows in the distance.

I break our mutual stare and look around. Anat and Lee are nowhere to be seen; the she-wolf and I are alone.

In the center of the circle, above the dark, smooth rock, the dome recedes slightly to create a small circular opening. A large round moon appears in the black sky.

The she-wolf and I raise our heads to the moon and howl.

Daphne sits up in bed, leans against the wall and starts writing in her dream journal. An image within an image? Recursion? Where had she heard those terms before? And what was the meaning of the repetitive whisper: *Where do I start?* In the dream, she was able to deliberately create the world around her. She called to the forest in her dream, and it came. She wanted to feel at ease, and she felt at ease.

The scenario could have been frightening had she not been in control. She wasn't scared.

It's progress. Her control over her dream world is growing stronger. She's embracing the process. *Need to discuss with Rotem*, she writes in the journal.

The three intertwined cases, all of them one case, have been haunting her for eight months, from the moment he killed Anat Aharon. Four months have gone by since the abductions, and not a sign of the babies since, not a word from Lee Ben-Ami or the person who snatched them. She opens the drawer of her bedside table, looks at Lee Ben-Ami's missing-person notice and runs her finger over the image on the piece of paper. Then she puts the piece of paper back in the drawer and takes out the one underneath it.

She's already very familiar with his face. She's sure she would recognize him if she ran into him even though the image from the hospital's security camera is of poor quality. His hair is hidden under his knit cap, and he's probably shaved off his beard since then. His eyes are blank and his mouth turns downward slightly. Twins. Yeah, right. A foolish thought. A strange dream. She's nothing like him. How could anyone even think like someone like that? Everything she's done was done only to save herself from those who wanted to enslave her. Mind and body. She's never sought to cause harm to anyone for no reason. When she called others to her rescue, nothing happened. When she begged to be left alone, nothing happened. She had to take matters into her own hands. That's the only thing that's ever really worked.

34.

She's sitting cross-legged on the floor, barefoot, watching a Channel 2 investigative report about restaurant kitchens that recycle unfinished dishes after they've been cleared off the tables. The presenter is describing how a half-eaten chicken breast that had come back to the kitchen was turned into a stir-fry meal for another diner, while the program's incognito reporter wanders around with a hidden camera, documenting the process and filming the roaches scurrying around on the floor. She finds herself drawn to cooking shows. Living on tinned food and cornflakes has turned hot dishes into a craving.

The Four are lying on a blanket she's spread out on the floor next to her. Two of them are asleep, and two are busy touching and tasting the soft toys for infants he's brought them.

"Their development up to the age of one is very important," he'd said. "It's good that you talk to them a lot."

She thinks about this afterwards. First of all: How does he know she talks to them a lot? She needs to be more cautious. And another thing: Why only "up to the age of one"? What's happening in eight months' time? What's he planning to do with them?

The door opens unexpectedly and he walks in.

"On the bed."

Lee looks at him but doesn't move.

"Move it! Get on the bed!" His tone of voice changes, his lips curling downward in anger. "I don't have time for games. Do you want me to kick one of them in the head? Two or three are sufficient for me. Get yourself onto the bed already."

She complies and handcuffs herself to the bed. She thinks about what would happen if he were to leave her shackled to the bed or even simply locked in the room one day, and never return.

He picks up one of the sleeping babies and turns back towards the door.

"Where are you taking him?" she asks, on edge. "What are you going to do to him?"

"A routine examination."

"What kind of examination?"

He exits the room without responding, leaving the door open. She stands up and tries to lift the bed to see if there is any way to slip the cuffs off the frame. Not a chance. She knows the bed is fixed to the floor with metal screws, but she's hoping for a miracle, nonetheless. The door is open, but she can't get out. She tries to listen to what's happening outside the room. She can hear the crying of a frightened baby and a sound she's familiar with from her work – the humming and clicking of an X-ray machine.

He returns with the sobbing baby some ten minutes later, then takes another one. Lee feels helpless, desperate. She's unable to comfort the screaming baby, and no longer able to hear what is happening outside the room. After returning the fourth crying baby, he sits down on the bed next to her, unaffected by their tears.

"What did you do to them?" she asks, clenching her jaw.

He ignores the question and closes his eyes.

"The human body is so complex, so beautiful. So fragile."

"What did you do to them?"

"They have beautiful bones. Beautiful little bones. Perfect little skeletons."

His eyes remain closed and Lee casts her eyes over the crying babies on the floor, looking for signs of injury, blood, lacerations. She doesn't see any.

"Are you running low on anything? Diaper cream? Diapers? Formula? Mineral water? Corn? Tuna? Pickles? Cornflakes?"

"What did you do to them?"

"X-rays."

"What for? Babies shouldn't be X-rayed for no reason."

"There's a reason."

"What reason?"

"Everything in due time, Guardian, everything in due time." He rises from the bed and heads to the door, tossing the key to her.

The moment the door slams shut behind him, she hurries over to the babies, who are immediately soothed by her presence. She picks them up, one at a time, and eventually they all stop crying. She has to find a way to stop him before he harms them. To him, they are lab rats. She runs her hand over her makeshift knife, which is still there, all the time, hidden in the elastic waistband of her flannel pants.

35.

"Four months and you still don't have a clue what's going on."

The police commissioner and the interior minister are the only people in the room, sitting on either side of a heavy, dark wooden table in the minister's bureau.

"No," the commissioner replies. "We don't know where they are. We have tire prints from the kidnapper's vehicle, his DNA from the four scenes, and footage of his actions at the hospitals from the security cameras, but we don't have an ID on him. Calls did come in following the release of the video footage from the cameras. And we followed up on every piece of information we received. But they all led nowhere. We've invested every possible resource. Now we're waiting for his next move."

The minister's eyes have dark circles around them and the commissioner notes to himself that he looks ten years older than last year. "And how has he not been identified yet if there's video footage of his face?"

"The footage is far from perfect. He was aware of the locations of the security cameras and made sure he passed by them from angles that would make it hard to identify him. We don't have a full-frontal image of his face. We've released all possible facial composites – with a beard, clean shaven, with hair, without hair – but nothing so far."

"And you still don't think it's nationalistically motivated?"

"All our findings indicate it's the work of a single individual, of European descent, carried out with sophistication after years of planning. It doesn't fit the patterns of Hamas or Islamic Jihad or Islamic State or any other organization in the Middle East."

The interior minister sighs. "This isn't just the private affair of my daughter and three other families whose babies have disappeared. The entire country is in a panic. People have become paranoid. Maternity wards are fortified with extra security. Mothers have stopped sending their children to daycare. It won't end until you catch the person responsible and return all the babies safe and sound."

"And Lee Ben-Ami too," the commissioner reminds him. "We believe he abducted her for the purpose of caring for the babies. It's a good sign."

"A good sign?" The minister is struggling to control his temper.

"It means he has a job to go to during the day. He's working alone and can't look after the babies all the time by himself. He's a criminal, but a calculating one, so we're likely to receive a ransom demand at some point."

The two cups of coffee on the table that were brought at the beginning of the meeting are getting cold, but none of the men are bothering to drink.

"Have you enlisted any outside help?" the minister asks.

"Come again?"

"Outside help? From the Shin Bet? The Mossad? Or is the foolish pride of senior police officers preventing any such cooperation?"

"We work with the Shin Bet concerning internal matters and with the Mossad with regard to everyone else around us. As for the cooperation thing, you can ask them if you lack faith in the police."

"I already have."

There's a moment of awkward silence. "We've done all we can," the commissioner continues. "All we can do now is wait. Wait for him to make a mistake or get in touch. The searches are continuing in the meantime, but – for your ears only – the ball's in his court."

The minister leans forward, stares directly into the commissioner's eyes and speaks in a low, cold voice. "He's holding my grandson. Find the son of a bitch and find him fast, or I'll make sure you're all replaced. You can record me if you haven't done so until now. I stand behind my words."

36.

She's standing close to the locked door, a can of food in her hand. She can hear him typing on the computer on the other side of the wall. He's been there for hours, and she's been in her same spot too, waiting for him. She needs to go to the bathroom but can't risk moving from her position in case he chooses to enter the room just then. She keeps shifting her weight from one leg to the other and passing the can back and forth between her hands, remaining alert and focused. From time to time, she practices quickly pulling out the knife. She can't allow herself to miss this opportunity. She's built up a measure of trust with him, but her desire to incapacitate him and flee from there hasn't faded for even a second.

He'll walk in and she'll hit him with the can at the base of his skull. He'll black out and she'll escape with the babies. He must have a car parked outside. She'll take them out one by one while he's lying on the floor and then lock him inside.

Once she's in the car, she'll get the hell out of there and call the police. She has no idea where she is; but in a country you can traverse widthwise in an hour and a half, and lengthwise in seven, how far could she be from a community of some kind?

And what if things go wrong? And what if he walks in and looks to his right and sees her lying in wait for him? What will happen to her then? What will happen to the babies? If the blow doesn't knock him out, she'll have to stab him with the knife. She touches her neck with her right hand, feeling her rapid heartbeat in the artery carrying oxygen-enriched blood to her brain. A stream of plasma, blood cells and hormones that keeps her alive. If she gets a chance, this is where she needs to cut him.

She's got no choice. Who knows what other tests and torture he has in mind for the babies? She's seen the pictures on the wall. The X-rays are just the beginning. She needs to put an end to it.

She hears footsteps and tenses up.

Key. Lock. A short click. The door opens and the stainless-steel trolley comes in first. He's pushing it in, his eyes pointing straight ahead, towards the cribs.

With all the strength she can muster, she slams the can against the point at which his skull joins the back of his neck and hears a loud noise, like an explosion. For a split second she thinks; the babies are sleeping.

He falls to the floor and blood oozes from the cut to his head. She doesn't think she's killed him. With the knife in her hand, she moves closer to make sure he's really lost consciousness and isn't about to spring at her. His eyes are closed and he isn't moving. She leans over, checking for a pulse and to see if he's breathing.

She drags him towards the bed, retrieves the handcuffs from his pocket and shackles his hand to the bed frame. She throws the key for the handcuffs to the other side of the room. She's overwhelmed with rage again. Let him get a little taste of his own medicine. A small accident with a blow to the head. Handcuffed to the bed. He should be grateful she doesn't break his arm too.

The Four are still asleep, and he isn't near the cribs. He won't be able to get to them even at a stretch. She pauses for a moment alongside the cribs to catch her breath. A small pool of blood begins to form under his head.

She pulls herself together and runs out of the room.

37.

"Hi, Doreen."

"Hi, Rotem. What's happening?"

"Living the dream."

"Excellent." Doreen, her boss' personal assistant, smiles at her. "You can go in. He's waiting for you."

"I thought you called me because he retired and I'm inheriting his corner office. I always liked this office. I like the '70s decor."

"You wish." Doreen smiles and gestures towards the office door.

She steps into his office. Considering his age, her boss has taken to technology quickly. There isn't a single sheet of paper on his desk. Arranged in front of him in a semicircle are three computer monitors; a slide presentation projector is fixed to the ceiling; and installed on a round side table is a video conferencing system. He ends a phone call and replaces the landline receiver. She sits down across the desk from him.

"Good morning, Rotem. How are you?" He puts his cup of tea on the table.

"Great."

"Working on anything interesting?"

"A look ahead at the Iranian government's possible course of action in the wake of the recent changes in US and North Korean policy. I'm amending the models – slight changes in terms of Ahmad Jannati and Ali Khamenei, moderate changes with regard to Sadeq and Ali Larijani, and a re-thinking when it comes to Hassan

Rouhani and Mahmoud Hashemi Shahroudi. Their models have changed completely and require reconstruction. I'll be presenting my findings at the quarterly next week."

"You appear to have acquired a new hobby: police work." He looks at her, stroking his white beard.

Rotem leans forward, places her elbows on the desk and rests her chin on her fists. She frowns and stares straight into 'Grandpa's' eyes.

"Gra-nnnd-paaa? Are you spying on me?"

"You're too valuable an asset for us not to."

She sits back in her chair and shrugs. "It's a personal favor for a close friend."

"The fact that you're playing cops-and-robbers a little doesn't bother me. But I am troubled by the possibility of you finding yourself in the line of fire if you deviate from providing anything more than just psychological profiling advice. You getting yourself hurt in the field the last time was more than enough for me. I don't want it to happen again. You're not a field agent. You're a divisional chief, for God's sake. If you're lacking thrills in your life, I can arrange a sky diving course."

"And you don't want any grief with the commissioner if word gets out."

"That's no longer a concern of mine, and let me tell you why—"

Rotem cuts him off, "Have no fear." She leans back and stretches her hands behind her head. "I have no intentions of launching an assault on the Babysitter; and to be on the safe side, when I'm with Daphne, I carry the weapon I got from Control. They made me undergo a refresher course before they gave it to me."

"Are you serious?" He raises his thick white eyebrows.

"It gives me a sense of security. And don't forget, we're dealing with a civilian psychopath, not a terrorist, so his access to weapons is limited."

"We need your skills here." He sighs, knowing that this is a lost battle.

"Don't worry. It's called multitasking. I'm a woman." She smiles.

"Who's seen you there? Who knows that we, in the form of you, are working on this case?"

"No one but Daphne Dagan. She won't leak it."

"I've just now returned from an interesting chat with the interior minister. With us in the room were the heads of Military Intelligence and the Shin Bet. The honorable minister – let's put it this way – delicately expressed his concerns regarding the Israel Police's ability to cope with the complexities of the case it has been trying unsuccessfully to solve for several months by now."

Rotem's eyes light up. "And he's given the Organization the green light to work on it in parallel? Can I wake the dragon? Can I discuss it freely with Control? With Operations? With Angel Fire? With Unit 8200?"

"Slow down. Don't get carried away. With all due respect to five abducted civilians, we have a greater responsibility for the safety of many more, and I have no intention of diverting resources disproportionately just because the honorable minister believes his grandson is worth more than others. I'm going to allow you to continue working on the case, but without the police knowing that we're involved. Continue working with Daphne Dagan; we'll move Nathan Shmueli aside, and you'll replace him to work on the case directly under the guise of an external investigator. We'll come up with a story for you."

"No need. If we aren't going to conduct things on a full scale, then the current format will suffice. I'm receiving updates directly from inside the Forensics Department; what I require in addition to that is the data from the other police divisions involved in the investigation. For it all to be channeled to me. And from my perspective, I'd rather they didn't know about it. My activity there should be on the sidelines, totally unnoticed. If I were to intervene directly and we were to get Nathan reassigned, it would only cause trouble. Just make sure that if I need access to other elements, and not necessarily within the police, I won't be hindered and they'll comply."

He blows lightly on his cup of tea and sips from it. "Consider it done. Look after yourself."

"Of course." She stands up and steps towards the door, blowing a kiss back at him before closing it behind her.

He waits until she's out of earshot and then picks up the phone and presses the speed-dial button for the head of the Operations Division.

"Yes, Grandpa?"

"Motti, I have a small favor to ask."

38.

Tonight, I'll remember my dream

Tonight, I'll lucid dream

I'm strong and can face up to any character who seeks to harm me in my dream

Tonight, I'll remember my dream

Tonight, I'll lucid dream

I'm strong and can face up to any character who seeks to harm me in my dream

Tonight, I'll remember my dream

Tonight, I'll lucid dream

I'm strong and can face up to any character who seeks to harm me in my dream

04:56

I'm sitting on a bench in an old, noisy train car. The smell of coal is coming from the chimney of the locomotive at the front. Next to me is a young girl in a Victorian dress, and I realize that I'm a child again. She's my friend; the same girl I was with in the pool, and who was lying opposite me in the tent. The rattling of the wheels on the tracks creates a monotonous background noise.

Tatack-tatack

Tatack-tatack

Tatack-tatack

She has a string of pearls around her neck and her dress hides her legs and shoes. I look at myself. I'm dressed in similar clothes. A long white dress. White gloves. A scarf.

Looking out of the window, I see two stone towers in the distance.

"The tracks will curve to the right soon and we'll start to move closer to the towers," the girl says.

"It happens sometimes," I reply.

"Want to go on a journey?"

"Yes."

She reaches her hand out towards my face, brushing strands of my hair back and caressing my cheek.

Tatack-tatack

Tatack-tatack

Tatack-tatack

There's a smooth sea in the distance. A cool breeze ruffles my hair. A setting sun. It's pleasant.

I'm in.

I'm at the cinema with Anat Aharon and I have to go to the bathroom. I tell her to come with me, but she says she'll wait for the intermission. I need to go now, so I get up and go to the bathroom, which is at the front of the cinema, behind the screen.

There's no gender sign on the door. Hanging there is a picture of a white mouse, with a note underneath that reads: Out of order. *Undergoing repairs – sorry for the inconvenience*. The note reminds me of something. A different bathroom perhaps. Maybe in a house that was never a home for me. Maybe at boarding school. Maybe in the home of the foster family that turned me into a slave. Before the fire.

Reality check.

I'm dreaming.

I go into the bathroom, which is lit by a powerful fluorescent light. The floor is soiled with black fingerprint powder. There's a long line of sinks, and my school geography teacher is leaning over one of them and throwing up. I know it's her without seeing her face. I feel sorry for her. I continue past the sinks and see Lee Ben-Ami standing in front of me in a white dress. Her eyes are black and very big, disproportionate to her face, like in the illustrations of children with huge eyes by an artist whose name I can't recall.

I hear someone whispering my name repeatedly. It isn't Lee because her mouth is shut, only her eyes remain open. She points to one of the toilet stalls and I open the door and see a lake in the afternoon light, just before sunset. There's a steep incline of a few yards on a dirt path with thick vegetation on its sides, and I descend and stand on the sandy shore.

The movie theater's popcorn smell, which turned into the smell of bleach in the bathroom, changes into the pleasant fragrance of perfume. I remove my shoes and socks and feel the warm sand under my bare feet.

A soldier in a green uniform approaches and tells me that I should put my socks and shoes back on. It's not safe here. I climb back up to the door. The soldier comes with me. In the bathroom he presses me up against the wall and kisses me. It's nice but a little scary. The door to the lake is still open and a cool breeze is blowing over us. His hands are strong. I sense that something is wrong. I move my head from side to side and tell him that he's making me feel uncomfortable. "Stop!" I say to him, and he takes a step back.

"I think I saw him once," he responds. "The guy you're looking for. I replaced him one Saturday. I know what he looks like. A crazy son of a bitch. Tell Rotem."

"And Nathan?"

"Only if he's come down from his branch and gotten dressed." The soldier laughs.

The door of the toilet stall opens and Anat Aharon is standing there. "Where did you disappear to?" she asks, then looks at the soldier. He turns around and goes back down to the lake, and I can tell that something that shouldn't have happened has just happened.

I lower my eyes and look at my feet. I'm still holding my shoes and socks in my hand. Anat asks if I want to go to Disneyland next week. I'm pleased she's not angry at me. I ask her if she wants to swim in the lake.

"Liquid bleach is made from sodium hypochlorite. Mixing liquid bleach with vinegar produces chlorine vapor, and inhaling that will kill you," she says.

We go down to the lake. There's a large rocking chair on the sand by the water and we sit on it together. We share a long kiss. Her tongue tastes of mint and strawberries. I slip my hand into her pants and she turns her head to look at a van that's approaching along the shore of the lake, raising a cloud of dust in its wake.

I know something's about to happen but I don't know what. It's an intense sensation.

The name Helen pops into my mind. Who is Helen?

Something is going to happen very soon.

In a perfect world, you can do anything and everything will turn out well. You can trust people without fear of being hurt.

Anat Aharon and I pass through the bathroom again. I stop at one of the basins to wash my face. I can feel the sand on my feet mixing with the black powder on the cool white floor. Footprints, fingerprints, drowning in a stormy sea, the savagery of nature, human nature, the State of Israel vs. Daphne Dagan, a minor. The prosecution's summation. The defense's summation. One thought follows the next, spinning in my head.

I wash my face, and when I lift my head, Lee Ben-Ami is looking at me from the mirror with huge black eyes. She's wearing the same white dress. She reaches out to me. Her face is pale. She doesn't shout. She whispers softly.

"Help me."

Daphne wakes up in state of panic and sits up. The door to the room is open and a figure is standing there.

"Mom!" Daphne shouts.

"It's me," Anna approaches. "Are you okay? You were screaming in your sleep."

She rubs her eyes. "What was I saying?"

"You said 'Stop' several times and then you yelled: 'Help me.'"

"Wow, sorry. Did I wake you?"

"Come on, I'm used to it by now." Anna smiles.

"I was having a really weird dream. I need to write it down before I forget."

"Can I make you a coffee?"

"Yes. Thanks."

Anna leaves the room and Daphne begins writing quickly. The

mirror was terrifying. She saw herself but not herself. Lee Ben-Ami, who looked back at her from the mirror, was the emotional reflection of herself in her subconscious. She knows she's read about it somewhere. A warning not to look in the mirror during lucid dreaming before you're in full control of your dreams and know how to wake yourself up.

She gets up, puts on a pair of sweatpants and walks into the kitchen just as Anna rests two mugs of coffee on the table. Anna's very presence, awake and by her side early in the morning, is comforting.

Anna tosses a pack of cigarettes onto the table and sits down. "What frightened you so much?"

Daphne wraps both her hands around the hot cup of coffee. "Let's say you're lucid dreaming. Wandering around contentedly in a world you've created for yourself and busy with various kinds of interesting activities. Now, you feel like looking into the mirror for a second to check that your lipstick hasn't smeared."

"Okay."

"Well, don't do it."

"Why not?"

"In dreams, the laws of physics fly out the window. If you look into a mirror, you won't see yourself the way you're used to seeing yourself. It's similar to looking at your hands during a reality check in a dream. It's not the reflection of light rays off the surface of the mirror like in the waking world."

"So what's it like in a dream then?"

"In a dream, you'll see yourself in the mirror the way your subconscious perceives you. You're glimpsing into your soul. And it's totally unexpected. Maybe you won't have eyes in the mirror. Maybe you won't have hair. Maybe you'll be a child or an old woman or have the face of someone else. A face can change too while you're looking at it. That's why you're meant to leave looking into a mirror to a stage in which you're in total control of your dream and can wake yourself whenever you choose."

"Is that what happened to you now? Did you escape from it in your dream?"

"No, you woke me up. And I hadn't planned on looking in a

mirror. It happened by chance. It's good that you woke me. I could have ended up stuck there for hours."

"You're crazy to be carrying on with your sleep experiments. You're starting to scare me."

"It's interesting. I'm learning a lot about myself."

Anna sips her coffee and looks at her.

"And eventually, it will help me get rid of the nightmare too. I'm sure it'll happen if I stick with it."

Daphne sips her coffee while Anna gets up and leaves the kitchen, returning with a joint. She sits down and lights it.

"Want a hit?" she asks, offering it to Daphne, who takes a drag and then hands it back.

"Anything new happening?"

"With what?"

"The Babysitter."

"In the waking world? No." She does a reality check before she continues. She's awake. "Nothing since the chocolate. We're waiting for him to do us a favor and show up again. But Anat and Lee are back in my dreams." She reaches out and Anna passes her the joint. "We've been assigned to another case for now. A new Volvo imported privately from Switzerland. Heroin hidden in the doors. Discovered during an inspection by the Customs Authorities, who were waiting for the importer to collect the vehicle. But no one showed up, and the owner's details are fictitious of course. It may have been a private initiative on the part of some workers at the Ashdod Port to supplement their income. We've been looking for evidence there for two days now, with no luck so far."

"The usual boring stuff."

"Yes. A welcome routine bit of criminality."

They both start laughing.

"Is there anything to eat? I'm starving."

Anna goes over to the fridge.

"Just this," she says, turning to Daphne with a cherry tomato in her hand. "There's one left."

"Half each."

They burst out laughing again.

39.

Lee runs barefoot from her room into the Images Room, and quickly through the X-ray Room and towards the door that leads to the outside. The door is locked. She pulls on the handle with all her might, screams and slams her fists against the door in frustration.

Her heart is pounding. She presses the palms of her hands against the door, leaning over and panting. She needs to focus. She has to find a way out. She can't afford to lose her cool. She turns and looks at the X-ray equipment. Breathe. Her respiratory rate returns to normal and she returns to the babies' room and stands over him. He's still out. She needs to backtrack now, but slowly. To pay attention to details. The only way out of here is to think. To look. To assess.

She leaves the room again, walking slowly this time, and studies the other side of the door, the one with which she isn't familiar. There's a lock that allows the door to be opened from the one side only. She looks at the image-covered walls of the room adjacent to hers. Hanging above the desk are sixteen numbered X-rays of the skeletons of the babies arranged in the shape of a large square.

The monitor on the desk is on. If he has an Internet connection, she can call for help. She moves the mouse to reveal that the computer is password protected.

Above the computer is a shelf she remembers, with a row of glass jars of various sizes. She didn't dare approach them the first time. Now, she picks one up and takes a close look. The fetuses of conjoined twins suspended in a clear solution. She shudders and returns it to the shelf. The other jars also contain the fetuses of conjoined twins, in varying stages of development. Some as small as a matchbox, others almost as big as premature newborns.

She leaves the jars behind and goes into the X-ray Room, walking past the silent machines towards the closed door. She tries once more, but again it doesn't open, and she stands there and examines the structure from up close. It's a thick steel door, like the door to an apartment, with a high-security cylinder lock that takes a dimpled key and not a key with teeth.

She goes back to her room, crouches down next to him and starts going through the pockets of his pants. She finds a single key, to her room. She stands up and places it next to the sink. In his other pocket she finds a small notepad and a very worn-down pencil.

About half the pages from the notepad have been torn out, and the remainder are lined and blank. She runs her fingers over the first page and then takes the small pencil and begins sliding the graphite tip back and forth across the page, quickly, but taking care not to apply too much pressure. After covering the entire page, she reads the letters that are revealed:

Sunday
03 / 25 / 2017
Ten in the morning
Status meeting
System integrity
Two open issues

She returns to the Images Room with the notepad in hand, places it on the desk and then begins a systematic review of the room, item by item. The objects on the desk, the computer, the keyboard, under the keyboard, the drawer, under the wooden desktop, inside the reading lamp. No key.

She runs her hands over all the photographs stuck to the wall, pressing against them to check if there is something hidden behind one of them. If the key isn't on him then it has to be here in the room with the photographs, or in the X-ray Room.

The sound of a groan followed by the rattle of metal startles her, and she runs back to her room. He's sitting on the floor, one wrist cuffed to the frame of the bed, his other hand pressed against the back of his neck.

"You should stitch my head. There's a special needle and thread in the first-aid kit in the cupboard on the right." He speaks in his usual dry and emotionless tone.

She takes a deep breath and tries to speak calmly. "Where's the key?"

"I'm sorry, but I can't tell you. It would compromise my plans."

"Then you'll remain just as you are. Shackled to the bed."

"Stitch the back of my neck in the meantime. It's uncomfortable to keep my hand here like this."

"Where's the key?"

"I've already explained that I won't divulge its location."

"You're going to stay cuffed to the bed, without food or water, until you tell me where it is."

"Stitch the back of my neck." He turns his head away from her and she sees the wound, which hasn't stopped bleeding.

She has a long look at the cribs. "Get on the bed," she instructs, "and lie face-down with your free hand under your stomach."

She can't believe what she's doing. She should slash his face; instead, she's going to play nurse to him. But she has to keep him alive so he can tell her where the key is. If he bleeds to death, or if the wound becomes infected and bacteria enters his bloodstream, he could lose consciousness and she and the babies would be stuck here with no way out.

He complies and lays on the bed as instructed, and she approaches him from the side of his cuffed wrist and examines the wound.

"Yes, you need sutures. Stay just as you are. Don't move."

She has to keep focused. She goes over to the cupboard and pulls out the first-aid kit.

She goes back to the bed and straddles his back, locking him between her knees. He isn't strong enough to throw her off him while he's lying like that on the bed, wounded, his arms neutralized. Then she proceeds to clean and stitch the cut, proficiently but not particularly gently. She wouldn't have administered an anesthetic even if she'd had one. He doesn't move or make a sound. He appears to enjoy the pain. Crazy psychopath. She's going to leave him here to starve until he lets her out.

When she's done, she gets off of him and returns the kit to the cupboard.

"Give me the mattress," she says.

"What?"

"Toss the mattress to me and stay there on the springs. I need a place to sleep tonight, and it certainly won't be with you."

He doesn't move. "I suggest you do the rational thing and release me now," he says. "The food will run out if I don't replenish the stock."

"Don't you worry. I'll find a way to get out."

He doesn't respond and she gives in. There's no point in arguing about the mattress; it's better to reserve that energy and look for the key.

The babies wake up in the meantime and she goes over to the cribs. He sits on the bed and watches her changing diapers, warming bottles, feeding them, talking to them, and washing the bottles and setting them out to dry. He addresses her again only when she's done.

"Bring me water."

"Where's the key?"

"I've been good to you until now. I've provided everything you need to live here in comfort. You're not repaying me in kind."

"You're forgetting the fact that you ran me down and abducted me and imprisoned me here. Apart from that, you've been the perfect host. But if you haven't noticed, you're no longer calling the shots. I'll give you some time to take that in. You'll get water and food when you give me the key to get out of here."

He doesn't respond.

"And I'm not leaving them here in the room with you."

182

She spreads out the babies' blanket on the floor in the Images Room and moves them there along with their toys. She also moves the four cribs, which, unlike the bed, he hadn't fixed to the floor, then she closes the door and locks him inside.

While the babies explore their new surroundings, she renews her search for the key. She goes through the Images Room thoroughly once again and then moves to the X-ray Room. She carefully picks her way through all the equipment and machinery. After hours of searching – she can't even tell how much time has passed – she gets down on all fours and examines the underside of all the surfaces and instruments.

From under the steel table of the X-ray machine, she pulls out a key.

40.

"Hello."

"Have you ever tried WILD?"

"Daph?"

"Have you ever tried WILD?"

"What's the time?"

"It's almost twelve. I've been trying to get you all day."

"Ah. Hmmm. I fell asleep on the sofa." Rotem sits up and looks at the fish swimming across the screen of her laptop on the living room table. "It's easier than you think."

"What do I need to do to experience a wake-induced lucid dream, to go straight from a state of alertness into a dream?"

"Set an alarm to wake you during REM – four and a half or six hours from the time you fall asleep – get up for an hour and a half, drink some water, go back to bed, but don't fall asleep."

"Do you mean get up after another hour and a half?"

"No, no, after sleeping for four and a half hours, you get up for an hour and a half, go back to bed, but don't go to sleep."

"Ah, okay."

"Lie in bed, think about all the muscles in your body, one by one, and relax them all. Toes, tummy, jaw – the lot. When you feel that your body is completely relaxed, and without moving in the slightest, you start counting in your head: I'm dreaming one dream, I'm dreaming two dreams, I'm dreaming three dreams. And so on. Nonstop."

"And what does that do?"

"It leaves your brain's center of logic active while you enter a state of REM. What you're doing, in fact, is tricking your brain – convincing it that your body is already in a state of sleep. It's very easy to lose focus and fall asleep at this stage and experience a regular dream. It takes a lot of practice to stop your thoughts from wandering. You need to focus on the counting until the landscape changes and then you'll realize that you're lucid inside a dream. You'll go through a number of stages. You'll see sparks, geometric shapes, circles of light or various other things like that, like you see when you close your eyes tight or press on them. You continue counting. Eyes closed. Body relaxed. Without moving. You'll hear voices. Someone calling to you. Someone whispering 'Shhhhh' in your ear, or someone whispering: 'What's that?' The doorbell ringing in the distance, the rustling of a carrier bag. Things like that."

"It sounds a little frightening." Daphne's in the car, driving back home. She's already passed the last trees of the Jerusalem Forest and on her right she can see the Paz gas station lights. She lifts one hand from the steering wheel and looks at her fingers.

"You get used to it," Rotem says. "You have to keep counting. Your brain is approaching REM. If you're struggling to focus at this point, start counting afresh and then you'll feel the stage of your body entering a state of sleep, when sleep paralysis kicks in. A buzzing-like sensation that runs through you when the brain turns off your ability to control your muscles."

"Can you genuinely feel it?"

"Totally. You may also feel tremors through your body, like an electrical current. And from that point, your body will be paralyzed and you'll go into REM."

"From a state of alertness straight into a dream without all the other steps?"

"Exactly. But no need to worry, your body experiences the same process a few times every night, only now you'll be aware of it. A few more tremors and you'll be inside a dream. The landscape changes, and you stop counting."

"And then a reality check?" Daphne looks at her fingers again, then opens the car windows a little to let the cold air in.

"Yes, you're dreaming and you're aware of it. The entire process lasts from ten minutes to half an hour at most. It rarely happens the first time you try it, so don't despair. It's an excellent shortcut from being awake to being in a lucid dream."

"Yes, thanks, that's what I need." She'd read about it but feels a lot more confident after hearing Rotem's explanation.

"I got a green light from my section chief."

"A green light?" The sharp change of subject throws Daphne.

"To work with you. We're an official team now."

"You, Nathan and I?"

"Just me and you. Carry on working with Nathan like usual, but keep me posted on everything you guys find, do, or are planning to do. At the same time, I'll be sending out feelers to other police divisions that are working on the case and additional elements outside the police too."

"Do you need me to speak to anyone to arrange access for you to computers and phones?"

"I'm already in. The computers, the phones and the emails of everyone at the police who's involved in the investigation. They're completely unaware of course, and you don't know a thing either…"

"Of course, of course."

"If I were to get involved in the investigation formally, I'd only hamper things. Egos would run wild. It's best I remain an unseen observer."

"Great!" Daphne smiles at the news, although she's a little sorry she'll have to keep lying to Nathan.

"Goodnight, Daph."

"Talk to you tomorrow."

"Bye."

Rotem picks herself up off the couch and gets undressed, adding her clothes to the impressive pile of laundry on the living room carpet. She looks at it admiringly. It'll hit the ceiling in a few weeks. She goes to her bedroom and burrows under the thick comforter. She toys for a short while with the thought of practicing a little lucid dreaming but drops the idea. Her life is wild enough in the waking world, and at night she simply wants to rest. Within a few minutes, she's fast asleep.

Daphne drives through the Lod interchange on her way home from the Forensics lab. It has been a very long day. A white family sedan, with a soldier in uniform at the wheel, passes her, and a large, yellow-eyed German Shepherd stares at her through the rear window. She almost crashes the car when she takes her hands off the wheel to do a reality check.

41.

Lee stands with the key in her hand. Force of habit causes her to brush her knees clean after getting up, though there is no need to do so. The X-ray Room is spotless. She approaches the door on the far side of the room and slips the key into the lock, taking a deep breath and praying it will work. The key turns to the right. With two clicks, the door opens onto a long hallway, lit up in a yellowish glow, with steel doors on either side. She bangs her fist against the walls. Just like in her room, the walls are concrete here too. She tries opening the doors one by one.

One of them, marked *Laundry Room*, opens. But all the other doors along the hallway are locked, including the one with a sign like in a movie theater shining above it that reads: *EXIT*. What is this place?

She bangs her fists against the door, kicking it repeatedly with the heels of her bare feet.

"Help! I'm locked in here!"

She stops to listen. She can't hear a thing from the outside. She runs back to the locked room, opens it, and ignoring him on the bed, grabs a can of food from the cupboard and slams and locks the door behind her again. She then runs back to the EXIT door and begins banging loudly with the tin can, pausing now and again to press her ear to the door and then picking up the screaming and banging again. Then listening again. And more banging. And again.

Nothing.

She gives up and goes into the Laundry Room. A large dryer is full of her flannel clothing. The industrial washing machine is empty. She opens the doors of the cupboard and finds rows of large one-gallon bottles of fabric softener and rows of large bags of laundry detergent. All neatly arranged. The spaces between the bottles and bags are even, as if they've been precisely measured with a ruler. Alongside the machines stands a metal bench with a laundry basket filled with folded white towels.

She turns everything inside out. There is nowhere in the room to hide a key.

Back in the hallway she tries the other doors again, pounding on them with the tin can to check if one is thinner. But they are all heavy metal doors, she can see that there is no way she's going to break through any of them. She has to find the key to the EXIT door.

She realizes that she's becoming hysterical; her breathing is rapid and shallow, her heart racing. She stops, returns to the metal bench in the Laundry Room and sits down, placing the can next to her, closing her eyes and breathing deeply. She's in control. Time is on her side now. Not his.

A few minutes later, she feels composed again. She stands up and goes into the Images Room and sits down on the blanket next to the babies. It doesn't look like it's going to happen tonight. She needs to be patient. He'll be a little more cooperative after a few days without food and water.

Yoavi is awake and lying on his back, his tiny hands clutching at the cloth figures swaying from the baby gym she placed above him. Omer is sleeping on the side of the blanket. Shai, who she named after her boyfriend because he looks just like him, is focused on a piece of cloth displaying a black-and-white image of a smiling face and is smiling back at it, and Rami is lying on his stomach looking at her.

She hopes their parents will like the names she's given them. She thought she was going to remain imprisoned with them for a long time, months, even years perhaps, but she's feeling hopeful now.

It won't be years. She recalls the survival Rule of Threes: You can survive three minutes without air, three days without water and three weeks without food. Another day or two or three without food and water and he'll break and let them go.

42.

Great. Everything is just great. Better than any scenario he's imagined. The road to redemption is paved with suffering. Everyone's. His, the Messenger's, and the Bearer of the Mark, in particular. *Surely he took up our pain and bore our suffering, yet we considered him punished by God, stricken by him, and afflicted.* All the misguided sheep, all the criminals and sinners, all the vile and the shameless, all the wicked.

He observed the feed from the camera he'd installed in her room on the computer screen in the Images Room – watching her standing behind the door with a can of corn in her hand, shifting her weight from one leg to the other, waiting for him. The pleasure he derived from the anticipation caused him to delay the moment as much as he could. She was so determined. So purposeful. From time to time, he tapped on the keyboard so she would hear him and keep waiting. He assumed the blow would be painful and that he'd probably lose consciousness. If not, he'd pretend to black out to see what her next move will be.

Lee continued to move agitatedly. He decided that if she broke down and went to the bathroom, he'd immediately get up and enter the room. To make her think she'd just missed her chance. Another small grain of suffering for the great mountain.

He continued to type and observe her at the same time. If she had any sense, she'd cuff him to one of the metal pipes in the showers or the iron frame of the bed and then she'd have to take care of him. Another reason why it was important for him to have chosen a doctor. She might hurt him, but she wouldn't be able to abandon him and refrain from helping him. Everything would become plain to her. He decided to allow her to move forward at her own pace. To experience the frustration one step at a time. Without rushing.

He got up and walked through the X-ray Room and into the hallway, where he checked that all the doors were locked apart from the one to the Laundry Room, where the dryer had just come to the end of its cycle and had switched off. He returned to the hallway and from there to the X-ray Room and then the computer.

And she was still there, waiting for him.

He locked the computer, got up from the chair, pushed it into place alongside the desk and approached her door. He paused momentarily in front of it, interlocked his fingers to crack his knuckles, then opened the door. He made sure to look straight ahead and not to the side where she was standing.

43.

The smell of wet earth.

Moisture hanging in the still air.

I'm lying in bed under a blanket and realize I'm there again.

I have to face up to him this time. I can't let him strangle me.

The banging on the door begins.

I throw off the blanket and run to the other room. I open the closet and remove the hanging rod. I run back to bed, and before I leave the room, I look back at the closet. The inscription says *Hopeless* in black letters.

I get back into bed, hiding under the blanket with the rod. Waiting for him.

Pale moonlight penetrates the fog and shines through the three windows of the hut. I hear the howling of a wolf.

I have to remember something.

I'm sure I have to remember something.

I can't remember.

The door to the cabin bursts open with a crash and footsteps approach me. The blanket is torn away and I swing the rod from the closet at his face as hard as I can. He catches the rod in mid-flight and flings it aside. It lands on the wooden floor with a hollow thud.

He sits on me.

"Did you think you could do something to me with that toothpick?"

He leans over me. His face is right in front of my nose. His eyes are bloodshot. His pupils are big and black. He smells of forest and death and swampland. He wraps his two large and dirty hands around my neck, smearing me with black mud. He tightens his grip and my air runs out. Everything goes quiet, and a continuous high-pitched sound rings in my ears.

Daphne sits up in bed, her hands stretched out in front of her to fight off her assailant. He isn't there. He was only in her dream. She's covered in sweat. Her heart is racing, pounding hard.

She gets up to go to the bathroom and from there she heads to the kitchen for some water. She glances into Anna's room. She's sleeping, cuddled under her comforter. That's good, it means she hadn't screamed in her dream. That counts for something. On the night table next to Anna's bed is Stephen King's *11/22/63*. Daphne borrowed it from the library and passed it on to Anna when she was done reading it, in a single weekend. Its hero tries time and time again to change the course of history and prevent the assassination of Kennedy. Maybe that's what is happening to her in her dreams with Anat Aharon. Sometimes, she appears beside her, alive; and other times, she merely observes her from a distance. Sometimes, she's lying on the road, as they'd found her at the scene of the hit-and-run. The image had etched itself into her mind.

As Daphne stands there lost in thought, Anna turns on her side in her sleep, takes one leg out from under the covers and rests it on the comforter.

44.

He's hungry but mostly thirsty. He isolates his sense of thirst and breaks it down into its components. A dry tongue. An empty, shriveled stomach. A headache. But perhaps the headache's related to the blow he received and not thirst or hunger.

It'll come to light over the coming few days. *To this present hour we are both hungry and thirsty, and are poorly clothed, and are roughly treated, and are homeless.* Ancient scriptures live inside him. Roots that dried up two thousand years ago are waking and nourishing his body. The history that everyone is quick to forget beats inside him. Just as she said would happen. The time for realizing the prophecy is now.

He lies on his stomach so that the wound on the back of his neck won't come into contact with the pillow. Her scent rises off the white linen, and he starts to grind his pelvis against the mattress but ceases immediately. He needs to concentrate. Not to screw everything up for nothing.

He sits up, retrieves the TV remote from the floor beside the bed and presses Channel 2. *Survivor.* In general, he doesn't watch television. Certainly not reality shows. He has more important things to do. But his only task now is to wait.

On the screen in front of him, people in bathing suits are conniving against one another for the purpose of being the last remaining contestant on the island and winning a million dollars. A harem of seals clap their fins for fish. A bunch of dumb hamsters running on a wheel in a cage. Their lives are empty. Nothing will happen when they die. They were born and will die without doing a single meaningful thing in their lives that will reverberate forever after their demise. A pathetic bunch. All of them.

He switches to a channel on which more insignificant people are being interviewed about an insignificant subject. Another channel and another channel, fools everywhere, until he finds a nature documentary and sticks with it. Three lionesses are stalking a herd of buffalo, and they launch themselves at one of them, a small and weak member of the herd that's lagging behind. It tries to flee and falls into a river, with the lionesses on its tail. They're straining to drag it to the bank when a crocodile emerges from the water, snaps its jaws around the buffalo's leg and pulls it in the opposite direction. The lionesses manages to get the buffalo out of the river; but in the meantime, the rest of the herd notices the animal's absence and returns to form a semicircle around the lionesses, whose backs are to the river. The buffaloes charge and push them back towards the water, where the crocodiles wait. The three lionesses are forced to flee, and the young buffalo is saved. Although he's injured, he's still able to continue walking with the rest of the herd.

The hunter turned into the hunted. It wasn't by chance that he saw the documentary just then. It's a sign. A sign that everything will work out. He'll give the Guardian four rings. For the fingers of her right hand. He needs to remember that. Later. Everything in its own time. Copper rings.

He touches the back of his neck and peels away a portion of dried blood, which he puts in his mouth and plays with on his tongue. It's a familiar taste.

The taste of childhood.

45.

If the Laundry Room contained acid-based detergents, she could use
them to melt the cylinder and break open the door. She could cut
a bottle of fabric softener in half, fix it to the door under the lock
and make sure to fill it whenever the level went down. Within a
few months, the cylinder would melt and she could get out of here.
According to her calculations, the cupboards contained sufficient
food for her and the babies for at least another three months, albeit
in small portions. He restocked the cupboards a week ago.

Her mind doesn't stop ticking for a moment.

She dismantles one of the metal pipes from the showers and tries
to use it to break down the door. All her banging is met with nothing
but deafening silence from the other side.

He's working alone.

If he had accomplices, someone would have showed up by now
to check on what had happened to him. But the concrete structure
she's in isn't something someone can build alone. And all the
medical equipment too. Too complex. Too big. Too sophisticated.
How did he get his hands on or purchase this place? Where are
they? In which region of the country? She's sure at least that
they're in Israel.

Her abductor hasn't had anything to eat or drink for three
days. He simply lays in bed staring blankly at the television. She's
stopped talking to him. She isn't going to give him the pleasure of
conversation. Let him stew in his own juice. The last thing she said

197

to him was: "As far as I'm concerned, you can give me the key or you can die." She hasn't unshackled him to allow him access to the bathroom either, so the room stinks. She blocks her nose whenever she goes in to check that he's still conscious.

In the meantime, she continues caring for the babies and looking for the key to the EXIT door. She's examined every inch of the Images Room, the X-ray Room and the Laundry Room, then conducted another search through the hallway, running her hand over the walls, the floor and the doors, trying to find a hidden switch or concealed slot that activates something.

And then, feeling around one of the lights along the wall, she finds it. A key fixed to the back of the light with a magnet.

She studies it for a moment and then slowly makes her way to the EXIT door. She inserts the key into the lock. It slides in. She turns it.

Click

Click

She presses down on the handle and the door opens to reveal a staircase. There are stairs leading down to what looks like another hallway and then a few more stairs leading up to another metal door. Fixed above that door is another *EXIT* sign. She runs up to it. The door is locked. Two cylinders and a keypad.

She leans her back against the door, allowing her knees to bend, and slides to the floor. Tears fill her throat; but no, she clenches her teeth, she isn't going to cry. He's not going to break her. She can't despair. She'll get the code and keys out of him even if she has to torture him. It's not only her life. It's theirs, too.

The babies are asleep in the Images Room and she lies down on the blanket next to their cribs. It's late at night already. The door to her room, which is his room now, is closed and locked.

She falls asleep.

46.

His mouth is dry and his lips are cracked. Every now and then he feels dizzy and perhaps a little feverish, he isn't sure. She turned off the television and took the remote, and she turned out the lights too. He remains in total darkness, shackled to the bed, choking on the stench of his own excrement.

It's okay.

The suffering he undergoes must be complete. He's getting closer to the moment at which the lack of fluids in his body will impair his ability to implement his plan. His weakness is already restricting him. He squirms and reaches out to run his trembling hand along the underside of the metal frame of the bed, the section against the wall. It has to be here. She couldn't have found it.

After feeling around for several long minutes, he locates the key, which is fixed to the frame with silicone. He tears it off and opens the handcuffs, rubbing the mark left behind on his wrist. He gets to his feet slowly, taking care not to fall over from the bout of dizziness which hits him. Step by step, he moves through the darkness towards the switch on the wall and turns on the light.

The sudden burst of light makes him blink repeatedly, and his head is throbbing with pain. It's good. He waits for his eyes to adjust and then moves slowly to the stainless-steel sink, opens the tap and drinks straight from the stream of water, just a little, no big gulps. He scrubs his hands with soap, dries them with a white towel and goes over to the cupboard. He takes out a box of cornflakes, reaches in for a handful and chews on them slowly and carefully. When he's done, he removes his foul-smelling clothes, throws them on the floor and steps under a stream of cold water in one of the showers. He's exhausted, but he soaps himself repeatedly, scrubbing his body, his head, his face. He knows she can't hear him. She's been asleep for two hours. He counted the minutes.

Once he finishes in the shower, he goes over to the closet, leaving a trail of wet footsteps in his wake, takes out a towel and dries himself. He drops that onto the floor too and then goes over to the light switch. He turns the light off and then on again ten times in succession, pausing for a second between each state. When the light goes on for the tenth time, he hears a low buzz, and the lock is released. He immediately turns off the light and slowly opens the door.

The Images Room is bare. She's removed all the photographs from the walls and stacked them on the desk. The computer is off. The Guardian is asleep on the floor in the short pajamas he'd given her. The Four are sleeping in their cribs, which she's lined along the wall opposite the desk.

He's engulfed by a torrent of rage. Blasphemy. She's ruined everything. He'll kill her and look for another Guardian. He'll hold a pillow over her face and press down on it with all his weight until she stops moving. Like back then, when he was eleven. Arms and legs flailing in all directions like snakes. Wildly at first and then just spasms, twitching, dragging. Until it was over. It had to happen. If he hadn't done it first, it would have happened to him. The two of them were one, and only one could remain. He looks at the white walls again. Sacrilege. He fills his lungs and slowly releases the air.

She's sleeping on her side, curled up in the fetal position. He kneels down and brings his face close to hers. His eyes are closed and he can feel her breath on his lips. The minty smell of toothpaste. The fragrance of shampoo and conditioner. Of soap. The smell of sleep.

He slowly gets to his feet again and goes over to the cribs. The Four look healthy. She's doing a good job. She'll live for now. He picks up the two keys and the notebook that the Guardian left on the desk, leaves the X-ray Room, quietly closes the door behind him and double locks it.

Click
Click

47.

Something's not right.

Something wakes her.

She'd been sleeping with a light on, just to be on the safe side, and she opens her eyes to the sight of the white wall from which she'd removed the gruesome photographs.

She looks around and immediately springs to her feet. A shudder of terror grips her body. The door to her old room is open.

She pulls the improvised knife out of the folded towel she's using as a pillow and walks slowly towards the dark room. In the light penetrating the darkness, she can see that the bed is empty. She flips the switch and the room lights up. Handcuffs on the mattress. Clothes tossed on the floor. A towel... and a trail of wet footprints leading to the door.

The footprints go into the Images Room, step on her blanket, and end outside the door to the X-ray Room. She looks at the desk. The keys and notebook are gone. She runs to the door. Locked.

He's back in control.

For the first time since finding herself here, she can't hold back the tears. Sobs that had been locked inside her for four months burst forth, tears streaming down her face, her entire body shaking uncontrollably.

She weeps until she hears a noise from the cribs. Yoavi wakes up and is grumbling for attention in baby talk. She picks him up and holds him in front of her face, and he reaches out to her with both arms.

"There's no time for crying now." The voice booms from the speaker, loud and metallic, ripping through the silence.

"Put the knife down. You don't want to hurt him."

She hadn't noticed that the knife was still in her hand when she picked up the baby, and she places it on the desk. She looks up to try to locate the cameras she didn't know were there until then. He can see what's happening in every room. He'd seen everything she did. The knife she'd made. How she'd waited for him with the can. The way she showers.

"What do you dream about?" the question echoes from the loudspeaker.

"Getting the hell out of here," she whispers. Yoavi reaches out to touch her wet face with his little hand.

"No, no. What do you dream about at night? Do you dream about walking and finding yourself in the same place over and over again? In the same dense forest? Walking in circles and tripping over that same branch on the ground again and again? Sprouting, growing, flowering, wilting, dying, rotting. It's a wheel that keeps turning, nonstop, and will keep turning forever until… Until we can make it different. More powerful. Stronger. Less quick. A symbol and continuation of God. *Then another sign appeared in heaven: and behold, a great red dragon having seven heads and ten horns, and on his heads were seven diadems.*"

She clasps Yoavi to her chest.

"I forgive your improper actions towards me. I, unlike you, uphold the rules of civilized conversation and behavior. Clean your room. Take the mattress into the Images Room. Scrub everything with towels soaked in soapy water. I don't want the Four to catch anything from the filth in there. Wrap the dirty towels and clothes in a sheet, tie them into a bundle and leave it on the mattress in the Images Room. Take a shower afterwards. And then, once you are clean and the room has been disinfected, replace everything you removed from there, including the Four. On the desk in the Images Room are four photographs of the walls of the room before you ruined them. Hang up all the images in their places with adhesive tape. When you're done, go back to your room and close the door behind you. I'll bring you a new mattress tomorrow. You can sleep on the floor tonight."

She takes a deep breath.

That's it. No more crying.

PART 4

THE LETTERS

NOVEMBER 2017

48.

Tonight, I'll remember my dream

Tonight, I'll lucid dream

I'm strong and can face up to any character who seeks to harm me in my dream

Tonight, I'll remember my dream

Tonight, I'll lucid dream

I'm strong and can face up to any character who seeks to harm me in my dream

Tonight, I'll remember my dream

Tonight, I'll lucid dream

I'm strong and can face up to any character who seeks to harm me in my dream

05:46

We're sitting in the front seats of a red car. We're both wearing school shirts. It's already evening and the car is parked in a large parking lot full of cars. A soft song by a singer with a velvety voice is playing on the radio.

"Want to go on a journey?"

I nod.

She opens the car door and steps out.

"Come quickly, the show's starting soon."

She takes my hand in hers and we run between the rows of cars to the theater. She pulls a pair of crumpled tickets out of her pocket and presents them at the entrance. We go in and sit in row 9, seats 11 and 12. The lights dim. The speakers announce that the show is about to begin and that filming or recording is prohibited. The audience is asked to please mute their phones. I take my phone out of my pocket and mute it, and I notice that my fingers curl around the device in a strange fashion. I'm dreaming.

A small gray bird flies through the hall and perches on a lighting beam near the ceiling.

The lights go out and those above the stage come to life.

Lee Ben-Ami, the dead Anat Aharon and my adult self appear on the stage.

Showtime.

On the stage, we're planning a jeep trip.

We're sitting on the roof of Lee Ben-Ami's apartment building eating pasta. Lee says she has a great idea – to drive from Tel Aviv all the way to Eilat on the dirt roads through the Judean and Negev deserts; and when we get there, we'll drink wine and eat tomato salad on the beach of the Aqua Sport scuba diving club and then return via Dimona.

Anat Aharon and I agree that it's a great idea and we decide to sleep at Lee's apartment so that we can set off early in the morning. As we lie together, Anat brushes her hand across her cheek and looks at her red fingertips. If she were alive, she says to me, we could be very close friends. Lee tells her that it truly is a shame. She says that after I rescue her, we'll keep in touch. "No one really cares. Only you. I know you'll find me. I'm relying on you."

My child persona in the audience is crying. My friend notices and hugs me, and I rest my head on her shoulder.

On stage, we set off early the following morning.

The drive passes merrily by the yellow-brown backdrop on the stage, and we loudly sing every Queen and ABBA song we can remember.

My child persona and friend in the audience join in and sing along with us.

When we come to the edge of the Ramon Crater, we stop. Our trail curves downward at a frightening angle and is strewn with boulders that have rolled down from the surrounding rocky slopes. A military sign reads *Dangerous trail. No entry to vehicles of any kind, including 4X4s* in half-erased khaki letters.

My adult self, Lee Ben-Ami and the dead Anat Aharon discuss our options.

Lee suggests circumventing the crater even if it means a longer drive.

I say that maybe we should cut through the town of Mitzpe Ramon.

Anat adamantly rejects the idea of extending our drive and says she wants her wine and salad at Aqua Sport; she'll drive and we can descend on foot behind the jeep. If the jeep flips over on the way down and falls off the cliff, it won't really matter since she's no longer alive anyway.

"You'll hear from him soon," Lee says, addressing my adult self on the stage. "And when you do, you'll know I don't have much time left."

Anat nods, the trail of blood on her cheek

shimmering under the stage lights. "You have to stop him before she joins me. I'm beyond help already."

All three turn to look at the audience at once. Their eyes fix on me.

I'm startled and reach my hand out in search of my friend's, only to find that the seat next to me is empty.

"It's coming closer," the three on the stage say in unison.

Daphne wakes and quickly records the dream in her journal before it's lost. Strange how the brain produces about ten dreams a night and erases them immediately. Just a few minutes, and half the dream is gone already. A few minutes more, and it's all gone. If you don't practice, you don't remember. They dissipate like smoke.

Anna is getting dressed in her room when Daphne passes her door.

"Coffee?"

"Yes, thanks."

She places her dream journal on the kitchen table and fills the kettle. While she's still busy preparing their coffees, Anna walks in, dressed in jeans and a black blouse. As she's not in the field, she has the privilege of spending most days in civilian clothes. She sits down and reaches for the journal. She doesn't open it, she simply holds it in her hand.

"Still writing?"

"I don't really know how to define it, it's like being in another life, which keeps changing. Like a parallel universe. It's frightening and beautiful at the same time."

Anna puts the diary down and sips her coffee. "You're trying to steal more dream time."

"What?"

"I'm on to you. You're going to bed earlier and getting up in the middle of the night. You're trying to work in more dreams every night. You're developing an addiction."

Daphne tries to respond, but Anna says, "It's the same with

junkies who always need another fix. Perhaps you should lower the dosage."

"Let me get to grips with the nightmare and then I promise I'll quit. I'm not doing it for any other reason. I have to get it out of my head."

Anna fixes her with a long stare. "Just watch yourself. I'm genuinely worried about you."

"It's fine."

Daphne lights a cigarette and stands at the window with her coffee in hand.

"Are you going to Jerusalem today?"

"Yes."

"Dress warm. The news says it's going to be freezing. In the low forties."

"Brrrrr."

49.

Lior Goldman wakes up and reaches for his phone to check the time. Five-ten in the morning. He sits up in bed and rubs his eyes. Rinat's side of the bed is empty, and there's no dent in the pillow to indicate that she slept for even a short while.

He goes downstairs to the living room. Rinat is sitting on a stool at the kitchen island with a steaming cup of coffee. But she isn't drinking from it. Her eyes are fixed on her cell phone and the landline's cordless handset that lie on the island in front of her.

"Nothing," she says without looking up at him. "No call. No knock at the door."

"Did you not get to sleep at all?"

"He said he would make contact after one year."

He stands behind her and hugs her, and she closes her eyes. "Why hasn't he called?"

"He's a psychopath, and you expect him to be precise to the minute?"

"I don't get it." Lior tightens his embrace, readying himself to hear what he's been hearing every day for an entire year. "How can the police not have found anything? He walked into Ichilov and took our child like he was walking into a supermarket for a bag of chips. Why didn't anyone stop him? How could they have let it happen?" She sounds exhausted, but her eyes remain glued to the phones. "How could they let it happen? How did they let it happen?"

He kisses her on her temple. "I'll go check outside, perhaps he left something."

Outside, the dawn is already rising, to the accompaniment of the lively chirping of birds all around. Lior walks down the pathway to the gate, casting his eyes over the front garden. He opens the gate – there's nothing on the sidewalk – and goes to the mailbox, reaching in to retrieve its contents. Flyers, the electric bill, the community center's annual activities booklet, and a white envelope.

He opens it, takes out a folded sheet of paper and starts reading; a moment later, he throws aside the rest of the mail and runs back into the house.

"Rinat!" he yells. "Call the police! Quickly! Call the police!"

50.

Dear Goldman Family!

I'm pleased to inform you that your little Rag is growing and developing nicely!

He's already a year old and certainly suits his name because he loves to crawl along the floor of the cell in which he's being held and gather up all the dust onto himself. He cleans the entire floor very admirably!

It's funny.

A few weeks ago, he found a piece of glass on the floor and put it in his mouth. Fortunately, I was right there! I pulled it out of his mouth and his tongue stopped bleeding a few minutes later. Tough baby!

When I yell: "Rag!" he looks at me and smiles. He already knows his name.

Soon, when he starts talking, I'll teach him all the profanities I know. I promise to be a wonderful father to him. We'll sit together in his cell and howl like dogs.

A few days ago, when I was changing his diaper (You can't believe how much he shits!), he jumped off the dresser headfirst, and I managed to grab his ankle at the last second before his head hit the floor. It was so funny. Lucky I wasn't drunk at the time.

I love red wine.

White wine too.

And vodka.

I think I'll allow him to drink a little too.

How long can a person drink only supermarket low-fat milk that has passed its expiry date?

What is he? A calf or something?

Huh!

Don't worry. I'm holding each baby in a different room so that they don't end up fighting over their living space when they grow up. Each will have his own room. Forever. I know that teenagers become territorial as they grow up. Like hyenas. Like dogs. If we allow them to run free, they'll kill one another.

I'll keep writing to you from time to time.

I think this is the beginning of a beautiful friendship!

Regards from Rag

51.

Along the winding road through the Jerusalem Forest, on her ascent towards the capital, she sees a naked body on a branch among the pine trees. Anat Aharon peers at her from behind a gnarled tree trunk. When she blinks, the vision disappears. She slows a little, takes her hands off the wheel for a moment and does a reality check. She's awake.

She presses her foot down on the gas again and her finger on one of the speed-dial numbers on her phone.

"Hi, Daph."

"What's up?"

"On my way to work."

"Me too. Remember you asked me if there's a character that appears in my dream and takes me into it?"

"Has one appeared?"

"Yes. In a few dreams already. A young girl."

"Who is she?"

"My friend."

"A friend in your dream?"

"Yes."

"Someone you know from the waking world? You as a child?"

"No. She looks Japanese. Black hair, straight bangs."

"What's her name?"

"I haven't asked her, but I know her name is Makoto. She appears in almost all of my dreams. She leads me into the lucid state."

"When you're with her, are you a child too? And when she leaves, do you return to your true age?"

"How did you know?"

"Does she try to persuade you to remain?"

"Where?"

"In the dream."

"No."

"Let me know when she does."

Makoto. And Anat's there too. And Lee. And Carlos. And the wolf that reappears sometimes. And the man who kills her again and again. The parallel world that takes shape for her at night.

"Sometimes, I have flashbacks during the day. I see Anat or Lee or something I've dreamed about for a moment and then they disappear."

"Makes sense. There'll be some spilling over now and then."

"It's really unpleasant." Daphne knows all about flashbacks. They already bother her at unexpected times. But now the dreams have joined them too.

"Look at it this way: That three-pound chunk of meat between your ears works."

Daphne laughs ruefully.

"The body is designed to soak up stimuli from the outside, and from within, and relay them to the brain," Rotem continues. "You have receptors precisely for that purpose – eyes, nose, tongue, ears, skin. But when it comes to internal stimuli, it's the opposite. There are so many internal systems to monitor that if we were to pick up on everything happening inside our bodies, the inner noise would drive us crazy."

The beep of an incoming call sounds on Daphne's end of the line, but she ignores it.

"Inside us are four sensations only – pleasant, unpleasant, stimulating and relaxing. These four sensations are coursing through our bodies all day, from the body to the brain, which convert them into emotions based on our past experiences. Fear, anger, disgust, love, happiness, everything. It's a little different in a dream, due to the fact that the brain's center of reason is shut down during the

216

REM phase. Those emotions are supposed to be blocked, but now you're aware of them. Bottom line, let me know when your friend starts trying to persuade you to stay."

The silence on the line is broken by the sound of another call-waiting beep. "Okay, thanks, Rotem. I need to hang up. It's Nathan."

"Bye."

Daphne reaches for her phone, which is resting on a car phone mount on the dashboard. She hangs up on Rotem and picks up the waiting call.

"Hi."

"Are you on your way?"

"Yes. Just past Motza now."

"He's made contact."

"The Babysitter?"

"Yes. Four letters. One to each family. They're here in the lab now and I'm about to begin examining them. You're welcome to join me. That is, of course, if you don't have more important things to do."

Daphne knows he hates call-waiting. She puts her foot down and starts zigzagging between the three-lane trail of cars on the climb to Jerusalem, sparking angry honks and hostile stares from the drivers around her.

"What does he say?"

"Sick sadist. I've only read one of them so far. He's tormenting them. He's enjoying causing them pain."

Pain. And intellect. The pain is mental. Just like Rotem said.

"What does the letter say?"

"I can't read it out to you over the phone. You'll see when you get here."

She veers from the left lane into the right, recklessly cutting in front of a truck in the center lane and drawing another volley of honking.

"Wait for me before you move on to the others."

52.

A little more than a quarter of the cases are fused from the upper chest to the lower chest. Some twenty percent from the upper thorax to the lower belly. Ten percent at the lower abdomen only. Ten percent in an asymmetrical fashion with the one totally dependent on the body systems of the other. And six percent can be conjoined at the back, front or side of the head but never the face or the base of the skull.

When the initial stage in the development of a new organism, the zygote, is impeded by a mitosis inhibitor and the fertilized ovum splits only partially, you don't get two separate identical twins but conjoined twins instead.

There are rarer cases too. Two faces on opposite sides of a single, conjoined head, or one head with a single face but four ears and two bodies. In general, these don't survive. There have been cases in which the lower half of the two bodies is fused, with the spines conjoined end to end at a one-hundred-and-eighty-degree angle. Sometimes, they're fused side by side with a shared pelvis. And sometimes they share only the skin and soft tissue from the neck down to the coccyx. Those are the easiest to separate; it's only skin and soft tissue.

Such foolishness. Why separate them? Something so rare. One in a hundred thousand. One in a million.

He's holding a series of postcard-size X-rays, and he places them one by one on the table in front of him, reciting the names.

Thoraco-omphalopagus
Omphalopagus
Cephalopagus
Xiphopagus
Omphalo-Ischiopagus
Rachipagus

He fashions the individual X-ray images into a square mosaic. From the desk drawer, he retrieves a large X-ray image and places it over the others, covering them perfectly. He's gone through the same procedure a thousand times by now. At least. He's perfectly familiar with each and every one of the images. Each and every bone. Each skull. Every connection point.

He reaches for a jar from the shelf above the desk and studies the fetus suspended inside. Large eyes under closed lids in an off-white body. Four small legs, a narrow spine with its vertebrae protruding through almost-translucent skin. Two hands, each with five fingers. One thumb tucked into the mouth. Frozen in time.

Before Thailand became Thailand, it was Siam. The conjoined Bunker brothers were the first to be called Siamese Twins. When one died just before the age of sixty-three, his brother knew his time was coming too. He yelled for three hours until he died. Medicine has come a long way since then, since 1874. His eyes are so close to the jar his nose touches the glass.

On the computer screen, the Four are sleeping soundly. The Guardian is asleep too, in her flannel pajamas. Her blanket moves slightly with each mint-scented breath.

They all need to have the same blood type. That information wasn't on the blue cards at the hospitals. He'll have to check. It's time to move on to the next stage.

53.

It must be so frustrating to hold such a senior position yet be unable to influence anything. You sit there in your office, with all the authority you have over those who are looking for your grandson, and you can't do a thing.

When your grandson grows up, I'll tell him how his grandfather did nothing for him despite serving in one of the government's most senior positions. He'll probably be very angry. He'll probably be so angry that it'll grow inside him like a bush of black thorns that will prick and stab his stomach until it kills him.

Minister of the Interior!

"Your grandfather is a loser," I'll tell him.

I'll tell him you didn't even try. That you weren't persuasive enough with the prime minister. With the police. With the official entities under your authority that are laughing in your face. You failed to convince them to make a concerted effort because you're incapable of doing so. Because you're a wimp.

They must have been able to invest more in the search, but they had more urgent matters to deal with. More important than your grandson. There's a police convention in Eilat. They have young female volunteers to sexually harass. They have donuts and coffee with two spoons of sugar to drink in their air-conditioned offices.

I'm sending a copy of this letter to your daughter and her

husband too. To show them the real you. To show them you haven't lifted a finger for them.

Huh!

A finger!

Maybe one of these days I'll send your daughter and her husband a small foot in a beautiful white box tied with a red ribbon.

That would be a laugh!

I'll attach a little note to one of the fingers that says: "A gift from Grandad. If he had made a little effort, this wouldn't have happened."

I didn't kidnap them for money or for gold. I have other plans for them.

You'll hear from me again soon.

54.

"Sick, delusional and totally fucked up. What does he have to gain from torturing them?" The letter is lying in front of Nathan as he wipes a white cotton swab over its surface.

"Pain and intellect. The families' mental anguish is part of what he's looking for." Daphne examines the first letter under a microscope.

"The families' mental anguish?" Nathan pauses his work with the swab.

"Yes, it's part of his plan. Suffering and pain as a precursor. A sacrificial offering to make something happen. He abducted a medical student because he needs medical know-how for whatever he's going to do to them. He'll force her to cooperate. The pain and suffering are prerequisites. Like he wrote in the letter with the chocolates. He's going to make a change. Something big. The entire world will be talking about it if we don't get to him in time."

Nathan looks at her, frowning.

"Where did that all come from?"

"I've been thinking about it." Her head is bent over the eyepiece of the microscope. She reaches for the button to adjust the focus. "How did he manage to get the letter into the interior minister's mailbox? Is there no security detail there?"

"Wearing a red shirt and carrying a mail bag. Baseball cap, sunglasses. Dropped the letter in and walked on. Footage from the security cameras offers nothing special. That's what they told me when I asked who'd touched the letter. Just him, the minister, and the minister's PA."

"And did all the other letters arrive without a postage stamp? Wouldn't it have been easier to simply mail them?"

"He probably wanted to drop them off himself, so that they'd all arrive the same morning. A day after the anniversary of the abductions. He couldn't have accomplished that if he'd mailed them."

"That's for sure. Half the things I order on eBay disappear in the mail."

Nathan sits down on the chair at the station alongside Daphne and places the letter he's been working on back in its evidence bag. "There's nothing there aside from the fingerprints of Lior and Rinat Goldman. And the only DNA is from these stains here, which are Rinat's tears. The same printer for your one?"

"Yes, the same steganography. It's not the same printer that was used for the letter with the chocolates. I'm capturing an image now and will run it through the database in a moment."

The microscope sends an enlarged image of a cluster of yellow dots. The decryption software scans the pattern for a few seconds, spits out several numbers on the screen and stops.

"That was quick."

"A Lexmark C510 from 2004. A real antique. Serial number 55C4MC5. Page count 1,022. This particular page was printed precisely two weeks ago. At two thirty-three in the morning." Daphne prints the results of the scan and hands them to Nathan.

"Strange that such an old machine has only printed 1,022 pages until now." He looks at Daphne. "What's the next step?"

She smiles at him. He still tests her from time to time, and she has no problem cooperating with his blatant didactics. "The Customs Authority computer," she replies. "If there's a record of it somewhere, it has to be there. Someone paid customs duty on that printer when they imported it into Israel; and if there's anything that's meticulous when it comes to recording serial numbers, it's the entity that makes money from doing so."

She wheels herself in her chair to a different computer station and enters the printer's serial number. Again, the response is almost immediate, causing Daphne to stare at the screen and scratch her head absentmindedly.

"What's up?"

"Imported for the military. Part of a shipment of five hundred of the same printers for the IDF in 2004. No further details."

"We'll have to check with the army."

"I can stop by the Defense Ministry compound tomorrow morning. Can you ask Investigations to coordinate that for me with the Military Police?"

"I'll take care of it."

"And what about the paper?"

Nathan returns to his computer.

"Old too. Fits the profile of an Israeli manufacturer. Hadera Paper, most probably. Almost all the components are identical. A4. Not recycled. Five-thousandth of an inch thick. Bleached with sodium hydrosulphite and a glucose-based starch. Pretty standard. Nothing to indicate where the paper was delivered."

"Should we move on to the next letter?"

"Yes. Give it to me and have a look at the envelope. I'll read it to you."

55.

Dear Gabbay Family!

Think for a moment. What would you be prepared to do to get your son back?

Huh?

Alex! If you kill yourself today, I'll return your son to Natalie. If I read in the paper tomorrow morning that you jumped off the roof of the building in which you live, I'll leave your son on your doorstep tomorrow night and disappear.

But I need proof. I need Natalie to film you diving off the roof headfirst and to post it on her Facebook page. That way I'll be sure you aren't working with the police and trying to pull one over on me.

I'm not stupid!

So what do you say?

Your life for your son's life? You've lived for more than thirty years already. Won't you give a chance to someone who has only just begun his life? Will you not give Natalie the chance to hold your son in her arms? Your son who she gave birth to?

Nahhhhhhhh!

Just messing with you.

You can jump off the roof for all I care, but it won't bring Jennifer back to you. Yes. I've named your son Jennifer and I dress him in little pink dresses.

It tickles me.

When he learns to walk, I'll buy him ballet shoes and he'll be our little ballerina. Each of the Four has a role to play when they grow up, and your Jennifer will be a dancer.

I'll take pictures of her with and without the dress and I'll sell them to interesting websites that are particularly fond of that kind of thing. Little Jenny will also have to do her bit for the sake of the livelihood of all of us. You can't just take and take and take. What have you done for us lately?

Huh?

I'll keep you posted.

The day after tomorrow perhaps.

Or maybe two years from now.

56.

During her first few months there, when she woke, before opening her eyes onto the row of showers and cribs, she still imagined sometimes that it was all a bad dream. That she'd press up against Shai, who was lying next to her, and cuddle him before they both got up and readied themselves for the day ahead. Work for him and medical school followed by a shift at the hospital for her. It would last for just a few seconds, until she remembered where she was.

Now, one year since her abduction, it no longer happens. When she wakes up, she knows exactly where she is, and the routine of another day begins.

She gets up to shower. She knows he has cameras and that he watches her, but he's never tried to touch her during the year that she's been there. She's caught him eyeing her now and then but never in a sexual manner, more like he was looking at a rare collectible or at the doctor who is caring for his children. The children he kidnapped.

She gets dressed and goes over to the refrigerator, which was added to the room a few months ago. "In the first year, they triple their birth weight. Give them a sliced hard-boiled egg, peeled and diced cucumbers, small pieces of cooked chicken, cheese and hummus." He didn't bring in a stovetop or oven. The cooked food for the babies was delivered ready on his stainless-steel trolley, packed in plastic containers and arranged neatly in the refrigerator while she was handcuffed to the bed. He still made sure to shackle her to the bed whenever he entered the room.

Months had passed since then, but she couldn't stop thinking about it. Why did he allow her to wait behind the door for him if he had cameras? She couldn't understand it. And how did he get out of the room? How did he unshackle himself? How did he open the door?

In the small hours of the morning, when she couldn't hear a sound from the other side of the door, she would turn out all the lights in her room, so she couldn't be seen on camera, and fumble around in search of hidden switches. In the cupboards, under the cribs, on the floor, in the showers, in the toilet. She'd searched through those same places hundreds of times, without finding anything, but continued to do so whenever she got the chance. But he'd managed to free himself, that's a fact, and eventually she'll figure out how he did it.

The babies will be up soon. She takes several plastic containers from the fridge and dishes out portions of cold cooked food into small plastic bowls. She has no way of heating the food, but they're used to it cold. They've never eaten anything different. She carries the small bowls over to the four highchairs that he's brought in and lined up in a row along the wall, alongside the cribs. She is placing the bowls on the trays when the door opens. He walks in pushing the stainless-steel trolley and begins stocking the cupboards with more cans of food.

Did he forget to throw the handcuffs to her? She's been working out every day. She's a lot stronger than he is now. She could jump at him again. Tie him up in a way that makes escape impossible.

And then what?

She's seen the locked EXIT door.

She knows what will happen. He won't talk even if it means dying of thirst.

She has to wait and see what comes next.

He stands there and looks at her, like he's reading her thoughts. "I'm not going to cuff you to the bed any longer. We'll all die here if you try to escape. You know that."

"What?"

"If you try to starve me to death, and succeed, you'll die of hunger in the end too. This place is fitted with door upon door, lock upon lock. Hallways and more floors all the way to the top. You may find a key or two, and you may get one of the key codes to a door right after thousands of tries, but you, too, will run out of food within a few months. You'll have to decide whether to allow the Four to die first, or all of you together, or you first and them after you. In any event, you won't get out of here without me."

"Where are we?"

"Somewhere no one will come looking for us."

With a black marker in hand, he goes over to the sleeping babies and writes on their foreheads.

A1

A2

A3

A4

He places the marker in one of the cribs, takes a cell phone out of his pocket and photographs the four faces. "Don't erase those. If they fade, go over them with the marker again. If you refuse, I'll give them permanent tattoos."

57.

Tonight, I'll remember my dream

Tonight, I'll lucid dream

Tonight, I'll have soothing and pleasant dreams

Tonight, I'll remember my dream

Tonight, I'll lucid dream

Tonight, I'll have soothing and pleasant dreams

Tonight, I'll remember my dream

Tonight, I'll lucid dream

Tonight, I'll have soothing and pleasant dreams

04:40

We're sitting on a park bench. Other kids are playing around us. An ice-cream truck playing music pulls up nearby and a line of children forms in front of its window.

"Want to see something funny?" my friend asks.

"Yes."

"Look." She points up at the sky and then claps her hands. And all at once, the clouds begin spinning quickly around themselves. Another clap of her hands and they stop.

"How did you do that?"

"It's easy. Try for yourself. You simply have to will it to happen the moment you clap your hands."

I clap, and the clouds start to spin. The children and parents in the park look up, point to the sky and cry out in amazement. I clap again and the clouds stop spinning. I clap my hands and the grass turns purple. Another clap, and a huge playground slide appears. The children scream in delight and some run to climb up the ladder. Others stay behind to play on the purple grass.

"Cool."

"Want to go on a journey?"

"Yes."

The park disappears. I'm standing alone in front of a closed compound surrounded by a fence. I'm cold even though the sun is shining. I walk along the mile-long fence of thick iron bars that are covered with a thick layer of shiny, viscous black paint. Behind it, a tall green hedge makes it impossible to see inside. I walk until I reach a gate. Sitting next to it in a white plastic chair is a white-haired old man. He smiles at me. "An adult ticket costs ten euros. There's a fifty percent discount for students." I hand him ten euros.

I pass through the gate and then through an opening in the hedge and come to a large square courtyard paved with basalt flagstones. In the center are four huge rectangular basalt slabs, rising high into the air, green vines climbing around them.

In the silence, I walk around the slabs, reading words that repeat themselves in small writing across them at eye level. The babies, says one. On another, the word Lee appears over and over and over again. The third says Anat. As I walk among them, they block out the sun, and I feel the cold rising from the paving stones.

"Welcome to the memorial site."

The sound of a female voice with a slight Russian accent startles me. It's coming from corroded speakers installed around the edges of the courtyard. "Thirty years ago, in August 2016, Anat Aharon was deliberately run down in the road. The driver fled the scene. No positive ID."

I step out of the shade of the giant slabs and the sun warms me for a moment. It's very cold between the rock faces.

"Lee Ben-Ami was struck in a similar fashion and abducted. The offender left the scene with her. No positive ID."

I lightly run my hand over the inscription in small letters on the fourth slab and my fingertips feel the word that repeats itself over and over again: *Daphne Daphne Daphne Daphne*.

"One morning, in November 2016, four newborn babies were kidnapped from four different hospitals in the center of the country. The kidnapper disappeared. No positive ID."

I move away from the slabs of basalt rock and walk towards a clear lake. Sitting down on a wooden bench, I look out across the water, ignoring the recording that continues to play in the background. I get up, dip my hands into the lake and drink from it. The water is cold and tastes good. I kneel down and drink some more, listening again.

"About a year after the abductions, and following extensive detective work, the location at which the kidnapper was holding Lee Ben-Ami and the four babies was found. The kidnapper was armed, and the ensuing gun battle, in November 2017, left four police officers dead, three males and one female."

I sit down on the bench again.

"A beautiful place."

This time, it's the voice of the old man from the gate that makes me jump. I look to my left and see him sitting next to me.

"Yes, it really is pretty here."

"He has good phonology. The one you're looking for."

"Yes."

"But it's different in the letters. Did you notice?"

"Yes. It's like he's trying to lower his IQ. To underplay himself. To make the police and families think they're dealing with someone else, with a different persona to the one he truly is."

"You're a clever little girl."

"Thank you."

"Did you feel yourself on your fingertips? That stone bears your name. You rest here forever."

We look at the ripples that the cold wind creates on the surface of the lake.

"This is one of the forks in the road," he says.

"What does that mean?"

"This is one of the possible outcomes. You can choose to remain in it, or you can go back to 2017 and continue from there at random."

"Are there many more like this?"

"An infinite number. Some even worse."

"I'll go back," I say and get up from the bench.

We walk slowly, side by side, watching the setting sun.

"Good choice," he says.

"Thanks."

"Your chocolate milk."

"What?"

He's holding a full half-gallon bottle of chocolate milk. I can't recall it being mine but have no desire to argue with the old man, or offend him, so I take the heavy bottle and continue with it towards the exit from the memorial site.

"See you, little girl," he says when we get to the gate.

He laughs out loud and then coughs dryly.

The alarm she set for eight wakes her up. She's headed to the Defense Ministry compound in Tel Aviv this morning, so she allows herself to sleep a little longer. No need to battle the traffic in Jerusalem today.

On the way to the compound she plays a lucid dreaming podcast she found on iTunes, but she isn't really listening to it. Her thoughts wander. She can recall her dreams much better now. The backdrops, the sensations, who was there and what they said. She's already able to remain lucid in her dreams, or a significant number of them at least. The narrator of the podcast talks about three levels of lucidity. At the basic level, you're aware that you're dreaming but have no control over what's happening. By the time you get to the second level, you are in control of yourself in your dream; and when you reach the third level, you have control over both yourself and the dream environment. At this level, the dream will become so palpable that it will be very difficult for you to distinguish between dream and reality, and you need to perform frequent reality checks and look for dream signs so as not to get locked inside the dream for an extended period of time. She didn't really understand what they meant by being "locked in the dream". She's already well into the second level. It is no longer like watching a movie that involves all the senses with no control over what's going on. She can now make decisions in her dream, change the course of it.

Nathan arranged a permit for her to park inside the compound, and the sentry at the gate examines her police ID before pointing her in the right direction.

"Hi, nice to meet you. I'm Noya." A Military Police corporal meets her at the entrance to the building and escorts her to a room with walls covered with old metal shelving laden with brown folders tied with black string. The desk in the middle of the room is empty aside from a large computer screen, a keyboard and a mouse.

"I was told you needed to look for something in the Logistics archive for an investigation you're working on, and to be nice to you." Noya smiles and her ponytail flaps slightly as she moves her head.

"Thanks. Yes. Printers that were purchased in 2004. Where they ended up. At which base." She hands Noya a piece of paper with the serial and model numbers.

"What's so important about this printer?"

"It's part of an investigation and will help us a lot."

"Cool. Don't let all the folders freak you out. The one for 2004 has already been scanned into the computer." Noya begins typing quickly, and Daphne sits down in the chair beside her.

Noya searches a large Excel sheet, then copies and pastes a long reference number into a SAP screen, and after a few more mouse clicks she leans back in her chair in satisfaction. "Yes, got it. It was part of a shipment of five hundred printers purchased in August 2004 for the various Field Corps."

"Which of the Field Corps?"

"Just a sec. In 2007, the same serial number appears in the Home Front Command. They must have passed the printer on to the Home Front Command three years later. They may never have used it at all and it may have sat in the Field Corps storerooms for three years before they passed it on. Every piece of equipment with any sort of value gets recorded in the transfers so that the various corps can offset their budgets."

"And where did it end up?"

"It doesn't say here. That means it remained in the Home Front Command until it was written off."

"Written off?"

"After seven years, printers are given a zero-value in the books so they can be thrown away without offsetting the budget."

"IDF bookkeeping at its best," Daphne mumbles to herself, leaning in closer to the screen.

"Absolutely," Noya smiles again. "From where I'm sitting, it looks like we have more lawyers and accountants than combat soldiers."

"So the printer was thrown away?"

"It doesn't say. Let me check with my liaison at the Home Front Command." Noya opens a Lync window, then closes it again after a brief correspondence.

"Her records don't show that the printer was thrown away, but that doesn't help us much. We don't have documentation from before 2010 pertaining to the location of every serial number. That printer did indeed go to the Home Front Command in 2007; but because it's perishable equipment, there's no record of where in the Command it was sent to. Worth less than a thousand shekels. She says that such an old printer was probably thrown away at some point, or donated to charity, or taken home by a reserve soldier who didn't want to see it end up in the trash."

"And is there nowhere else that keeps records about where the printer could be?"

Noya runs queries through several different programs, nibbling the tip of her fingernail while she waits for a response.

"Nothing. Sorry."

"So this printer could practically be anywhere."

"Yep. And if you are looking for it, then I guess you got a page it printed, so we can rule out the printer being shredded." Noya smiles.

"Thanks, Noya, this was helpful even though we don't have the exact location."

"Sure, glad to help."

Daphne says goodbye and leaves the compound on foot to go and meet Rotem, taking advantage of her parking space close to the

Sarona Center. She crosses the road and strolls among the small, gentrified stone buildings until Rotem arrives.

They buy themselves beer and hot dogs and find a quiet patch of grass.

"Thanks for giving me a break from the infinite boredom of the espionage industry." Rotem chomps down hungrily on her hot dog laden with sauerkraut, ketchup and mustard. "Did you bring them?"

"Of course." Daphne takes the four photocopied pages out of her bag.

"At least it's some kind of sign of life."

"Pain and intellect? Why is he torturing them like this? It's pure sadism."

"I don't know about the intellect thing, but pain is certainly a factor here. They arrived in unstamped envelopes, right? Not via the mail." Rotem was not asking, she was stating a fact.

"Why like that?"

"He wanted to see their reactions."

"What do you mean?" Daphne says with a mouthful of hot dog. Rotem is always a few steps ahead and Daphne feels she needs to catch up.

"He placed the letters in the mailboxes and waited outside to observe the families' reactions, or part of them at least. Whatever he could see from outside. He feeds on their pain. He needs to be there for that. It's part of the process he's putting them and himself through. I fear it's not going to get any better." A colorful ball rolls and stops next to them and a toddler follows it. Rotem hands it to him smiling and he grabs the ball and runs back to his family sitting on the grass nearby.

"This one we received directly from the commissioner." Daphne points to the letter that was sent to the interior minister. "Everyone's in uproar."

"And you didn't find anything on the pages or envelopes?"

"No. No DNA or fingerprints. The paper is standard and old, from a batch that's probably been lying in a warehouse somewhere for years. The printer is thirteen years old too."

"Steganography?"

"Yes. Printed two weeks ago."

"A printer suspended in time with paper from the past." Rotem sips her beer and places the glass on the grass again. "What's the gap between them?"

"Between what?"

"Between the pages. Each page displays the total number of pages printed on that printer, right?"

"Of course. But we didn't consider that. We saw they were all from the same printer, and that it hadn't printed many pages, but we didn't check the gaps. One sec. I'll ask Nathan." She sends a WhatsApp message, and her phone beeps with his response a minute later.

"1,022, 1,036, 1,053, 1,077."

Rotem simply nods and continues to drink in silence.

"Well?"

"It makes sense," Rotem finally says. "If the letters were a true reflection of his style, he wouldn't have had to make so many attempts between them. He's trying to convey a different persona."

Who else has said that to her? She knows she's heard it before. The old man. In her dream the previous night. He said the exact same thing.

Daphne looks around for a gray bird. Nothing. She does a reality check. She's awake.

"Are you telling me that he printed multiple drafts until he was satisfied? Why all the printing when he could have simply edited the letters onscreen?"

"He probably did edit each one first. Then printed it. And changed his mind. Made adjustments, reprinted it. And changed his mind again. And again. All of that multiplied by four and two weeks in advance. You could say he's highly self-critical. Aspirations of perfection."

"Neither of us questions the fact that he's a psycho." Daphne licks the ketchup and mustard off her fingers. "I'll have to be careful when filling in Nathan. He's been looking at me like I've grown feelers or something. It's a little insulting. Like he knows I couldn't have come up with such insights on my own."

Rotem chuckles. "Try to get him to think that they're actually his ideas that you're simply running with and expanding. Men love that."

Daphne shakes her head.

They stand up and begin walking across the lawn towards the elevator that will take Rotem to her car, a few levels below the street. The day is cool but sunny, and the Sarona Center is filled with people taking advantage of the good weather. Some are pushing prams, others walking and playing with toddlers or young children.

Just seven miles away, hidden from the sunlight, are four babies who'd spent an entire year without their parents and one young woman who has skipped an entire year of her life.

58.

One by one, he collects the large cardboard boxes from outside and brings them in via the labyrinth of doors, staircases and hallways. He stacks them carefully near the door marked *Temple* and then goes to retrieve the toolbox from one of the nearby rooms.

He kneels outside the door and closes his eyes.

It's getting closer. The Four are pure.

He won't forget a thing. He'll make sure of every detail. He'll implement the transfer soon. They'll have to lie there without any external stimuli aside from those he has in store for them. To see. To listen. To internalize.

He opens the locked door and carries in the boxes and tools. He cleans the hot tub with a damp cloth, covers it with a large sheet and starts working. From four large flat boxes, he pulls out television screens and hangs them on the room's four walls. From smaller boxes, he unpacks speakers that he hangs up too. He then runs the cables from the TVs and speakers through white plastic tubing that he fits to the walls and to a metal cabinet, which he attaches to the wall. Inside the cabinet is an amplifier and a laptop.

He takes his shirt off and uses it to wipe the sweat off his face before gathering up all the cable cuttings, wrappings and boxes and moving them out to the hallway. When he returns to the room, he sits down on the floor in front of the laptop and starts running a video on the four screens. He turns on the amplifier and the speakers immediately thunder:

...This is the matrix when the variable is on the right, X with two components of X and Y. We'll call this Matrix A. And here we have an unknown vector with two variables that later...

He turns down the volume slightly and plays a different file:

Today we are going to be focusing on fifteen questions that you should know. We will practice asking and answering the questions so you...

The volume is the correct level, the screens are calibrated, the picture is sharp.

Everything's in working order.

He turns off the entire system and places the remotes for the TVs and the amplifier in a neat row on top of the metal cabinet.

He vacuums the floor and then washes it. The door to the Temple is still open, and the speakers in the hallway allow him to listen to the Guardian playing with the Four. That will come to an end soon. A few more weeks.

The Temple is clean, and he goes over to the hot tub to remove the sheet covering it. When he turns back to the door, he catches sight of the reflection of his bare back in one of the inactive TV screens on the wall. Etched into his skin is a large Star of David, with a cross at its center. Not a tattoo. A series of burns made with a sharp object. He stops. The mark on his back feels like it's on fire, burning like white-hot iron. He's panting for breath as he recites through clenched teeth:

So the Lord said to him: 'Therefore whoever kills Cain, vengeance will be taken on him sevenfold'.

So the Lord said to him: 'Therefore whoever kills Cain, vengeance will be taken on him sevenfold'.

So the Lord said to him: 'Therefore whoever kills Cain, vengeance will be taken on him sevenfold'.

So the Lord said to him: 'Therefore whoever kills Cain, vengeance will be taken on him sevenfold'.

So the Lord said to him: 'Therefore whoever kills Cain, vengeance will be taken on him sevenfold'.

He goes quiet again and leaves the Temple, locking the door and moving the waste from the hallway to one of the nearby rooms. The door to the Laundry Room is open and he can hear the hum of the dryer. He closes the door and goes into the room on the opposite side of the hallway to prepare the package he promised to send to the interior minister's daughter and her husband.

He won't forget the red ribbon. A promise is a promise.

He leans over the table and places a layer of cotton in a small box.

59.

Marina sits motionless on the sofa in the living room. Jacob is talking to her, urging her to speak to him, but she isn't responding.

They'd waited for so long. Five years of trying, fertility treatments, agony, and a year ago he was born. Beautiful. Perfect. And less than two days later, he was taken from them.

Her father has done everything he could. He turned the world upside down, drove the police crazy, but nothing has happened. Aside from pathetic attempts to ask for the public's assistance in locating an indistinct figure in black-and-white, they haven't done a thing. And it has eaten him up from the inside. Her father is used to having his instructions followed. He's someone who gets things done. A bulldozer. When he wants something, he gets it.

But not this time.

Marina and Jacob have watched him wither and fade with every passing day. They know he took the failure personally and can't forgive himself for the fact that his grandson and three other babies had yet to be found.

And a year later, that horrific letter. Her father could barely bring himself to read it to them over the phone. And then he tried to encourage them by defining it as a sign of life. But what kind of sign? Why such cruelty?

They knew about Lee Ben-Ami, who was abducted in all likelihood to care for the babies. Please God, at least they aren't there alone with him. But why is he doing all of this? At no stage has he asked for money or anything like that. What does he want from them? Why is he torturing them like this?

And now?

Marina threw the box aside the moment she realized what it contained, and it's still on the floor. Despite the police's clear instructions not to open or touch any letter or package from an unknown source, she had untied the red ribbon and looked inside…

Cotton lining the bottom.

A red stain at its center.

And resting on it, a small foot.

"The police are on their way. They'll be here soon," Jacob keeps saying over and over again. But Marina doesn't hear him. He hugs her and feels her entire body trembling.

60.

Lying on the metal table in the Forensics Laboratory at National Police Headquarters in Jerusalem is an open police evidence bag and, alongside it, the closed box that has been removed from it.

She photographs it from all angles and dusts it with black powder, which reveals a generous collection of fingerprints. She captures images of all of them.

"I bet you none are his. You open it. I have enough nightmares as it is." Daphne moves to a workstation at the far end of the lab, removes the camera's memory card and uploads the images to the computer. "And turn up the heat. I'm freezing."

Nathan raises an eyebrow. "Anything else, Your Highness?"

"Excuse me, but I'm not accustomed to examining sawn-off limbs, especially not those of babies." She runs the prints through the identification software. The interior minister's daughter and her husband, a number of police officers, all in the database. No unknown prints.

She doesn't look when Nathan opens the box.

"You have to see this." Nathan's voice is relaxed, it irritates Daphne, who would be acting completely differently if she was the one doing the opening.

"No, thanks."

"You must," he repeats calmly.

"Leave me alone already." She's already prepared for the lecture that's coming her way – that it's part of a forensic technician's job and that she needs to toughen up and deal with it.

"Look, it's not a baby's foot; it's rubber." Nathan raises his eyes from the evidence, looks at Daphne again and signals her to approach.

She remains in her chair and wheels herself quickly over to him. "Huh?!"

"Look, he's drilled a hole in the leg of a doll and attached a bone to it. A chicken bone it looks like. And he's poured blood or dye around it and onto the cotton. I have to admit it looks pretty real but clearly it isn't from up close."

She leans towards the box. "He's going to some lengths to cause the families pain."

"But he's doing so without harming the babies."

"For now." She sighs.

"I don't even want to think what the next level will bring." Nathan keeps staring at the rubber foot.

Daphne photographs the contents of the box.

"Does it look like real blood to you?" Nathan asks.

She leans closer and sniffs. "Smells like blood but let's see." She opens a DNA test kit, dips the nylon brush into the vial of saline and rubs it over the red stain on the cotton. She then applies a barcode sticker to the brush, with a sample identification number, which she scans into the computer before laying the brush down to dry. She repeats the procedure with a second brush, and this time she dissolves the suspected blood in the vial and places it in the hematology analyzer, which begins processing the sample.

"Who opened it at the house?"

"The mother."

"And did she see anyone leave it outside the door?"

"The detectives don't know. She isn't talking. She's in a state of shock." The machine spits out a short strip of paper, and Nathan reviews it. "It isn't human blood. Based on its composition, it looks like cattle blood. I'm calling Investigations so they can let the parents know straight away." Nathan goes over to the phone while

246

Daphne sits staring at the rubber foot, with its layer of dried blood and the protruding sawn-off bone.

"Coming for a smoke?"

"No," she replies, wheeling herself in her chair back to the computer at the far end of the lab. "I want to check something first. Don't wait for me."

Nathan leaves, and Daphne starts searching online, following her instincts. When Nathan comes back, he parks himself in a chair alongside her. On the screen in front of her are pictures of babies.

"And these are?"

"This one looks most like it, doesn't it?" she asks, pointing at the feet of one the babies on the screen.

"Very similar. What are they?"

"Reborn dolls."

"Dolls?" Nathan takes a closer look. "They look so real."

"That's the thing about these dolls. They're made of silicone."

"Weird."

"There's an entire online market for dolls like these – either ready-made, or you can buy the parts and assemble them."

"Why would anyone want to buy a silicone baby?"

"Based on what I read online, they're bought by parents who have lost a baby and want something to help them cope, or by people who want something to remind them of a baby who's grown up. And then there are the regular collectors. They're expensive dolls, handmade."

"They give me the shivers."

Daphne chuckles. "Touch it, touch the foot – it's soft silicone. Ecoflex or something similar. He may have ordered a complete doll and dismantled it, or he could have ordered a kit and colored the foot with special paint for silicone, like Psycho Paint."

"Does anyone in Israel manufacture them?"

"I just had a look but couldn't find anything. I think they're all imported. He must have ordered it on eBay or some other site. We can have a look through the Customs Authority computers, but I don't think he would have brought it in without concealing the details or simply calling it a doll."

"We'll pass it on to Investigations. They can try."

"Okay." She pushes her chair back from the desk and stretches. "I'm going out for a cigarette. Back soon."

Once outside, she lights up and calls Rotem to update her, but there's no answer. She looks at the leaves that the wind is blowing along the sidewalk, at the gray skies above her, at the National Headquarters building with its covering of Jerusalem stone. She moves closer and touches the wall of the building. Her fingertips recall the feeling of the engraved basalt slab, and she remembers the words she read there.

Daphne – Daphne – Daphne – Daphne.

61.

Sitting on the floor in the Images Room, he opens the cardboard box marked *DJI Matrice 100*, removes all the parts and lays them out in front of him.

Fuselage. Four motors. Battery. Camera. Remote control. He assembles and activates the quadcopter drone, which rises quickly to a height of three feet and hovers steadily in front of him.

According to the information he found online, the Matrice 100 offers up to forty minutes of flight time without an additional payload and can carry a weight of up to eight pounds. He'll need it to carry four and a half pounds for just a few minutes, so it'll do.

He lands the drone and turns it off. He'll have to try the GPS outside. *To fully charge the battery, attach a four-and-a-half-pound payload and fly it around for a few minutes along a course of around three and a half miles.*

He can hear the television in the Guardian's room next door.

He could have removed the TV from her room. Made her live on baby formula and baby food. Shackled her to the bed. Have forcibly impregnated her so that he'd have another baby as a back-up. He didn't do all those things because they weren't necessary. Because he's focused only on what is required. He avoids the pleasures of the flesh. He endures the suffering before the advent of the Messiah. He'll suffer now so that afterwards he can lead them. All the fools in the world. Today, they mock him; tomorrow, they'll bow down at his feet. *But this crowd which does not know the Law is accursed.*

For now, he will suffer. Along with the Guardian. And the Four. And the families of the Four. And those who are looking for them, and her, and him. All of them.

> *Shall I bring to the point of birth and not give delivery?*
> *says the Lord.*
> *Or shall I who gives delivery shut the womb?*
> *says your God.*

Every action has a purpose. Every palm. Every heartbeat. Every white bone.

There will be one entity.

One entity that is four.

62.

After imprisoning her in the room again following her escape attempt, he refused to return her notebooks and pen. He said that she could use the pen as a weapon and stab him with it. She promised him that the pen would be left at the sink whenever he entered the room and that he could check via the cameras before he came in. She also said that the writing helped to maintain her sanity because she had no one to talk to. In the end, he consented and returned the blue Pilot pen and pile of spiral notebooks, on condition that her writing doesn't come at the expense of caring for the babies.

The babies are busy exploring and tasting the toys scattered on the floor in their room-sized world and Lee is sitting cross-legged on the bed writing when she hears the two clicks that herald the opening of the door.

He comes in with the stainless-steel trolley, upon which is a white towel. This time, he doesn't go over to fill the cupboards with groceries or freshly laundered clothes but approaches her with the trolley instead.

He lifts the towel to reveal a second white towel below it, and resting on it are four empty syringes, with needles. Each syringe bears a sticker: *A1 A2 A3 A4*.

"Take blood from them."

"You must be kidding!"

"Take blood from them. You know how. I don't want to have to cuff you to the bed and do it myself. It would be a lot messier."

"What for?"

"To send for testing, to check that everything's okay. That they're developing well and are getting the right nutrition."

She knows that he's probably lying to her. He needs their blood for something else. They're healthy and developing just fine, despite their circumstances, and there's nothing to warrant taking blood from them now.

"There's no reason for them to get sick. We're in isolation."

"Take blood from them."

She stands in front of him, inadvertently clenching her fists. He takes the handcuffs out of his pocket. "Lock yourself to the bed while I take the blood."

She doesn't budge.

"Guardian, you have a key role to play in the creation of something wondrous. I know that you're suffering. You're tormented. It's hard for you. I read what you write now and then. The families of the babies are suffering. The people looking for me are suffering. Suffering is part and parcel of the birth into the world of something new. After the Rebirth, you'll be free to go. I promise you that. But if you become more of a burden to me than a help, I'll have no choice but to replace you. Not release you – replace you. You have no choice. The time is approaching. The time when you will learn why we are all here."

"Why are we here?"

He doesn't answer.

"When are you reading my notebooks?"

"While you're asleep."

"Who gave you the right to do so?" The absurdity of her words strike her as she hears herself speak them.

"Take blood from them."

She gets up from the bed, picks up the first syringe and approaches Omer. A1.

63.

He's in the Laundry Room, standing in front of the dryer, a distorted reflection of his face staring back at him from the concave glass. He inhales as deeply as he can and expels the air again in the form of a scream.

And again.

And again.

He screams and screams and screams. His voice turns ever hoarser, until his vocal cords cease to cooperate and the scream turns into a rasping breath. He tries to say something to his distorted image; nothing but a whisper rises from his throat.

Excellent.

He goes out into the hallway but halts in his tracks after a few strides. He almost forgot the cooler box. A picnic. Like going out for a picnic. He recalls that on the very odd occasion, when no one was around, late at night, she would take them both outside. One of them would hide in the trunk of the car and the other would sit next to her in the front on the half-hour drive to the forest. To the one sitting in the front seat, the drive was a short one. To the one in the trunk, it felt like forever. She would lay out a large sheet on the forest floor and give them boxes with whatever she'd taken from the refrigerator, and she'd bring a bottle of wine for herself. She would sit there and watch them wander through the trees. Never did she move or call to them, even when they wandered out of sight and ventured deeper into the living forest; they always found their way back. Like wolves. They'd return to her before first light, shrouded in the scent of the earth and the trees and sweat, and drive home before the neighbors woke up. *"Then two female bears came out of the woods and tore up forty-two lads of their number,"* she would say to them every time they emerged from among the trees. *"Who slaughter the children in the ravines, under the clefts of the crags,"* they'd respond. Always the same.

He backtracks, grabs the cooler box off the bench next to the washing machine and walks out of the compound.

PART 5

THE INTERROGATION

NOVEMBER 2017

64.

The Messubim police station wakes up to a peaceful Saturday morning. The morning shift replaces the night shift, the automatic irrigation system feeds water to the row of potted plants under the pergola at the entrance, and Deputy Inspector Oleg is making himself a cup of Turkish coffee when a man in a white T-shirt, jeans and sneakers enters the building.

"Good morning," he whispers.

Oleg puts down his coffee and looks at him across the front desk.

"What was that?"

"I'm hoarse. Bronchitis. I said good morning."

"What can I do for you?"

"A blood test," he whispers again, placing a small cooler box on the counter.

"You must be confused. This isn't a medical clinic. You've come to the police."

"I'm not confused. You'd better inform your superiors. I'm the man who kidnapped the four babies a year ago."

Oleg sips the coffee and looks long and hard at the face of the man in front of him. Bearded. Cropped hair, which could have been hidden by the knit cap in the famous security camera footage. He puts down his coffee and releases the safety strap of the gun holster on his hip.

"What's in the cooler box?"

"Four test tubes of blood for testing. One from each baby. Check the DNA with that of the parents, and you'll see I'm not lying."

Deputy Inspector Oleg is accustomed to offbeat visits to the station on the part of eccentric individuals with fantastic tales to tell, but his gut tells him this isn't one of those. The man standing in front of him appears level-headed. He chooses his words well and doesn't blink nervously or display any other twitches or tics to suggest that he's lying or tripping on something.

The man lifts the lid of the cooler for a moment.

Oleg places his right hand on the butt of his weapon.

"Take a right here along the hallway and go into the second room on the right."

The bearded man does as instructed, and Oleg follows him into the Interrogation Room, his hand still on his pistol.

"Take a seat and I'll get the detectives who are handling the case. We'll soon find out if you're genuine, and you'll be held accountable by law if you're having us on. And if you are the Babysitter," Oleg stops and shakes his head, "God help you."

The man doesn't respond and sits down with the cooler; but before Oleg closes the door, the man beckons him closer. Oleg leans towards him.

"What's your name?" the man whispers.

"Oleg."

"Tell them to come quick, Oleg. I've placed a bag of ice cubes in the cooler and I don't want the blood in the test tubes to heat up and coagulate. Tell them it's vital for the health of the babies. I'm concerned that they may have caught bronchitis. They're coughing incessantly. Do you understand the urgency, Oleg?"

Deputy Inspector Oleg says nothing. He leaves the room, locks the door and wipes his forehead with the back of his hand. Despite the cool air in the station, he's sweating. He takes a seat at the front desk again and picks up the phone.

"Tel Aviv District Command Room."

"It's Oleg from Messubim. Someone's just walked in here with test tubes filled with blood claiming to be the Babysitter."

"Another one under the influence of *IT*? Does he have a clown's mask too? We've been getting a hundred of those a day since that movie came out." The policewoman on the line sounds amused.

"He's not one of those. He seems very serious. His cooler box does indeed contain four test tubs with a liquid that looks like blood."

"Just a moment, I'll put the duty officer on the line."

"Great."

He sips his coffee, which is cold by now, and listens to the elevator music while he waits for the phone operator to return.

"Oleg, you there?'

"Yes."

"Assulin, you there too? Go ahead, you can talk."

"Listen up, Oleg. The man claiming to be the Babysitter, is he at the station now?"

"Yes. I've locked him in one of the interrogation rooms."

"Okay. Don't open the door. Just ask him if he remembers the first line of the letter he sent with the chocolates."

"I'll have to open the door. He's hoarse and can only whisper."

"Okay, ask and lock him back in again."

Deputy Inspector Oleg places the receiver next to the phone. He returns a minute later.

"Great upheavals in history don't occur slowly."

"Son of a fucking bitch!" The yell in his ear startles him. "Hold him there, Oleg. Under no circumstances are you to open that door again. Is there anyone else there with you?"

"There's two of us."

"Close the main entrance to the building and the gate outside. I don't want anyone coming in. You're closed today. I'm on my way."

65.

08:11

The sun has just set and I'm standing on the edge of a cliff facing the sea. Black clouds drift slowly above me in the remains of light, while waves transform into white foam as they crash loudly on the black rocks below. The salty spray rises up to me, wetting my face. I'm barefoot, wearing a long white sweater that reaches my knees and a pair of leggings. A cold shiver courses through me.

The cliff is high.

I spread my arms out and take a deep breath.

I hear a crackling sound behind me and turn around. There's an electricity pole in the distance, and sparks are shooting off a transformer that's wet from the moisture in the air. The noise of a car engine comes from somewhere. The hum of electricity in high voltage cables.

I turn back to look at the black sea below. My nails scratch at my thighs through my leggings.

There's no vegetation at all along the entire coastline, only sharp black rocks, but the soles of my feet don't feel them.

An old car approaches on the path I followed

to the edge of the cliff, its windows covered with moisture and spray. I can't see who's inside. The car pulls up alongside me and the driver's window slides down. A young woman looks at me. Her face keeps changing and I can't recognize her. Her hair is long and black and tied up for a moment, then short and doesn't reach her shoulders.

A small gray bird lands on the ground next to me and looks at me.

I look at the palms of my hands, which look bigger than usual, and blue and black stripes appear on them and then disappear. I touch my left palm with my right forefinger, and it goes straight through.

I'm dreaming.

The woman at the wheel of the car gestures me in, and I walk around to the other side and get into the car. For a moment, I think she's going to put it into gear and drive us both off the cliff into the crashing waves.

The thought brings a sense of serenity.

Perhaps it really is time.

She looks at me. Green eyes. Brown. Black. Freckles appear. Disappear. Her hair is fair now. I make a concerted effort to recognize her but to no avail.

She puts the car into reverse and backs up, away from the edge of the cliff. The car turns around and we drive over an old bridge that has lights along its sides reminiscent of large lampshades, then the path goes through a cotton field that's engulfed in blue flames but isn't burning.

"Do you remember what you have to do?" she asks me.

I'm aware that I'm dreaming.

"To find a doll that's missing a foot. Or an old printer perhaps."

"You're going in the wrong direction." She looks at me in sorrow. "Think harder. Think how the letters can tell you where he's writing them from."

"I don't know."

The car is moving fast. A heavy rain is falling. The sky is dark.

"There were others before her. Before Anat."

"What do you mean?"

"It's all over him."

"What?"

"The place he comes from is all over him. On his clothes. In his hair. He's the place where he's at, and the place where he's at is him. Peel one layer off him and you'll get to the place where he is. Use the crumbling world around us."

Now she has a white woolen hat on her head and black leather gloves on her hands. The vehicle fills with vapor that smells like bleach, but we drive on to the end of the path. There's a baby's crib in the middle of the path. She stops the car a second before we hit it and turns towards me.

"Let me explain. You need to—"

The phone on the bedside table rings.

"One sec, Nathan. I'll get back to you," she snaps, abruptly hanging up. No rest on a Saturday either. She has to record the dream before it fades.

She writes quickly, then calls him back.

"Sorry, I was having a dream about how to get to the Babysitter, and you woke me just as someone was about to give me a clue." She gets out of bed and pulls on a robe, the phone jammed between her ear and her shoulder.

"We don't need clues. He's come to us."

"What?" Daphne almost drops the phone.

"He walked into the Messubim station two hours ago."

"What?!"

261

"Yes. Showed up out of the blue. Just like that."

Daphne sits down on the bed and performs a reality check to make sure she isn't still dreaming. Wide awake. "And are they sure he's not an imposter?"

"He knows details that haven't been released."

"And are the babies okay? Is Lee okay? Have they been found?" She stands up again, finding it hard to stay in the same spot.

"I don't know. Investigations say they transferred him to the Salameh station and that he came in voluntarily and is being questioned as we speak. Nothing more."

"I can't believe it."

"I thought you'd be happy to hear he's in their hands before someone leaks it to the media."

The news certainly justifies waking her on a Saturday, but this is too weird. Something must be wrong. Her gut feeling tells her this is not a good turn. "Something doesn't feel right to me. Why would he give himself up? He's playing a game with us," she says, getting up again and pacing around the room as she speaks.

"Everything about this case is crazy."

"Do they need us? We'll have to examine him and his clothes to match DNA and collect fibers."

"Let's see what he has to say in his interrogation. Don't disappear."

"Bye."

"Bye."

66.

Chief Inspector Assulin is sitting in front of the strangest interrogation subject he's ever encountered. He speaks in whispers only, closes his eyes from time to time and stops responding, and seems, for the most part, to be enjoying the situation. He's seen his fair share of crazies, but the one across the table from him now tops them all.

"Let's start over; and let me advise you again to cooperate. What's your name?"

"You can use the nickname the police pinned on me – the Babysitter. Although I'd prefer a different one."

"Like?"

"God," he whispers, "the Creator." He closes his eyes and opens them a second or so later. "Have you sent the blood for testing?"

"Yes. We'll share the results with you in return for information. What's your name? Where are you holding the babies? Cooperate and we'll consider lessening the charges. It's in your hands."

"Yes," he responds, closing his eyes again. "It's in my hands. You'll be releasing me soon. I'll be out of here in a day or two or three with the results of the blood tests and no charges."

Assulin is a large man, 6 foot 3 inches high and weighs two hundred and twenty pounds. If he plunged his fist into the smug face in front of him, he would send him flying straight from the chair into the wall. Assulin does his best to control himself from executing this.

"What makes you think we're going to let you walk?"

"The babies. I'm not going to tell you where they are, and if you don't release me soon, their food will run out."

"Are you holding Lee Ben-Ami? Did you snatch her too? Is she with the babies now?"

"The Guardian is with the Four."

"Where are they?"

"Forging them would be detrimental."

"Forging what?"

"The tests. Let's say I need to give them blood because they're anemic and you've recorded the incorrect blood type. They could die. Do you know what happens when you administer an infusion with the wrong blood type? It's called AHTR. The body quickly destroys the blood cells it receives. A quick death for someone just a year old."

Assulin clenches his fist and then releases it, tries to remain calm. "I suggest you tell us where the babies and Lee Ben-Ami are being held and we can make do without the blood tests. We'll take care of them if necessary."

The Babysitter leans forward, stares into Assulin's eyes and speaks slowly, "Every person is said to die four times. The first time – when the physical body ceases to function and decomposes. The second time – when the name of that person is spoken by someone for the last time. The third time – when all the descendants of that person die too. And the fourth time – when that person's works disappear from the face of the earth. A building he built, a tree he planted. But I'm going to live forever."

"Listen up, whatever your name is." Assulin's patience is wearing thin. "We've been sitting here now for half an hour and we're getting nowhere. I've been asking you the same questions and you've been responding in riddles. I'm going to walk out of here soon and others will come in. And they won't use words to get information out of you. They have other methods. For your sake, I strongly advise you to start talking. We have been authorized by the interior minister to use all means at our disposal to get the location out of you, and we will get it."

"The interior minister," he responds, opening his eyes wider and leaning even closer towards Assulin, "will have one less grandchild if he leaves me here too long. Tell him that. Bring him here if you're afraid to tell him yourselves." He leans back and closes his eyes again.

"Why are you doing all of this?"

"I could spend the entire day explaining it to you, but you don't have the mental capacity to understand. Don't be offended. I'll wait for the others you promised would come, and I'm not going to answer any more of your questions. You're wasting my time and yours. Go catch some car thief or buy yourself a donut. I have no intention of talking to you."

67.

A big orange sun begins setting in the west. Couples in bathing suits are playing volleyball on four courts marked out in the sand. The *puck-puck-puck* sound of beach bats punctures the air as Rotem and Daphne run side by side along the water's edge.

"They called and told us to be on call tomorrow to collect samples from him."

"They didn't call you in today because they're still working on him. But they don't have anything. I have access to the summaries they upload to their systems. They'll probably try sodium pentathol, but it doesn't do any good on interrogation subjects like him. They've already sent a mail to the Shin Bet, to put them on call too."

"Subjects like him?"

"Psychos."

Daphne doesn't respond. He certainly is one, but of a type that no one has seen before.

"They'll keep pressing him harder and harder, I suppose," Rotem continues.

"He hasn't provided any information, and the blood samples are indeed from the babies."

"Yes, I saw the report, cross-referencing with the DNA you collected from the parents."

"He's hoarse and can't speak, and he told the detectives he and the babies have bronchitis. I don't know what that has to do with the blood tests he asked for. Nathan tells me they've beaten him and that he isn't talking yet. Just whispering."

The noise of the beach bats fades into the distance, replaced by the sound of their rapid breathing. It's already November, but the beach at dusk is full, and they move away from the crowds. Two lines of footprints trail in their wake.

"He's not who he appears to be."

"What do you mean?" Daphne asks. Rotem jumps ahead too fast sometimes.

"The hoarseness is intentional. He doesn't want his voice to be recognized."

"So it's not really bronchitis?"

"No."

Daphne runs with the idea. "So he's disguising his voice now because he doesn't have a wig on or anything else to conceal his identity? So he can disappear again if they release him?"

"Not if they release him. When they release him."

Daphne feels frustrated. "And you don't think they'll get it out of him?"

"No."

A couple of middle-aged joggers pass them from the other direction and Rotem waves a friendly hello. She waits for them to be further away before she continues.

"It's good that he doesn't want to reveal his voice. That means he comes into contact with other people. At a job perhaps, or some other framework. He's not a hermit in some hut in the desert. It plays into our hands. It's a constraint we have on him. An opening to expose him."

It doesn't make sense to Daphne. After all, the police are soon going to announce that they've arrested a suspect and his face will be plastered all over the news. She waits for an explanation, but Rotem's train of thought takes a different route. "He's not doing it for money," she continues. "The families aren't wealthy. He didn't bother to check that beforehand. He snatched random babies. The fact that one of them is the grandson of the interior minister is an unintentional bonus."

"A bonus? Why is it a bonus if he's not asking for money?"

"Pain and intellect. Pain for everyone involved in the case. The pain is also the police's frustration, which only intensifies if the grandson of a senior minister is one of the victims. It serves his purpose and feeds his need for pain. He's playing with them. He doesn't need the police for a blood test. He could have gone to a private clinic and received the results within an hour, but he deliberately chose to go to the police for the purpose of humiliating everyone working on the case, of making their lives a misery. Not only did you fail to catch him, but you're going to have to release him even after he turned himself in. Do you know what that's going to do the interior minister, to have to release the despicable criminal who's holding his grandson? The entire country will be up in arms over this."

"And why does he need to know their blood types?"

"I've no idea, but it's certainly not out of concern for their well-being. He's planning something."

The wind turns chillier as evening falls but running warms them. The sea is still calm. The sun is approaching the watery horizon, and a sailboat passes by in the foreground to create the perfect picture postcard image. But Daphne is oblivious to everything around her, trying to make sense of the last insights from Rotem.

"I need to talk to him," Rotem says.

"Why?"

"I think I'll be able to get more out of him than they'll get from the standard interrogation. He's not the kind of person who's going to break under physical pressure. He's waiting for it. Longing for it. The police are going to throw in the towel today, and they'll call in the Shin Bet, but their doctrines are tailored to terrorism and don't suit this case."

"Have you already asked to sit in on the questioning?"

"No one's going to approve that. I need to get to him myself. Will you help me?"

"Of course." Daphne doesn't hesitate for a second.

"I've already organized a police ID. I only need a uniform."

"I'll give you one. No problem. You can come in with me tomorrow."

"Excellent. Because we won't have much time before the minister issues an order to release him."

"You think so?"

"I'm one hundred percent certain."

"How so?"

"I once profiled the honorable minister. Don't ask me to explain why."

"So he'll break and order the release of the Babysitter because his grandson is one of the kidnapped babies?"

Rotem marks a zipper over her mouth with her fingers, smiles, turns her gaze forwards and keeps running next to Daphne without saying a word.

68.

The taste of blood on his lips reminds him of home. He licks his split lip and stretches as best as he can, which isn't very much with his hands tied to each other behind his back and to the chair too, to prevent him from falling off it when they beat him. He hopes they are soon going to up the level of violence against him. The first interrogator bored him, and he simply stopped answering his stupid questions. The second team was a little harder, with kicks, punches and even a headbutt, which has probably left him with a broken nose. Those who followed employed more painful means and he almost blacked out a few times, but they managed to keep him conscious. He thanked them for that, but only in his thoughts of course. It's important that he doesn't miss a single second of pain inflicted upon him.

But the two men who just walked in don't look like professional torturers. More like businessmen in suits.

"Hello," one of them says as he places a suitcase on the table. "I'm Dr. Sharoni, and my colleague here is Dr. Ben-David. We're going to give you a small shot soon, after which you'll tell us everything we want to know. There's no point in trying to resist. It would be a shame for you to tear a vein. Keep your arm steady."

They release his hands from behind his back and cuff them to the arms of the chair. He looks at the needle that pierces his arm and the clear liquid that is forced into his vein. The world soon turns foggy, gray, transparent and lit up all at once. Truth is singular, one and only. He'll answer each and every question. There's no need for him to resist. Resistance is worthless.

"Where are you holding the babies?"

His head is heavy now. Spinning. Their words are coming to him through blurred curtains of white lace.

"In the Temple."

"And where is the temple?"

"Under the ground. Like him. Under the ground. Like she wanted. Days under the earth. Like moles, the eyes grow accustomed to the dark. One person, one entity, two that are identical, two that are one. We killed the cats. The dogs. We cut them up. She read to us from the two Holy Scriptures every day. Morning. Evening. Night. She knew one of us would become the last Messiah. Only one would remain. Cain and Abel."

"What's your name?"

"Which is which? She said we would find out ourselves. He was exactly like me."

"Where are the babies?"

"When the dog died that night, I looked him in the eyes and knew. He knew too. Whoever falls asleep first will die. Only one can remain. He fell asleep before me. It's his fault. Afterwards, I buried him under the earth. I buried half of myself."

"Who did you bury under the earth?"

"She didn't say anything. But she branded me with a nail she had heated in the stove flame. With the mark. The seventh descendant in the Cain dynasty is Enosh, mortal man. We're all descendants of mortal man."

"Who marked you?"

"On the chair in the kitchen. I didn't move, didn't make a sound. No one asked. She didn't allow us to leave the house together. Everyone thought we were one. Two who are one. The one who will bring redemption. The one who will assemble the last Messiah."

"Where are the babies?"

"Under the ground."

"Did you bury them?"

"No. They are in the Temple."

"Where is the temple?"

"In the safest place in the world. Where nothing can disturb them or the Guardian. Behind many doors. Many walls. Deep under the earth."

"Where are the babies?"

"In the Temple."

"What is the temple?"

"Soon. Soon they'll go in and everything will begin."

"What will begin?"

"The Rebirth is about to begin. The next stage in the evolution of mankind. *For by Him all things were created, both in the heavens and on earth, visible and invisible, whether thrones or dominions or rulers or authorities – all things have been created through Him and for Him.*"

"Where's Lee Ben-Ami?"

"Under the ground."

"Where under the ground? In which city?"

"In a city of concrete."

"Where are Lee and the babies? At what address?"

"They're all in the Temple. *The Lord said to me, This gate shall be shut; it shall not be opened, and no one shall enter by it.*"

"Where's the temple?"

He leans forward suddenly and the pair of investigators lean in, too, in anticipation, but he simply whispers again: "Under the ground, like him, under the ground."

"Where under the ground?"

"They have beautiful bones. White. So beautiful."

"Did you see their bones?"

"Yes. I took pictures."

"Of the bones of the babies?"

"Yes. Of the Four. So beautiful. Four sides of a square. The four corners of the earth. Four spirits."

"Of Lee Ben-Ami too? Do you have pictures of her bones too?"

"Of one bone only. In her arm." He looks at his forearm and tries to lift it. He looks surprised that it doesn't respond.

"Did you kill the babies?"

272

"No. No. They're on their way to becoming something much greater than any one of us. They'll live forever. *But He, having offered one sacrifice for sins for all time, sat down at the right hand of God.* Nothing monumental occurs without suffering. That's what she used to say. She taught me. The more you suffer the more impervious you become; the longer the sacrificial blade hangs over your head the less sleep you get, the more you torture your body with whips and scorpions, so your greatness will emerge and develop. The greatest act requires the greatest suffering and sacrifice. Mine. Everyone's. She said that all the time. Even when the Angel of Death came to the hospice. Sprouting, growing, flowering, wilting, dying, rotting. You'll put an end to it one day. You. The creator of the last Messiah. Assembling the parts into a single whole. Cain."

His head slumps to his chest, as the interrogator slams his hand down on the table.

69.

"...the public's help in finding the man you see in these pictures. This is the man who abducted the four babies from hospital maternity wards in the center of the country more than a year ago. Anyone who may know anything that could be of assistance in locating him is requested to contact the Dan Region Police at 03-6104444, or the police emergency hotline centers, 100, throughout the country. Please note, even if you haven't seen this man today, but have encountered him in the past, it's vital for us to know where. The photographs you can see are recent and precise. This is the man who abducted the babies."

The police announcement continues to run across the bottom of the screen, but the news studio is engrossed in a discussion about how the police can have gotten their hands on recent photographs of the suspected kidnapper, how they can be so sure that he is indeed the man, and, if it is him, why they need the public's help to locate the missing babies and why there seems to be a gag order on his name.

"...and on a very different note, North Korea announced that yesterday it carried out—"

Lee mutes the TV and gets out of bed. They've caught him. They've finally caught him. That's why he disappeared two days ago. He was there every day recently. How did they get him?

She's agitated and begins pacing around the room to gather her thoughts, dodging the babies, who are crawling constantly around her, pulling themselves up on the furniture and exploring every corner of the room.

Why aren't the police here? Why are they asking for the public's help? Could they not get him to tell them the location? How could that be?

She goes to the sink to drink water. Her hand trembles as she lifts the glass to her lips. The implications of the news broadcast she's just seen aren't necessarily good.

What if they hold him there? What if he's told them he killed her and the babies? What if he doesn't lead them back here? She's already discovered that he can tolerate pain and remain silent. And lie. And invent crazy tales. And that he doesn't care if they die. A1 A2 A3 A4. They aren't even human beings to him.

She opens all the kitchen cabinets and checks the food supply. There is enough there for about two weeks.

The news frees her to keep looking for the mechanism that opens the door to the room while the lights are on. For the thousandth time perhaps, she runs her hands over the walls, pats the sides of the cupboards, tugs on the tap handles, presses down on the floor tiles. Despite the babies around her, Lee is entirely focused on her objective. If he managed to get out of the room, something must open the door from the inside.

70.

"Wow, it fits me perfectly," Rotem says, looking at her reflection in the mirror, turning to the right and then the left. "We really are the same size."

"You look good in uniform," Daphne says.

Rotem examines herself from all angles while Daphne outlines the plan: "If they happen to address you first, we're from the Forensics Unit at National Police Headquarters, and we've come to take DNA samples and prints from him so that we'll have ten high-quality prints in our database."

"Okay."

"And if they start asking too many questions, you'll realize just then that your wallet is missing and you'll leave to go look for it, and I'll take the samples and we'll think about what to do next. I hope they don't suspect you're not police. I just hope there's no one there who works closely with the Forensics Unit and knows all of us. This is such a small country, and with my luck…"

Rotem pulls herself away from the mirror and places her hands on Daphne's shoulders. She looks into her eyes with a reassuring smile. "Everything will be fine. I'll walk in slightly behind you, you'll flash your ID, I'll smile at the cops who are guarding him, and we'll both go in. Do you have any red lipstick? And perfume?"

Daphne takes a lipstick out of her drawer and hands it to Rotem, then grabs her perfume from her dresser, saying, "After I take the samples, we'll sit down and talk to him."

"Not together, sorry," Rotem says, taking the bottle of Forbidden Euphoria, spraying it on her wrist and smelling it. "I need to be alone with him. The presence of anyone else in the room will only hinder the process. Go back to the car with the excuse that you forgot to bring something from your forensics kit and give me as much time as you can alone with him. Sit in the car, go to the bathroom, do whatever you want and we'll drag things out for as long as possible, until the cops outside decide our time is up."

"But I—"

"Sorry, Daph. Only me. And don't worry, I will fill you in on every word." She pats her pants pocket. "I'll get it all on tape."

"I hope you do manage to get something out of him. According to what Nathan hears from Investigations, he's driving them crazy. The drugs were of no use. He spoke about them all being under the ground, and about their bones. The detectives there are pretty sure he's killed and buried them all. He also spoke about a twin brother he once had and who he killed as a child, or at least that's what it sounded like."

"A truth serum doesn't always get the truth out. It's like being really, really drunk, it lowers inhibitions, but it's not like you see in the movies. When you're in that state, you might confess to things you've dreamed about and seem real and lead the investigators down the wrong path." She straightens her collar and looks into the mirror with satisfaction.

After she parks, Daphne takes out her forensics kit from the trunk and they walk in together in silence.

At the front desk, Daphne says, "Hi. Where are you holding the Babysitter?" She flashes her police ID with confidence.

"What do you need him for?" The policewoman behind the desk looks at them indifferently.

Daphne raises her evidence-gathering kit to show the policewoman. "We've come to take DNA samples and prints from him. To make a positive identification and add it to the database."

"Take a left here, to the circular building. Second floor. They'll take you in to him."

They turn left and wait a minute for the elevator. When they get to the second floor, they make their way down the winding passageway until they reach the only room that's being guarded.

"Is the Babysitter here?"

"Good morning. Who are you two?"

Daphne explains the purpose of their visit once again, and Rotem flashes a red smile at the two policemen outside the door.

"Do you have any weapons on you?" They don't appear concerned about the risk of the Babysitter making a run for it; they're far more concerned that some cop will decide to part with a bullet or two for the sake of a dead Babysitter.

"No."

"Okay. Go in."

"Great. It'll take a little time because after I collect a sample of saliva, I have to make sure it isn't contaminated, and I want to collect two clean samples so that I don't have to go all the way back to National Headquarters only to have to come here again. Is that okay?"

The policeman nods. "Fucking psycho. Didn't say a word during his interrogation but screamed all night like a banshee without anyone near him. He's not going anywhere. Take your time."

They walk in and close the door behind them.

The smell of sweat, blood and urine slaps them in the face. The room is airtight, windowless, and he's sitting in the middle of the space, his hands and feet shackled to a metal chair fixed to the floor. His shirt is covered in blood stains, which also appear on the chair below him. His face looks similar to the blurry image they know so well, aside from a few new bruises and a swollen nose. Rotem assumes that under his clothes, in places that no press photographer lurking outside can capture, his condition is a lot worse.

> **Sit here on the chair**
> **I won't tell you again**
> **Sit here on the chair**
> **You'll be tied up here all night**
> **Until you learn**
> **Not to touch the food of others**

Dirty thief
You'll eat what you get
Only what's put on your plate
"Leave me alone!"
"Don't touch me!"
"Don't touch me!"

Rotem places a hand on Daphne's arm and plucks her out of the memory that had risen with such intensity. She takes a deep breath, then again, and again. Rotem, meanwhile, opens up the forensics kit on the table.

Daphne pulls herself together a few seconds later, takes what she needs from the kit and approaches him. "Hold out your hand." He complies, stretching his shackled hand out towards her as far as he can, and Daphne takes a full set of fingerprints from him.

"Open your mouth."

He does so, and she runs the long swab along the insides of his cheeks.

Daphne notices that he still has all his teeth. Their interrogation hadn't involved the use of maximum force. Fresh needle marks appear on his arms. They used sodium pentathol. The strong smell of urine suggests they haven't changed his clothes, but the floor is dry. They've wiped it down. No scruff marks on his wrists or ankles. He hadn't twitched or pulled on the shackles. He didn't resist. He accepted it.

Daphne remembers her lines. "I forgot the second kit in the car. I'll be right back."

She goes out and closes the door behind her.

Rotem continues to scan her eyes over the room. Apart from the table, there are three more chairs randomly positioned. Light, cream-colored walls that are easy to clean. Worn floor tiles. A bright white light. She returns her focus to him.

"Do you want something to drink?"

"Yes," he whispers.

She takes a bottle of mineral water out of her bag, twists off the cap and holds it up to his lips. He drinks.

She says, "You've changed your appearance."

She pulls up a chair and sits down in front of him, her legs crossed, and places the bottle on the floor next to her.

"Your appearance and your voice, so that no one will be able to identify you from the police tapes. Not your neighbors and not your work colleagues and not the pizza delivery driver. Do you wear a wig to go about your daily routine? A different nose? A different set of teeth? Stick on a beard? How did you cause yourself to lose your voice the first time? Did you drink something scalding hot? Is it also part of the pain and anguish that come before the redemption?"

For the first time in two days of interrogation, he responds.

"*And He will wipe away every tear from their eyes; and there will no longer be any death.*"

Rotem waits a few seconds before she replies: "*There will no longer be any mourning, or crying, or pain; the first things have passed away.* Revelation, Chapter 21, Verse 4."

His eyes widen in surprise.

"You're not police," he whispers.

"That's right."

"You're an imposter. I could shout for them to come get you out of here."

"Whisper, you mean," she reminds him. "They won't hear you. And you don't want to do that anyway. I'm keen on having a chat with you. Like you said, I'm not police; so if I'm not police, this isn't an interrogation. They think you've killed the babies and Lee Ben-Ami. I don't."

"Why do they think that?"

"You spoke about their bones and said they were all under the ground."

"When they drugged me?"

"Yes."

He flares his nostrils and breathes in deeply with his eyes closed, then opens his eyes again and responds.

"I haven't killed them."

"I know. They have a role to play. You have a role to play."

"Yes." He looks at her in amazement. "Everyone here is so stupid."

"We're pretty much in agreement about that."

"Do you know the age of the girl who was the youngest-ever victim of a kidnapping?"

"It was a boy. Elijah Evans. His mother, Debra, was ninth months pregnant when her ex-boyfriend murdered her and removed him from her womb. He was placed in the care of a woman who pretended to be pregnant so that everyone would think she gave birth to him."

"Is this a subject that interests you or did you read up about it in my honor?"

"I read up about it in your honor. I want to get a better understanding."

"What's your name?"

"Rotem." She runs the tip of her tongue along her upper lip and tastes the lipstick. She's not used to makeup. His eyes are fixed on her, studying her every movement.

"When a baby is created, Rotem, it's pure. It remains in a closed system for nine months, receiving nourishment and oxygen via the umbilical cord, shielded from all germs, viruses or bacteria. During the course of the birth, that shield is compromised. The bacterial load is formed already in the birth canal. The bacterial signature of each and every one of us that will accompany us all our life. If I could have left them in the womb for the rest of their lives, I would have done so, but it's biologically impossible."

"Why four?"

He doesn't respond.

She leans towards him and gently touches his wounded face. "They shouldn't have treated you like this." She can see him struggling not to peer down her blouse.

"Suffering is part of the process. Part of the construction. Part of the path to redemption."

"Pain and intellect."

"You've read my letter. How did you do so if you're not a cop?"

"The woman I came with is police. We're friends. She told me about you and I told her I have to get in to see you somehow. Not everyone gets a chance to speak with greatness. With someone who is going to bring profound change to this world."

"You asked her to leave so you could stay here with me alone."

"Yes."

He closes his eyes and inhales deeply from his nose, releasing the air from his mouth. He looks at the bottle on the floor and Rotem, who is tracking his every gesture, brings the bottle to his lips for another sip of water.

He swallows and continues, "Your friend. Your friend who froze when she saw me."

"Yes."

"It wasn't because of me."

"Is there anybody else here?"

"She was looking at my shackles and wet pants, it carried her elsewhere."

"Well observed."

"She was abused as a child. She was tied to a chair. She was beaten. Maybe more. My appearance, the smell of the blood and the urine, it carried her back. She drifted off. She wasn't here until you brought her out of it with a touch."

She merely looks at him without responding.

"You know what they did to her. Tell me about it before we continue."

Rotem nods. She's never asked Daphne for permission, but she's sure that for the sake of the investigation, Daphne would consent. "Her mother disappeared and her father abused her. She managed to run away from him and was placed in foster care. She was abused there too and ran away again."

"How did she manage to get away from her father?" he whispers, sounding almost lustful. "Was she successful the first time she tried? Did she save up money for bus fare and travel far away somewhere? Did she call welfare services? Did she stick a knife in his throat?"

"She smashed a bottle of arak in his face when he was drunk.

282

They worked on him in the ER for hours, stitching his face back together. She was twelve. She hasn't seen him since."

"She had the courage to make change. To violently alter the course of her life. *Between her feet he bowed, he fell; where he bowed, there he fell dead.* It continues to haunt her to this day."

"Yes. Her act freed her from a vortex that would have killed her. Judges, Chapter 5, Verse 27."

"You see things correctly. You understand. You're not like the others, Rotem. You're not a fool. I'd be happy to get to know you under different circumstances."

She notices that he's examining her from head to toe.

"You asked them to conduct blood tests. They'll have to comply before they release you. It's part of the pain."

"Of all of us – mine too," he whispers. "*For I consider that the sufferings of this present time are not worthy to be compared with the glory that is to be revealed to us.*"

"The Epistle of Paul to the Romans, Chapter 8, Verse 18. What is going to be revealed to us?"

"Everything in due course, Rotem, everything in due course. It's a process that started years ago and is now in full swing. It will take years still, but it will happen in the end."

"How is Lee? Is she okay?"

"The Guardian. The Guardian of the Four. She's in good health."

"Unlike Anat."

"Who's Anat?"

"The one you ran down and killed before Lee."

"An unfortunate incident. It almost delayed the start of the process. There were others before her."

"Who?"

"Others who didn't survive the blow or couldn't adapt to captivity. It took time to find the right Guardian. Three years. One needs patience. The creation of a perfect entity is no simple matter."

"The creation of one entity from the four?"

"Ezekiel, Chapter 10, Verse 21."

"*Each one had four faces and each one four wings, and beneath their wings was the form of human hands.*" Rotem's photographic memory doesn't let her down. "You had a twin brother."

"How interesting, Rotem. You are not police, yet you are sucking from their breasts. You try to shake me a little with a fragment of truth that I may have given those nice doctors who drugged me. All they have are fragments, else we would not be sitting here and the crude feet of policemen would be stomping around a place I would prefer to keep hidden. I am above this, Rotem. I am no match for them. Now back to our conversation, you asked about twins. Twins are the first level. Conjoined twins are the level beyond that. Just imagine the power of four brains in one body. One brain that is four. That's the pain. The joining of the Four, and the pain of those around them. That will produce the greatest effect of all. *You also became imitators of us and of the Lord, having received the word in much tribulation.*"

Hearing this, Rotem draws a deeper breath, trying to conceal the thoughts running through her mind as she digests the new information. She is well aware that he notices.

"The First Epistle of Paul to the Thessalonians, Chapter 1, Verse 6. You're about to—"

"Hope, Rotem, is a cruel thing. For as long as you hang on to the hope to live, you will do everything to keep life going. I'm assuming she'll eat them one after the other as long as she still hangs on to the hope that I'm going to open the door and walk in." His eyes are fixed on hers. He slowly runs his tongue over his lips and swallows. "All the cards are in my hands, Rotem, all of them. I'm sitting here with the police and they have no idea who I am or what I look or sound like when I'm on the outside. The Guardian is waiting for me. If I don't get back in time, her food will run out. She's probably already wondering where I've disappeared to and if I'm coming back at all, calculating how long the food I've left will last for her and the babies, debating whether or not to continue feeding them or to save the food for herself. Or perhaps the food I left has already run out? Perhaps the babies are starving by now? Just imagine. Closed off in a room with four babies screaming incessantly for food. How long can she hold out under such circumstances? Our conversation is going to end here, Rotem. I enjoyed talking to you. A refreshing change from the police. Farewell to you."

He closes his eyes.

Rotem sits there looking at him for a few more seconds, then stands and takes out her phone, sending a text message to Daphne.

Then she picks up the bottle and moves over to him. He keeps his eyes closed but cooperates when she holds the mouthpiece to his lips.

Daphne enters the room and waits in silence until the Babysitter has drunk the remaining water, and Rotem returns the bottle to her bag.

"We'll see each other again," she says to him. He doesn't move or open his eyes.

They turn towards the door, and before Daphne knocks to ask the guards to let them out, they hear him whisper: "When an artery is ruptured, pressure is applied. When someone suffers a head injury, pressure is applied. Sometimes, Rotem, in order to fix one thing, something else has to be sacrificed."

71.

For the first few minutes of the ride after they settle into the car, Rotem sits in the passenger seat with her eyes closed and moves her hands as if she's arranging the pieces of an imaginary puzzle. Daphne drives and doesn't disturb her until she's ready to talk.

"They're alive and he's going to do something terrible to them." Rotem speaks in a steady voice, but her eyes are fixed on the window as if she's still lost in thought. "After they release him, he's going to press ahead quickly with his plan. You didn't get samples from his clothing, did you?" she asks, turning to Daphne, "From his shoes? To try to ascertain something about where he's come from?"

"They didn't give us his clothes. Just the prints and the DNA."

"Yes. They thought he'd spell it all out for them during the interrogation, with no need for the lab," Rotem confirms. "Apparently, they were wrong."

"We can ask for them now."

"No, it's better to check him out without arousing his suspicions. If he thinks the police have a lead, he won't return to his hideout immediately after he's released. He'll take his time until he manages to get away and they lose him. He's far from stupid."

"How do we do it without examining his clothes?"

"By knocking the particles off him. He doesn't have a problem with beatings; on the contrary, he enjoys the suffering. The interrogators need to beat him but without injuring him. We don't want him bleeding again, and we want him to be able to go back to the babies. Dry blows with an open hand. They know how it's done. And we need a filter on the air conditioner's intake vent. It'll catch whatever flies off his clothing, and that's what you examine."

Daphne has never encountered the technique before. "I'll speak to Nathan, and we'll see what we can do."

"But carefully. Nathan can't know it comes from me."

"Okay, it'll come from him," Daphne responds, remembering the instructions.

"We don't have much time. His plan is in place. He's going to join them together, to form them into a single entity. That's why he abducted a doctor, to do it for him."

"Join the babies together? How? Why?" Daphne can't imagine such a process and she isn't certain she really wants to know.

"I don't know. I haven't figured it out yet."

"And what's with the tests he requested?"

"It's part of his plan, and they're going to have to give him the results without any games. If they lie to him, and don't stop him in time, he could kill the babies without meaning to do so. He doesn't want to kill them; he wants to transform them into something else. To connect them to one another; I don't have a clue how. But I believe him."

"Can I hear the recording?"

"Yes, just a heads-up though; we speak a little about you."

"About me?" Daphne is taken aback.

"Yes. He asked about you and I told him the truth. He would have known right away if I'd lied."

Rotem pairs her phone with the car's Bluetooth. Daphne hasn't heard his voice before, and a moment later it's echoing through her speakers. But it isn't his real voice. It's a conversation between Rotem and a hoarse person who says terrible things in a whisper. When the recording gets to the description of her escape from home, Daphne's eyes immediately well up with tears.

Rotem looks like she doesn't notice. She's listening to the conversation, too, focused, her eyes closed, searching for nuances she may have missed the first time. Daphne knows she's thinking perhaps, between the lines, he did let something slip that she missed in real time.

Daphne quickly wipes away the tears with the back of her hand and doesn't say a word.

72.

Nathan and Daphne are in the Forensics lab. Nathan takes the time to sort a pile of evidence bags and Daphne is feeding the DNA samples and fingerprints into the system.

"He's keeping them alive. Why would he want their blood tested if he's already killed them? It doesn't make sense."

"This case hasn't made sense, Daph, from the second we started working on it," Nathan replies.

"They're going to release him in a day or two. I can guarantee you, the interior minister isn't going to allow his grandson to starve to death. Investigations are going to let him walk and they'll put him under surveillance." She takes out the DNA samples and fingerprints from her forensics kit.

"Do you think he'll lead them to the babies? He seems far too sophisticated to do that." Nathan is sitting on the chair next to her, watching her scan the fingerprints into AFIS. "What's he like?"

"In what way?"

"What does he look like? How did he act? What did he say to you?"

"Didn't say a word. They say he screams at night but remains silent during questioning. Looks like your next-door neighbor. Listen to what I'm saying – he's working an angle and messing with everyone."

"I got a call earlier from someone from Investigations. Chief Inspector Assulin."

Daphne remains quiet, focusing intently on the work in front of her and hoping that Assulin didn't say anything about the two forensics investigators who'd turned up to collect samples.

"He wants us to run all the prints through our database, to see if they show up anywhere else, and through the biometric database too. By chance, perhaps, we may stumble over his details."

"We know he isn't in the biometric database from all the prints at the scenes."

"He asked us to check all the same. And the DNA too."

"Obviously."

"So you don't think he's murdered them? He's just playing with us all?"

"I mean he is playing with us all but not like that."

"Why?"

"Why would he kidnap them just to kill them all?"

"Why abduct someone to raise them?"

"Who knows how many girls he killed before Anat Aharon?"

"I think you're going a little too far now."

"I'm going to look into it. I have a hunch."

She can't tell him anything about the recording she heard in the car. There were more before Anat. More unsolved cases that can be solved now, but she has to find Lee first.

"They're alive. He's holding them somewhere. Perhaps there's more for us to work with and we're missing it. There must be some way of tracing where he came from." Daphne hopes Nathan will take the hint.

Nathan goes quiet for a while. "His clothes," he finally says.

"His clothes?"

"We didn't examine them at all. They might bear residue. He brought the blood, so he was with the babies. There's a possibility that he changed into different clothes a second before walking into Messubim station—"

"Should we take his clothes for examination?" Daphne interrupts. "I hadn't thought about that."

"Yes. No. Actually, no. If we do that, he'll figure out our

objective right away, and he won't lead us to the babies. We need to get it done without his knowledge."

"How are we going to collect particles from his clothes without going over them with adhesive tape?"

Nathan looks at her intently.

"Perhaps," Daphne suggests, "we can tell them to beat him until he blacks out and then we can do it."

"No. That could make him suspicious too, and I don't need too many fibers for the test. We need to get the particles off him. To shake him, that's for sure, and to somehow suck up the dust that comes off his clothes."

"Something that will filter the air in the room…"

"The intake vent! We'll place one of our filters in the air conditioner's intake vent. They can rough him up but not beat the crap out of him, and we'll collect the dust. We can remove the filter when he's out the room and examine it here."

"That's brilliant," Daphne enthuses. "I think it'll work. You're right."

"Let's go now. Bring some sterile gauze pads for the air-conditioning vent. I'll give Assulin a call."

Daphne goes over to the equipment cupboard and allows herself a secret smile. Rotem was spot on. She takes out a few rolls of strong adhesive tape and listens to Nathan issuing instructions on the phone.

"…you'll come up with some excuse, we only need a few minutes.

"No, leave his clothes on. Just as they are, yes.

"Exactly, like a carpet beater.

"No, we don't need saliva and blood.

"No feces either. It's fine.

"I'm sure you can arrange for those too, but there's no need. Thanks. Just blows that will give his clothes a good shaking.

"Yes, we're heading your way now. We'll be there in an hour and a half or so."

He turns to Daphne, who is already waiting for him with her mobile kit and a bag with the accessories he requested. "Should we go in two cars, or just mine and then come back here to examine the findings?"

"Of course we're coming back here. I want to be here for the examination. I'll leave my car."

"Let's get going."

73.

It's two in the morning, and Lee's entire body aches, but she finds something. Nothing of any use to her, but something new, nevertheless. Under the bed, on the underside of the iron frame, she discovers silicone residue. That's where he must have stuck the key with which he opened the handcuffs three days after being shackled to the bed.

She goes through every inch of the room all over again but still fails to locate any hidden switch to press or handle or hook to pull. She empties all the cupboards, arranges their contents on the floor and checks to see if they contain anything for the thousandth time. Nothing.

How did he get out of the room?

Lee can feel the despair creeping up from her stomach towards her throat and forming a lump that chokes her. Tears lurk behind her eyes. He's out there in police custody and she's locked in here with an ever-diminishing supply of food that will soon run out.

She stands up and leans back against the door, trying to scan the room from a different angle. Maybe her brain will pick up on something. She's exhausted and can barely keep her eyes open. The babies are sleeping soundly in their cribs. She begins playing with the light switch, trying to wake herself up, to refresh her thoughts.

On.

Off.

On.

Off.

The orange-red light that appears and disappears actually soothes her. Her eyelids close.

She's almost falling asleep standing up when she suddenly hears a buzzing sound. The door opens and she falls backwards onto the floor of the Images Room.

The blow startles her, and for a moment she thinks someone has attacked her. That he's back. She springs to her feet and looks around for him, but no. She's alone. After a few more seconds of confusion, she realizes what happened. The door opened on its own. No one opened it. No, she did. The light switch.

She leaves the door open and flicks the light switch on and off again, counting in her head. When she reaches ten, a soft buzzing sound comes from the doorframe.

Sophisticated, but so simple. That's how he got out. He had an escape route ready. He guessed she would cuff him to the bed, and that's exactly what she did. He got into her head. But she won't dwell on it. Now she has to figure out how to get out of there. How the other doors open.

The weariness is suddenly gone. Her eyes are no longer heavy, her body is filled with energy. She peeks into the cribs – they're all snug in their beds, breathing softly. She gulps down a glass of water over the sink and gets working.

From the Images Room to the X-ray Room. She feels along the underside of the metal surface and retrieves the key. He hasn't bothered to move it elsewhere. That's a good sign. The key in the hallway, hidden behind the light fixture, is still waiting there too. Now, she can continue the search that was interrupted eight months ago.

She's going to find a way out of here.

She walks down the hallway, humming Miri Mesika's 'November'.

74.

"Remember the definition of dust?" Nathan asks.

"The thin sediment of the universe that crumbles under the forces of nature. In the words of one of our professors at least." She tries to recall who said that to her recently. She could have sworn that someone discussed it with her. She does a reality check. She's awake.

"An interesting definition."

"Outside, for the most part, it's soil particles, volcanic eruptions and man-made pollution; in homes, it's mostly pollen, clothing fibers, skin particles and hair and paper fibers, in addition to the dust from outside that mixes with all of them. Plant pollen can tell us if someone works in an office, for example. And I can't believe you're still testing me after two years of working together."

"And I'll probably never stop." Nathan grins and reaches into the transparent evidence bag for the strip of gauze they'd planted in the intake vent. He then applies a strip of clear adhesive tape to the fabric, pressing it down firmly before carefully pulling it back and fixing it to a thin plate of glass.

He places the small glass plate on the tray of the electronic microscope. "Assulin had a word with me when we went out for a cigarette," he casually remarks.

"About what?" she responds, trying to sound nonchalant as she prepares another sample from the fabric.

"About your visit this morning to the Babysitter."

"Was he so impressed by my professionalism and well-mannered approach that he couldn't get me out of his head?"

"The thing that impressed him and that he couldn't get out his head was the appearance of the young woman who accompanied you and whose telephone number he asked for. When I avoided the subject, he thought I was brushing him off because I didn't want him messing with my female officers."

She thought she and Rotem managed to keep their work under the radar. Damn. She tries to figure out a way to control the new situation. Best treat this as a non-issue and hope Nathan won't take it too hard.

"Ah. That." She remains completely focused on the fabric, on which particles from the Babysitter's clothing are mixed up with everything else that had come off the interrogators and was flying around the room.

"I seem to recall a conversation we once had. You told me about some friend outside the police who you wanted to consult about the investigation, and if I'm not mistaken, I told you not to even consider it at all."

"Ahhh." Her eyes are still fixed on the screen of the electronic microscope.

"I have a feeling that this friend of yours was with you. Assulin told me you were there for quite some time. Collecting prints and taking cheek swabs takes two minutes."

Daphne lifts her head from the microscope and looks at Nathan. "Do you really want to know who was there with me?"

"No. It's better I don't know."

"Are you sure?" She keeps looking at him.

"I haven't made up my mind yet." His gaze is fixed on her, and she can't work out if he's angry or deep in thought. "You've had some very interesting insights lately, and I kind of guessed they weren't all yours."

"It's hard to tell if that's a compliment or an insult."

"A bit of both. You're an excellent investigator, but you're not a psychologist, and you did exactly the opposite of what I asked you to do." Okay, anger then.

"Okay, look. My friend received special permission to look into the case from the organization where she works. It wasn't my initiative. We just happen to be friends, and we just happen to be working on the same case, and she received instructions to look into it quietly, in parallel with us, and not to share her involvement with anyone but me. Yes, I know it sounds problematic, but that's the way it is. And as far as the Babysitter's concerned," she continues to speak rapidly so that Nathan can't respond, "his day-to-day appearance is different from the one he's presented to us. He showed up hoarse deliberately so as to conceal his true voice. He screamed during the night when he felt his voice returning. The babies and Lee are alive. Before Anat, he was responsible for the deaths of other young women over the past three years. He's about to do something terrible with the babies and needs to be stopped quickly. He quotes passages from the Bible and New Testament all the time. He sees himself as a prophet of sorts who's going to change the world. A lunatic through and through, but an intelligent one."

"And all of that you got from him this morning?"

"She got it from him alone. I waited outside."

"So you leave a civilian in a room with that psychopath and go wait outside?"

"She's not a civilian…"

"Forget it. I don't want to know. You should have told me about it earlier."

She doesn't respond. There's no point in telling him that she wouldn't have hidden it from him had he not objected to the idea in the first place.

"Okay," Nathan continues, "we need to bring Investigations up to speed. They're going to be a little put out by the fact that he chose to share this information with two forensic technicians of all people and not their own officers, but life's a bitch."

Daphne turns back to the microscope, relieved that she's put this issue behind her and can focus back on her work. "It's not an office. Not enough paper fibers or printer toner dust. I see clothing fibers, mostly his probably, maybe some from Lee and the babies, but they won't get us anywhere. Carpets or drapes perhaps. We'll have to check. Hair follicles – head and body. Skin cells. Mostly his probably. No talc or cosmetic powder – just basic bathroom facilities probably. No flour, spices, starch, so no kitchen. A small amount of saliva and blood particles, all his probably. What I do see a lot of are these gray particles. What are they?"

Nathan takes a look too. "They look like cement particles."

He carefully cuts off a piece of the fabric and places it in a particle analyzer.

"As for your friend, I don't care who gave her license to work in parallel with us; keep working with her. She seems to be able to do a better job than Investigations has done. But let's keep it to ourselves."

"Of course."

The analyzer spits out a strip of paper and Nathan reaches for it. "Chalk, sand, plaster. They're cement particles that have come off concrete. He's in a concrete structure."

"And judging by the quantity of the particles, he's there a lot. What is it? A bomb shelter? A basement? Some sort of public building? I'm ruling out a standard safe room because there wouldn't be enough space for him and his victims."

"Could be. I'll send a sample to the Standards Institute. They have a large number of samples from public institutions. Maybe we'll get lucky, though I'm not counting on it. We can't rule out a safe room."

"I'll pass on samples to Biology so they can check which germs are present. Maybe an interesting culture will jump out at us in three days' time."

"Do it."

"Okay." She cuts off another piece of fabric and seals it in an evidence bag.

"Daph."

"Yes?"

"Do you have a recording of her interrogation of him? Of their conversation?"

"No."

75.

Again he spends the night shackled to the same chair he's been sitting in for several days. But this morning is different.

Instead of an Interrogations officer, a policeman enters the room, carrying a black plastic bag.

"In here are fresh clothes and shoes and the results of the blood tests you asked for. I'll take you to shower in the locker room of the gym here in the building. Put your dirty clothes in the bag and take them with you. The results of the blood tests are in the pocket of the pants. Your wallet and keys are in there too."

The shackles around his wrists and ankles are removed and he rises slowly. His entire body aches from the beatings and prolonged sitting.

They're pure. They're strong enough. The big night is approaching. The sacred union. He won't look at the results now. Only when he gets to the Temple. Only after he loses them. He'll restrain himself for now. They're going to try to follow him, and he's going to vanish into thin air.

He takes the bag. "I'd be happy to meet with the minister of interior and tell him all about his grandson. About a week ago, I overheated his bottle of formula in the microwave and didn't notice that it was boiling. Do you know what happened to him when—"

The policeman's face twitches with anger. "Shut it. He won't meet with you. Maybe when you're behind bars, after they free everyone you've kidnapped."

"That's a shame," he says, still whispering. "We could have had an interesting chat."

He showers and puts on the fresh clothes, after which he's driven out of the building in a patrol car, lying on the back seat and covered with a blanket to avoid being seen, even by chance, by the swarm of press and photographers who've gathered.

When the car is a few hundred yards from the station, the policeman behind the wheel turns to look at him.

"Where do you want to go?"

"I'll get out here."

He steps out of the patrol car on the corner of Salameh and Sderot Yerushalayim Streets and starts walking.

Three teams of detectives are assigned to tail him in person. The tiny tracking devices sewn into the pants and shirt he's wearing already display his precise location on a screen in the Command Center. He's a red dot moving north.

He walks until he reaches a hostel on HaYarkon Street. He goes in, steps up to the reception desk and pays up front, in cash, for a room for two nights. He buys two bags of salty peanuts and a bottle of mineral water from the vending machine in the lobby, goes up to his room, polishes off the peanuts, drinks the water, lies down on the bed and falls asleep.

76.

Tonight, I'll remember my dream

Tonight, I'll lucid dream

Tonight, I'll have soothing and pleasant dreams

Tonight, I'll remember my dream

Tonight, I'll lucid dream

Tonight, I'll have soothing and pleasant dreams

Tonight, I'll remember my dream

Tonight, I'll lucid dream

Tonight, I'll have soothing and pleasant dreams

05:18

We're both young girls.

We're sitting on maroon-colored velvet chairs.

A thick, red velvet curtain with tassels painted in
a soft rosy hue by copped spotlights hides the stage.

There's a heavy smell of old things. I get the feeling that I've been in this theater before.

"The show's going to begin soon," my friend says. "I'm scared."

Her black hair is shiny. Her eyes are gleaming.

"I'll look after you," I say to her, offering her a snack from my bag. She smiles and takes it.

"Thanks." She nibbles on it like a little mouse. "How about staying here with me a little longer? We always see one another for such a short time." She rests her head on my shoulder.

The curtain opens to reveal a large wooden stage. My friend, Makoto, shrinks into her chair. "Want to go on a journey?"

"Yes."

"Are you sure?"

"Yes. Let's get going."

I pull back the sheet and get out of bed. The lights of the city at my feet flicker through the large glass windows that stretch from the floor to the ceiling.

I walk towards the window and open it. A gust of cold wind peppered with rain blows in and wets my white dress. White curtains on either side of me flutter in the wind. A small gray bird lands on the windowsill.

Reality check.

I'm dreaming.

I stretch out a bare foot and stand on the narrow windowsill that wraps around the entire building. I'm on the fortieth or fiftieth floor. So high. I almost stumble and manage at the last second to regain my balance.

I need to wake up.

The windowsill is slippery from the rain. A

loud clap of thunder sounds and a bright flash of lightning strikes the building opposite me. The air shakes and shudders and I lose my balance and fall.

The fall goes on endlessly. Fear paralyzes me.

I must wake up.

Lee Ben-Ami reaches her hand through one of the windows and stops my fall. I stand outside the window and look into her room. Four babies are playing on the rug by the bed. All at once, the Four raise their heads to look at me with empty eyes, and I realize they're dead.

I must wake up.

"Why didn't you come to rescue us?" Lee Ben-Ami yells and pushes me. I fail to grab hold of something and fall again. I look down at the sidewalk that's rushing up to meet me. Anat Aharon is lying there and looking up at me. A thin trail of blood runs down her cheek. The blood collects on her lips and colors them bright red, like lipstick. I smell hot candle wax. She reaches her hand out to me. "Come, join me, we'll die together."

I must wake up.

I can't wake up.

I slam down onto the sidewalk, on my stomach. My cheek is pressed to the ground. I'm facing Anat, who's lying next to me. She says, "She's surrounded by concrete. You've seen it. Go there quickly, before it's too late. Before he harms them irreparably. Before they suffer the same fate as me." Anat sits up and places a cold hand on my forehead. "You're running out of time."

Daphne wakes before the alarm goes off. She's already gotten into the habit of falling asleep and waking four and a half or six hours later. An internal wake-up call of sorts. Her dreams have become even more palpable and she recalls more and more details each time. She was lucid in that last dream and tried to control it but wasn't able to. Knowing that she was dreaming didn't alleviate her fears. The situation was as real as reality itself.

She wants to go to the bathroom, but her body won't respond. Suddenly, she has trouble breathing. There's pressure on her chest, her heart is pounding. Why can't she move? What's happening to her?

Soft whispers sound all around her, but as hard as she tries to listen, she can't make out the words. A figure runs across the room from the door straight to her bed. Her heart is like a jackhammer in her chest. He leans over her.

Her eyes refuse to open but she can still see the man above her. His head is hidden under a priest's hooded robe, and his eyes are mere dots of dull red light. Wait. Her brain is playing tricks on her. She's in sleep paralysis.

The man vanishes in an instant. Now a set of identical twins, bald, are leaning over her, looking at her, their faces ashen, their eyes browless and black. They start walking towards the door. The left hand of one and the right hand of the other drag over her body, heavy and cold, leaving black streaks of ink in their wake. They pass through the room's closed door. There's barking in the distance, and a chill invades the room. A white mist hangs in the air.

She tries to move her toes, and they slowly respond. The man with the hooded robe is back. He looks at her closely, then raises his head towards the door. She hears the sound of a rush of air and he moves with incredible speed and disappears through the closed door. Now she can move her feet, and she pulls herself up into a sitting position. The shadows, the whispers and the strange sensation coursing through her body disappear.

Daphne opens her eyes.

Fuck! What the hell? This dream frightened her more than her usual nightmare, and the sleep paralysis was unbearable. She's horrified. It's going to have to come to an end, she feels unstable.

She gets up to go to the bathroom and drinks a glass of cold water, her heart rate gradually returning to normal. Back in her room, she records the dream and falls asleep. When she wakes again at seven, she reads what she wrote, then gets dressed and drives to Cinema City to meet Rotem.

At the coffee shop she orders a bagel with smoked salmon and cream cheese and a Turkish coffee. She's halfway through her bagel when Rotem arrives.

"Sorry I'm late. I got stuck in a meeting that went on longer than expected." Rotem sits down in the chair opposite Daphne and gestures to the waitress.

Daphne doesn't wait a second. "Last night I had a scary dream and then I experienced sleep paralysis. It freaked me out."

Rotem takes Daphne's hand and holds it between her palms. She looks into her eyes, "I really think you need to put the lucid dreaming aside until we finish the investigation."

"I'll push it just a little bit longer. I have to try and get rid of that nightmare and I feel like I'm really close."

"Is the girl already trying to persuade you to remain in the dream?" Rotem still looks a bit worried.

"Hmmm, yes, she's been trying recently. I forgot to tell you."

Rotem takes her jacket off and gets settled at the table as she digests this, then asks, "What technique do you use to induce lucid dreaming – MILD or WILD?"

"Only MILD. Other techniques don't work for me."

The waitress comes over and Rotem orders. "Hi. I'd like a good strong Americano with some cold milk on the side. And do you have a cake with an obscene amount of sugar? Something truly decadent?"

Rotem turns her attention back to Daphne. "When she's with you in the dream, are you both children?"

"Yes. Why is that?"

"She's a reflection of you in the dream. An aspect of your personality. Think of it as a temporary multiplicity of personalities when you aren't in a conscious state of awareness. It shouldn't be of any concern to you, unless she manages to persuade you to remain in the dream and not wake up."

"And then I won't wake up? Ever again?"

"You will wake up, but you'll wake in the morning at an incorrect reference point in the waking world."

Daphne frowns. "And in simple language that us humans can understand, please?"

The waitress comes back to their table with Rotem's Americano and a huge slice of chocolate cake. Rotem puts a spoonful in her mouth. "Damn. This is good." Daphne takes a spoonful too and Rotem continues talking, "Let's say Makoto convinces you to remain in the dream. You travel all around the world, learn to fly, complete a film course at university, have sex with whoever you want, take a skydiving course, a scuba diving course, spend a month in Zanzibar, and you don't have to work in the dream. See what I'm getting at, right? There's a trick going on here. As the brain perceives it, dream time is the same as reality time. They've proved it scientifically with experiment subjects who experienced lucid dreaming and then—"

"Just a sec. They were able to communicate with someone who was dreaming?"

"Ah, yes, that's simple. When you dream, your entire body is paralyzed except—"

"Your eyes. Yes. Sleep paralysis." Daphne shudders.

"You get used to it," Rotem says, pausing for a moment for a sip of her Americano before continuing. "So the experiment subjects communicated with the researchers who were conducting the experiments by way of eye movements. They were asked to dream and, while they were dreaming, to look right and left and count the seconds, and they saw that a second in a dream is the same as a second in reality but that the time sequence is different. Sometimes, you seem to have dreamt the events of an entire day in the space of one hour of dream time. It happens to everyone all the time, but someone who plays around with dreaming like you, and lucid dreams, can prolong that, like recursion. A sixty-four-disc Tower of Hanoi. A picture within a picture. I screwed up once and spent a few months on a trip around the world in a dream that probably lasted an hour. It was fun, but when I woke up, I had to catch up on work material I could no longer remember because my brain hadn't dealt with it for months of dream time. Do you get the logic?"

Recursion. Where had she heard that word?

"Sort of." Daphne answers with a mouthful of cake.

"Makoto is you. And when you get to a point at which you try in a dream to persuade yourself to remain there, that's the time to take a step back."

Daphne leans back in her chair and sighs. "I still haven't been able to go lucidly into the nightmare that led me to start all of this. I know that if I'm able to do so just once, it'll never come back again. But it's not happening. I'm lucid in other dreams but not the nightmare."

"We're getting closer to the point at which I'll be able to help you with that. I'll arrange for you to pay us a visit on a day when the Alpha room is free. Meanwhile, the next time you dream of Makoto, ask her what her name is."

"But I know her name."

"True, but it will serve as a trigger for you to recognize in your dream that she is you. You'll be able to go on from there."

Daphne finishes her bagel and sips her coffee, wishing she could smoke. "I've had really weird dreams since starting with the lucid dreaming. Really, really weird."

"You've always had them, it's just that now you're aware of them. Use them to your benefit. You can learn a lot about yourself if you analyze them."

"What did you use it for?"

"What?"

"The lucid dreaming."

"Work-related things. There's a benefit to be had sometimes by approaching a problem from a different angle. Ah," Rotem continues, "and to practice my tennis. I spent hours playing in a dream to improve my playing in reality. An experiment of sorts I conducted on myself and it actually worked well. My serve improved."

They sit in silence for a moment as the noise of the coffee shop continues around them.

"I don't want to stop it," Daphne eventually says, "but I'm scared it's going to pull me in completely. I already find myself waiting all day for the moment when I can lie down and get back into that world."

"Talk to her, to the girl in your dream. Conduct a conversation with her that goes beyond a few sentences about going into a dream. And if she doesn't agree to talk, then stop your lucid dreaming. If you aren't able to set boundaries, it'll mess with your life."

"But how? How can I simply stop dreaming?"

"You can regress. As soon as you stop recording your dreams and scheduling times to wake up and memorizing dream signs and doing reality checks, things will go back to how they used to be."

"How's that possible?"

"The moment your brain realizes that it is no longer a priority for you, you'll keep dreaming a number of dreams every night and forgetting them the moment you wake up. Like you did your entire life until you started experimenting with lucid dreaming. The brain is a fascinating thing." She peers into her empty mug. "I need another coffee, or a shot of insulin. That cake killed me." She waves to the waitress and points at her mug.

The waitress signals back, and Rotem turns to Daphne. "Tell me, what's their blood type?"

"The babies'?"

"Yes."

"Three O positive and one A positive."

"Hmmm."

"What?"

"He spoke about the four becoming a single entity. If he plans to transfer blood from one to the other, he has one baby who isn't a match. He may choose not to use him."

"You mean return him to his family?"

"Or get rid of him. Remember, we aren't dealing here with someone who thinks like a normal person."

"Shit. But what could we—"

She's interrupted by her phone. She looks at the screen before taking the call and sees Nathan's name.

"Hi, Nathan.

"Yes, I'm with her.

"When?

"Where did they do that?

"Yes.

"I'll be there in the early afternoon. Around one.

"Bye."

Rotem is watching her intently as she speaks. "They released him," she guesses.

"Yes, this morning, just now. They've got him under surveillance, assuming he'll return to the babies."

"They're going to fail." Rotem scoops up the last remains of the chocolate cake with her teaspoon.

"Why are they going to fail? They're on him."

"They merely think they're on him. They have no idea what his next step will be."

77.

He undresses in front of the mirror on the door of the cheap closet at the hostel. His body is patterned all over with the marks of his interrogation. Cuts, abrasions and bruises from the beating in various colors. Purple and blue from the last twenty-four hours, yellow and brown from the days before.

Excellent. Everything is just as it should be.

He goes into the bathroom and stands under the stream of hot water in the shower for a good hour. And after tossing aside the white towel, covered now with pink stains, he dresses again in the clothes he received from the police.

He locks the door behind him and goes out into the street, choosing the first café he comes across to sit down and order breakfast even though it's already past noon. It's a bright winter's day, and the café has a nice view of the sea. The sun sparkles on the water and warms his eyes. He knows that for a good plan to come to fruition, you need to devote eighty percent of your time to the planning and twenty percent to the execution. He put everything in place before entering the police station with the blood tests, and now he must move ahead with the implementation.

When he's eaten breakfast, he returns to the hostel to collect the bag with his dirty clothes. He has no doubt that he's being followed. He doesn't even bother to check by whom as he walks to the station's parking lot. He weaves his way among the cars and stops behind a silver Kia Picanto. He retrieves a key and remote control from

310

inside the exhaust pipe. He gets into the car and drives out of the parking lot. In his rearview mirror, he spots two men shouting into their two-way radios. When he hits the road, he immediately puts his foot on the gas.

Above him, he can hear the faint chopping sound of a helicopter's blades. They clearly have no intention of allowing him to disappear on them. The Kia zips through traffic, moving eastward away from the coastline, until it turns into the Sarona Center parking garage.

His tires squeak around the corners underground. -1. -2. -3. He parks close to the elevator, scatters the clothes from the bag on the backseat and takes a blue jerrycan out of his trunk. He douses the backseat in gasoline and throws the empty jerrycan into the vehicle. From his pocket, he pulls out a box of matches that he took from the hostel, lights one, tosses it into the car and runs.

He races up the stairs to -1 and to a white Mazda, which also has a key waiting for him in the exhaust pipe. He reaches into the car for a bag of clothes and shoes, gets undressed and changes everything that he's wearing. After pulling the test results from the back pocket of the pants and tucking them into his new jacket pocket, he throws the pants onto the floor of the parking garage with the rest of the discarded clothes and gets behind the wheel.

He turns the car on and drives quickly towards the exit onto HaArba'a Street, taking note of the silver Renault that's stuck to his tail. Just before the barrier at the exit, he brakes, puts the Mazda in reverse, jams his foot down on the gas as hard as he can and slams into the Renault. He reaches into the glove compartment for a gas mask, puts it on and jumps out of the car, running back to the stairs.

The parking garage is already filled with black smoke, and people, coughing and panicking, pass him on the stairs on their way up. On -2, which is empty by now, he stops next to an old white Mitsubishi, takes the key from the exhaust pipe and gets into the driver's seat. Waiting for him in this glove compartment is a black curly wig, which he takes out and replaces with the gas mask. Looking in the rearview mirror, he fits the wig to his head and then starts the car and drives carefully towards the Kalman Magen Street exit.

The barrier is up. The parking garage guard and a group of police officers are directing the flow of cars and studying the faces of the emerging drivers. He slows, opens his window and addresses the policeman standing nearby.

"What's going on? Was there a terror attack?"

"No. Just a fire. Keep driving. Move on."

And move on he does.

He needs to disinfect himself before the sacred union. To remember to antisepticize the tubes and make sure the needles are sterile. Swimming pool chlorine. Iodine tablets. More bleach.

Things are progressing exactly as planned. He'll wait to read the results of the tests. He'll look at them in the white place, the clean place. Not now. Patience is something he has, though it's lacking in all the other fools around him. Patience and determination. Mrs. Maroz once asked him what he did for a living, and he saw the small, familiar, contemptuous smile that crept to her face when he told her that he was a maintenance man. An invisible man. A small cog in a machine. *And if He were to transform into vapor, would you not breathe in His flesh? And on that day, the Four will come to crush your skulls.*

78.

Scattered on the floor are small board books, colorful building blocks, a xylophone with a small stick, and a wooden rod stacked with plastic rings of various sizes. The Four are playing as Lee continues her search. She's already gone through the Images Room and its computer again, as well as all the equipment in the X-ray Room and the hallways, and she's tried to open the doors to the other rooms.

Temple
Food Store
Medical Equipment
Communications
Office
Generator
Pumps

The Laundry Room, like before, is the only one with an unlocked door. The washing machine and dryer are silent. The cupboards are neatly arranged as if waiting for inspection.

The key behind the wall lamp in the hallway affords her access again to the stairwell, and she ascends to the EXIT door. But it's locked. She isn't expecting anything different, but she tries, nonetheless. She goes down the stairs to the hallway of the floor below her. There, too, all the doors are locked except for one, at the end of the hallway, to a room marked *Emergency Equipment*. She goes in.

Cupboards cover three of the walls. She opens them all. Gas masks. Medical equipment. Flashlights. Batteries. Work tools. She rummages through the items, feeling between them, running her hands down their sides, searching for another key or switch, but she finds nothing. The equipment in these cupboards have also been meticulously arranged. In one, a sign reading *Fetuses* hangs over a metal shelf supporting rows of jars of yellowing formaldehyde solution.

The police haven't gotten to her yet, and that means he isn't talking, or he's been talking – and lying. Maybe he's told them that he killed her and the babies; and finding their graves is less urgent.

She has to get out of here. She can't despair.

She takes a break from her searching to check on the babies. As she's coming up the stairs, the click of a lock sounds from the door at the top of the upper staircase. She thinks momentarily about running to the door and calling out, but what if it's not the police at all, what if it's him? Or an accomplice he's sent in his place? A rescue team would have already called out to identify themselves, she would have heard sirens, a megaphone – something.

Her walk turns into a run. She flies up the stairs, along the hallway – hearing the door above open – through the X-ray Room and Images Room and into her room, taking care to shut the door as quietly as she can.

She flops to the floor beside the four babies and smiles at them, trying not to pant. It wouldn't escape his cameras and microphones. She hopes her face isn't flushed from the run and quickly holds her hands to her cheeks. Time to play some peekaboo.

She needs to wait patiently. At least she knows now how to get out of this room.

PART 6

DREAM ON

DECEMBER 2017

79.

Tonight, I'll remember my dream

Tonight, I'll lucid dream

Tonight, I'll have particularly interesting dreams

Tonight, I'll remember my dream

Tonight, I'll lucid dream

Tonight, I'll have particularly interesting dreams

Tonight, I'll remember my dream

Tonight, I'll lucid dream

Tonight, I'll have particularly interesting dreams

The building is eight stories high and we're sitting on the edge of the roof, looking down at the cars moving along the roads below, swinging our legs in the air and singing songs by Mashina. There's something

I've forgotten. Something important I'm supposed to do and I can't remember what it is.

My friend looks at me and smiles. "Want to go on a journey?" she asks.

"Just a moment. I need to remember something."

A flock of pink flamingos passes overhead. I look at my hands and they look strange. Translucent. I'm in a dream. What was I supposed to remember? Ah, I know.

"What's your name?"

"Mine?"

"Yes."

"It's not important."

She looks at me and smiles. She has a hair band on her head that changes color. Stripes that look like a beam of light refracted through a prism run along the hair band in a wavy motion. I suddenly think I know who she is.

"Your name is Makoto."

She laughs. "*Your* name is Makoto," she says.

I place my hands on her shoulders and look her in the eyes. "Tell me who you are."

She laughs loudly now, flashing her white teeth. "I'll kick you out of this dream. Don't be annoying. You are Makoto."

I remain silent and the penny drops all at once. I keep my eyes fixed on hers.

"Did I make up the past two months in my dream? Has everything happened only inside my head?"

"Yes."

"Did I dream up Anna? Is she not real?"

"It's all a dream."

"When I wake up, will she no longer exist?"

"It's all a dream."

"And Nathan?"

"A dream."

"And Rotem?"

"Rotem is real. You didn't make her up. You really did meet her a few years ago when you were in the army, but you haven't seen her recently."

"And my job with the police? And the abduction of the babies? All made up by my brain?"

"Yes."

"And you too?"

"Yes. I am you. Pleased to meet you. You can call me Daph." She touches her finger to the tip of my nose.

She laughs. I take my hands off her shoulders and turn away from her. The landscape has changed and we're sitting on the edge of the roof of a high-rise in Chicago or Montreal. The streets below us look like black stripes with silver dots moving along them, reflecting the sunlight in a display that looks like faraway sparkles. Transparent wings like those of a dragonfly appear on our backs. She flaps hers rapidly and takes to the air, reaching a hand out to me. I flap my wings too and we fly hand in hand.

I say, "I can't forgo them. They're a part of my life. My work at the police is a part of my life too. And so is this investigation. I have to find them. Lee. The babies."

"If you wake up, they'll disappear. Everything will end and you won't remember anything. The writing exercises, the dream signs, the reality checks – they're all part of this singular dream that you're dreaming. The moment you wake up, everything will be erased within minutes. Forever. You'll have no knowledge of dreaming about them at all. Lee is you. The babies are you. The Babysitter is you. The predator is you."

No. That's not possible.

"If you stay here with me, they'll still be here

with you. In your head. You won't forget them. You'll be able to call them and they'll keep coming back. You can go on with the life you've created for yourself. With the investigation you're handling. With your job at the police Forensics lab."

"But the dream will come to an end at some point."

We fly over a frozen sea. The light from the sun crashes onto the ice crystals, shattering into millions of fragments that bounce in a multitude of colors. Kaleidoscopes of bold purple-blue butterflies swirl around us.

"It doesn't have to end. The time dimension here is different. How many times have you been in a dream for an entire day only to wake up and discover you napped for just ten minutes? Time here works in another way. Like recursion. An image within an image forevermore. You can live here for an entire lifetime while your body goes through its last state of REM over a period of an hour and a half. As far as you're concerned, there's no need to wake up."

The ice below us is replaced by lakes surrounded by trees. We land on the shore of a lake and walk barefoot along the white sandy beach, our feet dipping in the chilly water.

I don't say a word.

She says, "And what do you think – that they won't cotton on to you?"

"About what?"

"About what you did to your foster family? Those who abused you. Those who tied you up. Starved you. Tortured you. Left marks on your body. About how you exacted revenge on them years later? How you took the law into your hands. Do you remember the smell of gasoline that wouldn't leave your hands even after you scrubbed them with a scouring pad and green Palmolive dish soap when you got back to the boarding school? The smell of the smoke. The hair on your forearms that was singed. The black smear of soot across your cheek. The clothes you got rid of in the blue trash bag with the yellow ties. The long, boiling hot shower afterwards, with the soot residue spinning at your feet into the drain."

"What? How do you know all of this?"

"I told you already. I am you. Pleased to meet you."

"I didn't do anything to them."

"It's only a matter of time before they get to you."

"You don't know that. You're lying."

"They'll work it out in the end. They'll get to you in your room and lead you out in handcuffs. That's what will happen."

"No."

I wonder if I should stay here. If I'm lucid, I can stay here with Anna and Nathan and Rotem and everyone else. I can catch the Babysitter. Free Lee Ben-Ami. The babies. Maybe it's a good idea. I don't know who I am outside my dream – who I know, where I live, what I like. Who will I be when I wake up? Could the police really discover what I did? Do I even work in the Forensics Unit outside my dreams?

"If you don't want to play with me, then we won't play." She turns her head to the side. The folded dragonfly wings on her back vibrate. We continue walking along the shore of the lake until, a few minutes later, she turns her face to me and I can see the tears in her eyes. She stops, taking my hands in hers. She looks me in the eyes. "I'm waking you up," she says.

I wake up in my big double bed, wrapped in soft sheets with a delicate, pleasant scent. I stretch, place my feet on the heated parquet floor and then get up and walk into the brightly lit living room. The panoramic glass wall looks out over a forest, and for a few moments I watch the sun rising above the golden-red treetops. I go to the kitchen and use the coffee machine on the island to make myself a cappuccino. The coffee tastes great. It was such a long dream and I'm already starting to forget parts of it. They're vanishing from my head like fall leaves blowing in the wind. Did I go to university? Have I studied something? Computers perhaps? Or chemistry? Not my style. I hear the chirping of birds outside. I had friends there. I think I dreamed about working for the police and that we were investigating something? We were investigating something. What was it? It's all gone. I know that the dream was interesting, but I can't remember what happened in it.

Never mind.

I go over to my favorite armchair, the one in front of the glass wall, and sink into it. I look out at the woods, at the flowing stream, at the pool, at the trees losing their leaves. I'm warm and snug. I drink my coffee and then get up and place the mug in the sink. Iris will wash it later.

The telephone on the island rings and I lift the receiver.

"Hey, babe."

"Hey there, sweetie."

"You asked me to wake you at eight. You're meeting your friends at the country club at nine, right?"

How could I have forgotten? That long dream has left me confused.

"Wow, thanks. Good that you remembered; we're doing an aerobics class. I'm meeting with a client later in the afternoon. When will you be back?"

"At around six."

"I'll be getting back around the same time."

"Great. We'll have dinner together. I'll order something for us."

"Bye, babe."

"Bye."

I replace the receiver and step into the studio for a moment. I have a quick look at the sketches laid out on the table. I don't have

321

too many changes to make. I'll have time to get them done after the aerobics class. I sink back into the armchair.

"What's wrong with that?" Another armchair appears to my left and a young girl is sitting there.

"Who are you? What are you doing here? How did you get here?"

She stands up and leans in closer until her forehead touches mine. It all comes back to me.

"What's wrong with this?"

"With what?"

"With what's around you. Isn't it better than a room in a rented apartment with an empty refrigerator and a roommate?"

"No."

I feel really strange. I'm someone else. I'm a different me. Why is everything moving? The world around me is swinging back and forth.

Back and forth.

Back and forth.

"Come on already, Daph, get up…"

Anna is sitting on her bed and shaking her gently, then less so, until Daphne opens her eyes. Anna's here, and she's completely real. A wave of joy washes over her. The world in which she lives genuinely exists. Genuinely? Dream and reality swirl together in her head, she's struggling to tell them apart. She does a reality check to make sure she's awake and then hugs Anna tightly.

"You haven't disappeared from my life."

Anna laughs in surprise and hugs her back. "You're losing it, Daph. You need to slow down with that dreaming thing. Take a break."

"I've missed you."

"Okay, okay," Anna says, squirming out of the embrace. "Come on, get up, we'll have some coffee."

"I'll just get dressed and I'll be there."

"And brush your hair," Anna shouts as she leaves the room.

Daphne laughs and checks her reflection in the mirror. Her hair really does look like she had a rough night. She gets out her notebook and quickly records the dream before she forgets it. She does another reality check, just to be on the safe side.

Anna and two cups of coffee are waiting for her in the kitchen. "What's that? Chocolate?"

"My parents just got back from a trip to Barcelona."

"Pass on my deepest love to them."

She breaks off a row from a slab of chocolate the size of a small shelf and bites into it.

"Wow, it's delicious!"

"They think I'm too skinny; they're trying to fatten me up. What did you dream about?"

Daphne swallows her mouthful of chocolate. "What?"

"Why did you hug me like that when you woke up?"

"Oh my God, it was so weird. I dreamt that everything in my real life is a dream and that my dream was reality. I was worried that you'd disappeared from my life."

Anna shoves the shelf of chocolate in her direction. "You're the one getting thin."

"Thanks."

"No, you're *too* thin. And pale. You haven't been doing anything lately, Daph, aside from working and dreaming. It's not good. You need to go out and walk around, to start running again on the beach. To eat like a normal human being."

"Hmmm."

"Don't hmmm me. And you need to have some fun. When was the last time you went out on a date, huh? You've turned into a nun."

"Don't worry. I'm fine – really."

Anna gives her a long look but decides to let it go. "And the Babysitter?"

Daphne feels a stab of regret at the reminder that Rotem's prediction had been proven right. "He's fine too. Really fine. Free and happy, and once again we have no idea where he is. We're waiting for an analysis of the concrete samples and germ cultures we collected from him."

"Concrete samples?"

"A shot in the dark. That's all that remains for us to do after the surveillance screw-up. The Standards Institute is sifting through its databases. Thousands of concrete samples and nothing computerized. It's like the Middle Ages over there. They need to go through sample by sample and compare them under a microscope until they find a match, if at all."

"I can't believe they let him go."

"As long as there's a chance that the babies are still alive, no one's going to risk holding him for very long. Certainly not when one of them is the grandson of—"

"Right." Anna gulps down the rest of her coffee and stands up. "He may have murdered them all and is now wandering around free and laughing at us all."

"No, we're sure he hasn't killed them. But if we don't get to them soon, bad things are going to happen."

"Do you know what he's going to do with them?"

Daphne looks her in the eye. "Yes. But I can't say. Sorry."

Anna nods. "I'm going to go take a shower."

"Did you turn on the water heater?"

"Yes."

"Don't turn it off."

80.

He opens the door and presses the light switch. A row of low-wattage bulbs come to life, and the Temple reveals itself in an orange-red glow. The hot tub's filter system is humming as it should, and he dips his hand into the water.

Warm.

Pleasant.

He shakes the water off his hand before reaching into his pocket for the paperwork. He unfolds the pages and reads.

A1 – O positive
A2 – A positive
A3 – O positive
A4 – O positive

Excellent. Three of the four are suitable for the procedure. He can move ahead.

"What if God, although willing to demonstrate His wrath and to make His power known, endured with much patience vessels of wrath prepared for destruction?"

If the investigator he met the day before yesterday were here, she'd respond: The Epistle of St. Paul to the Romans, Chapter 9, Verse 22. He'll look for her. And find her. Rotem. He'll bring her here. She's the only one who understands. But not now. In a few years' time. When they're at a different stage.

He leaves the Temple, locks the door behind him and makes his way through the X-ray Room to the Images Room, where he sits down at the computer. On the screen is a live stream from the video cameras in the Guardian's room. Two-twenty in the morning. Everyone's sleeping. She's under the blue woolen blanket he brought for her not long ago, naked. Her clothes are lying on the floor next to the bed. The Four are covered with blankets that they will soon no longer need.

He reaches into the desk drawer for several sheets of blank paper and starts jotting down ideas for essential sentences he wants to include in a new series of letters to be sent to the families. Maybe he'll attach a dirty diaper to the letters this time. That would be more authentic. More aromatic. More intimate. The parents would be able to hold onto something that entered the Four, passed through the mouth, esophagus, stomach, small intestine and colon, and exited the other end. A bacterial signature. A genetic signature. Best regards.

- Attached is a photograph of your son. I have to admit that I was a little careless once and he fell and suffered a slight blow to the head, but this picture is from before it happened.

- Just so you know, it's very important not to fill the bath with water that is too hot. Very important. I've made a note to myself so that it won't happen again. Hope I don't forget. Huh!

- Attached is a photograph of A3. Your son. Or maybe he isn't yours actually. Have a look at the letters I sent to the other families and try to guess who belongs to who. Put the four pictures on a table and you can play a game of sorts. Like a memory game. Or you can make cards with their names, their pictures and their blood types and play Guess Who? Good luck!

- I may need you to send me some money in a secure and anonymous fashion. Being a father of four isn't easy. I'll think about it and let you know soon. Or not so soon.

- A1 looks a little yellow today. I edited the photo with Photoshop so as not to worry you too much. He'll be back to his normal self after the infusion, like always.

He leans back and suppresses his laughter. The letters, at this stage of the infliction of pain, genuinely amuse him. He can already imagine the reactions of the parents, reactions he plans to capture like he did the time before, from afar, using a telephoto lens.

He removes his shoes and dims the light, then opens the door to the Guardian's room. Taking his phone with him, he slowly steps inside, carefully so as not to make a sound. He leans over and photographs the sleeping Guardian from up close without using the flash and then he takes pictures of the Four from various angles – faces, bodies, feet – before leaving the room again and quietly closing the door.

He immediately transfers the images to the computer and prints them all on an old black-and-white laser printer, one of the ones on which he'd printed the letters. He lays out the pictures of the babies and selects which of them he will send to the families. They came out blurry. Dark. Desperate.

He also cuts out four close-up shots of the Guardian, numbers them and fixes them to the wall alongside the matrix of X-ray images of the babies. He turns up the light and surveys the results, then he opens the Guardian's door again, without bothering to be quiet this time.

He sits down on the bed and watches her wake up from the movement and the light streaming in.

He says, "I've been busy with a few errands over the last few days."

* * *

327

She opens her eyes and lies still. He's here and the police aren't. He got away from them. Or they released him, which means they think that she and the babies are alive. They haven't lost hope. She can't allow herself to lose hope.

"I saw on the TV."

"Yes, I assumed you would." She notices that he's hoarse and feels a flicker of concern that he's ill. But that doesn't make sense. He wouldn't bring germs into the room.

"The video and pictures they aired won't do them any good," he continues. "I look like that here, and in their pictures too; but when I go out and walk around among all the fools on the street, I look completely different."

He looks at her as she sits up, and she moves as far away from him as possible, unnerved by his gaze.

"What's your first memory?" he asks.

"What?"

"Your first memory. From childhood. The one before which there's nothing."

She wonders what he really wants to know, and she can't remember him ever having asked her a personal question before, about her life before he ruined it. Despite herself, she desperately needs conversation. To talk to someone. Her solitude has become a physical ache. So she answers him.

"I'm three years old and I'm being driven to a new daycare for the first time. We get out of the car and my mother holds my hand and takes me into the daycare. It's a private home. The daycare was on the second floor, with a wooden staircase leading up to it on the outside of the house. And I try to climb the stairs, but because I can see the ground below through the spaces between the stairs, I'm scared, and a few steps up I freeze. I can't move, neither up nor down. I'm paralyzed. My mother notices that something's wrong and asks me what's happened, but I'm too scared to even speak."

He's looking at her with interest. "And did she pick you up and carry you to the top? Was she mad at you? Did she speak to you with pursed lips and order you, in a soft but restrained voice, to keep going? Did she make you feel that she was disappointed in you?"

"I don't remember. I only remember the stairs, and that my legs wouldn't listen to me, and the lump in my throat that wouldn't allow me to speak."

"After you went up to the daycare together, did she turn around and leave? Did she stay there with you for a short while? Did she exchange a quiet word with the teacher? How much time did she devote to you?"

His questions overwhelm her. "I don't remember."

"Our memories begin to form at around the age of three. In general, people don't remember anything from before then. Freud called it 'childhood amnesia' and associated it with sex. We know today that it's because prior to the age of three, the brain has yet to develop sufficiently to create an efficient storage mechanism. The structure of the neurons doesn't facilitate the creation and efficient preservation of memories that are more than mere sensations."

"What's your first memory?" she asks.

A boy is bouncing a basketball on the sidewalk. The ball hits the curb and rolls into the road. The boy runs after it without looking left and right. A white Subaru, plate number 364-518, hits him and throws him into the air, and he lands a few yards down the road. The boy tries to sit up, then vomits.

"I don't have childhood memories."

"At what age do your memories begin?"

He doesn't answer her question.

"They won't remember you," he says, pointing at the cribs.

Why's he saying they won't remember her? Is he taking her from here? Is he going to do something to her? To them? She notices his bruises and abrasions. They beat him. How did they get to him? Why did they release him? Why haven't they gotten here by now?

"Follow me." He stands. "We need to celebrate. Today's a big day."

She remains where she is, sitting down, wrapped in the blanket, and waits for him to leave the room. But he goes no further than the doorway. She gets up and dresses with her back to him, aware that he's stopped, sensing his eyes on her. When she's dressed, she follows him into the Images Room.

She notices the four new photographs on the wall but doesn't say a word.

They go out into the hallway, where he opens an unmarked door. As they go in, she takes in the stacks of khaki-colored mattresses along one wall and folded military camp beds along another. On a sheet of wood resting on iron legs stands a row of old black telephones.

In the middle of the room is a table. On it are four lit candles, glasses of wine, two white plates and serving bowls filled with food. Real food.

She begins salivating. She hasn't smelled cooked food in a very long time. Pasta in sauce. Grilled chicken. Fresh salad. *I don't care if you poison me* is the only thought that crosses her mind.

"Sit," he says, gesturing towards one of the two chairs at the table.

She sits down, fills her plate to the brim and begins eating. She feels like she's losing control, swallowing too quickly, barely chewing, but she doesn't care. She's too busy savoring the taste of food that didn't come out of a tin and isn't cold and flavorless. The food tastes of sanity.

He doesn't eat but merely sits across the table from her in silence, drinking wine and watching her.

After polishing off everything on her plate, she cuts herself a slice of cake with a plastic knife.

"What are we celebrating?" she asks.

"They're all the same blood type apart from one."

"Who?"

"The babies. The Four, who are now three. Thirty-two percent of the Israeli population has the blood type O positive, and thirty-four percent A positive, with the remaining thirty-four percent divided among the other types. So statistically, at least two should have been the same blood type and that would have required me to collect additional babies until I had three, which is the minimum. But that's not the case. I have three."

"What do you mean they're three now?"

"You won't have to care for four. One of them is of no use. We don't need A2 any longer."

"Yoavi?" She could feel the good taste of the food disappearing.

"The names you came up with are irrelevant to the process."

"But—"

He cuts her short as loudly as his hoarseness permits him to: "Three laborers are working on a railroad track. They've got their backs to an approaching train and don't realize it's about to kill them all. If you press a button, you'll divert the train to a different set of tracks where just a single laborer is standing. If you divert the train, he'll die. Would you do it?"

"Yes," she responds at once. "I'd save three at the cost of one."

"Three laborers are working on a railroad track. They've got their backs to an approaching train and don't realize it's about to kill them all. You're stopped in a car on the road in front of the lowered barrier. There's one car ahead of you, with only a driver inside. If you use your car to force him onto the tracks, he'll stop the train. The three workers will live, the driver in the car in front of you will die. Would you ram into him from behind and push him forward?"

She hesitates. He's crazy, but she knows she has to remain cooperative. She simply has to. She tries desperately to think what the right answer is.

"You haven't offered an immediate response to a question that from a logical perspective is identical to the previous one. You failed to respond because your brain has been influenced by years of social programming, due to which, although you know the answer you should give, it's still difficult for you to do so. The lives of three versus the life of one. The same calculation. The same result. Only in the second instance, you have to take action. To push a man to his death instead of pulling a handle or pressing a button."

She stares at him and he blankly stares back. "I'm not afraid to be active. I'm creating something different here. Something powerful that appears in the ancient scriptures, something that's never been done before, something great."

He closes his eyes and recites: "*For though the twins were not yet born and had not done anything good or bad, so that God's purpose according to His choice would stand, not because of works but because of Him who calls, it was said to her, 'The older will serve the younger.' Just as it is written, 'Jacob I loved, but Esau I hated.'*"

He stands up. "Follow me."

"What are you going to do with Yoavi?"

"Nothing. Just add the word 'superfluous' alongside the A2 on his forehead."

They leave the room and he locks the door. The crying of a baby sounds from a speaker in the ceiling as they walk back to her room. She goes in, he remains outside. "Sleep well. You're going to have to be focused soon."

81.

Daphne and Rotem meet outside the Tel Aviv Museum of Art and walk together to 2 Berkowitz Street, a single-story building that stands out from the concrete and glass buildings around it.

"That symbol looks familiar," Daphne says, pointing to the depiction of a square and set of compasses set into the wall of the building.

"The Freemasons. Nothing to do with us. There's an entrance here to one of our institutes, which is, of course, a civilian institute concerned with the science of aging, established for the purpose of encouraging and promoting studies to improve the quality of life of the Third Age."

"Of course."

They go up a short flight of stairs and Rotem waves hello in the direction of a camera lens above the door. A low buzz sounds a moment later and she pushes the door.

"Good morning, Rotem," the guard sitting inside says with a smile. "And who are you?" he asks Daphne.

Rotem answers for her. "Hi, Yoel, she's with me. I booked an Alpha room for three hours from nine. Is it free yet?"

"Yes, I'll take you there."

They follow him down a flight of worn-out stairs into a passageway with plaster crumbling from its walls and gray filing cabinets along both sides. Towards the end of the passageway, the guard pauses and looks up at what looks to Daphne like a smoke detector on the ceiling. Two cabinets against the wall next to them slide aside on rails to reveal an elevator door behind them. It opens and they follow the guard in.

Daphne feels the elevator go down, but there is no way of telling how many levels. It comes to a halt and they step out into a very different passageway. She takes in the shiny gray epoxy floor, bright white walls and the light scent of incense. A small computer screen alongside each door displays the room's booking schedule.

"Room eight. It's yours until twelve."

"Thanks, Yoel."

The guard heads back to the elevator and Rotem leans towards the small lens fixed to the door. The words *Welcome, Rotem Rolnik* appear on the screen and the door opens with a buzz.

The room is entirely black: walls, floor, ceiling. Two black single beds with black linen stand side by side with a black armchair between them. In front of the armchair is a black table with a computer screen, black too.

"Spooky," Daphne whispers.

"Effective," Rotem replies. "Sensory deprivation." She points to one of the beds. "Take off your shoes, strip down to a level at which you're comfortable and cover yourself. I'm turning the heat up."

Rotem sits down at the computer and the screen lights up. Her fingers race over the touchscreen. There's a soft hissing noise and warm air begins to flow into the room. While Daphne gets undressed and sits down on the bed, Rotem explains the process. "Soon you'll hear a low and resonant bass sound that will continue for as long as we are here. They're alpha waves. They'll help you fall into a trance. Don't worry. You'll get used to the sound in a minute and won't even notice it." Rotem's fingers continue to move across the screen and the bright white light is replaced by a dull orange glow, like a sunset. The bass sound resonates around them, as if emanating from all the walls at once.

Daphne gets under the black comforter and lies down on her back, her arms tight against the sides of her body and her eyes fixed on the ceiling. Rotem starts laughing. "Take it easy, Daph. You look like a condemned woman." Daphne forces a smile. Rotem reaches into the desk drawer for a wireless microphone and headphone set and puts it on. "Testing. Testing." Her voice echoes in the room. She turns towards Daphne. "Listen, I'll be right here next to you, in the other bed. The light in the room will fade almost completely soon, my voice will be a little *deeper* and my intonation a little *different*. That's intentional. It'll take about fifteen minutes to take you in, and we'll go from there." She touches the computer screen and it goes black. The lights in the room dim even further. Rotem removes her shoes and lies down on the adjacent bed.

"Ready?"

Daphne says, "You're going to look after me, right? You're sure nothing will happen to me?"

"I'm good at this."

"Okay."

Daphne closes her eyes.

> Breathe in slowly and deeply...
> And release the air slowly...
> And while you're doing it, relax...

Rotem's voice turns slow, deep and soothing, until it sounds as if it's flowing from the walls with the bass sound.

> Let all the tension in your body dissipate as you breathe in slowly again...
> And release the air...
> A deep breath in...
> And release...
> You're relaxing more and more...
> Deep breath in...
> And slowly, slowly releasing the air...
> When you breathe in, open your eyes...
> And when you release the air at the very end, close your eyes...
> In with your eyes open...
> Out with your eyes closed...

You'll notice that when you breathe in, your shoulders rise a little...

And when you release the air, at the very end of your exhale, they drop back down...

Perhaps you barely notice the way your shoulders rise and fall...

With your breathing...

And you know you shouldn't think about it...

You continue to relax...

Every breath makes you feel more and more relaxed...

Every breath helps your body to unwind more and more...

Every slight movement of your shoulders takes you deeper and deeper...

And makes you feel better and better...

Let it happen with each breath...

Allow your shoulders and upper body to unwind and relax...

You're more and more relaxed...

You continue to breathe in and out deeply...

In and out...

Allowing the pleasant sense of relaxation to wash through your body...

With every breath...

You feel so good...

Tranquil...

So at ease...

Warm and cozy...

You feel a wonderful sensation rising from your shoulders to your head...

Soothing you...

And you realize now that every time you take a breath, your eyes become heavy...

You feel so relaxed...

As you breathe in and out...

You feel wonderful…

Tranquil and relaxed…

Safe and protected…

Still breathing in and out…

So peaceful…

As you sink deeper and deeper…

As you breathe deeply in and out…

Allowing your eyes to become heavier and heavier with every breath…

In with your eyes open…

And out with your eyes closed…

And you can tell that your eyes are heavy…

So much so that you could simply fall asleep…

Close your eyes now.

Relax…

You're sinking deeper and deeper…

You're safe and protected…

The deeper you sink the better you feel…

And the better you feel the deeper you sink…

Let yourself go all the way down now…

Deeper than before…

Let everything go and relax…

And no matter how relaxed you become, you'll continue to hear *my voice*…

And you'll be able to respond to *my words*…

To ignore everything else…

Now, I'm going to count down from ten to one…

And when I get to one, you'll find yourself in a deep hypnotic state, a trance…

With every number I count out…

Ten…

Nine…

Eight…

Seven…

Six…

Five…

Four...
Three...
Two...
One...
You're in a deep hypnotic state now...
The feeling is peaceful...
You're focused only on my words...
You can move your body into a more comfortable position at any moment if you want to...
And of course, if you want to talk to me, you can do so easily...
Now I want you to focus carefully *on my words*...
Every time I snap my fingers and say *"Sleep"*, you'll go back to that wonderful feeling of a deep hypnotic state and feel at ease...
Every time I snap my fingers, it'll feel good to relax and fall even deeper into the trance...
You'll feel peaceful...
Safe and protected...
Now I'm going to count to five...
When I get to five, you'll wake up and open your eyes...
One...
Two...
Three...
Four...
Five...
Wake up and open your eyes
– Snap –

Rotem snaps her fingers

Sleep
Close your eyes now...
Go deep...

Rotem goes through several rounds of putting Daphne into a trance and bringing her out again, taking her deeper each time. Then she gets off the bed and moves to the armchair. She leans towards Daphne and studies her eye movements under her closed lids, then leans back again.

> Now you may notice a tickling sensation in your fingers…
> Or your toes…
> If this happens, you'll know it's the feeling of relaxation you experience when going under hypnosis…
> Let your body continue to relax…
> With each breath…
> Let go of all worries and fears…
> Relax more…
> It feels so good to let go and relax…
> You'll feel a few tickles in your body now…
> They're of no significance…
> Ignore them…

Rotem leans over Daphne and observes her calm face from up close. She makes sure there are no hand movements under the comforter and that the only movement is the rise and fall of her chest. She opens the desk drawer and takes out five wireless electrodes, carefully lifting the blanket and fixing them gently to Daphne's body. One on each hand, one on each temple, and one above her heart.

> Your body is so relaxed now…
> Your legs are relaxed…
> Your arms are relaxed…
> Even if you try to move them now, you won't be able to…
> Because you are so relaxed and tranquil…
> Safe and protected…
> Allow yourself to sink deeper and deeper…

With *every word* you hear…
Now focus *only on my voice*…
And ignore everything in the background…
Let my voice fill your head…
As you allow your brain to empty…
As you relax and focus *only on my words*…
Feeling so relaxed and allowing my voice to take you deeper and deeper…
Every time I snap my fingers, you'll return to the exact point at which you are now, peaceful and unwound, safe and protected…

Daphne's eyes are closed and her breathing is slow and calm.

"Now I want you to take yourself into the nightmare. I want you to be in the cabin before the man who kills you gets to it."

"The predator. I call him the predator," Daphne says. Her voice is calm and steady.

"Let's see how we can crack this thing. You're able by now to be lucid in your dreams. Look around you. Tell me what you see."

"I'm in the bed under the comforter."

"Where are you?"

"I'm in a secluded house in a forest. It's dark outside and there are no other houses nearby."

"How can you tell that you're inside the nightmare?"

"I can sense it." She gasps. "I'm scared. I don't feel well, I'm nauseous, I want it to end."

"Just a little longer," Rotem coaxes her gently. "What do you see around you? Peek out from under the comforter."

"It's a living room with an antique wooden floor. I'm in a big double bed. Candles are burning. White sheets, a white comforter. I can see three windows in the wall in front of me. I see him at one of them now! Enough! Enough! Get me out of here!" Daphne's breathing quickens.

"What else is there outside?"

"He's not at the window now. He's coming in! Get me out of here!"

"What more can you see through the windows?"

"There's always a mist outside and then his face appears suddenly at a window, or sometimes he passes by all three windows and looks inside through the last one before he starts banging on the door. He's approaching the door now. I can hear his footsteps."

"Have you managed to see his face?"

"Yes."

Her breathing turns shallow and urgent. Her body shakes.

"What does he look like? Who does he resemble?"

"I don't know. He's blurry. His face is distorted. It's like I'm looking at him through the bottom of a bottle. Like he has a layer of ice on his face. I remember a bad smell and yellow teeth. He doesn't look like anyone I know. I'm getting up."

"Just a moment. Do you always peek out from under the comforter?"

"Yes."

"Are you standing on the floor now? Any sensation?"

"Yes, I'm on the floor. It's cold. No! No! He's kicking the door. He's in! He's coming towards me!"

–Snap –

Sleep

The shaking stops at once. Daphne's breathing turns relaxed again.

"You're back in a deep trance. In a calm and pleasant place. You're safe and protected." Rotem wipes the sweat off Daphne's face with a small black towel. A red heart that's flashing rapidly on the computer screen turns yellow, then green a few seconds later.

"Okay, it repeats itself but not sufficiently. It could throw you off during reality checks."

"What do you mean?"

"How do you usually get out of bed? Not in the dream, in the waking world."

"Quickly. I'm a snappy riser."

"And in the nightmare?"

"It's slower in the nightmare."

341

"So it won't do any good in the meantime. You can't practice those reality tests because you aren't in bed or barefoot during the course of the day. Let's go on. I'm taking you back into the nightmare from the start. You can wander around the cabin. You're inside now. Get out of the bed."

"I'm inside."

"Can you open the windows in the living room? Or just one of them?"

"No, they don't open. Sometimes, I smash one of the windows with the clothing rod that I take from the closet in the other room. Sometimes, I kick one of them out and cut my leg, and sometimes he grabs me and breaks the window with my head before throwing me onto the bed and sitting on top of me."

"Okay. Let's go on. You get out of bed. What would happen if he were to get there soon?"

"He kicks the door and I know he's going to break it down with his heavy shoes. It's a wooden door and it isn't very strong. He always manages to open it."

"And what do you do in the meantime? What are you doing now?"

"Something different every time. Sometimes, I hide under the bed until he grabs my legs and pulls me out. Sometimes, I bury myself under the comforter and he throws it off me. Sometimes, I try to block the door with the bed but I'm never able to because it's too heavy and I can barely drag it a few inches. Sometimes, I break one of the windows and jump out and that's the worst because I think I've managed to escape and then he appears suddenly in front of me and takes me back to the house after he beats me. It always ends on the bed with him strangling me and then I wake up. He's here next to me now!" All at once, Daphne's voice breaks, and she shouts: "He's back inside again! How did that happen? I didn't hear him at all! He's taking me to the bed! No! No!"

– *Snap* –

Sleep

Daphne's body relaxes. Rotem studies the computer screen; the array of graphs settles down. Indicators that had turned red return to yellow and then to green. She waits, and Daphne's heart rate drops from one-seventy to one-thirty, to ninety-two, to seventy-six, to sixty-four.

"You're in the cabin again. You said you smash the window sometimes with a rod you get from the adjacent room. Where's the rod?"

"Yes, I always look around the room next door before I try to escape. It's part of the dream but different every time."

"So there are two rooms in the house?"

"Yes."

"Okay." She pauses for a moment before continuing: "Is there a door between the rooms? Because then you can practice doing reality checks in the real world every time you open a door. That could be good."

"No, there's no door. Just an opening. I'm stepping through it now."

"And what's in the next room?"

"A closet. I'm opening it now. It's empty. There's a clothing rod, but there aren't any shelves or drawers. There's always something written on the back of the closet, on the inside. In chalk. In blood. In coal. Engraved with a knife once. It's not consistent apart from the fact that it's terrifying. And the writing says: 'Tonight, you will die', or 'There's no escape', or 'I'm going to strangle you tonight', or something to that effect. Now it says, 'He's behind you.' No! No! Oh my God! Get me out of here! He's here in the room, get me out of here now! He's coming closer! He's touching me!"

– *Snap* –

Sleep

Rotem waits again for the indicators to stabilize and sips from a bottle of water she retrieves from her bag.

"You're inside again. You're standing in front of the closet in the

343

other room. Does the closet have doors? Do you open doors before you look to see what's written inside?"

"Yes. I'm opening them now."

"Are there always doors?"

"Yes."

"Excellent. We've found the way in."

"Oh my God! He's behind me again! He—"

– *Snap* –

Sleep

Rotem wipes Daphne's face and neck again, giving the indicators on the computer screen time to return to normal.

> Now I'm going to count to five…
> And when I get to five, you'll wake up, feeling alert and energized…
> You'll be able to remember everything that happened when you were in the trance…
> You'll remember how wonderful it felt to sink so deeply…
> You're safe and protected…
> One…
> You're moving slowly towards being awake…
> Two…
> More and more so…
> Three…
> Starting to become aware of your surroundings…
> Four…
> Almost awake…
> Five…
> Wake up and open your eyes…
> Move your hands…
> You feel so alert, fresh and ready to go, full of energy.

"I'm cold."

"I'll turn up the heat. Lie there for a little longer. Don't try to get up."

Rotem comes over to her. "I attached some sensors to you, and I'm removing them now." She leans over and removes them one by one, from her temples, her hands and her chest. It feels odd. Daphne hadn't felt her attach them.

Rotem returns the electrodes to the drawer and runs her hand over the computer screen, and the orange light grows gradually brighter. The low sound of the alpha waves stops abruptly, reminding them of its existence. It had become part of the room by then. Part of them.

"That was incredible," Daphne says.

"You were great." Rotem sits down next to her and caresses her head. "Sorry I threw you back in there again and again. I needed to figure out the key you use to enter that dream lucid."

"And did you?"

"Yes. Can you sit up?"

Daphne slowly pulls herself up into a sitting position, still wrapped in the comforter. Rotem hands her a bottle of water, and she drinks cautiously. Her hands are shaking even though the room is very hot. She takes two sips and hands the bottle back to Rotem. "That was very quick. Just a few minutes."

"Two and a half hours."

"What?"

Rotem smiles. "Don't worry. We still have another half an hour before they kick us out of here." She moves away from Daphne and lies down on the other bed. "You have a way of entering that dream lucid. The closet doors. This is what you need to do when you're awake: You need to open closet doors once every hour and follow that immediately with a reality check. At home, you can do it with the doors of your closet, whatever one most resembles the one in your dream. When you're at work, you can open cabinets in your office, in the lab, firehose cupboards in the hallways, whatever you find. At least once an hour. I think that will be the most effective."

"Okay."

"Unless you want to ask your roommate to strangle you every

hour and do a reality check at the same time. But I don't really advise that."

Daphne laughs. "Wow, Rotem, you're a genius. I'm going to get started right away." She looks around the black room. No cupboard. "Okay then, the moment I get out of here." She lies down in her bed again and covers herself with the comforter, only her head peeks out.

Rotem is still sitting on her bed facing Daphne. "When you become lucid in your nightmare, you must always remember that you're fighting against yourself and that you know yourself best. You also know better than anyone how to frighten yourself. He'll do terrible things to you, but you'll know you're dreaming. You're going to have to repeat to yourself in your head over and over again – it's a dream, it's a dream, it's a dream. He'll start killing you, and you'll be running on automatic – it's a dream, it's a dream, it's a dream. And then you'll see that you continue to live. That he can't really kill you. It'll suddenly become clear to you. And then you can steer the continuation of the scenario in any direction you please."

"I only need to get in once. I know it. I just hope it works now with the closet doors." Daphne feels relaxed now. The room no longer seems menacing, it actually feels like it cuddles her with safety. She could fall asleep if she wasn't talking. Suddenly, she feels so tired.

"It'll work," Rotem says, still carefully observing Daphne's reactions. "Have you learned any tricks to prevent yourself from waking up too soon in a lucid dream? So that the excitement doesn't wake you."

"Yes, it happened to me the first few times and then I went for the technique of spinning myself around in the dream, or shouting 'Focus', and it helped." She speaks softly and yawns.

"Try to remain calm. To explore the dream environment and attempt to map out what you see around you. To touch something to create a sensation that will keep you inside. If the dream starts to fade, then spinning yourself around is a good idea. A movement, a touch, a smell, talking to yourself in your head during the dream – one of them, or a combination. And don't forget to do a reality check afterwards to make sure it worked and you haven't woken up."

"And if it doesn't go well and I do want to wake up? I had such a terrible nightmare before we met the last time. I wanted to wake up from it but couldn't." Daphne yawns again and closes her eyes.

"To wake up quickly at will, you need to decide on a wake-up code for yourself. There are various options. Shouting 'Home', for example, or falling asleep in the dream, clapping your hands, halting your thoughts and simply staring into space, or focusing your attention on a marginal item until the dream dissipates. Check what works for you in a regular lucid dream and then apply it to the nightmare. And do a reality check the moment you wake up because it could be a false awakening, which is merely a continuation of the dream."

Daphne nods. She has a lot more to do, but first she needs to digest what just went on here. "Thank you, Rotem. I owe you big time," she says, half asleep.

"You don't owe me a thing, Daph. I want to beat this nightmare with you."

Daphne doesn't respond. Rotem reaches out to touch the computer screen and turns the alpha waves on again. "We have another thirty minutes; let's sleep a little at their expense," she says to herself and curls up under her comforter and drops off at once, into a deep and peaceful sleep, devoid of dreams.

82.

Something causes her to open her eyes.

It isn't his presence. She doesn't feel it now.

She knows he has visited her several times during the night. Entering in his socks, dimming the light in the Images Room so that she and the babies won't wake up.

He always thinks she's sleeping.

But sometimes she's awake when he comes in. She continues to breathe peacefully, but her heart races when she senses him leaning over her. Sometimes, he's close enough for her to feel his breath on her skin. He always watches, but he never touches her. And then he moves away from her and wanders around the room, stopping for several long minutes in front of the cribs to look at the babies, until finally she hears the soft click of the door. She waits, counts to fifty, makes sure he isn't still in the room, and only then does she open her eyes again in the dark. She always sleeps facing the wall so that the cameras won't catch her opening her eyes.

Again, she waits for him to leave, waits a little longer, then gets up to go over to the sink. She drinks straight from the tap, wipes her hand across her mouth and approaches the cribs. Everything appears fine. Omer is sleeping on his back, Rami on his side, Shai on his back. Yoavi is also lying on his back, his eyes open. He's looking at her but isn't moving.

His skin is blue.

The word *Superfluous* appears on his forehead in black marker.

Lee wakes up in a panic. She gets out of bed at once and turns on the light. The room is quiet, everyone is asleep, but the dream was so vivid. And so terrible. She goes over to the row of cribs. One of them is empty.

One of the babies isn't there.

She looks around; perhaps the baby woke up and fell out of his crib and didn't cry. Maybe he's crawling around somewhere.

It takes a few seconds for the realization to hit her. He came into the room and took him. He was here and took him while she was sleeping. Maybe she woke up just as he was leaving the room? She runs her hand over the bare crib mattress. It's still warm.

"Bring him back!!!" she yells towards the ceiling.

"Bring him back right now!"

"I know you can hear me, bring him back right now!"

Her yelling wakes the babies, and they burst into tears. She doesn't go to them but stands in the middle of the room, her hands clenched into fists at her sides. She looks at the closed door yelling: "Bring him back now! I swear to you, I won't look after any of them if you don't bring him back *righ-t n-ow*!"

Her screaming and the crying of the babies echoes through the room. "Bring him back! Bring him back now! Bring him back!"

The loudspeaker in the ceiling suddenly comes to life. "You're frightening the babies. Calm them down."

"Bring him back right now!" she yells towards the ceiling with all her might.

"He's a liability now, not an asset." His tone is as moderate and as cold as ever.

"I don't give a fuck! Bring him back now!"

"I have no need for him."

"Oh yes, you do!" She pauses for a moment to swallow, her throat already sore. "If you want the three to live for the purpose of your plan," she continues loudly but no longer yelling, "you'll bring him back here right now." She moves towards the kitchen cupboards. "Watch closely with your cameras because this is what's going to happen whenever you replenish the food supply if you don't bring Yoavi right away." She takes a container of baby formula out of the cupboard, opens it and turns it upside down, scattering the white powder on the floor. She tosses aside the empty metal container and reaches for another one, which she empties too, and then another.

"Stop that."

"Bring him back and I'll stop," she says, opening another container and dumping its contents. "There'll be no food left soon, and I'll do the same when you bring more."

She grabs a bottle of mineral water and empties it over the mound of powder on the floor. By then, the three babies are standing up in their cribs, crying helplessly in terror. She doesn't look at them. She can't allow herself to break. Her feet are wet with the gray mud that has formed on the floor when the door opens.

He stands in the doorway.

"That's enough."

"We'll all die," she snaps back, eyes on fire, "me, and the three who you want. I won't eat or drink and I won't feed them. Your insane plan will go to Hell. What were you on about earlier, huh? Train workers being run down and sacrificing one for the sake of three? If he doesn't come back here right now, you'll be sacrificing four for the sake of one. *Four*," she stresses, waving four fingers in his face. "Me and another three. We're not dealing with reason here. We're not dealing with logic. Bring him back immediately!"

"Okay. Enough." She notices that this is the first time she sees him angry and not his unemotional self. His face twitches with anger as he tries to say the words without shouting.

"Bring him here now."

"I'll get him. Stop destroying the food supply."

"You have a minute."

He turns and leaves. She waits, breathing heavily, counting the seconds.

He returns to the room with the baby in his arms.

"Take him. I don't have the patience now to deal with your rebellion. We'll get back to it when the time is right."

She quickly gathers Yoavi into her arms and he smiles at her, seemingly unmoved by the desperate crying that fills the room, oblivious to the fact that she just saved his life. She hugs him, her body shaking.

She lays him down in his crib and then turns her attention towards the others. She has no way of picking them all up at once, so she caresses, hugs and kisses each one in turn and begins singing one of the songs they love.

"And clean up all the mess you've made here." That's all he says before he leaves the room and slams the door behind him.

83.

He forces the thumb of his left hand towards his wrist. The skin stretches, and he bites the section between his thumb and forefinger until he can taste blood. He smells the marks his teeth leave in his skin, then wipes the blood on his upper lip. That fool in there could ruin everything. After all his work and preparation.

He paces back and forth in the Laundry Room while clothes swirl in the dryer. He opens the cupboard. The items are as neatly packed as ever, but he straightens them, nonetheless.

Fool. The next time she falls asleep, he'll go in with a hammer and smash it down on her head until she stops moving. She deserves it. Is this her way of thanking him for choosing her? For everything he's done for her? She will, after all, go down in history. In the next chapter of the Book of Gospels. He'll replace her. She's just like all the rest. Unable to comprehend. He'll replace her with someone capable of understanding what he's doing here.

Now after He had risen early on the first day of the week, He first appeared to Mary Magdalene, from whom He had cast out seven demons.

Let her keep the baby for now. He's going to kill her. He's definitely going to kill her. Soon. When her role is done, he'll kill her. Not with a hammer. He doesn't like the thought of having to clean the room afterwards. He'll simply leave her there after the

Three are moved to the Temple. Her and the useless one. And after they starve to death, he'll remove them in trash bags. They won't weigh much.

Insolent girl. She'd better clean up. She'd better clean that fucking floor in her room just like he always cleans up after others. You can't live in filth. Dirty girl.

84.

"A banana, for instance."

"A banana?"

"Yes, one before bed. The potassium and magnesium in a banana have a soothing effect on the muscles. The L-tryptophan amino acid in a banana turns into HTP-5 in the brain, and that HTP-5 in the brain then becomes serotonin and melatonin again."

"Which is great for sleeping." Daphne knows this all too well.

"And if you add a hot bath, with the water let's say at around one hundred and five degrees, an hour and a half before you go to bed, your body will be better prepared for sleep. Make sure your room isn't cold, and go to bed dressed, or in pajamas anyway."

"Yep. I've being doing that for a while. It really works."

"And don't eat a lot before going to sleep. If you tuck into a steak, you'll do nothing more than snore like a hog and screw up the entire process."

Daphne laughs. "Yeah right, I'm just the kind of person who would eat a steak before bed. That's me." She switches gears as her old Fiat struggles with the ascent to Jerusalem.

"Cheese is better." Rotem's voice sounds in the car speakers again.

"Really?"

"Half an ounce or so of cheese half an hour before bed. Try various kinds. Each one will draw you into different dreams."

"You're shitting me."

"Not at all. There've been very serious studies conducted into the effects different types of cheeses have on the contents of dreams, and apparently every different type of cheese releases chemicals that act on the brain in different ways. If you're looking for the strangest dreams, go for Stilton. I'll be at my base soon and will have to turn off my phone. Any progress with the nightmare?"

"No, it hasn't come back yet. But I'm opening doors and doing reality checks all day."

"Good, keep me posted. And when I get to the office, I'll check if the police or Shin Bet have made any progress on the Babysitter. I haven't had time to deal with the case over the past two days. Bye. Have to go." Rotem hangs up.

The pine forest winds up the road to Jerusalem alongside her, and Daphne opens the car window. The morning chill blows in, cooling her face. She inhales deeply through her nose, out through her mouth. Maybe Rotem will allow her to spend an entire night in the black room. Maybe there, under laboratory conditions, the nightmare will manifest and she'll be able to fight it. Not alone. If Rotem is there to watch over her.

The Babysitter's disappeared; no new findings have arrived from any of the scenes, so they spend most of their time in the Forensics lab analyzing the items and data they already have in a frustrating wait for something new to happen. She could take a day off. Maybe Nathan would agree.

A phone call interrupts her thoughts.

"When will you be here?" Nathan says.

"Approaching Motza. Waze says forty minutes."

"Are you driving twenty miles an hour?"

"Something like that. I'm in the forest, with the window down, romantic surroundings. If only I allowed myself to smoke in the car, the drive to the cabin would be perfect."

"Very nice." Nathan loses his patience. "Get a move on. There's a surprise here for you from the Babysitter."

"For real?"

"A drone."

"A drone?"

"Just came in from Investigations. I just hope it hasn't been touched by every possible detective in the Tel Aviv District."

"Did he send anything with it?" Please let it be another rubber foot, she prays to herself. Anything but the real thing.

"Nothing. Just the drone. Nothing attached to it."

"Why send us a drone?"

"He sent an email to Investigations, to Assulin directly. He said he needs three 17-ounce bags of O-positive blood and told them to meet him in Rabin Square at exactly four in the afternoon yesterday. His instructions were to send it with a tall man wearing a red baseball cap, in the center of the square. They deployed a sea of undercover cops so as not to lose him again after the handover, but he didn't show."

"Why the fuck would they wait a whole day before letting us know? Does it hurt them to let Forensics know this in real time?"

"You know Operations," Nathan answers. "They like keeping all the glory for themselves. They update us when they feel like it or when they need something from us."

"He must have seen they were waiting for him," Daphne responds.

"No, no. They were waiting there in the square and then a drone carrying a note written on a piece of cardboard landed next to the detective with the red cap. Let me read it to you: *Isn't it frustrating being so stupid? Attach the portions of blood to the hook on the underside of the drone. I've attached a bag of zip ties for your convenience. Don't try to keep up with the drone. You're liable to cause an accident or two and I'll simply give you the run-around through half the streets of Tel Aviv until I've had enough.*"

"Wow. So they took the drone?"

"Yes. They had no intention of giving him the blood anyway. After he was released, I shared your friend's insights with Assulin. To allay any suspicion, I presented them as our ideas. But I told him everything he said about his plans to do something to the babies, to perform some kind of medical procedure on them. So they decided they weren't going to give him anything in any event."

"Have they checked where the email was sent from?"

"Tel Aviv. Somewhere near HaYarkon Street. He stopped outside the Sheraton Hotel, connected to the hotel Wi-Fi and sent it from there."

"And he asked for just three portions of blood?"

"Yes."

The line goes quiet. Daphne considers the significance of the number.

"Who are the parents of the child with A positive?"

"Ruthie and Yonatan Heller. He's the one who was taken from Beilinson."

"I hope no one leaks it."

"Me too."

Silence again.

"I really can't believe all this went down yesterday and we're only hearing about it now," Daphne says.

"Good morning again, Daphne Dagan. You're Forensics. Not the head of the Special Investigations Team."

"Maybe we could have—"

"Okay, just get here as quick as you can," Nathan interjects before she can continue complaining, "I'm starting to go over the drone. Can you get me a pack on the way?"

"Marlboro Red?"

"Yes."

"No problem."

85.

He was initially planning to dismantle one of the baby chairs from the hot tub but decides in the end to leave it in place. It's more symmetrical, even if only three will be occupied. He tests the quality of the water, adds a touch of swimming pool chlorine and iodine and allows the mixture to swirl. He also thinks about removing one of the screens from the wall, deciding against it for the same reason. Symmetry and backup.

He feels wonderful.

He hasn't felt so alive in a long time. He's fulfilling his destiny. The bruises and abrasions he suffered during the interrogation no longer bother him, and the extra bags of blood for back-up that the police refused to send aren't a source of concern either. Even his rage towards the Guardian has subsided to a level at which the ways he plans to end her life appear in his thoughts only every now and then and sometimes even include less painful methods.

The time has come.

He goes to the Laundry Room, folds a pile of dry white towels and takes them upstairs to the X-ray Room. Waiting for him there is the stainless-steel trolley, and he places the stack of towels on its surface and wheels it into the Images Room, humming a merry tune to himself.

* * *

The door to the Guardian's room opens.

He says, "The usual drill."

Lee is sitting on the floor with the babies and watches him throw the handcuffs onto the bed. She stands up and cuffs herself to the iron frame and watches as he wheels in the trolley. Two of the babies crawl quickly behind her towards the bed. A third remains playing on the blanket, and the fourth approaches him, following his every move with interest.

He places the towels neatly in the cupboard, replaces the full trash bag with a new one and loads a bag of laundry onto the trolley. After pushing the trolley out the door, he returns to pick up the baby who is following him.

"What are you doing?"

"It's time."

He leaves the room.

"Time for what?" she shouts in his wake.

He doesn't respond.

Although she already knows that it's hopeless, Lee lifts her hand and tugs at the handcuffs, rattling them in frustration.

He returns a moment later and picks up Rami.

"Where are you taking them?"

"To the Temple."

She remembers the sign she saw in the hallway.

"What's the Temple?" she asks. "What's there? What are you going to do to them?"

But he's already gone.

She stands up, grabs the bed frame with both hands and tries to drag it towards the door. But it's impossible, the bed's fixed to the floor. The handcuffs cut into her wrist, dotting the floor with drops of blood.

He returns to collect Shai. He, too, appears relaxed and curious. They aren't afraid of him. On the contrary, his rare presence adds variety to their very limited world.

"What are you going to do with them?" She speaks firmly but doesn't yell so as not to frighten the babies.

"Join them together. And you're going to help me."

He slams the door, and she sits down on the bed again. Yoavi, who is playing on the floor at her feet, smiles and reaches out to her. She leans over and lifts him with her one free arm. "It'll be okay, sweetie," she whispers into his soft hair.

He makes his way to the Temple with Shai in his hands, reciting to himself:

Then she shall remain in the blood of her purification for thirty-three days; she shall not touch any consecrated thing, nor enter the sanctuary until the days of her purification are completed.

After entering the Temple, he undresses the baby and places him in a chair in the hot tub, alongside the two others. Their chairs are tilted at a comfortable angle, allowing their entire bodies apart from their heads to be immersed in the warm water. The lights are dim, soft classical music is coming through the speakers and colorful shapes flicker on the four television screens. He gathers up the babies' clothes and diapers into a trash bag and places it by the door, then undresses down to his white underpants.

Nor shall he go out of the sanctuary, nor profane the sanctuary of his God; for the consecration of the anointing oil of his God is on him: I am the Lord.

From the metal cabinet against the wall he retrieves a glass bottle filled with a yellowish liquid. He opens the cap and pours the liquid over his head. The oil drips down his body and he puts the bottle down and rubs it over his skin, his hands, face, neck, nape, chest, stomach, back, legs. He uses paper towels to wipe up the drops on the floor, before stuffing them, along with his clothes, into the trash bag. The Star of David and cross on his back glisten under the oil.

He goes back to the cabinet, retrieves two needles and sticks them into his hands. One in the center of his right hand, the other in his left. He pushes them through until their points emerge on the other side.

Pain.

He leaves the room and closes the door, the needles still embedded in his hands.

86.

We're both jumping from one sofa to another and laughing. It's night now and we're in a closed branch of IKEA and it's all ours. In the game we're playing, you're not allowed to touch the floor.

My friend leaps from a double bed and lands in a soft armchair and then we spring back and forth between two children's beds with colorful bedspreads, jump our way to a large sofa and sit down on it, gasping for breath.

The lights in the store dim gradually and the white fluorescent glow turns into shades of a sunset. There's a low resonant sound all around us. It reminds me of a place I've been to.

Safe and protected.

Makoto is sitting next to me. She turns to me.

"Want to go on a journey?"

"Yes!" I say.

We're in a dark place. The floor is soft like wet clay. It's warm, and the mud seeps between my bare toes. There's a pleasant smell of smoke. I can't see a thing.

"Are you here?" I call out.

"Yes." I recognize the voice of Lee Ben-Ami.

"Yes." Anat Aharon responds next.

"Let's try to get out."

There's a noise above us. A kind of rolling thunder that doesn't stop.

I stretch my arms out in front of me and feel my way through the darkness, walking slowly until I encounter a soft wall.

"I've found something!"

"Me too."

"Me too."

The three of us run our hands over the wall and look for something that will help us get out of there. I come across a handle and press down on it. A door opens and light streams in to reveal a large circular room. The wall around it is black and made of soft, thick fibers, and the floor is milky white. The sound of thunder outside is louder now with the door open. We leave the room and find ourselves standing in a warm pool of liquid.

The noise is very loud.

I look up to see a flame as high as a multi-story building. We're standing on a giant candle. We've emerged from its hollow wick into the pool of molten wax around it. The flame is burning high a few yards above our heads and the noise drowns out all the other sounds around us. We're hot but not too hot.

I watch Anat Aharon form a megaphone with her hands and yell: "This way!" I can barely hear her.

She starts walking towards the rim of the candle, and we follow.

We walk through the pool of wax for a few minutes before it gets shallower and we step out onto a firmer wax surface. We look up at the burning wick. Our legs are covered to above the knees in a layer of warm, white wax, and we stand there and peel it away.

We turn our backs to the flame and look out at the

landscape before us, beyond the rim of the candle. We're above the clouds. The sky is blue, and snowy mountain peaks rise up here and there among the clouds below us. The pillar of fire is at our backs.

Where do I begin?
A picture within
A picture within
A picture
Forever.

"Follow me." Anat Aharon spreads her arms and dives over the edge.

And we follow.

Daphne's phone rings. She reaches out and gropes her hand over the bedside table until she finds it.

"Hmmm."

"Are you awake?" Rotem asks.

"Apparently so." She twists her neck, turning her head to one side and then the other. "What's the time?"

"Seven-thirty."

"What day is it?"

"Saturday."

"Ah."

"Updates have come in."

"On a Saturday morning?" She yawns.

"Yes, listen up, it's interesting. Remember the printer you looked into? The one they told you was purchased originally for Home Front Command?"

"Initially for the Field Corps Command. And then given to Home Front Command." She rubs her eyes.

"So last night, one of the police's email accounts that I follow received a message with a report from the Standards Institute that says the concrete particles you sent them are very similar in composition to a concrete sample from a Home Front Command military bunker. I don't expect anyone from the police to be reading the report before tomorrow morning."

That's it, Daphne is wide awake now. "How close is the match?"

"Almost identical. But they take into account the aging of the concrete in the structure, so it's a match as far as they're concerned, and they've stopped examining additional samples."

"Well, that doesn't really help. Do you know how many Home Front Command bunkers there are? And bomb shelters? And concrete basements? Every army base from Mount Hermon down to Eilat has one. It'll take us a year just to get authorization to go into those places. I'll check with Nathan tomorrow morning to see what we can do. Maybe the interior minister can fast-track the permits."

"Or you could let me finish…" Rotem admonishes her.

"Okay, sorry, go on."

"I'm on with the lab that's testing the germ culture you sent them."

Daphne frowns. "On with the lab?"

"Let's just say connected to their computer network, and I can see they already have partial results that have yet to be sent to Investigations. They're probably waiting for the final report before they send anything."

"And...?"

"And there's just about every germ and bacterium that exists in the universe more or less. An eight-page PDF file with names such as staphylococcus, cndida albicans, streptococcus, stenotrophomonas maltophilia, MRSA, you name it. A catalog of every bacterium on Earth."

Daphne sits up. "He works in a hospital."

"Exactly."

Daphne stands up and start pacing the room. "In a hospital built with concrete that served the Home Front Command. The same contractor perhaps, the same construction company. I'll tell Nathan to have a word with Investigations, get them to go through the files of employees at every hospital in the country. HR departments should be able to check out all their male staff members, who was absent from work while he was in custody. We have a picture of him, we have DNA. That's great!"

"No."

"What? Why?" Daphne asks.

"There's no time. We need to act now. Get ready, I'm on my way. We'll start with Beilinson. We'll check in the order in which he took them from the four hospitals. My gut tells me he works at one of the hospitals. That's where he got the idea from."

"But you aren't going to find anyone there from Human Resources on a Saturday morning. There are fewer workers on weekends in general."

"We don't need them. Things are sometimes simpler than they appear."

"What do you mean?"

"At the entrance to each of the hospitals, at the guard station, you're going to flash your police ID and then we'll ask just one question."

"What question?"

"Where's the Home Front Command building?"

"You're messing with me." Daphne closes her room door, puts her phone on speaker and keeps talking while getting dressed.

"Every hospital is required to be prepared for an emergency situation. The Home Front Command and Medical Corps are jointly responsible. There are bunkers for treating large numbers of casualties, soldiers from the battlefront or from an aerial assault on the home front. These bunkers are stocked with medical equipment, generators, underground operating rooms, you know, all those optimistic things. Are you getting dressed?"

"Yes, yes." Daphne puts on her blue police shirt.

"Dress in uniform and get one ready for me too."

"Five minutes."

Rotem hangs up. Daphne runs to the bathroom and does a reality check in front of the mirror. She's awake. She quickly brushes her teeth and washes her face. Back in her room, she pins her metal name tag to her shirt and then prepares a uniform for Rotem.

87.

Lee's wrist is bleeding, but she can't bring herself to stop trying, in vain, to pull her hand through the hoop of the handcuff. She already knows how to get out of the room, but that's no good to her with her wrist shackled to the bed. A fox, she thinks, would have already chewed its leg off.

She puts Yoavi on the floor and he begins to play with his tower of rings, smiling at her and babbling away. They've all learned to say "Lee", or so she thinks. "Dada", they could already say, without it meaning anything.

She knows he'll want to eat soon. What's she going to do?

Her thoughts are interrupted when the door to the room opens, revealing him standing there in just his underwear, anointed from head to toe in oil. She gasps. That's it. He's lost his mind completely. How's she going to save herself? The babies?

"To maintain pure intellect, you need to turn off the body's sensations. Arms and legs fixed together. Filtered feces. Water at body temperature. Chlorine and iodine in the water to prevent infection. Antibiotics into the bloodstream. From one to the other. Artery to artery. Vein to vein. A closed circuit, like with conjoined twins. One body with three brains. One heart composed of three hearts. Artery to artery. Vein to vein. Like hooking up a battery. Pure intellect. A superior entity. Three who are one. Combined heartbeats for a common bloodstream will also cause brains to vibrate at the same frequency. Brains that will never see the light of day but will create and build an entire world."

She waits for him to finish his speech. She knows she must continue to cooperate with him.

She makes every effort not to scream and to speak calmly as she says, "It doesn't make sense. You'll kill them."

"I won't kill them. And you know that too. They have the same blood type. I'll give them antibiotics to prevent infection. The water will be sterilized regularly. The power of three brains joined to one another. You don't understand. You couldn't understand. It came to her in the revelation, and she told me that morning, when she branded me with the sign. The mark. She told me word for word. Maintenance man. Carpenter. Messiah. She saw it when we were still in her womb. Before we were born. Before the sign. She saw them lying in the water, joined to one another for thirteen years. God's voice told her. God himself. Thirteen years and then it will occur."

"What will occur?"

"Let them be as a snail which melts away as it goes along, like the miscarriages of a woman which never see the sun."

She looks at him and tries to diagnose his condition. He's crazy, that's for sure, but she wonders if he is experiencing a full psychotic episode now. He spreads his hands wide and she notices the needles through his hands.

"I need you to connect them. Your time has come. The Guardian. The time has come for you to fulfill your purpose." His voice is the same as always, cold and impassive.

She says, "Okay, I'll do it. You need to know how to get into a vein, particularly when dealing with such small ones. If you try it yourself, you'll hurt them."

He approaches her and opens the handcuffs. The sight of her bleeding wrist makes him smile.

"The agony of redemption, Guardian, the agony of redemption."

As he turns towards the door, she launches herself at him.

He took the improvised knife from her a long time ago, and the cameras haven't allowed her to make another one. But concealed in

367

the waistband of her pants is a lid from a tin can. It, too, is a sharp piece of metal that can slash. It, too, is a weapon.

She leaps at him, aiming for his neck. He raises his arm to protect himself, but the piece of metal pierces his flesh with all the strength and rage she can muster.

88.

"There aren't any bunkers at Mayanei Hayeshua."

Sammy turns a key in the lock at the center of the door and then a different key in another lock below.

"There are two more big ones near here. One in Ichilov, which is relatively new, and one at Tel HaShomer, and the rest are scattered all over the country."

1 – 9 – 6 – 8

He taps the numbers into the keypad and the door opens with a buzz.

Daphne says, "And this is manned here 24/7?"

"Negative. Eight to five, including weekends. I get here in the morning, check all the systems to ensure everything's in working order. Check expiry dates on the kits, turn on a generator, dust. And the rest of the time, which is practically all the time, I read books, play on the computer and sleep. There's a communications test at ten in the morning and that's it, no one bothers me for the rest of the day. A dream job. I live really close by too," he winks. "Come on, I'll give you a guided tour."

"Are you the only one with the dream job, or do others have it too?" Daphne asks as they're going down the stairs.

"Just me."

Daphne sees Rotem run her hand over the butt of the pistol that's on her right hip.

"And what if you're ill?" Daphne keeps questioning him as

the three of them ascend the long staircase. Sammy leads the way, Daphne next to him and Rotem a few steps back, her eyes focused on Sammy for any suspicious movement.

"They'll send someone from Command if it's for more than a few days. It's just an emergency bunker, not a Combat Ops Room."

"And you're a career soldier?"

"A civilian employee of the military. Up until a few years ago, they used soldiers, but the IDF started outsourcing. Like they did with all the army mess halls. Little by little, everything that doesn't explode or get fired from a weapon has been shifted out for civilians to deal with."

"So you're here seven days a week?"

"Every other Saturday, then the Command sends soldiers to do the weekend I'm off."

They walk down an underground hallway with incandescent lights on the walls, passing one closed door after the other.

"Where's the logic in being here from eight to five?" Daphne wonders out loud. "What if war breaks out in the middle of the night?"

Sammy flips a switch and another dark corridor lights up on their right. "First of all, we're talking about the army, so don't expect too much logic. But I think they figure that between the time the war begins and the time the injured and the black body bags start pouring in, I'll have enough time to get here. To set all the emergency systems into motion takes two hours at the most, and I know the procedures by heart."

Daphne looks around while they keep walking, her gaze crosses to Rotem who replies with a nod. "Are there any other levels here?"

"A machine-room level below us."

"Okay," Rotem interjects, "let's do a quick check through all the rooms."

"All of them?"

"Yes." Rotem sounds adamant.

"There are a lot of them."

"So quickly then." Rotem smiles.

He consents and begins opening the doors one by one and turning on the lights. Laundry room. Emergency equipment room. X-ray room. Underground ER. Wards for patients. A morgue.

"What are the showers here for?" Daphne points at a row of shower heads in one of the rooms they visit.

"In the event of a chemical warfare attack."

"Why like that, without curtains?" The row of exposed showers sparks unpleasant memories in Daphne.

"Believe me, if you've been hit by phosphorus or mustard gas, the last thing you're going to care about is privacy."

They go down to the lower level and the guard opens all the doors there too.

"This isn't the place," Rotem says as they leave the last room.

"True," Daphne agrees. The place is prepared for war, but nothing out of the ordinary seems to be happening there.

"Tell me, Sammy," Rotem asks on their way back up, "you said you do a communications check at ten, right?" Now she walks next to him, her hand no longer ready to draw her gun, and Daphne climbs a few steps behind.

"Affirmative. In an hour or so."

"And when you do the test, can everyone hear everyone else?"

"Affirmative. The duty officer goes through all of us one by one and everyone responds in turn, from Rebecca Sieff Hospital in Safed, down to Yoseftal in Eilat. It takes two minutes."

"Have you been here for the past two weeks?"

"Affirmative."

"And when you did the communications checks during that time, was there anyone who didn't respond? Someone who was missing?" Rotem fires questions one after the other.

He stops to think, frowning.

"Affirmative. Perry. Poor guy. Came down with bronchitis. He was at home for three days and he's still hoarse now."

Rotem turns towards Daphne and their eyes meet. "Where is he?" they ask in unison.

"Probably at home now."

"No," Daphne almost shouts. "Where does he work? Which facility?"

"Tel HaShomer."

"Thanks."

They race up the remaining stairs towards the exit, but when Daphne opens the door, Rotem turns around and runs back towards Sammy, who is lagging behind them. "Listen," she pants, "when you do today's communications check, don't breathe a word about us being here or anything we discussed. And not on the phone in any conversation or to anyone either. Got that?"

"Affirmative."

"It's really, really important," Rotem reiterates.

"Not a word. I swear to you."

"And is the facility at Tel HaShomer identical to the one here?"

"Don't know. I've never been there."

They run to Rotem's car. As they leave the parking lot, she checks to make sure that Daphne is buckled before slamming her foot on the gas. "We'll be there in ten," she says.

Daphne does a quick reality check. "I'm letting Nathan know," she says.

"Cool."

She calls.

"Nathan, we know where he is."

Rotem is driving while Daphne provides Nathan with details about the emergency bunkers and daily communications checks as the car races through the empty Saturday morning roads, which are just beginning to fill with cars.

"No, I didn't see a weapon on him. And not in the facility either. Unarmed guard duty. Maintenance, in fact."

"No way! I'm not waiting for anyone. We'll be there soon. Five minutes."

"Yes, I'm with her."

"We're carrying."

"There's no way they can get there before us."

"No, Nathan, we don't have time to waste… Hello? Hello? I can't hear you, there's no reception here, you're breaking up."

She hangs up.

Rotem doesn't say a word but speeds through another intersection just as the yellow light turns red.

89.

He looks at the folded ring of metal that pierced his arm. Blood is dripping from it and sliding over the oil. *Not now*. He leaves it stuck in his flesh and shoves the Guardian with his other hand.

She's strong. She's dangerous. She could put an end to the plan. That's not an option.

He takes advantage of the second during which she loses her balance a little, runs for the door and slams it behind him. He'll do it alone. Traitor. She can die there in the room without food. Die for all he cares.

Back in the X-Ray Room, he goes over to the treatment table. With one tug, he pulls the piece of metal out of his arm and then he pours alcohol over the cut straight from the bottle. It burns. The agony of redemption. The pain rises and redemption approaches. The blood washes onto the floor. He places a strip of medical gauze on the wound and fixes it in place with a white bandage. When he's done, he slips his arm into an elastic bandage, which holds the dressing underneath in place.

He goes to the Temple and opens the door. The Three are splashing in the warm water and watching the screens around them inquisitively. They're warm, they're comfortable, they have no reason to complain. Resting on a tray are the required instruments, waiting for the Guardian but now ready for him. Everything's sterile. Pure. IV needles are attached to their polyethylene tubes, transparent and flexible. Bottles of baby formula are ready, mixed with a small amount of ibuprofen.

* * *

Ten
Nine
Eight
Seven
Six
Five
Four
Three
Two
One

A brief buzz and the door opens.

Lee holds back for a few seconds, making sure there's no response, and then she steps into the Images Room, gripping a tin of corn tightly in her hand. She stands still and listens. Apart from her own heartbeat, she can't hear a thing.

After he bolted from the room, she assumed he would keep an eye on her with the cameras, so she went about her business as usual. She prepared a bottle for Yoavi, placed a few baby biscuits on the blanket for him among the toys, and only then did she open the door. Now, she looks back. Yoavi is on the floor, drinking from his bottle. "I'll be right back," she mouths silently and closes the door.

The trail of blood on the floor leads her to the X-ray Room. It's empty. She goes out into the hallway and walks slowly. The noise of the dryer echoes through the open door to the Laundry Room. The door to the Temple is open. A pale orange light is visible through the opening, and she can make out soft classical music too. Lee's fingers tighten around the tin can. Walking on tiptoe, she approaches the doorway and peeks inside.

It's the first time she's seen the Temple. The screens on the walls, the hot tub. She can see the three babies inside. They're naked, strapped in, but they are not crying. She feels comforted by this momentarily.

He's standing with his back to her, but from the sounds she can hear she knows he's fiddling with medical equipment on stainless-steel trays. The cut on his arm is bandaged. The awful sign on his back terrifies her. She watches him wash his hands meticulously with alcohol-soaked cotton. One finger at a time. And then he puts the cotton aside and picks up an IV needle.

She has to act now. No, she'll wait for him to move closer to the hot tub, to bend over. He'll have to remain really focused to find a vein in a baby's arm. Or leg. Or neck. And just when he's totally focused on the task, she'll launch herself at him again. Her eyes are fixed on his back as he approaches one of the babies.

Kuperman stations, Kuperman here. Testing, testing, testing. Do you read me? Over.

The voice sounds distant behind her, like it's coming from behind one of the closed doors. She jumps, startled, and just before he turns she manages to dash behind the open Laundry Room door. She stands there, pressing herself to the wall.

One here. Loud and clear. Over.

She hears him mutter something and realizes that he's left the Temple. He's barefoot, but she can hear his wet footsteps on the hallway floor. Then the footsteps stop. She can see him through the crack between the hinges and the wall, standing in the doorway. He sniffs the air. She holds her breath.

He walks into the Laundry Room.

He stands in the center of the room and spreads his arms out. His eyes are closed, and he raises his face towards the ceiling. And then, with his eyes still closed, he pulls the needles out of his hands and throws them onto the floor.

Two here. Loud and clear. Over.

He goes over to the storage cupboard, removes a bottle of fabric softener and opens it; and out falls a commando knife.

Three, do you read me? Over.

He sniffs the air again.

Three, do you read me? Over.

He leaves the room and turns in the other direction, away from the Temple. She hears a key turn in a lock, a door open and then his voice: "Three here. Loud and clear."

She comes out from behind the door and runs as fast as she can to the Temple, where she lies down flat on the floor behind the hot tub. She waits a few seconds and then cautiously sits up, her back against the side of the tub.

Four here. Lou—

The radio goes silent. She can hear her own rapid breathing. She presses the tin can against her chest in an effort to ease her panting. Through the sound of the water in the hot tub, the music and the babbling of the babies, she won't hear him approaching. He'll walk in any second. Maybe he's here already. Maybe he won't hear her.

"I can smell you." His voice freezes her. "I smell your toothpaste. Your sweat. The shampoo I bought for you. The softener on your clothes."

Daphne presses down on the handle and pushes the door. It doesn't budge.

"Should we buzz him on the intercom?"

"We can try. I don't expect him to open."

Daphne presses the button with the bell sign on it. There's a buzz.

No response.

Again. Then several longer and more agitated buzzes.

Rotem draws her weapon and aims it at the door.

"Back up. I'm firing."

It takes four bullets to shoot out the bottom lock. Another five for the top one. Rotem presses down on the handle again, but the door still won't open. She empties the magazine into the keypad, and the door finally opens to reveal an illuminated staircase.

They begin their descent.

Lee hears a short buzz sounding above her, followed by a series of longer ones.

There's a moment of silence, then loud bangs echo from above. Is it finally happening? Have they finally come to rescue her? She's too scared to believe it.

She hides behind the hot tub, knowing he's already moving

towards her, that he's on her scent like an animal, but the buzzing causes him to stop in his tracks and she hears him hurrying out of the Temple.

When the stairs come to an end, Daphne leads the way down the hallway at a run. Unlike the facility they've just visited, the rooms here are all locked. They go from door to door until they find one that opens to reveal a large room with X-ray equipment. The same as they saw in the previous bunker. But there's another door here. They run across the room.

He follows them from the far end of the hallway, the knife in his hand.

Yes, he recognizes them. The two women who came to the room when he was shackled to a chair, beaten and bruised. The genuine policewoman who, at the sight of him, abruptly revisited a childhood trauma, and the fake policewoman, Rotem, who could recite verses.

The anger that made his hair stand on end when his plan was interrupted transforms into hope. There are no more footsteps on the stairs. There are just the two of them here, wandering around his facility on their own. Excellent. They may not have said anything to anyone. They may want to take credit for finding him and the Four. This is his chance to upgrade the Guardian. He tightens his grip on the knife handle, feeling a stab of pain where the needle punctured his hand.

He wonders how they found him. And if they have, perhaps others can as well. He'll have to question them after he contains the situation by trapping them in one of the rooms. He'll kill the genuine policewoman and take the other one, Rotem, to serve as his new Guardian. He'll explain the plan to her. All the details. She'll understand. She's not like all the other fools. And when she gets it, she'll participate and maybe even become an active player in the project. Two to kill, and one to keep. He peeks at them from

377

a safe distance. They do not look his way, too busy exploring the rooms they enter.

"What the fuck..." the policewoman whispers as they walk into the Images Room, her eyes moving over the walls and shelves.

"Wow." Rotem moves forward and takes a close look at the X-ray images. "He really is planning to join them together somehow."

They think that they're alone but pressed up against the wall in the X-ray Room, close to the doorway, he can hear them. And when they go into the Guardian's room, he slips into the Images Room behind them. He spots the pistol Rotem has in her hand. He'll have to be careful. Something already went wrong. The Guardian managed to get out, and she's wandering around freely. He smelled her in the Laundry Room and the Temple, but where is she now? She's dangerous. He needs to make it quick with these two and then go back to deal with her before she does any damage. Backstabber.

"There's a baby here!" The policewoman runs over to A2, who is sitting on the floor sucking vigorously on his bottle. "Hi, sweetie," she says, bending down towards him. He doesn't appear distressed or very impressed by their presence. Rotem goes over to the empty cribs. She shakes the comforter on the bed, then hurries over to the door to the toilet and opens it.

"Three of them are gone. And Lee was here."

He moves towards the door with the intention of slamming it closed and locking them in.

The policewoman caresses A2's head. He can tell she's trying to read the faded ink on his forehead.

"Let's go on," Rotem says. "We need to find out what's happening with the others. We'll come back for him."

He realizes that he isn't going to make it to the door without them noticing. So he runs back to the X-ray Room and hides inside. They pass him and go back out into the hallway.

"Look." The policewoman stops outside the room, squatting and examining a wet footprint. She reaches out and touches it with her finger, which she then holds up to her nose. "It's olive oil. Did he step in olive oil?"

"Sacred oil," Rotem responds immediately.

"What?"

"This was the dedication offering for the altar from the leaders of Israel when it was anointed: twelve silver dishes, twelve silver bowls, twelve gold pans."

"What?"

"It's either a sacrificial rite or he's taken another step towards becoming the new Messiah. Whatever the case, it's not good. Come on, let's go."

But the woman is still focused on the floor. "The prints go in both directions; he's wandering around." She leans in close to Rotem. "Maybe he's following us now," she whispers.

Rotem looks up and down the hallway and raises her voice a little. "I'm looking forward to talking to him when he reveals himself to us."

Of course he's going to reveal himself to them. He's going to reveal himself to everyone. But everything in good time. He needs to explain to her first that this isn't a sacrificial rite. She's wrong. For a moment, he wants to get up and tell her right now, so that she'll understand, but he stops himself and waits for them to move away.

They head towards the Laundry Room.

"There's blood here too," the policewoman whispers, pointing at the floor. Rotem simply nods.

He peeks out from behind the door, then takes advantage of the dryer noise and races to the Temple. He knows he's taking a gamble, but it pays off. They don't notice him. They are both focused on the Laundry Room, examining the large dryer filled with snow-white towels, the obsessively neat equipment cupboard, and discovering the blood-stained needles on the floor.

He enters the Temple and presses himself against the wall alongside the door. Closing his eyes, he inhales deeply. The smell of the Guardian is still here. She's hiding here, behind the hot tub. There's nowhere else she could be. He'll check soon. Meanwhile, he stays absolutely still where he is. In the low orange light, they won't spot him right away. He hears their footsteps approaching the Temple. He can smell them.

* * *

Lee doesn't move. She hears him come into the room again, then she thinks she hears talking, but perhaps she only imagines it. He's barefoot, his footsteps are quiet. She doesn't dare lift her head and peek. Someone infiltrated this locked facility – of that she is certain. She decides to stay where she is and let whoever came in deal with him. She saw the knife in his hand. She doesn't really have a chance against him with a tin can. As long as he doesn't touch the babies, she'll remain flat on the floor.

She hears footsteps approaching the room. Shoes.

Daphne enters first.

Before them are three babies immersed up to their necks in water. Daphne runs towards them without hesitation. As she leans over the hot tub, Rotem suddenly sees him appear and kick her in the back. Daphne stumbles and falls forward, her head slamming against the corner of the tub; she drops to the floor before she even has time to cry out in pain.

Rotem shouts, "Don't move. Police."

He turns back towards her. Slowly. "Hello, Rotem. It's not very polite of you to break in here like this."

She stands in front of him, the muzzle of her gun pointed at his chest. She hopes he won't notice that the slide is pulled back, which shows that there's no bullet in the chamber. Her eyes race over the room, trying to take in everything at once. His skin gleaming with oil, his bandaged forearm, blood smears on his body, a tray with medical instruments, the babies in the water, screens on the walls. The stigmata signs on his palms. Daphne lying motionless, blood trickling from her forehead onto the floor.

She says, "You're going to join them together. To connect their circulatory systems."

"To create a superior being," he responds. "You understand. A superior entity. Pure. Infinite intellect." He looks her in the eyes, ignoring the gun, not brandishing the knife. "I was hoping to get the chance to talk to you again. *And it shall be in the last days, God says, that I will pour forth of my Spirit on all mankind; and your sons and your daughters shall prophesy, and your young men shall see visions, and your old men shall dream dreams."* He steps towards her, but she raises the gun to point it at his head and he stops.

"The sun will be turned into darkness and the moon into blood, before the great and glorious day of the Lord shall come," she says.

He stands still, his gaze fixed on her. "Everyone goes on about us taking advantage of no more than ten percent of our brain's capabilities," he continues. "Nonsense. We use most of our brain. But no one has thought about what could happen if we were to join several brains together. Bodies that are connected to the same circulatory system and constantly absorb the same knowledge. Bodies that are free of the burden of physicality and exist instead in a world of pure intellect. That's my creation. I'm creating the first brain comprised of several brains. Like computer processors with several cores. And when I harness the knowledge and power that will be created here in the Temple, I'll then be able to fulfill my destiny to alter the face of humankind. I'll create an empire. Just think what would happen if the most powerful brain ever created was there to serve your every objective. Armageddon is approaching."

Rotem holds his gaze. "Until what age do you intend to leave them like that?"

"That's a dumb question, Rotem, which I didn't expect to hear from you."

Lee peers out from behind the corner of the hot tub. The policewoman on the floor beside her is unconscious. She isn't sure if she's even breathing. She needs urgent attention.

He's standing with his back to her, speaking to the other policewoman, who has a gun pointed at him. He can't see her; he's focused on the policewoman. Lee rises slowly. The policewoman must have spotted her, but she doesn't let on in any way.

He says, "Let me put it differently. When do you think they'll be at the stage of being able to fully exploit their brain potential as a single entity? When will the learning end?

"I'll be switching soon to gastrostomy tube feeding so they won't get hungry and waste time eating. They'll be learning at a fast pace. All the material has already been prepared for screening. You can help me with this project. I'll release the Guardian and we'll work together. You understand what we can create here."

Lee gets to her feet and advances slowly, step by step. She knows he can smell her, that he can sense the air moving. She raises her right hand very slowly, her fingers gripped tight around the can.

"Sounds like a great idea," Rotem says. "I think that—"

Lee slams the can against the back of his neck with all her might, and he collapses to the floor, unconscious.

"Third time's the charm," she mumbles and then rushes over to Daphne. She turns her over onto her back, making sure her air passages are clear and that she has a pulse. "Shoot him if he moves," she instructs Rotem, who is still standing over the Babysitter. "He appears to be out, but he could be faking it."

"Gladly, only I don't have any bullets." She returns the pistol to its holster and plucks the knife from the Babysitter's hand. "I'll stab him if necessary."

"I can feel a pulse." Lee sits down next to Daphne and lays her head on her thigh. She studies the wound to her forehead and lifts her eyelids. "Her pupils are dilated. Find me something to stop the bleeding."

Rotem looks around.

"Is there no ambulance here?" Lee says, she can feel her anger building. "Did you come here alone? That's who they sent? Two policewomen? No offense, but you don't look like a SWAT team."

"They'll be here in a few minutes." Rotem hands her a package of gauze pads that she found on the stainless-steel tray.

"Okay." Lee carefully wipes the blood off Daphne's forehead. She checks her pulse again. Weak, but there.

Rotem looks at her curiously. "You look pretty calm for someone who's just been released from a year and a half in captivity."

"Only because I'm concerned right now with preventing your friend from dying. I'm a doctor. Or rather, I was studying medicine until this creature here abducted me. I'll allow myself to fall apart afterwards. Yoavi! Go get Yoavi!"

Rotem doesn't have time to respond before three men in civilian dress burst into the room with their weapons drawn and take in the scene.

"Hi, Rotem," one of them says.

"It took you five whole minutes to get here," she remarks dryly.

"You need to get going. The police are on their way. Before they start taking names."

"Are they bringing an ambulance?" she checks.

"Of course."

One of the men approaches the Babysitter, kicks him in the ribs to confirm that he's indeed unconscious and then cuffs both his ankles and his wrists. The third man goes over to Daphne.

"There's one more baby, shut in one of the rooms," Lee says as the man crouches beside Daphne, checking too that she's breathing.

"Should we take her upstairs?" he asks.

"No," Lee responds firmly. "We'll wait for the gurney. I don't want to risk causing her any damage."

The man who cuffed the Babysitter approaches the tub to make sure all the babies are alive and then turns his attention to looking for a switch to turn the light on.

"Come on, I'll accompany you upstairs," the man standing next to Rotem urges her.

She gets down on her knees and hugs Lee. "It was nice to meet you," she says, "and I'm sure we'll meet again. But now I need to disappear from here." She strokes Daphne's cheek and then stands up, and she and the man from the Organization quickly exit the room.

Moments later, the room fills with uniformed police officers and paramedics and a SWAT team and forensic technicians and social workers and even a negotiations team. Only after seeing them take care of Daphne and find Yoavi – and after hugging and kissing him and Omer and Shai and Rami – does Lee agree to leave the room and be taken to sit in one of the ambulances.

And only on the short drive to the ER, when the ambulance team gives her the chance to call her parents, does she allow herself to cry.

PART 7

A SMALL
GRAY BIRD

DECEMBER 2017

90.

No.

No, no, no, no, no.

Not again.

Silence.

The smell of old wood.

I'm in bed, with the comforter over my head.

I have to peek out.

I'm paralyzed by fear. My heart is pounding wildly.

I peek and they're there. The three windows, the mist beyond them hanging thickly in the air. The old wooden floor. The walls of the cabin. Palpable fear like a blunt object.

Silence.

Nothing's happening.

Maybe I'll just go back to sleep this time?

A shadow flits by outside, but the face doesn't appear at the third window.

Silence again.

The smell of candle wax. Shadows dancing on the walls.

His face appears all of a sudden at the middle window and I jump out of bed in my pajamas.

"Wait, I'll be right there," he yells, and the sound of heavy, rapid strides comes from outside.

I run to the other room. This time, I'll break one of the windows with the clothes rod, then dash back afterwards to hide in the closet. He'll think I've jumped out and he'll go looking for me. And while he's doing so, I'll escape through the door in the opposite direction. Maybe I'll get far enough to call for help before he doubles back to look for me.

I open the closet doors.

A good night to die, says the writing on the back inside panel.

Reality check.

I turn my head away and then look forward again.

The writing has disappeared and now there's an illustration of a skull.

"What is it?"

I look at my hands and see that they are surrounded by a halo of light.

I'm dreaming.

I'm lucid in my nightmare, at last.

I don't bother with dismantling the clothes rod. I shut the closet. I head slowly back to the other room, feeling the coolness of the floor against the soles of my feet.

I'm dreaming.

I stand in front of the door to the cabin and wait. My legs are steady. My hands are clenched into fists at the sides of my body. I'm ready.

The kicking begins, until the door bursts open with one powerful blow and he's standing in front of me.

I'm dreaming.

He moves forward and stands right up close to me. Just an inch or two between his face and mine. His foul breath on my skin. He realizes something has changed, that I don't fear him this time, and he immediately grabs for my throat.

I'm dreaming.

I'm dreaming.

I'm dreaming.

It's just a dream.

His hands try to close around my neck but they can't. They slide off my skin like river water.

I'm dreaming.

He steps back and pulls out a knife.

I'm dreaming.

I'm dreaming.

Relax.

Breathe deeply.

Don't wake up.

Stay in the dream.

He stabs me with the knife and the blade slides through me.

I'm dreaming.

It's a dream.

He's taken aback. His eyes widen and he tries to slash at me again and again. I stand there looking at him and don't budge.

I'm dreaming.

It's a dream.

Deep breath.

He backs away towards the door. I feel as if the cabin, the outside and the entire world are mine, under my control. There's nothing I can't do. My power is limitless.

He's scared. The fear impairs his focus. The ice-like layer that blurs his features begins to melt. The mask drips off him and I see his face for the first time. I'm gripped by an irrepressible sense of rage. I promised myself I'd remain calm when I got to this stage, I've been waiting for this for years, but I'm so angry. It's him standing in front of me. Him. I break my vow.

I'm too worked up.

I'm starting to lose the dream.

I'm waking up.

The cabin around me begins to fade.

I stamp my foot down hard and scream: "*Focus!*"

A shockwave spreads out in ever-widening circles from the foot that strikes the floor, smashing out the three windows and flinging the predator through the open door. I hear a cracking sound as his ribs break. He struggles to his feet and begins limping away along the path leading from the cabin into the forest. He can run as much as he likes. I'll deal with him later.

I look at my hands. They're glowing like small suns. Satan has fled, and now it's time to take care of Hell. I spread my arms out to the sides and raise them skyward. The roof of the hut is ripped away to the sound of the creaking and snapping of wooden beams. The mist outside and the darkness inside disappear, and there's a white sun shining in the blue sky. The roof flies off and swirls faster and faster until it turns into a gray dust that spins around like a tornado, creating static electricity charges that are released in the form of bolts of lightning all around. I shout with all my might. The walls of the cabin disintegrate. The floor disappears and a circle of grass appears under my feet and spreads rapidly in all directions, painting the previously black and muddy earth a light green.

The cabin is gone.

I walk barefoot across the grass towards the hills. The dark forest has been swallowed up by the earth, to be replaced by new trees with green leaves that shine and glitter in the sun. The grass spreads, turning the hills around the forest into a green meadow. The chirping of birds sounds all around me. Just a single oak tree remains on one of the hills, and I walk towards it without really touching the ground, light as air.

I sit down in the shade of the oak and a small gray bird lands next to me and pecks at the grassless earth around the roots of the tree.

Reality check.

My hands are still glowing.

I'm dreaming.

I look to my right and my friend is sitting next to me.

"You know that dream will never come back again, right?" she says.

"Right."

"Only if you summon it."

"Yes."

"And will you summon it?"

"When the time is right."

"You know, there you're a forensic investigator for the police, and here you're God. There you play by the rules, and here you create the world and write the rules of the game."

"I know."

We lie on the soft grass, holding hands and looking up at the sky. The sun flickers and dances for us through the branches moving in the gentle breeze. Small white clouds drift through the blue sky. I can hear the sound of a babbling stream in the distance.

Never before have I felt so at peace.

91.

"It's a little ironic."

Lee looks up at the woman who's just walked into the room. "What's ironic?"

"One of the babies was taken from here at Tel HaSomer, the Babysitter held you here, and Daphne's in the hospital here now. The ambulance that evacuated her drove for a minute from one side of the hospital to the ER on the other side."

"It's you – you were there with me." Lee's eyes widen. "You're the other policewoman." She stands up from the armchair and embraces her, not letting go for a long time.

"I didn't recognize you without the uniform," she says, as she sits back down.

Rotem perches on the edge of Daphne's bed, making sure she isn't squashing Daphne's legs.

"How are you?" Rotem asks.

"I'm good." Lee doesn't feel like elaborating. "I can get up and walk around at least."

"Yes." Rotem nods and looks anxiously at Daphne. "Anything new?"

"No," Lee responds. "No change. There's brain activity, but she hasn't regained consciousness. It's like she's shut off in a box. I saw her eyes moving earlier, but she didn't open them. I think she's dreaming."

"That's a good sign."

Rotem turns away from Daphne and looks around the dark room at the bouquets of flowers, greeting cards, gift baskets. "Do you think anyone's going to eat this chocolate?" she asks, pointing at the Mozart chocolate pralines on the dresser.

Lee smiles. "I think we are. Now that I think about it, I haven't eaten a thing all day. I'm starving."

Visiting hours are long since over, and the rustling of the cellophane echoes loudly through the silence on the ward. "We'll buy you more when you're up. Promise," Rotem says to Daphne as they devour the chocolate.

"Hi."

They both jump in surprise, caught red-handed by a new visitor arriving.

The woman chuckles. "It's okay. She doesn't like Mozart anyway. I'm Anna, her roommate."

"Oh, hi, I'm Rotem. From the police."

"And I'm—"

"Everyone knows you," Anna smiles. "You've been on every possible TV channel."

"They didn't give me a chance to breathe. And I felt bad saying no; everyone's being so nice to me. And this weekend, all the families are getting together and they've invited me."

"The families of the babies?"

"Yes. I don't know if they're really up for it, but the psychologists have advised the four families to go their separate ways gradually and to have contact with me too over the coming month. A disengagement in stages."

"It's complicated. You must need it too," Rotem says.

Lee thinks of the babies and feels a wave of sadness go through her. "Yes, perhaps."

Anna approaches the bed and kisses Daphne on the forehead. "Hi, sweetie. When are you getting up? I'm bored without you."

The three of them go quiet, as if waiting – hoping – for an answer.

"I'll get another chair." Lee breaks the silence and stands up and leaves the room.

"How is she doing?" Anna asks as she plants herself in the vacant armchair.

"No change."

"Did you see the news? They've transferred the Babysitter to the psychiatric wing at Ayalon Prison. His defense lawyer is claiming insanity."

Rotem clicks her tongue. "He won't get off so lightly. Have a chocolate."

Lee returns with another chair and sits down next to them. "So you come to visit only at night?" she asks.

"Work," Anna responds.

"A lot of work," Rotem says.

"I'm incapable of being anywhere else," Lee admits.

Anna hands her a Mozart praline. "Here. This one is the best."

Lee smiles.

The three of them remain in the dimly lit room, sitting and talking, Daphne lying beside them, her face soft and serene.

92.

An empty classroom. Green Formica tables. School chairs. The two of us are sitting there in our school uniforms watching the blackboard fill itself unaided with words in white chalk. I realize they're pairs of letters that designate the names of elements in the Periodic Table.

I say, "Can I call you Makoto? I know you're me; it's just that it'll be easier for me like that."

"My name is Anna. Anna-Sophia."

We're sitting in a boat on a deep, wide river. The water is clear and I can see orange fish swimming. The river flows and I can hear the calls of parrots from the treetops along its banks.

"Anna?"

She laughs. "It's okay. It doesn't matter what you call me. Makoto is fine too, just as long as you know who we are."

"Where are we?"

"In between."

* * *

"She knew she'd find you." Nathan and Lee are sitting in the hospital room, single-use cups filled with instant coffee in their hands. The shutters are almost fully closed, and the sun's rays draw lines of light from the cracks to the bed.

The flowers have changed, the chocolates have changed; the only constant is Daphne.

Lee answers, "How?"

"She wouldn't let it go. Wouldn't brush the case aside and off her agenda even though we'd already been assigned to other crime scenes. Even during the months in which the investigation was going nowhere, you were always on her desk. Your photograph sat in front of her all the time. She swore she'd find you."

"And the babies."

"Yes." Nathan sips his espresso and swallows hard. Hospital coffee. "But she was so persistent because of you. Not them."

"Why?"

"I don't know the whole story, only fragments. I know that she was abused as a child. I think she was left locked up for some of the time. She relived it all over again through you. Through your case."

Lee places her cup on the shelf that serves as a food tray for the patients and stands up to straighten the blanket, wrapping it snugly around Daphne. She strokes her cheek and studies the very familiar medical equipment. Saturation – normal. Pulse – normal. She looks at the liquid trickling and dripping from the IV bag, the standard 0.9 percent saline solution. Everything is as it should be. But she won't wake up.

Lee needs to know that everything is running smoothly, that Daphne is being well cared for. She's used to going between patients during her shifts, but she's part of the story this time. She leans over Daphne again, gazing at her peaceful face. An electronic buzz sounds from the IV machine, indicating that it's time to replace the bag.

"She's strong," Nathan says, watching her. "She'll pull through."

* * *

A glass of orange juice drops onto a white marble floor and shatters. Fragments of glass and yellow shrapnel disperse through the air in slow motion, and splashes of juice wet our legs. A tall concrete dam is blocking a river. An empty gray boat is anchored in the middle of the lake. We're standing on the dam wall and looking at it. She takes my hand in hers. The dull toll of a bell sounds faintly in the distance.

"I need to talk to you," I say.

The two of us are standing in an antique store and looking at a semi-decomposed snake in an old jar of formaldehyde. Outside, a piece of newspaper swirls in the wind in the parking lot, gets caught against a pole, sticks to it and stops. In the restaurant across the road, a man and woman are sitting in silence on either side of an empty table. The light above them flickers and burns out. Three silver candlesticks stand on a dusty shelf behind us.

"Want to go on a journey?" Makoto motions towards the store door.

"Only if it has a timeframe."

* * *

They walk in together, holding hands.

"She's so pretty." The woman slips the bouquet they brought into the vase next to the bed, adding red roses to the cluster of orange marigolds.

"Shhhh." The man puts a finger to his lips and nods towards the armchair bed against the wall under the window. Lee is lying there, sleeping, a thin hospital blanket draped over her. The ward is empty at night, outside visiting hours, but the nurse agreed to allow them in as long as they were quiet and didn't wake anyone.

"She doesn't leave her side – Lee," the woman whispers.

"Should we wake her?" he asks.

"No way. Let her sleep. We'll see her next week. She's been through so much as it is. I think her way of dealing with it all is by taking care of others."

They stand at Daphne's bedside in silence for several minutes,

holding hands and looking at her. Before they leave, the man takes
an envelope out of his coat pocket and places it alongside the vase.

* * *

I'm three years old. The candles on my cake burn,
then flicker and go out. Birthday hats made from
cut up boxes lie scattered on the floor. The party is
over and only the two of us are still here. My friend,
Makoto, and I. On the table are plates of leftover
chocolate cake.

"Why a timeframe? There are no restrictions here."

"I can't."

"Why?"

We're eleven years old, standing on a hill, next
to a rotating wind turbine. The shadows of its large
blades move over the ground. We hear the sound of
them slicing through the air. A column of ants winds
its way along the ground below us, carrying a huge
green leaf. Hundreds of wind turbines twirl on the
hilltops all around us.

"I can't be drawn into your world. I need my
world too."

"It's more fun here with me."

We're eight years old, sitting on an old wooden
bench. A mass is being held in the huge church.
The voices of the choir and the sound of the organ
envelop us. Thousands of white candles are burning
in translucent red-glass holders on long tables, their
flames dancing. Colorful rays stream in through the
large stained-glass windows, slicing through the dust
floating in the air.

"I know, but that's my decision. You know it's
my decision. You are me."

An old woman on the bench next to us leans over.
"Shhh, girls, no talking now. It's bothering me."

Around us are stretches of grass and a forest in the distance. We're standing exactly where the cabin used to be, where the predator tortured and killed me anew each time. Flying through the air here now are blue-yellow-purple butterflies.

"If you don't agree, I'll have to stop dreaming. Or in other words, stop remembering my dreams and going back to the way things were. I don't want to. It'll be very difficult for me. And terribly sad."

Am I crying?

I do a reality check to make sure I'm still dreaming. Everything seems so real.

She offers me her hand and we walk towards the forest.

We enter the forest and the trees block out the sun. A mist rises off the ground and reaches as far as our knees, hiding the earth. It looks like we're floating on a cloud. She stops and turns to me. She smiles.

* * *

There are no words strong enough to express our gratitude towards you. Lee told us everything that happened, all you did to rescue them. You're the bravest person we know, and were it not for you, our son would no longer be with us. We love you. If you are reading this now, that means you have woken up... Call. We will always be here for you. Ruthie, Yonatan and Yoavi Heller.

On the back of the note is a telephone number. Lee slips the piece of paper into the envelope again, places it on the shelf and wipes her eyes. She didn't think she would miss the babies so much. But they'd become a part of her, and it was so hard to say goodbye to them. She folds her sheet and blanket and returns the armchair to its upright position.

She has a quick look at Daphne's vital signs. No change. Yawning, she goes over to the metal cabinet against the wall to get her toothbrush and toothpaste. She opens the cabinet and finds a large carrier bag inside, attached to which is a note with a drawing of a red heart and the words: *We thought you might need these.* Inside the bag are sweatpants, shirts, socks, slippers, shampoo, conditioner and another bag filled with snacks.

* * *

"Okay," Makoto says.

"So you agree?"

"Yes. And we'll continue to meet."

"Awesome!"

Rays of sunshine find their way through the branches of the tall trees, adding color to the mist at our feet.

"And I'm very sorry," she says.

"For what?"

"For driving you crazy earlier. For lying to you. I was trying to lure you into being with me. I shouldn't have done that. I wanted you to stay with me only, and that was selfish. I hope you forgive me."

"I forgive you."

She moves closer to me until our noses touch and tickle one another, and we both start to laugh.

"Want to go on a journey?"

"Yes."

I'm in.

A warm wind. Salt. Sand. The sound of small waves washing over and shifting seashells on the beach. Sunshine.

I feel so good.

I'm on the beach in Eilat or the Sinai, naked.

Reality check.

I pick up a shell and throw it into the air. It hovers above my head.

I'm dreaming.

I walk across the hot sand. Tracy Chapman's 'Talkin' Bout a Revolution' is playing in the background. I imagine a big circus tent and it appears in front of me, the waves washing up to its entrance. I go in. Inside there's a circus ring and above it a trapeze rig. There aren't any spectators.

I climb the ladder dressed like an acrobat and grab hold of the swing's horizontal bar. I hang on it and swing, before letting go suddenly and falling. The circus ring below races up to meet me and turns into a huge trampoline. I keep bouncing higher and higher and almost reach the roof of the tent. It's fun.

"Haven't you had enough?"

"Hi, Mia!"

She's sitting in one of the audience seats watching me. I leap high and land in the chair next to her.

"You haven't dreamed of me in ages," she says. "I was starting to miss you."

I stroke her cheek. "What's up with you?"

"Same old, you know. Studies, studies, and not much time for myself."

My little sister is already in her first year at university. Time flies by so fast.

"Are you happy?" I ask her.

"I think so," she smiles.

"I'm happy. It's very important to be happy. Do

you need anything? Help with your studies, a place to live?"

"Thanks, Daph, I'm doing just fine."

I hug her.

"See you again next week. I have to see what happened to the babies."

* * *

"You have no idea how much I miss you."

Anna is doing her best not to cry. The large bandage on Daphne's head has been replaced by a gauze dressing that's held in place over the sutures with strips of surgical tape. Anna leans over and kisses her on the forehead.

"She's going to be like Harry Potter. The exact same scar in the shape of a lightning bolt on her forehead," Lee says, in an effort to cheer Anna up. She doesn't say anything about the other scars she's seen while taking care of her. She wonders if Anna is aware of them, but some questions are better left unasked.

Anna sits down on the side of the bed and caresses Daphne's face. "How much longer is she going to be like this? When's she going to wake up?"

"She'll be okay." Lee genuinely believes so. "There's no reason why she shouldn't wake up. Her brain activity is normal. The MRI they did came out fine. No cerebral contusions. She's suffered a trauma and needs time to recover."

"I miss her."

Lee smiles. "And I'm waiting to meet her. We didn't even get a chance to talk before he launched himself at her."

"I can fill in for you if you like. Don't you want to get out of here for a while?"

"I'm here until she wakes up," Lee insists, "but thanks for the offer. The only time I leave her is when I meet with the babies' families. They set up a room here for us to get together. Want a cookie? They keep handing out treats on the ward."

"I have something better," Anna smiles. "Open the window. We'll have a little smoke."

* * *

*S*he gives me a kiss, gets up and leaves. I imagine a gate. The Forensics lab is on the other side of it, and I walk through it dressed in jeans and a colorful sweater. It's night, and there's no one here. I wander around in the dark among the evidence shelves, the microscope tables, the deserted computer stations.

I want to give Mia one last hug before I continue with this dream.

I summon a gate back to the beach but find myself in Tokyo, with a joint in my hand, wearing a black dress and black pantyhose. My hair is purple and my lipstick is black. I look at my hands. They're covered in tattoos. Some in Japanese and some in languages I don't recognize. I take hold of the hand of my boyfriend who's standing on the sidewalk next to me, and we watch the pictures change on the huge digital signs on the facades of the skyscrapers. I take a drag on the joint and we kiss.

"今何時ですか ?" he asks.

I glance at the screen of my phone. "Two-thirty in the morning."

"家に帰りまｉしょう ?"

"I don't want to go home. I feel like wandering around outside some more. I'm having fun. It feels good."

I summon a gate that will take me back to a happy place, with lots of sun, sand and water, but find myself on HaNevi'im Street, outside the building where I live with Anna. Naked again. I lie down in a yard across from the building and look at it, the grass tickles my back. Through the walls, I can see what's happening in all the apartments. Almost everyone's asleep. Anna's lying down reading a book, a steaming mug of coffee on the dresser next to her bed. I stare at the sky above me for a good hour. The stars form themselves into sparkling images, the last of which is the smiling face of a fairy.

I'm safe and protected.

* * *

"I look like something the cat dragged in. Do you mind staying here for a bit while I shower?"

"No problem," Nathan says, leaning back in the armchair, "I'll keep an eye on our Sleeping Beauty in the meantime."

Lee grabs a towel and goes into the room's shower cubicle, and Nathan gets up to take a close look at Daphne. "Daph." He touches her shoulder. "I don't know if you can hear me or not, but I hope you can. That was the dumbest thing you've ever done in your life." He waits, but she doesn't move. He starts to cry. "Who do you think you are? You and that imaginary friend of yours. Walking into his trap like two fools. It should never have happened, you hear me? The moment you wake up, I'm firing you. You can be sure of that." There are more things he wants to say, but he isn't able to. "Stay with me," he simply whispers, and he sits back down in the armchair just as the nurse walks into the room.

"Family?"

"Sort of," he responds.

"Where's Lee?"

"Showering."

The nurse has a quick look at the readings on the instruments and records something on the form hanging at the foot of the bed. "Everything's fine," she says. "Tell Lee to come by the nurses' station, okay?"

"Okay."

93.

Rotem waits patiently for the ritual to run its course.

"Cup of tea?"

"No, thanks, I'm not ill."

He always offers. And she always declines.

They're sitting at the small round table in the corner of his office. "We're going to need a series of profiles," Grandpa says, pouring a measure of dark tea from a flask into a thick glass mug.

"Of whom?"

"Senior executives at airports in Europe. Whatever you can get from the Net and open sources. Standard profiles. Weak spots, skeletons in the closet, phobias, something that can crack them. Start with Schiphol, Heathrow, de Gaulle, Frankfurt, Suárez. We'll move ahead based on whatever we can use to our benefit from those. If you need help getting into their Facebook or Gmail accounts, speak to Control."

"I'll assign someone good to it."

He sips from his mug and peers at Rotem through the steam. "How are things going? All good?"

"Everything's fine," she confirms.

"How's your friend?"

"Still in a coma. I'll be visiting again this evening."

Grandpa frowns and sips from his tee. "You shouldn't have gone in there on your own. You had a team ready no more than a minute behind you. You should have signaled them to join you."

"And they would have dragged me to their car, driven me here and called the police along the way. You and I didn't meet just yesterday."

He sighs. "That last time you were hurt was enough for me. If Carmit hadn't been there to treat you, we wouldn't be talking now. You're not a field agent, Rotem. You're a lot more than that. I don't have to spell out the value you bring to the Organization. You're putting yourself at risk unnecessarily just to satisfy some inner need for thrills."

She shakes her head, not daring to interrupt him but tired of hearing the same speech over and over again.

"Stop placing yourself in the line of fire. There are others of less significance who will do so better than you."

"Okay." She folds her arms across her chest, raises her eyebrows and fixes him with a long stare.

He starts to laugh. "You're impossible."

"That's why I'm here. Anything else?"

"That's all for now."

She stands up to leave, stopping at the door to turn to him.

"I wonder if it would have worked."

"What?"

"Connecting the circulatory systems of the three babies. It's possible, of course – in theory. It's just that no one's ever tried it before. It probably wouldn't have created a higher being or something to that effect, but I wonder what it would mean from a cardiovascular perspective."

Grandpa looks at her and sips from his tea again before responding. "You scare me sometimes, Rotem. When was your last psych evaluation?"

"I don't remember. Yours?"

Now it's his turn to raise his eyebrows.

Rotem smiles. "I don't think I've ever been put through the tests I've compiled. Could be interesting."

94.

The shelf is located in a bell-shaped ice cave in the middle of a large glacier in Iceland. We walk through a tunnel of ice, hunched over, to reach it, our bare feet wading through a stream which grows warmer the closer we get to the center of the cave. This is one of our favorite places.

We sit on the ice shelf, eating potato chips and swinging our feet in the air. My friend and me.

The light from the sun shines a deep blue through the glacier walls and creates the sense that we're in another world, outside of the Earth. Every now and then, a chunk of ice breaks off the ceiling, falls into the pool with a loud splash and sprays water over us. Every time it happens, or whenever the geyser of hot steam in the cave erupts, we cry out in unison: "Woo hoo!"

When we finish the potato chips, I fold the empty packet and put it the pocket of my freezing cold jeans. We make a point of keeping our bell cave clean.

"Want to go on a journey?"

"No. It's late already. I need to get up."

I'm no longer on the shelf of ice but lying on something soft. My friend is no longer with me. I feel a hand stroking my hair even though there's no one here. "Shhhh," someone whispers in my ear, their breath warm. A current courses through my body. The dream starts to fade. And before I can turn around or yell "Focus!" I wake up.

LET ME FINISH WITH A FEW THANKS:

To Etty, Noam and Yuval, thank you for the patience needed in coping with a strange person who disappears in the middle of family activities in order to type an idea for a new chapter before he forgets it. You are my muses.

To Einat Niv for the trust and the warm home at the Tchelet Publishing House.

To Tirza Flor for the great editing. It was really fun working together!

To Talia Marcos for the email you sent me with the article about lucid dreaming. "That's for you, I know you," you said, and you were absolutely right.

To David Belder for the expert advice in the area of forensic medicine.

To Dr. Dganit Zicin-Gensher for the early reading and constructive comments.

To The Deborah Harris Agency and Rena Rossner, who in addition to being a particularly energetic literary agent is also a great writer.

To Stephen LaBerge for your research and books on lucid dreaming and the invention of the MILD technique that definitely did the work for me. You have opened a door to a new world for me. To whoever wants to experiment with lucid dreaming, I recommend Stephen's book, *Exploring the World of Lucid Dreaming*.

Rotem's explanation of emotions (in Chapter 51) is based on

the book *How Emotions Are Made* by Lisa Feldman Barrett, which I warmly recommend. Thank you, Lisa!

The opening poem is 'free style' based on a Brazilian folk song.

Allow me to apologize for a few inaccuracies and small lies I've put into the story:

First of all, please excuse me for stretching the borders of lucid dreaming. There is no fear of being 'locked in dream time'. That's my invention. Also, there is no figure like Makoto that leads you into a lucid dream. Sleep paralysis, however, is very real and a pretty scary experience.

In Chapter 60, Daphne and Nathan examine a package that arrived directly from a crime scene, a thing that wouldn't have happened in reality. In Israel, body parts collected from crime scenes are sent directly to the Institute of Forensic Medicine and not to the police Forensics labs. I apologize for this trick I used in order to speed up the plot.

In Chapter 37, I mention 'Angle Fire', a secret system I 'stole' from the Americans who developed and used it while fighting in Iraq. There's no such beast in Israel, and no, I'm not giving away any homeland secrets.

The location detection based on concrete samples held in the Israeli Standards Institute. Well… there are no such samples.

In Chapter 81, I mention the Freemasons building at 2 Berkowitz Street. The Grand Lodge of the State of Israel Freemasonry is actually located in the adjacent building, Berkowitz 4, on the fourth floor of the Museum Tower building, but the smaller building suited me better for the story and it does not have (of course) any underground floors, labs or Alpha rooms.

Any connection between the organization which I call 'the Organization' and actual Israeli intelligence agencies is nothing but pure coincidence.

I hope you liked this book. I'd love to hear your thoughts about the story and lucid dreaming in general. My email is nirhezroni@gmail.com and you can also find me on all kinds of social networks.

If you enjoyed what you read,
don't keep it a secret.

Review the book online and tell anyone
who will listen.

Thanks for your support spreading
the word about Legend Press.

Follow us on Twitter
@legend_press

Follow us on Instagram
@legendpress